KATIE'S CHOICE
READER REVIEWS

"Reading this book was a pleasure. I couldn't put it down!"

— Alisha Bassett, Student in California, age 18

"*Katie's Choice* captures the reader's attention from cover to cover with believable characters and an engaging story about a girl who wants to believe that there is something better out there than the dull life to which she has surrendered. She makes some unwise decisions and must choose to deal with the grief-filled consequences or be stuck feeling that she deserves no better. Through new acquaintances she is able to view a different lifestyle that includes love and acceptance. But only she can make the decision to accept that love and be healed. This story is worth reading and re-reading and can give you a different perspective on life and the importance of friends and family."

— Christina Slike, Reader in Colorado, age 26

"This story of a girl who struggles with the aftermath of an abortion is so realistic that the reader is drawn into the lives of the characters. Tracey Langford is a gifted storyteller who brings her characters to life. During our two decades of pastoral ministry Kathy and I have counseled many girls with stories just like Katie's."

— Don Hawkins, D.Min.
President, Southeastern Bible College

Please turn the page for more reviews.

Katie's Choice

Katie's
Choice

A Novel by
Tracey Langford

CLADACH
Publishing

Printed in the United States of America

Scripture quotations are taken from HOLY BIBLE, NEW INTERNA-
TIONAL VERSION. NIV. Copyright 1973, 1978, 1984 International
Bible Society. Used by permission of Zondervan Publishing House. All
rights reserved.

Song lyrics:
ALMIGHTY by Wayne Watson ©1990 Material Music (Admin. by Word
Music, Inc.) and Word Music, Inc. All Rights Reserved. Used By Permis-
sion.
A BEAUTIFUL PLACE by Wayne Watson ©1993 Material Music (Admin.
by Word Music, Inc.) and Word Music, Inc. All Rights Reserved. Used
By Permission.
FRIEND OF A WOUNDED HEART by Wayne Watson/Claire Cloninger
©1987 Word Music, Inc. All Rights Reserved. Used By Permission.

Cover Design by Deanna Bouveé

Library of Congress Control Number 2003103911

ISBN 0-9670386-4-2

CLADACH
Publishing

For all the many faithful people who willingly and daily re-open old wounds so that others might heal.
May God bless you.

Katie's
Choice

KATIE'S CHOICE

PROLOGUE
❋

1970s Chicago

DARIA MONTGOMERY STARED INTO THE REARVIEW MIRROR of her yellow Volkswagen beetle. "Just what I thought," she muttered, disgusted with what she saw. "Those are the eyes of a desperate woman." Taking a deep breath, she conceded she needed a little pep talk. Her only companion was a two-month old baby. But she'd been doing a lot of things by herself lately. Maybe, if she were lucky and played her cards right, that would all change.

"Come on, girl, get a grip. You've planned this for weeks. And you've made it this far, haven't you? You never thought you would, but you did; and now you've got your chance."

A soft cry from the seat next to her interrupted Daria's musings. "Hey, little one, did Mama's crazy talk disturb you? I'm sorry, baby. Go back to sleep, sweetie."

The soothing voice and a few strokes on a chubby, pink cheek did the trick, and the baby once more slept peacefully. Stopping at a traffic light, Daria gazed at the pretty bundle beside her. She pulled the soft, white blanket up under the tiny chin. Daria wondered at the smallness of her daughter's hands compared to her own. "Amazing," she whispered. "Just amazing."

A horn blew. With a start Daria moved her foot to the gas pedal and resumed her mission. The May sun shining through the windshield warmed Daria. Briefly she allowed herself to enjoy the summer sights. All the good things in her life seemed to happen during the summer: her birthday, for one; and no school, for another. Best of all, summer was the season when she'd met T.J.

11

It was two years ago. She was 18 and had just finished high school—barely, but she graduated. Her friends wanted to celebrate. Most of the students were taking a senior trip to the coast, but that wasn't Daria and her friends' thing. The sooner she forgot about East Central High School the better. Besides, she couldn't afford the trip. Some things were not meant to be. Daria prided herself on being a realist. Kids from her economic standing were wasting their time dreaming about a better life.

So Daria chose to celebrate her release from the last twelve years of "prison" by going out drinking with her friends. After all, she'd earned the right.

They went to The Groove, a club that catered to an early-twenties crowd. Daria had no trouble getting in. Everyone she knew had carried fake I.D.s for years.

Dressed in hiphugger jeans and black tank top, Daria followed her friends through the crowd until they found an unoccupied table. Guys glanced as she passed by. Maybe she didn't turn as many heads as her friend Sonya, but she turned enough, thanks to the tight jeans and clingy top. She smiled to herself.

Daria sat at the table while her friends headed to the bar. Seeping out of the din and the cluttered sea of bodies was an unmistakable air of desperation. People tried too hard to have a good time, laughed too loud, smiled too big, and drank more than was wise. Daria never would have admitted to her friends that she would have preferred a quiet evening with someone she could really talk to, not just small talk. But she pushed the thought from her mind. Girls like her would take what they could get, and they'd better be satisfied with it 'cause that's all there was.

Daria's friends returned with the beers. She grabbed a mug and took a sip, then swung round in her chair as the MC introduced the live band. She silently reprimanded herself for her somber mood and determined, just as the Midnight Ride band struck the first chord of its opening number, to have a good time and celebrate. Daria looked up with a false smile. Then she found herself staring. The lead guitarist, practically swallowing the microphone as he sang, had the most perfect mouth and wavy brownish-blonde hair that fell across his forehead and almost covered his left eye. Long sideburns outlined a beautifully chiseled jawbone and the V-neck shirt revealed just enough of a masculine chest that Daria found herself wondering what the rest of it looked like.

Wow, she thought to herself. She was actually having a hard time catching her breath. With sweaty palms she reached for another drink of her beer. *Oh, this can't be happening! I've never believed in all that love at first sight garbage, but then again I've never seen anybody or anything so perfect in my life!* As if reading her thoughts, the lead singer began crooning in a sexy, raspy voice.

> I've been searching all my life
> for someone like you
> I didn't know if it would happen,
> didn't know it could be true . . .

Feeling her face redden, she looked down at her hands. Was this handsome, godlike musician looking at her while singing about searching for the right person or was her imagination playing a cruel trick on her? She must be mistaken. Stuff like this didn't happen. But when she willed herself to look up, two perfect blue eyes stared directly down at her. And was that a smile and a wink?

Sonya leaned over and whispered, "Dare, isn't he incredible? And he's looking right at you!"

"Oh, come on, Sonya, he's probably looking at somebody behind me or something."

"Well, if you really believe a guy that good looking would wink at a pot-bellied ex-jock like the one sitting behind you, then I guess you could be right."

"Oh, Sonya, you're terrible," Daria mumbled, unable to conceal the thrill in her voice. "What should I do?"

"Well, if I were you, I'd get up and start dancing in a real sexy way. But since you won't do that, why don't you try smiling back at him?"

Wishing she had some of her friend's brazen confidence, she whispered, "Okay, I'll give it a try." She slowly exhaled the breath she'd been holding.

"Yeah, go get 'em, tiger," Sonya mocked.

Daria wanted to rise to the challenge of the singer's eyes. She hardly ever succeeded at anything. Life seemed to come hard for her. She even had to work at having fun, something as natural to Sonja as breathing. At the moment, even breathing came hard for Daria. She consciously drew a deep breath, then forced herself to look up and lock eyes with the ones that were, incredibly enough, still gazing at her from the stage. She smiled timidly. The singer warmly returned her smile. And that was the beginning of her relationship with T.J. Nichols.

Now, two years later, Daria was once again breathless at the thought of seeing T.J. Nichols. She pulled to a stop across the street from the dingy gray clapboard house T.J. and his bandmates called home. His black van sat in the driveway. "Well, baby girl," she whispered, "wish me luck." She cracked the windows a bit and got out of the car. She smoothed her thin blue sweater and hoped T.J. would still be impressed at the sight of her in tight jeans.

"Okay, this is it." As soon as the barely audible words were out of her mouth, Daria cringed remembering how T.J. hated that habit she had of talking to herself. Shakily she knocked on the door.

Daria unconsciously ran her fingers through her long reddish-brown hair, which she had just this morning brushed until it shone, all the while dreaming of the many times T.J. had run his hands through it as they made love. She shuddered with the memory. T.J. may not have been her first lover, but he was the only one that mattered. Daria never dreamed anyone could make her feel as special and beautiful as she did when she was in T.J.'s arms. He would caress her and tell her how perfectly the two of them fit together, and then he'd start singing

a new song lyric he was working on, telling her she inspired him like
nobody else. She naïvely assumed life would go on like that forever.
But then came the opportunity for Midnight Ride to go on tour and
T.J. would have no part of her going with him. He said he wouldn't
have time for her and she'd just be bored; she would be nothing but
a distraction for him; he didn't want anyone holding him back from
his big chance.

At the time Daria hadn't understood. If she inspired his music
so much, how could she hold him back? It took a while for her
to figure it out; but after much arguing, she realized what he really
wanted was a fresh start with no strings attached. If the tour failed
miserably, he could always come back to her; if it succeeded he wanted
to be available to explore other options, as they say. The last scene
before he left was pretty dramatic, with her screaming and crying
hysterically, telling him she loved him and could never survive eight
months without him. He had shaken his head and told her to grow
up. Then with a quick kiss to her tear-stained cheek and a brisk wave
of the hand, he climbed into the van and was gone.

A smooth voice interrupted her thoughts.

"Hey, babe. Man, it's good to see you." He reached and pulled
her into an affectionate embrace, which she readily returned. His
hands moved over her shoulder blades and came to rest on the small
of her back. He pulled his upper body away just far enough so he
could look into her face. "Mmmm, you always did feel good in
my arms."

"Oh, T.J. you don't know how much I missed you."

"Well, then, welcome me home." Leaning, he found Daria's
mouth with his, in a lingering kiss full of familiarity. When they finally
came up for air, T.J. grabbed her hand and pulled her down until they
were sitting side by side on the stoop. "So, I guess you want to hear
all about the tour, huh?"

She looked at him with questioning eyes and T.J. leaned back
on his hands.

"Oh, no, here we go again. I know that look. Why do you have to be so serious all the time?"

"Because I thought we were serious, T.J."

"Yeah, but I just got back and I'm still kind of winding down, babe. I can't deal with anything heavy right now. I just need someone to listen and be there for me."

"Yeah, I know what that's like, T.J.. I've been wanting someone to be there for me for about eight months now." Daria was fighting hard to keep the tears back. Tears never worked around T.J.. "And since you're finally back, I need to know where things stand. I can't go through this again."

"Hey, things are just the same as before I left."

"Is that really what you think?" Fear began to replace the tears now. "That everything is the same? After the things you said to me before you left? I mean, T.J., I thought we had something special going on and then it was like you just threw me away when you left. How could you do that?"

"Come on, that's not fair. You knew from the beginning that music was my gig, not relationships. The only permanent people in my life are the guys in the band. You seemed fine with that before I left."

"Oh, T.J., that can't really be how you feel, can it? I mean the guys in the band are great and all, but what about a family? Don't you ever think about that?"

T.J. laughed mockingly. "Certainly you're not gonna give me some speech about putting down roots now, are you? 'Cause I gotta tell you, babe, you'd be wastin' your breath."

Desperation welled up inside Daria. "But we're so good together." She managed to choke out the words and still retain some semblance of dignity. "You always said so. Besides, you always said I was like a part of the music inside you."

T.J. looked unhappy with the direction of the conversation. The set of his jaw hardened. "I won't argue that we've had some good times, and we were certainly good in bed together, but if you're thinking I can't find that somewhere else, you're sadly mistaken." He raked his hand through his hair. "I like you, Daria, I like you a lot and I hope you don't do anything to mess up what we've got. But I have to tell you, I don't want anything more than we've got right now."

"But, T.J., what if it's already more?" She decided to come right out with it.

"What? I just told you how it was."

Slowly getting to her feet, Daria held out her hand to T.J. "Come here. I've got something I want to show you."

T.J. hesitated, then grabbed her hand and let her lead him down the sidewalk and across the street to her car.

"I want you to meet somebody." Daria opened the car door and stepped out of the way. Inside, the baby girl lay swaddled in pink and white. The tiny eyes were just opening after an obviously restful sleep.

"I ... I don't understand. Daria, what's going on?"

"This, T.J., is our daughter. Her name is Katie."

A world of dread, fear, and uncertainty lifted from Daria's shoulders. Her secret was out. This was her final play, her trump card. If baby Katie's perfect little face didn't change the mind of T.J. Nichols, nothing would.

"You've gotta be kidding." T.J. had already said it three times, but he was like a robot programmed to say nothing else.

"You've gotta be kidding. What are you doin' with a baby?"

"What are *we* doing with a baby, you mean, don't you?" She smiled, but T.J. didn't notice.

"You sure it's mine?"

"How can you even ask me that, T.J.? There has been no one else in my life since I laid eyes on you. Katie is your daughter." Daria softened her voice. "And she's a good baby, T.J. Would you like to hold her?"

T.J.'s face grew red and his voice rose. "No, I don't want to hold her. Why didn't you tell me about this?"

"Because I didn't know I was pregnant before you left and then I didn't know where to reach you. You never even called to check on me, you know. If you had, then maybe I could have told you about it."

"Well, I certainly wouldn't have told you to keep it. Daria, how could you be so stupid?"

"It takes two to make a baby, Terence!"

"Don't call me Terence. You know I hate that. And I wasn't talking about getting pregnant. I was talking about why you kept it. You could have easily gotten rid of it."

With an exasperated sigh, Daria tried to explain. "I just didn't feel right about an abortion. T.J., this baby is part of you. I didn't want to get rid of it. I liked knowing I was carrying your baby inside me." Daria didn't notice T.J. slowly shaking his head back and forth. She continued her reverie. "We could have such a good life, the three of us. Katie's a really good baby, and I've got a decent job. It's not like I'm asking you just for money, babe. I want to be there for you and support you and all that stuff. You don't even have to marry me; just tell me you'll be a part of our lives. That's all I want, T.J."

"You just don't get it, do you?"

"What?"

"I'm gonna have to spell it out for you, aren't I?" He took a deep breath. "Daria, I don't want any of this—none of it. I don't want a baby, I don't want a wife, I don't want any strings. Nothing. I can't imagine what was going through your head when you decided to keep the thing. But it was your choice, not mine, so live with it and leave me out of it."

Tears streamed from Daria's brown eyes. T.J. looked away. "I'm going back in the house now. Get in your car and take yourself and your little brat home. I don't care to see either one of you ever again." He spoke slowly and plainly as if Daria were mentally impaired.

She bit her lip. Without turning to look at the man she loved, the father of her baby girl, Daria Montgomery got into her car and left. She didn't have to look at him; she had every inch of T.J. Nichols memorized. His image was emblazoned on her heart and always would be. It wasn't until she had rounded Cornell Street that the shaking started. She had to pull over.

"Oh, god. What am I gonna do?" she cried, dropping her forehead onto the steering wheel. "Everything is ruined. Oh, baby girl, my little Katie. You weren't enough. I thought he'd take one look at you and fall in love, just like I did, but he didn't. He didn't even look at you. I was counting on you to change his mind. But you just drove him away."

She knew in her heart that the words were unfair. But it's hard to see reality through the anguish of grief.

PART ONE

1

Stoughton, Wisconsin, 17 years later

THE WIND BLEW GENTLY and leaves fell steadily from the trees lining Jamison Street. The brisk air was a stark reminder that football season had rolled around once again, that the holidays loomed right around the corner, and that life kept repeating itself over and over. Stoughton, Wisconsin, just outside Madison, was nothing more than a cycle, like a ferris wheel going round and round. Sometimes you found yourself on the top looking out over your life thinking, *This is good; I could go on like this forever.* But as soon as you'd get really comfortable with that thought, you'd feel yourself slowly slipping over the edge, descending toward some unknown yet familiar pit that consumed you until you felt the wheel slowly ascending to the top again.

These were the feelings of the young girl getting out of the black Camaro that pulled up to the curb. An enshrouding restlessness came over her without warning until she thought she couldn't breathe. But, just when she was about to finally suffocate, ever so gently the feeling disappeared, leaving her to wonder if she'd really experienced it.

Katie Montgomery had learned to ride out these emotional storms so gracefully that no one ever knew of the battle that raged within. She leveled her emotions day in and day out, causing no waves and bringing no attention to herself.

"Hey, I'll be back to pick you up around 6:30 for the game, okay?" said the guy in the driver's seat of the car. Katie leaned through the open window and gave Eric a quick kiss on the lips. "Thanks for the ride."

21

"For you, baby, any time."

With that, Katie turned and started up the walk to the front door of her apartment building, an old, three-story Victorian home converted into separate apartment units.

Eric watched her for a moment, and, indeed, he liked what he saw. Katie may not have been the most fun girl in the school—in fact she was really a little too quiet for his taste—but she sure did look good. At five-feet-five-inches she fit perfectly under his arm as they walked through the halls at school. With her slim figure she could have been a model had she been taller. Her brown hair with its soft blond highlights reached to the points in her shoulder blades. Today, wearing faded blue jeans and a white sweatshirt, she presented a picture of the quintessential all-American girl.

Not a bad little prize I've got there, Eric smirked to himself. *I know a lot of guys who wish they were in my shoes.* With one last wave of his hand out the window, he sped off, squealing the tires of his car in the hopes it would impress Katie and anyone else within earshot.

Katie slowly opened the third-floor apartment door and quietly called, "Mama?"

"She ain't here. She don't get off work till five." The owner of the voice appeared in the room as Katie closed the door behind her.

Rick's southern drawl grated on Katie's nerves. For some reason she never believed it was genuine. Why would anyone want to talk like that on purpose? But she'd given up trying to figure him out and just accepted the fact that her mama wanted him around.

"Well, you sure look pretty today, little Katie."

Repulsed at the sight that met her, Katie mumbled "Thank you" and then said a little more loudly and clearly, "I have some homework to do. I'll be in my room."

"You tellin' me you're gonna do homework on a Friday night? Now, I don't know much, but I know a pretty little thing like you must have better things to do on a Friday than homework, now ain't that so?"

"Well, I am going to the football game with Eric, but I just wanted to get my homework over with so it wouldn't be hanging over my head all weekend."

The dark-haired, bearded man broke into a sly smile. "Well, that Eric sure is a lucky boy, now ain't he? I can remember going to my high school ball games down in Georgia. OoooWeeeee! We'd sure have us some wild times. Chasin' the girls, drinkin' a little . . . well . . . okay, drinking a lot!" He bellowed as if it was hysterically funny.

Whatever the joke was, frankly, Katie didn't get it.

"Yeah," he continued, lost in nostalgia, "I remember this one game. Our team was losin' so bad—"

He kept talking, and Katie knew this was her time to escape. With any luck he wouldn't even notice she was gone. He was already pretty wasted. She quickly ducked through the door off the kitchen into the closet-sized storage space she had claimed as her room.

Closing the door, she sighed, shook her head, and flopped down on the mattress that lay on the floor. A small chest of drawers just fit into her little cubbyhole, and she had installed hooks in the wall for hanging clothes.

Katie kicked her tennis shoes off and stared up at the ceiling as if looking for answers. She'd never found any during all the countless hours she'd spent in this very same position in this very room. But again today she looked. She searched that ceiling, sure she must have missed the answers to all of life's questions in all those little whirling patterns. It was such a perfect picture of life. A series of swirls going round and round, no beginning and no end, just an endless cycle; not good, not bad, not leading anywhere. The occasional crack, like the ones in the plaster above her head, and the intermittent dark stains cast a gloomy glow on everything. But she threw a thin towel over the lamp in her room, and it dimmed the light just enough to make everything seem almost ethereal.

Katie marveled at the change an old flour sack towel made. She lay back and re-studied the ceiling. This time she saw no cracks and no ugly stains, just pretty little swirls like you might find in a pond on a breezy day; or the marks left by an ice skater pirouetting across a frozen pond. She closed her eyes, took a deep breath and held it to the point of being uncomfortable, then slowly released it. When the last drop of air had been expelled, she opened her eyes and whispered to no one in particular, "I wish I could throw something over my life to cover all the cracks and imperfections ... and be ... beautiful." The last word wasn't audible, just a faint expulsion of air released almost reverently into the atmosphere—the closest thing to a prayer that had ever crossed her lips.

Katie slept and when she awoke, she had an urge to not move and just be totally silent. She could almost hear the words *Be still* filling her tiny room. Acquiescing to the unbidden desire, Katie remained motionless for several minutes. *Why am I doing this? What is this going to accomplish?* But still the desire deep inside her won out. After another moment or so, Katie vigorously shook her head and began to rise. She then noticed the clock sitting atop her chest of drawers. It said 6:05; she sprang to life.

Rubbing her hands over her face to wipe away the last remnants of sleep, she muttered, "I try to be philosophical about the meaning of life, and all I end up doing is being late!" Semi-laughing at herself, she entered the kitchen.

"So Sleeping Beauty finally awakes, does she?"

Katie smiled at the woman sitting at the small, square kitchen table. "I can't believe I slept for over two hours!"

"Rick said something about a football game." The woman cocked her head toward the snoring mass sprawled on the blue and tan plaid sofa in the living room.

Katie crinkled her nose. "Yeah, Eric'll be here to pick me up in about twenty minutes."

Daria Montgomery frowned in frustration at her daughter. "Well, don't you think you should be getting ready, sweetheart? Guys like Eric don't come along every day; and if you want to keep him, you'd better fix yourself up a little."

"Mama, it's a football game, not the prom!"

"Well, scoff all you want, but mark my words, men don't stay around long if you don't do something to make 'em want to stay."

Katie had heard all this before. She knew to tread lightly. "Well, what if I'm not sure I want Eric to stick around? I mean, he's nice and he's certainly good looking, but ... I mean ... well, Mama, I'm only seventeen. You make it sound like I should be getting married or something."

Daria took a drink of her soda mixed with bourbon. Then she leveled her gaze at her daughter. "Well, I do know this much, Katie: I've been with a man and I've been without a man. And trust me, even with all the trouble they bring, it's still better with than without. Bein' alone is no sweet ride." With a wave of her hand she added, "So you go do like your mama says and doll yourself up a little."

Katie saw the sadness in her mother's eyes and knew she wasn't thinking about her and Eric. Daria often retreated to some far away place in her mind. Katie was fairly certain that mysterious place had something to do with her father. He was never mentioned; Daria made it quite clear she didn't want to talk about him—ever. So Katie rarely brought it up. At least she wouldn't have to "doll" herself up: her mother was now oblivious to everything except the amber-colored liquid in her glass and her tortured memories.

2

✿

"Ooooo, YUK! I hate these stadium bathrooms. They're so disgusting," Kristin wrinkled her nose, rolled her big blue eyes, and tossed her bleached blond hair. "I wouldn't even come in here, but you know how it is—when you gotta go, you gotta go!"

"Well, hurry up about it, okay, Kris? I don't like being in here any better than you do." Katie glanced around at the overflowing trash can, the explicit graffiti on the walls, and the used feminine hygiene products littering the floor. *Why do people do that?* She felt her stomach churn and tried not to focus her eyes on anything.

Kristin's voice answered from within one of the stalls. "Oh, you just can't wait to get back to Eric, that's all."

"Eric will be just fine without me for a few minutes."

"Yeah, well what about you?" Kristin came out of the stall tucking her shirt. "You must be crazy about him; I mean, who wouldn't be, with his dark hair and eyes, and that car of his! You must feel like a queen having Eric chauffeur you around in such a hot car! You are the luckiest girl I know, Katie Montgomery."

"You mean I should be head over heels in love with him because he's got a great car? Isn't that a little shallow?"

"So are you gonna tell me you're not crazy about Eric Martin?"

Trying hard to disguise her frustration Katie replied, "Sometimes I think Eric looks at me as a trophy or something. I just wonder how he really feels, you know. He never asks what I'm thinking. It's always about where we're going next or who we're gonna hang out with. Never anything personal, just . . . It's just so unsatisfying."

26

"Do you know what I think?" Kristin primped in front of the mirror, applying more make-up to her already heavily painted face.

"No, but I'm sure you're gonna tell me."

"You're right. I'm gonna tell you because you're my best friend, and I want to see you happy. You always seem so dreary. I think you get it from your mom. I've noticed she's like that a lot, too. It's like she's mad at the world or something. What's her prob—?"

"Okay, okay. I think we're getting way off track here. Let's just leave my mother out of this." Katie made for the door, but Kristin grabbed her arm.

"I'm sorry. I know you're close to your mom. But I can't believe you're not happy. You're dating the coolest guy in school, you're beautiful, and you've got me for a best friend." Kristin tried to put lightness back into the conversation. "What more could you want?"

"I don't know what I want. You know, Kris, you're saying the exact same stuff my mom's always telling me. She thinks I'm waiting for some fairy tale, too. Maybe I am." Katie sighed. "There's just an emptiness inside and even Eric doesn't make it go away. I know I should be grateful that he likes me—"

"Girl, we're just gonna have to shake off these blues! I say it's time to party!" Kristin's eyes danced. "Who cares about this stupid football game? It's already the fourth quarter, so why don't we ditch it and go back to my house? My parents won't be back till real late, so the house is ours. We'll relax and have a good time and make you forget all your woes."

Mentally reprimanding herself, Katie forced a smile. A nasty stadium bathroom wasn't the place for a heart-to-heart discussion and besides, Eric was waiting for her.

"That does sound good." In fact maybe that's exactly what she needed—a really good time. It's what everyone kept telling her anyway—her mama, Kristin, Eric, even Rick. They couldn't all be wrong, could they? Katie only knew of one way to find out.

❄ ❄ ❄

Kristin unlocked the door of her parents' four-bedroom ranch-style home in one of Stoughton's upper-middle-class neighborhoods. "You guys go on down to the rec room while I get some snacks from the kitchen. Katie, will you help me?"

"Sure."

"I'll be waiting for you," Eric whispered into Katie's ear. There was a strange glint in his eye. He gave her a quick kiss and a little squeeze to her backside that unnerved her. It wasn't that he'd never acted this way toward her before, but something was different tonight. She stared blankly as Eric and Jason headed downstairs.

"Come on. Let's get the food," urged Kristin.

"Oh yeah." Katie stammered.

Kristin touched Katie's arm. Softly, she said, "You're not still upset over that crack I made about your mom, are you? 'Cause really, I didn't mean anything by it. Honest."

Katie looked into her friend's eyes and saw genuine concern there. She was thankful to have a friend like Kristin Jarvis. She could make her laugh when nobody else could, and she really did seem to care. She never made a big deal about Katie's lack of a father or her lack of money. And, until tonight, she had never made a crack about Katie's mother. Kristin had always overlooked these things despite the fact that she herself had grown up as the youngest of three kids in a nice neighborhood with two parents who had been married for twenty-seven years. Katie didn't want to do anything to jeopardize this friendship—not even defend her mom, who for all practical purposes deserved any criticism she received.

"I know that," Katie smiled. She reached over and gave her best friend a hug. "My mood has nothing to do with you, I promise. I don't know what's wrong with me."

"Is it Eric?" Kristin pulled a bag of potato chips from the cupboard.

"I guess so, but I don't know what it is that bothers me. I wish I could stop thinking so much and just live."

In a matter-of-fact tone with a slight edge of irritation, Kristin said, "Look, Katie, I think you spend way too much time analyzing life and missing out on all the fun!" Then she attempted to lighten the mood. "Hey, wouldn't it be neat if we could share our personalities?"

"What are you talking about?"

"Yeah," Kristin's eyes twinkled. "Just think of it! I could give you some of my party-girl attitude and you could give me some of your studiousness and responsibility." She laughed. "Boy, would that ever make my dad happy! He's always telling me I should take life more seriously, study hard, and forget about boys until I'm, like, thirty years old!"

Kristin adopted a deep masculine voice—a poor yet humorous attempt at impersonating her father. With her left hand on her hip and shaking her index finger she continued. "And don't wear so much make-up, young lady. You look like a tramp. You'll be attracting the wrong kind of guy that way, and the way you wear your jeans so tight, it's a wonder you can even sit down!"

Katie laughed, but secretly she had to agree with Mr. Jarvis on those last two points. When it came to having a good time, though, Kristin was a master at it; and Katie didn't see anything wrong with that.

"Okay, okay!" laughed Katie.

Kristin abandoned her "father" stance and pulled herself up onto the counter. She sat for a few moments, then looked right into Katie's eyes and said, "Katie, stop saying you want to change and just do it. If you want to have more fun, then do it." She slid down from the counter and grabbed the chips. "Come on, let's take these snacks downstairs, have a few beers, play some pool, and let those guys down there make us feel beautiful and desirable and sexy. That sounds like a good time to me. How 'bout you?"

"I guess so."

"Well, I know so. There's nothing better than having a guy

29

fall all over himself to impress you." A thought seemed to dawn on
Kristin. She opened her eyes wide and said, "You have gone all the way
with a guy before, haven't you?"

Katie suddenly felt cold although the house was very warm.
Lamely, she answered, "Yes." It was a true statement, but it wasn't
anything she was proud of or excited about.

"But not with Eric?" Kristin couldn't conceal the surprise in her
voice. Katie shook her head no. Kristin looked ready to laugh, but
checked herself. "I can't believe it. Nobody would believe this. You two
have been dating for like, what, two months? And you haven't slept
together? I'll bet Eric doesn't want that getting around school." She
hesitated, then added, "Do you mind if I ask why, Katie?"

3

KATIE THREW BACK THE COVERS, pulled herself out of bed, and stumbled to the chest of drawers, fumbling for her alarm clock. Hitting the snooze button, she returned to the warmth of her bed. *Ten more minutes before another day starts all over again.* She pulled the pillow over her head, trying to shut out the memory of the night before.

The pillow muffled her groan. "Why doesn't anything ever change?" Even Katie was surprised by the intensity of her emotions. She sat up, trying to brush away the last residue of slumber still clouding her brain. It was then that it all came charging into her consciousness with a vengeance—every word spoken the night before, every action, and every silent plea she had hurled into the darkness hoping to be rescued from the abyss into which she was falling. Yes. It was like watching a movie starring Katie Montgomery. She could feel the heroine's pain and longing; indeed, she could empathize with her but to no avail. She couldn't—no matter how hard she tried—jump into the movie screen and rescue the poor girl. She couldn't even change one word of the sleazy script.

Katie had tried to explain to Kristin how she hoped for a deeper relationship with Eric. Actually, it wasn't about Eric so much as her need to connect with anybody on a deeper level. Katie had talked of kindred spirits and soul mates, but Kristin could never get past Eric's dark eyes and wavy hair. It had been like talking to a brick wall, a very persuasive brick wall.

Abandoning the idea of getting through to her best friend, Katie joined the party downstairs, which consisted of several six-packs of beer and lots of sexual innuendoes. Apparently, Eric and Jason had decided not to wait for the girls before beginning "the fun." An already-tipsy Eric couldn't keep his hands to himself, and Katie found no aid in Jason or Kristin, who were busy having a party all by themselves.

Much to her disgust, Katie had given in. She didn't know what else to do. Everyone kept telling her this was what life was all about. You took what you could get, whatever made you feel good. And she honestly tried to "feel good" in the midst of it all, but she kept coming up empty. If this wasn't what life was meant to be, then what was it supposed to be? The question kept pounding in her head until it actually hurt. In fact, at one point, Eric raised up and stopped his sensual caresses. "Hey, what's going on? You seem really distracted."

The longing in his eyes made her want to weep. Not because she knew he cared about her and cherished her, but because she knew this was enough for him: pure physical pleasure. *He really doesn't understand*, Katie cried out in her heart. The physical pleasure Eric was offering simply wasn't enough for her. *Life would be so much easier if it were.* Then the tears came. Not for Eric, but for herself.

"Katie, what's wrong? Are you all right?" asked Eric.

Unable to stop the tears and unable to articulate their origin, Katie simply nodded.

"Well whatever it is, it can't be all that bad, can it?"

Katie shook her head "no."

"Well, how 'bout if I just hold you for a while, okay?" After Katie's approving nod, Eric asked almost timidly, "Hey, this doesn't have anything to do with me, does it?"

For a moment Katie was taken aback. It was such a selfish statement. But then again, why should this surprise her? That's how everybody lived their lives, wasn't it? Right then she made the con-scious decision to get over it—to simply have fun, like Kristin had implored her to do.

"Yes, Eric, it does have to do with you," she whispered in a throaty voice. "I still can't believe someone like you would want to be with someone like me." Oh, wouldn't her mama be proud. "I can't tell you what this means to me."

"I had a feeling this was gonna be a special night."

"Oh, Eric, I'm sorry if I made you think I didn't like you," purred Katie. "But I've been with guys before who only wanted one thing, and I needed to make sure you would still be around afterward. You will be there, won't you?"

"Baby, you can count on it." Eric was breathless. "This is how I've always wanted us to be. You're worth the wait."

He kissed her deeply. There was no turning back now. Eric would be like all the others. But, so what? She'd chosen her path. So, lying on the floor of her best friend's rec room with Eric lowering himself over her, Katie had surrendered to the dark voice inside her—

The snooze alarm startled Katie out of her reverie. She'd have to get a move on, to make it to her job on time. She jumped up and grabbed her robe. She hated the way Rick looked at her when she had on nothing but her T-shirt and boxers.

"Well, girl," she muttered to herself, "you've made your bed, and now you have to lie in it." It was a favorite expression of her mother's. She had charted a course and now had to stick with it or drown. Katie knew it wasn't the fairy tale life she so often dreamed of, but she couldn't deny that anything was better than the emotional torment that had plagued her for so long. Besides, Eric was a pretty good catch. She smiled.

With a new resolve and a little spring in her step, Katie got a quick bite to eat in the kitchen before heading to her weekend job as a cashier at the grocery store.

For a Saturday, business at the Pic-n-Save was slow. Katie liked it better when she didn't have so much time to stand around and think. She contemplated asking for an early break, then spotted Kristin approaching, juggling four or five items.

"Hey, come on over to my line. . . . please!" Katie said, rolling her eyes. "I'm about to die of boredom."

"Has it been slow?"

"Unbelievably slow!"

"Well, my mom needed me to pick up a few things, and since I knew you'd be working, I went ahead and came out here, even though it's farther from my house than Kohl's Grocery." Kristin deposited her purchases onto the conveyer belt, and Katie began scanning them. "Wow, you're really fast at that. I'm impressed."

"It doesn't take long to get the hang of it, especially when it's busy and you have one customer after another. These scanners make it easy, unless, of course, they quit working when your line is backed up. Believe me, that's no fun!"

"I don't think I could stand having to work and I wouldn't have a good attitude about it like you do."

"Well, money is the main motivation; and since your parents keep you supplied with that, I guess you don't have the same incentive."

"Yeah. So what's the damage?"

"$18.26. Your mom uses plastic bags, doesn't she?"

Kristin nodded. "Hey, none of these things are perishable, so why don't we go grab a bite? Can you take your lunch now?"

Katie bit her bottom lip and bagged the groceries. "Yeah, I think I can since it's so slow, but I brought a lunch to eat in the break room."

Kristin fumbled in her purse for the twenty dollar bill her mom had given her. She didn't miss the slightly embarrassed look on her friend's face. She handed Katie the twenty.

"You know, I never paid you back for all the help you gave me with my algebra homework last week. I would have surely failed the test if you hadn't crammed with me, so why don't you let me take you to lunch? I've been wanting to try that new deli down the street."

"You're too much, you know that, Kris?" Katie handed her the change. "You don't have to pay me back for studying with you. It's

34

what friends do, and besides it helped me as well. I wouldn't have gotten as high a grade as I did if I hadn't studied so much with you."

With a twinkle in her eyes, Kristin responded, "Well, then, maybe you should buy me lunch!"

"Hey, let's not get carried away!—unless you want to dine on half of a peanut butter sandwich and peach yogurt."

"Aaaahhhh! Not yogurt, please. That stuff is nasty! Just go tell your boss you're taking your break now."

Chuckling, Katie headed toward the manager's office calling over her shoulder, "I'll be right back." Then she thought to herself, *Thank you for not making me feel bad about never having money, and thank you for being such a good friend.*

Seated at a bistro table in the Park Lane Deli and Bakery, Kristin wasted no time in getting to the point. "So, give me the scoop, and I want all the details!"

"What are you talking about?"

"How can you be so dense, Katie Montgomery? I want to know about you and Eric. You guys left last night before we had a chance to talk."

"Oh, yeah," came Katie's sheepish reply. "Since I had to work today, I asked Eric to take me home a little early."

"Oh, Katie, I think this job is ruining your life! I mean, it's your senior year, you're out with the best looking guy in school, he's all over you, and you say you have to get home early because of some silly job as a grocery checker! I can't believe I'm hearing this!"

"Kris, I wish you could understand. I really want to go to college; and, unlike you, I don't have anyone to pay my way. I know you think it's demeaning to work at a grocery store, but they were willing to give me the hours I needed. Plus, my mama works there too."

"I know, I'm sorry. But it is our senior year, and you only get one of those, you know."

"You know, Kris, a job might be just what you need, too. It might give you a little of that responsibility your dad is always talking about." Katie's eyes gleamed.

"Now, don't you start in on me, too. I already have two parents; I certainly don't need another!" She laughed. "But I will tell you this: if I were to get a job, it would have to be at the mall so I could meet lots of cute guys—maybe even in a men's shop. Yeah, now that would be more my style, don't you think?"

"I think it would hurt Jason's feelings if he heard you talking about meeting other guys."

"Oh, come on. You know I'm not crazy about Jason. I do like him—a little."

"Yeah, well, it's pretty obvious he's got it bad for you. You shouldn't toy with his emotions like you do." Even as Katie said the words, a sick feeling crept into the pit of her stomach. Hadn't she done that very thing with Eric the night before? She looked down at the chicken salad sandwich she had been nibbling.

"Well, not all of us can be so lucky as to have a god like Eric for a boyfriend."

Hearing envy but no accusation, Katie breathed a sigh of relief and forced herself to look into Kristin's eyes. She saw herself mirrored there and it reminded her to stay on course. "You're right. . . . and I'm sorry. Sometimes I forget how lucky I am. So, you wanted to know about last night?"

"Yes! And don't leave anything out!"

And so Katie told her. She didn't lie. The fact of the matter was that physically Eric was a great partner. She just conveniently left out the part about the emptiness she felt inside when Eric dropped her off in front of her apartment.

4

�֎

"KATIE, IS THAT YOU?"

"Yeah, it's me, Mama."

Daria looked up from the cutting board where she was chopping celery. "Did you remember to get the groceries?"

"Yes, I did," said Katie with a little grin. "You only reminded me three times before I left for work this morning."

"Come on, you know cooking isn't my strong suit."

"It's gonna be great, Mama." Katie pulled items out of the sack and set them on the counter. "I can't wait to get started. Mr. Brinker tried to get me to stay and work late, but I told him I had to get home and help you with the meal."

Daria put down her chopping knife and gave her daughter a quick hug. "I know you could use the money. Thanks."

"Well, I have to admit, I was pretty anxious to get out of there tonight. I have never seen it so packed. It was like a madhouse. You simply would not have believed it."

"Have you forgotten I've worked at a grocery store for the past ten years? The day before Thanksgiving is always a nightmare. I never would have got the day off except for all that overtime I did when half the staff was out with the flu."

"Hey, are these the pecans you want? They had whole ones, halves, and chips. I didn't know, so I got the halves."

"Yeah, that'll be fine. I remember my grandmother putting pecans on the sweet potatoes, so I thought I'd try that."

Turning so her mom couldn't see her, Katie's face gave way to a huge grin. Seeing her mother in the kitchen trying to cook up a big holiday meal was comical, but thrilling. "There, that's the last of the groceries. What can I do to help?"

"Do you really want to help?"

"Of course I do. We've never had a big Thanksgiving dinner before." Katie's mind produced a mental montage of their past Thanksgivings consisting of cold cuts and beer in front of some football game on TV. Usually, her mom's boyfriend would get drunk and, if they were lucky, pass out. If they weren't so lucky, they'd have to endure an unintelligible monologue about the inadequacies of the Montgomery women.

"Rick promised there would be no drinking this time, Katie. He's really trying. He's even working a little late tonight to make some extra money to pay me back for the turkey."

"Well, it's about time. All he ever does is eat or drink up all your money."

"Katie, please, give him another chance. I need him, and I know you don't understand this, but I love him. And I just want everything to be nice, for once."

Katie's eyes filled with tears. Often Katie felt more like the parent than the child. "Oh, Mama, I will try—I will, really. It's just that I love you so much, and I hate the way Rick treats you. You're always doing things for him and spending money on him, and for what? What does he ever do for you?"

"Well, for one thing, Katie, he's here, and I don't have to be alone. I don't expect you to understand, but that's the way it is. And he really does want to pay for the turkey."

"It would be nice to celebrate like a real family."

"Well, standing around talking isn't helping, so why don't you grab those onions over there and start chopping."

"Oh, sure," laughed Katie, "give me the job that's gonna make my eyes all red and puffy!"

"Well, somebody's got to do it, and I've got seniority!"

Katie basked in her mom's good mood. She usually seemed burdened and sad. Whatever Katie could do to ease her load and make her smile was worth it—even the dreaded task of chopping onions. She reached for the knife.

"Mama, we've never done the holiday thing before, so why are you intent on doing it now?"

Daria sighed. "Well, you're a senior in high school now, always talking about going off to college. You've got a boyfriend and a part-time job." Squeezing her daughter's shoulder, Daria looked straight into Katie's eyes and continued. "You are such a good daughter to me; I know I don't deserve you. But you're not my little Katie girl anymore, and well, uh . . . I think this dinner is my way to tell you that I'm sorry."

Katie swallowed a sob. "Sorry for what, Mama?"

"Oh, this isn't easy for me, sweetheart." Daria pushed a wayward strand of hair behind her daughter's ear. "I know I haven't been a very good mother to you. I never did any of those traditional mom things like cooking fancy dinners or baking cookies or any of that stuff, and I'm sorry." She shook her head. "Time flies. I turned around the other day and saw how grown up you were. I realized you're not going to stay around here with me forever, and I found myself being sad because of everything I've missed along the way and made you miss as well. I want to try to be a good mom to you—finally."

"Oh, Mama." Katie threw herself into her mother's arms. "I think you're a great mom. I understand. I know it hasn't been easy. I don't blame you one bit for anything that's happened. You've done the best you could. And I think having a Thanksgiving dinner this year is a wonderful idea!" Pausing to catch her breath and wipe the tears off her face, Katie smiled broadly at her mother. Suddenly no task in the world seemed sweeter than that of chopping onions.

❅   ❅   ❅

The doorbell rang just as Katie put the stuffing into the oven. "I'll get it, Mama, if you'll set the timer for 45 minutes."

"Sure, hon."

Katie waltzed to the door. It had been a great evening. Rick still wasn't home from the garage where he was a mechanic, so the entire night had been mother and daughter. They had laughed and kidded each other about how little they knew when it came to cooking. At one point they pretended they had their own cable mother/daughter cooking show. Katie had tied a flour-sack towel around her head as a makeshift chef's hat and Daria had adopted a French "Julia Childs" accent all the while giving a blow by blow description of how to make the world's ugliest sweet potato casserole.

"Oh, dear me," Daria had dramatically cackled, "it seems as if something has gone terribly wrong here. I don't believe this mixture is supposed to be quite this shade of green. In fact, it's not supposed to be green at all, but a wonderful, autumn orange. What do you suggest we do, my dear assistant?"

"Well, I think the only thing we can do, dear mother chef, is put some food coloring into it until we get the right color. After all, presentation is everything, you know."

"Ah, quite right, dear. And you out there in television land, remember: whatever it takes to make it look good, do it! If it's pretty enough, no one will even notice how bad it tastes!"

And with that Katie had burst out laughing. "Oh, if only that were so! What do you think we did wrong; 'cause this stuff looks very unappetizing."

They had worked on the dish for a while until it didn't taste too bad and actually began to look a little more appealing as well. But Katie was having so much fun, she didn't care how it tasted. She was still smiling when she opened the door and found Eric standing there.

"What are you doing here? It's 10:30 at night!"

"Well, I was out cruisin' around and came on a party over at Ryan Beckel's house. I came to get you so we could go. What is that thing on your head?"

Stifling a giggle, Katie pulled off her "chef's hat."

"It's nothing. Mama and I were cooking for tomorrow."

"I thought you said you guys never did anything special for Thanksgiving."

"Well, normally we don't, but my mom wanted to this year. I think it's kind of nice; I'm glad."

"Yeah, whatever; but we better get a move on if we're gonna make it to Ryan's."

"Eric, I just told you I'm busy helping my mom. I can't leave." Katie stepped into the hallway and closed the door behind her so her mom wouldn't hear the exchange.

"You mean you're not going with me?"

"I really need to stay here, Eric."

"Yeah, but I need you with me, babe."

"Oh, come on Eric, you see me all the time. What's one little night away from each other gonna matter?"

"Look, I don't want to be alone, okay? Is that so hard to understand? My folks left for my grandparents, and they said I didn't have to go. I was really counting on us being together, that's all. I thought girls liked that kind of stuff."

"Girls like to know their boyfriends want to spend time with them, but we also like a little advance notice. I've made plans with my mom to spend tonight and tomorrow together."

"You actually want to spend time with your mom?"

"Sure I do. We're having a great time." Katie giggled again while Eric shook his head. "Look, Eric, if you want to come in for a while, you're more than welcome. Mom and I are probably gonna be up cooking for at least another hour or so, and then we're gonna watch an old Cary Grant movie on TV."

"Uh, no thanks. Sounds lame, if you ask me. Besides, I don't think I could stomach being around your mom."

"And just what is that supposed to mean?"

"Oh, come on, Katie. You know every time I'm around it's like she flirts with me or something. It's strange."

"She does not! She likes you, but there's nothing wrong with that. Would you rather she hate your guts and tell us we can't see each other anymore?"

"Calm down, Katie. Whew! Kristin said you were protective of your mother, but that's an understatement."

"And just why were you talking to Kristin about my mother?" Katie's face had turned a dark shade of crimson.

Eric held his hands up as if in surrender. "Look, I just came over here because I was lonely for my Katie-girl. I never intended to get into an argument about this."

"Well, saying that about my mom was just plain cruel. She's all I've got. You've got two parents, but you never spend time with them, Eric, not even at the holidays. I don't want it to be that way with my mom and me. I want us to be close, and this Thanksgiving is important to her. I'm not gonna run off to some party and leave her, no matter what you say."

Daria stuck her head out into the hallway. "Oh, Eric, hello. Katie, why are you making your boyfriend stay out in the hall where it's so cold? Come on in the house, the both of you." She stepped back and beckoned them.

"Oh, no thank you, Miss Montgomery. I just came by to wish Katie a happy Thanksgiving. I need to be shoving off. I'm gonna go hang with some friends of mine. I was hoping Katie would come. All the other guys are bringing their girlfriends, but she seems to want to stay here."

"Now, Katie, don't you stay here on my account. Rick'll be home soon, and we're practically through cooking for the night. So, if you want to go, you run along. If I were you, I wouldn't be able to turn down a handsome boy like Eric."

A sick feeling crept into the pit of Katie's stomach. Eric had been right. Her mom was flirting with him. How had she not seen

42

it before? Maybe she was so used to it that she'd never thought twice about it, but here it was plain as day. Daria Montgomery couldn't function properly in the presence of a man, even if he was still in high school. Reason left her; all that mattered was making sure the guy—any guy—was happy no matter what. Maybe this was some kind of disease like Katie had seen on those sleazy talk shows: "women who love men who abuse them" or "women who fear being alone" or some other strange phenomenon.

Clearing her throat while simultaneously trying to clear the unwelcome thoughts from her head, Katie said at last, "Mama, I don't feel like going out. I worked at the store for six hours today, then came home and started cooking with you. Vegging out in front of an old movie sounds like about all I could stand tonight. But, Eric, like I said, if you want to join us, you're more than welcome."

"Oh, yes, please do," echoed Daria.

"Thanks, but I'll pass. Can I call you tomorrow, Katie?"

"Sure, and if you want to come and eat, dinner's gonna be about two o'clock."

"Well, maybe I'll come, I don't know. I'm gonna take off now." Eric cast a sheepish glance toward Daria.

"Well, I'm gonna go back in the kitchen and check something on the stove. You two carry on." Daria closed the door.

"I've got one last chance to make you change your mind and come with me." Before Katie could say anything Eric had her pinned against the front door kissing her passionately and running his fingers through her hair.

"Now, that's more like it." He was breathless. "I much prefer kissing you to arguing with you." He leaned down and let his hands roam over her body.

"Eric, stop that, not here. We're in a public place!"

"Since when has that ever stopped you before?"

"Eric, we have never done anything out in public."

"So, you like the back seat of my car, do you? Well, it's right down that stairwell, just waiting for you."

Trying to sound lighter than she felt, Katie countered, "Boy, you sure do know how to sweet talk a girl, don't you, Romeo?" She tried a little laugh, but it sounded stilted.

"Man, what is wrong with you tonight?" Eric backed away from Katie, glaring. "You won't go out with me, then you won't even kiss me back, and on top of all that, you make cracks about my charming nature."

"Or lack thereof. You're not yourself tonight, either, Eric, so why don't you go on to that party? It's what you want to do."

"What I want is for you to come with me. Everyone else'll be paired up; I don't wanna be the odd man out. Please, Katie, say you'll come with me." He practically begged. Katie might have laughed if it hadn't been so pitiful.

"Eric, the answer is no. I've made my decision."

Eric's eyes flashed. "You're doing everything you can to mess up what we've got, you know that?"

"And just what do we have, Eric? Are you gonna tell me you love me and can't live without me? What? Or are you just gonna tell me how much you enjoy sleeping with me?" She paused, but no reply came. "Well, what is it? Just what do we have that I'm trying so hard to mess up?"

Looking confused, Eric stammered, "If you have to ask, then obviously you don't have a clue how good we can be together. Why don't you take a little time and think about it—alone!" He turned on his heels and strode off. Just before reaching the staircase he called over his shoulder, "Have a good time with your mom," practically spitting out the last word. Then he descended the stairwell into blackness.

❄ ❄ ❄

Katie clicked the remote and watched as the TV screen went black. "Happy Thanksgiving, Mama."

"I guess technically it is Thanksgiving Day, isn't it?"

Katie glanced at her watch. "It's 12:55. . . . I just love that movie, don't you?"

"Yeah, it's a good one, but anything with Cary Grant in it would be good to my way of thinking."

"Do you realize, Mama, that Cary Grant is about the only guy you and I agree on?"

Daria chuckled. "Now that you mention it, I guess you're right. We do have pretty different views on men, don't we? I still can't believe you chose to stay here with me instead of going out with Eric. He seems like such a nice kid, and he certainly isn't bad to look at either. I confess, had I been in your shoes, I think I would have gone with him instead of staying with my mother."

"Well, I'm not you. I think I made the right choice."

"Well, whether you wanted to or not, I'm glad you did." Daria smiled at her daughter. They both sat slumped on the sofa with their feet propped up on the coffee table, a huge, half-empty bowl of popcorn nestled between them. "If you hadn't stayed, I would have been alone. I guess Rick isn't gonna make good on his promise. He should've been home two hours ago."

"I really am sorry, Mama."

"Well, this certainly won't be the first time he's let me down. It won't be the last either, I'm sure."

"So, why do you put up with it? It doesn't have to be this way. You could find somebody better, I'm sure. I mean, you're attractive, funny, you've got a lot going for you."

"And you think Cary Grant's out there waiting for a 37 year-old grocery checker like me?" Daria threw up her hands in disgust. "Haven't I raised you to be more sensible than that? People like us, Katie, have to make do with what we can get."

"You expect to be treated like dirt? You can't really believe that, can you, Mama?"

"Oh, don't sound so shocked, and don't be so naïve. You've got too many romantic notions in your head. Maybe I should ban you

45

from these old movies; they're not good for you. Katie, these movies are strictly fantasy, nothing more."

"Oh, so I'm naïve and living in a fantasy world because I'd like for a guy to genuinely care about me and to enjoy talking to me as much as he enjoys kissing me? When did that become some romantic notion as opposed to reality?"

Daria knit her brow and sat up. "Then, Katie, tell me one couple you know that meets your standard of romance."

Katie slumped her shoulders and frowned. "Just because I can't think of one doesn't mean it's not possible. You don't have to see something to believe in it."

"Katie, listen to me. I may not be a great mother, but I am going to give you some advice right now because I see you headed for a world of hurt. Give up these romantic notions of yours and be content with what you have."

"Why is it so difficult to believe things might turn out differently for me than they have for you?"

"Oh, sweetheart, I don't want to rain on your parade, but I don't want to lie to you either. I used to believe in life and love; but it isn't wise, Katie." Daria's eyes glazed over as she retreated to her faraway place. Normally Katie would let her go there alone. But tonight she felt compelled to journey with her.

With trepidation Katie asked quietly, "My father is the one who hurt you, isn't he?"

Daria Montgomery sat motionless. Katie half expected her mother to grow angry at this blatant intrusion of her privacy, and so was relieved when she remained docile. Katie dared to continue. "Was he the one who crushed your dreams?"

Slowly Daria nodded. She stared straight ahead, transfixed, as if she was seeing her past emblazoned on the blank wall in front of her. Katie had to know what was there. "I know you don't like to talk about it, Mama; but please, I want to know what happened. I want to know about my father."

Daria spoke in a near whisper and Katie leaned close to hear. "He was incredible. He was Cary Grant and more. He knew just how to make me feel good. I wasn't smart like you are. I didn't have much going for me except a decent figure and a pretty face. I was from the wrong side of the tracks. I never fit in at school or at home for that matter. The only place I really felt like I fit was in T.J.'s arms." She sighed wearily.

"So my father's name is T.J.?"

"Yeah, Terence Joseph Nichols. He hated his full name, would only go by T.J. He was a musician, a good singer. He thought T.J. was a better stage name. I guess he was right about that." Daria gave a soft laugh. "He loved his music, that's for sure. I had to learn the hard way that he loved it more than he loved me."

"What happened? Why did you guys break up?"

Daria's eyes instantly flashed. "Do you really want to know?" The question was spoken almost as a threat.

"Y-yes, I do."

"Well, to make a long story short, your father took one look at you and said 'so long' to me."

The matter-of-fact statement caught Katie off guard.

"What did you say?"

"You wanted the truth, you got it. I never wanted to tell you, but there it is. The truth. If it hadn't been for you I could have had the love of my life. I could have had my own Cary Grant—only your father was better looking. But instead, I'm a single mother living with the likes of Rick McBride. And you wonder why I don't believe in fairy tales." Daria got up to make herself a drink.

Katie's head reeled. She was having difficulty taking it all in. *I'm the cause of all my mother's pain. All these years, all the pain, it's all been because of me.* Katie dared to glance at her mother's face. What she saw made one thing startlingly and painfully clear: Daria Montgomery would have preferred having T.J. Nichols in her life over her own daughter. Katie had difficulty catching her breath.

"I'm s-sorry, Mama," she stammered as she rose to leave the room. "I didn't know. . . . I'm s-so sorry." She fled to her room and closed the door behind her. With her back against the door, she sank to the floor and buried her head in her hands. She wept. She wept for all her mother's pain, for all her mother's lost dreams. And she wept that Katie Montgomery had ever been born.

5

✳

"SO, HOW WAS YOUR THANKSGIVING?" asked Kristin, sliding into the desk next to Katie's in Monday morning chemistry class.

Katie hesitated before answering. Thanksgiving had been a disaster. There was the fight with Eric—she hadn't heard from him since—and Rick had stumbled in around 3:00 a.m. and managed to stay drunk all weekend. The turkey never got cooked, and the rest of the food wasn't fit to eat. Not that anyone besides Katie had noticed. Her mom had joined Rick on the drinking binge and seemed to forget the entire conversation she'd had with Katie about her dad.

"It was typical, I guess. How was yours?"

Kristin's eyes danced. "Oh, I had a great time. I went to Ryan's party. It was a blast! You should have been there."

"I thought Jason was out of town. Eric said Ryan's party was a couples thing."

Kristin's face reddened. "W-well, it kind of was. He had this neat hayride thing planned, you know, since they own all those horses. Anyway, it was romantic, and you'd feel strange without somebody."

"Yeah, that's what Eric told me. Guess I should have listened to him. I probably would have had a better time there. She shrugged her shoulders. "Well, no sense crying over spilled milk. So, who did you go to the party with?"

"No one you'd be interested in. I don't want to talk about it. You'll just lecture me about sneaking around behind Jason's back."

"You're right. I don't think I want to know."

Kristin cleared her throat. "That's probably best. Now, to

change the subject, Eric said you two had a big fight."

"Well, to be honest with you, Kris, I didn't think it was all that big a deal, but he didn't call me all weekend. I guess I really did make him mad. . . . How'd you know we had a fight?"

At that moment Mr. Reynolds instructed the class to take out their textbooks and turn to page ninety-five.

Katie looked at her best friend who shrugged her shoulders and smiled. This gave Katie an uneasy feeling inside. She normally enjoyed chemistry class, but today she couldn't wait for it to be over.

❋ ❋ ❋

Negotiating the hallways of Stoughton high school was a fine art at best and an exercise in futility the rest of the time. Today Katie could barely stay within earshot of Kristin as they muddled through the mass of ambulating bodies.

Kristin arrived first at the locker they shared. "Kristin!" Katie shouted. "Wait for me!"

"I can't. I've got to get to psychology early. Tricia's gonna let me copy her homework. I'm in a rush. See ya."

Katie mindlessly reached into the locker to grab her history book. She had study hall next period and wanted to cram for the history test she had after that. She wouldn't be able to do anything about her best friend until fifth period when they had lunch together.

❋ ❋ ❋

With her elbow propped on the lunch table Katie combed her fingers through her hair, from her forehead all the way back. Finally, she rested her chin in her hand and gave it one last shot. "Come on, Kristin, this is getting ridiculous. Why won't you tell me what's bothering you?"

"I told you already; nothing is bothering me."

"Look, I know you like a sister. Something is wrong."

"Okay, you win. I'll tell, but promise me no lectures?"

"All right, I promise."

Taking a deep breath, Kristin began, "Last Wednesday night, Eric came over to my house. He was really upset over the fight you two had. He told me how the comments he made about your mom really upset you. I have to be honest with you, Katie, your mom is a little strange when it comes to men. I mean, how many boyfriends has she had just in the five years I've known you?"

Remembering her promise, Katie struggled to keep her anger in check. "So what's the big deal? So she can't find the right person. I don't think that gives Eric or you or anybody the right to call her strange. She's just lonely, that's all."

"Well, call it what you want, but Eric was pretty upset that you chose your mom over him. He was counting on you to go with him to that party."

"Maybe he should have told me about it beforehand."

"It was just a spur-of-the-moment thing. You'd have known about it if you weren't always running off to that job of yours."

The contempt in Kristin's voice was not lost on Katie. With effort she replied, "I've explained that to you and to Eric. I need the money. I want to go to college, and there's no other way. Why do you guys fight me so hard on this?"

"Haven't you heard of student loans?"

"Oh yeah, right. Like I want to still be paying for my education when I'm forty. No thank you!"

Kristin exhaled loudly, not attempting to hide her irritation. "Look, I only know what Eric told me. He's getting tired of always coming in second in your life. He thought things would get better when the two of you started . . ." Kristin looked around to make sure no one was listening, then continued, "When the two of you started sleeping together. But he said nothing has changed. He said the sex is good, but you don't seem too interested in the relationship."

Fury rising inside her, Katie clenched her teeth to keep from screaming. "What does he mean I'm not interested in the relationship?

I try to tell Eric what's going on in my life, and he doesn't care. I try to explain to him about my hopes for the future or my feelings for my mom, and he doesn't care. All he wants to do is make out! I'm not even sure he understands what a relationship is all about!" Katie was too charged up to stop. "I know you guys make fun of my mom, but the truth of the matter is that you are all pursuing the same kind of relationships she has with her boyfriends: all sex and no substance. Take Rick for instance: he couldn't care less about my mom! He never talks to her or dreams with her; he just sleeps with her and occasionally gives her a present to keep her off his back. But he sure expects her to be there at his beck and call whenever he wants her. That's exactly what Eric wants from me. Well, I want something deeper." Katie's voice had softened by the end of her tirade, and tears were in her eyes.

Kristin closed her eyes and shook her head. "I knew this would turn into a lecture."

"I'm not lecturing." Katie's voice quaked. "You just think I am because I don't agree with you. You think relationships are about getting to go out and have a cute guy hold your hand; I think they're about sharing your life with someone, even the bad stuff, maybe especially the bad stuff."

"Whatever your reasons for treating Eric the way you do, you're going to lose him if things don't change."

"Okay. I'll think about it, and I'll talk to Eric."

"That's a good idea, Katie, a real good idea."

While Kristin went to dispose of her lunch tray, Katie couldn't help thinking, *I wonder why she thinks I'll be the only one losing out if Eric and I break up?* With a frown, Katie glanced around at all the commotion of the cafeteria. She was in the middle of a sea of people and felt like she was all alone and drowning. She wanted to stand up and scream, *Doesn't anybody see me? Doesn't anybody out there feel my pain? Am I not worth anything to anybody?* But Katie masterfully hid these thoughts and finished eating the ham sandwich she had brought from home.

6

✿

KATIE LAY ON HER BED that evening, staring at the ceiling. She made no attempt now to cover over the ugly stains. That action had come from one who still held hope that things could change, that certain cycles might be broken. No, on this night Katie took great comfort in the dingy, gray atmosphere closing in around her. It matched her mood and her life. In the silence she let her mind wander; yet it always came back to a little, ugly stain in the middle of a swirling ocean. She was that little stain, and she was drowning in that ocean.

With a mirthless laugh, she spoke into the silence. "Can things get any worse? It really would be funny if it weren't so painful." Her mom didn't understand her; even the sight of Rick made her stomach churn; Kristin had taken Eric's side in their argument and made no attempt to see Katie's point of view; and now she desperately wanted to break free of the trap that had become her life. She felt it her destiny to be like some helpless animal caught in a hunter's trap, whose only way free was to chew off its own leg.

This realization startled Katie. In a mortified voice she blurted, "Do I have to chew my own leg off to break free?"

Still breathless from the savage vision inside her head, Katie didn't hear her mom come into her little room.

"Katie, did you say something? Are you all right?"

Surprised by her mother's nearness, Katie tried to answer calmly, "Oh, yeah, I'm fine. I guess I was dreaming."

"Well, I certainly hope so," chimed in her mom, "but I think nightmare is more like it because I could have sworn I heard you say something about chewing off your leg! That's a pretty strange thing to be dreaming about."

"I'm all right. We . . . uh . . . saw some pretty gruesome films in biology. I guess they affected me more than I thought." Katie hated lying, but her mother would never understand. This way was a lot easier. Her mom wouldn't even realize she had taken biology two years earlier and now had chemistry.

Katie was right. The whole comment was lost on her mother. "I thought only horror films gave people nightmares! Who would think school films would do that!" scoffed Daria.

"Really, Mama, I'm okay. What time is it anyway?"

"Almost seven. Do you want some dinner? We ordered pizza; it should be here any minute."

"So that means Rick is here?"

"Yes, Katie. He does live here, you know."

"Oh, I know all right. I was just asking, that's all. But the truth is Eric is supposed to be coming by tonight."

"Have you two made up then?" questioned a hopeful Daria as she sat on the edge of her daughter's mattress.

"Not exactly. He avoided me all day at school today, but Kristin told me why he was so upset. I tracked him down after school and asked if we could talk. He said he'd come over. That's all I know."

"Well, why is he so upset with you?"

Not wanting to get into it with her mom, Katie simply answered, "It's a long story, and if I take the time to tell you, I won't be ready when Eric gets here." She smiled slightly at her mother anticipating what was coming next.

And sure enough, as if they had rehearsed, Daria said, "Well, if you're interested in keeping Eric around, dolling yourself up a little might do the trick." With that, she rose. She turned just before leaving and, in a sincere tone, told her daughter, "I certainly hope everything works out between the two of you. I like Eric."

When her mom was gone, the words "might do the trick"

echoed in Katie's mind. *I'm not interested in tricking anyone into staying. I want someone to stay with me because they can't imagine being anywhere else. Is that too much to ask?*

Fearing it was, Katie moved to stand in front of the full-length mirror attached to the back of her bedroom door. She gazed at her reflection. Even though she had on a pair of old sweat pants and a sweatshirt, Katie couldn't miss the fact that she was a pretty girl. She reached up and tugged on the scrunchy holding her ponytail in place. She let the light brown hair cascade over her shoulders and down to the middle of her back. "Oh, why bother? Eric's not even on the same wavelength as me."

She brushed out her hair and pulled on her favorite pair of Levi's, the old ones with the hole in the knee. Her mother hated them, but she didn't care. She left on the sweatshirt; after all, who was she trying to impress? They were just going to talk. It shouldn't matter.

For a brief moment Katie considered calling Eric and telling him to forget the whole thing, that they weren't meant to be together. The thought actually caused her to sigh with relief, but clinging to the heel of that pleasant thought came the unbidden recollection of Daria Montgomery's words from a few days earlier: *I've been with a man and I've been without a man. And trust me, even with all the trouble they bring, it's still better with than without. Bein' alone is no sweet ride.* Try as she might to put the words out of her mind, they continued to reverberate. Especially that last line: *Bein' alone is no sweet ride, bein' alone is no sweet ride, bein' alone is no sweet ride.*

Shaking her head in an attempt to shut out the unwelcome cadence, Katie purposed to do everything she could to make Eric understand she really did want him to stay in her life. Anything sounded better than being alone.

❄ ❄ ❄

Katie sat tensely in the front seat as Eric brought his car to a stop in front of Paine Park, a secluded place this time of night. He turned toward Katie who sat staring at her hands folded in her lap.

"Here we are," Eric broke the tense silence. "I thought this would be a good spot for us to talk and sort some things out."

Katie gave him the slightest of smiles as she looked up. "Yeah, you've already said that," she reminded him.

"So I have," he laughed softly. "I guess I'm a little nervous about this conversation. I feel like maybe our whole relationship is riding on this." He looked at her with hope and adoration in his eyes.

Katie twisted her hands. "I suppose you're right. Well, let's get started."

"You are direct, aren't you?"

Katie shrugged her shoulders and responded, "We might as well get it over with. No sense wasting time."

"You don't sound like you have much hope for us, Katie. Do you want to break up with me?" Eric asked tentatively.

Katie hesitated. "It's not that I want to break up, but I do know I don't want to keep going the way we are." She felt a brief moment of relief just having said the words.

"Katie, I don't understand. I've heard you say that before, but I don't know what it is you want. It seems to me we have everything we need." He spoke quietly and controlled, but there was no mistaking the frustration in his voice.

"And that's my point exactly, Eric. You see, I want to know you're with me because you care about me and not just because you need a girl to accompany you wherever you go or because you need a girl to fill the backseat of your car whenever you have the desire. Anybody can do that for you, Eric. I want more. I don't know what else to say."

"But Katie, I want it to be you, nobody else. I could have most anybody I wanted, but I want you."

Katie shook her head. "Can I ask you a question?"

"Sure, anything. Ask me anything."

"Why do you want me to be your girlfriend? You said yourself you could have any girl you wanted, and I believe you, Eric, I do. I'm not blind. I know how popular you are and how the girls are always flirting with you, and I saw how unhappy they all were when you started dating me exclusively. So it just makes me wonder why you'd give all that attention up to be with me."

"People date in high school; it's what everybody does. You find someone you like and you date. What is so difficult about that? Why don't you understand? Why do you have to make everything so complicated?" He stopped for a moment, looking thoughtful. Then with a softer voice he continued. "Katie, you really are special. There is a quality about you that I can't define, a gentleness maybe. Whatever it is, I like it. I think maybe the reason I want you for my girlfriend is that I feel good when you're with me, if that makes any sense. It feels right, you know? You're different than any other girl I've been with. I feel I can trust you and stuff."

"You can trust me, Eric, if only you would. I'd like to know what you're thinking and what you're dreaming." Katie now had a faraway look in her eyes. "I want you to open up to me, and I want the freedom to open up to you without being told I'm wrong or that I'm living in some kind of fantasy world."

"We talk about stuff like that all the time, Katie."

"No, Eric, we don't."

"Oh, yes we do," replied Eric in a louder voice.

"Eric," said Katie in an even tone, "the only time you ever open up to me is after we've had sex. And then all you do is tell me how you're gonna make it big someday and have tons of money. That's not opening your heart, that's opening your mouth." Katie practically spat out those last words and immediately regretted how harsh they had sounded. She lowered her head, so she missed the heat rising in Eric's face. "I'm sorry," she offered contritely. "I didn't mean that the way it sounded."

"It's always the same with you, isn't it, Katie? It's never enough, never quite what you're looking for. I think you want too much. And you're never gonna find it, Katie, never."

Anger growing inside her, Katie passionately retaliated. "I don't see why everybody thinks I'm asking for too much. But I'll tell you what I think. I've watched my mom for years with all her different men, and I've watched Kristin go through boyfriend after boyfriend, and the problem is that nobody wants to be there for the bad times. The minute it starts getting a little sticky, they're out the door. Eric, don't you see? I need someone I can go to and talk about my fears or my problems—someone I can trust is going to be there for me when it's all over. But if I tell you something about my mom, you just say she's looney, like that solves everything. But I still have to live with her and, whether you understand it or not, I love her. But do you ever care to know how I feel? No! Don't you see how selfish that is?"

"Selfish! You think I'm selfish!" Eric was practically shouting now. "It seems like I'm always waiting on you to finish something important to you."

"Like what?" demanded an equally irate Katie.

"Oh, please, Katie. How many times have you turned down going somewhere with me because you had to go to the library to study or because you had to work or because you wanted to stay home and babysit your mom! How dare you say I'm selfish. I've never put up with garbage like what you dish out! Most girls rearrange their schedules for me, Katie. You don't know how lucky you've been these past four months or how good you've had it!"

Katie could not believe her ears. She was not going to take this without a fight. "Eric Martin," she began in a surprisingly calm and even tone, "you are the one who made the choice to not be with me on most of those occasions. I've always asked you to come and study with me or to stay with my mom and me, just like the night before Thanksgiving. But you chose not to do those things. You didn't want to give up your agenda. It's always been your way or no way, and you know it."

"Oh, really? Well, Miss Self-Sacrificer, what exactly have you given up for me? Tell me that, if you can."

Katie did not miss the mocking tone of his voice. She took a deep breath and ventured her response. "Well, for one thing, I gave my body to you."

He looked at her with a shocked expression, as if he couldn't believe she had said that. Then his expression changed to one of annoyance. "So now you're going to tell me that you got nothing in return for that?"

"Oh, don't worry, Eric, your reputation hasn't suffered any. You gave me a lot of physical pleasure. You're very good at what you do." Her words were controlled now.

"So then, what's the problem?"

"The problem is that I thought a physical relationship would bring us closer together; but in the end, all it did was give you more of what you wanted and leave me feeling cold and alone—Oh, don't get that defensive look on your face. I'm as much to blame as anybody for my present state of mind. And I'm not even mad at you, Eric; really I'm not."

They sat in silence a long time. Eric stared out the windshield. Katie had that faraway look in her eyes again. After a while she spoke. Her voice was placid as if she were thinking out loud.

"I knew it was wrong from the beginning," confessed Katie. "I let everyone else talk me into it, but I knew I wanted something you couldn't give. I just didn't have the courage to say 'no.' I even convinced myself it was all right." She looked over at Eric with tears in her eyes. She continued in a slightly muffled voice. "I owe you an apology, Eric. I never should have expected you to be something you're not. You never pretended with me. I was the one who was playing a game. I never wanted a superficial or sexual relationship. I just did it to fit in. And now you're having to pay the price as well as me. I'm sorry."

"Look, Katie," came a voice not even sounding like Eric's anymore. "I'm real sorry, I really am, for whatever has happened in your life to make you feel the way you are right now, but you've got to understand that I don't need any of this. You make it sound like I've been using you or something, and it sounds to me like you've been using me."

"You're right, Eric. That's why I was trying to apologize. I never should have pretended to feel things that I didn't. I thought I could be happy if we were dating. Everybody told me I would, and, stupid me, I believed them." She shook her head.

Katie was ashamed of what she had done and somehow wanted to make it up to him. But how could she? The damage had been done several months ago in Kristin's rec room. It had all been a big lie, and now they were both miserable. All she could think of to say was, "You should be with someone who can truly appreciate you, Eric. You at least deserve that." Katie sighed loudly.

Eric seethed. "Don't you go worrying about me, Katie Montgomery. In fact you can rest your pretty little head about the whole matter. I've already found someone that can 'appreciate' me, as you say. As a matter of fact, she's already shown me just how appreciative she is." He looked at her.

Katie looked him straight in the eye and gently reached out to touch his hand. "Oh, Eric, I hope so, I really do."

Eric Martin gaped at his former girlfriend. "Either you didn't hear me correctly or you don't believe me. If you want to make sure I'm gonna be okay, all you have to do is ask Kristin. She can tell you." He smiled tellingly.

"Why would Kristin know?" came the innocent question.

"Why don't you ask her about last Wednesday night? I was going to keep those events a secret, because I actually felt bad about it. But after all you've said tonight, I think you deserve to know.

"After you turned me down last week, I went to see Kristin to hash some stuff out, you know, unload some emotions. Let me just say Kristin is an expert at consoling depressed guys. She knew exactly what to do to make me feel much better and to forget about the way you treated me."

Realization came slowly for Katie, not because she didn't think Eric capable of cheating on her, but because her heart refused to believe Kristin would do that to her. However, conversations with her best friend gradually replayed themselves in Katie's mind. It dawned on her that Kristin had been hinting for months that she wanted to be with Eric. Katie could almost feel her heart exploding inside her chest—not just breaking. Then the sobs Eric had been waiting for came. Although she couldn't think straight, one thing was clear: Kristin had no problem playing the game. In fact, it came easy for her. She had been doing it for so long she couldn't even stop when her best friend's heart was at stake. That was the hardest blow of all.

Katie cried for some time before looking up and searching Eric's eyes. Seeing nothing but pity and a smug satisfaction, Katie shook her head and said, "You know, a few hours ago I was thinking my life probably couldn't get any worse. Now I know I was wrong." She choked on the chuckle her last statement brought. She then reached to open the car door. "I think I'm gonna walk home now."

"Katie, we can talk about this; you shouldn't be walking in the dark by yourself." There was concern in his voice, but it didn't sway Katie's decision.

"Eric, it's okay. You go on home or to Kristin's or to some party or wherever it is you want to go. I'll be fine. I think I need to be alone right now." As soon as the words were out of her mouth, she saw the irony in them and burst out laughing. Less than two hours ago she had purposed to do whatever it took to keep from being alone. It was so ridiculous that she couldn't stop laughing. If she did stop laughing, she would sob all the way home.

7

✳

DARIA MONTGOMERY POURED HERSELF A SECOND CUP of coffee. She heard the shower turn on. It was Katie. Rick was still snoring in their bedroom. Slipping into one of the kitchen chairs by the window, Daria fingered the white eyelet curtain beside her. She remembered the day Katie had proudly walked in with her purchase saying, "We need something to make this place look a little more homey." Her daughter had stood back and admired the finished product. What Daria's mother-heart had admired was how Katie had spent money from her first paycheck from the grocery store to buy the little curtains. They weren't fancy or expensive—just from the local WalMart—but they did lend an airiness and femininity to an otherwise drab and dull room.

Daria pushed the edge of the curtain back to see outside. She was greeted by a sheet of white. It must have snowed a foot overnight. Something about a fresh snow made Daria want to smile. Everything looked so pristine and pure, so unadulterated; even death took on a whole new light after a freshly-fallen snow. Dead grass was covered over with a blanket of soft cotton; and barren trees looked all snug and warm wrapped up in their winter clothing. It was almost enough to give a person hope—almost.

But Daria was a realist. The world had taught her it was safer that way. She knew all good things come to an end, and you were left with nothing but a mess. The snow would turn brown as people walked over it or kids played in it, and the snowplow would come along and push big dirty mounds to the side of the road. And then the world would once again look as it did before; the winter wonderland lasted for only a few very short hours. You had to enjoy it while you could, if you were lucky enough to find the time to do so.

This morning was one of those rare occasions when Daria had the time to sit and relax while drinking her morning coffee. Usually she was rushing to make it to work on time. This morning, however, she had awakened early and couldn't go back to sleep, so she'd gone ahead and gotten up. Her few precious moments of solitude had been much needed. She had been worried about her daughter for several weeks. Ever since she had broken up with Eric and learned about Kristin's betrayal, Katie hadn't been the same.

In her otherwise bleak world Daria's daughter was a ray of sunshine. Katie always made things more beautiful. Daria absently stroked the curtains while once again remembering Katie's satisfied smile over the simplest of things. "Oh, my Katie girl," whispered Daria into the bare room, "are you ever gonna be yourself again? Where's the light that used to be in your eyes? What's going on inside you? And why don't I have the guts to try to find out?" She sighed, knowing she would cry if she dwelt on her inadequacies as a mother. There wasn't time for crying when you had a job waiting for you in a little less than an hour.

Just then Katie, hair still wet and slicked back, came into the kitchen. "Morning, Mama," she said flatly.

"Hi, sweetie. Do you want something to eat? I brought some doughnuts home from the grocery store last night."

"Thanks, but no. I'm not feeling too great this morning. My stomach's a little upset, so I think I'll skip breakfast."

"I hope you're not coming down with that nasty old flu that's been going around."

"No, I don't think it's that. Probably just something I ate." Katie was speaking in a disinterested tone.

Stifling her emotions and trying her best to keep the conversation going, Daria ventured, "Did you notice the snow outside? We got us a good one last night. It's really pretty."

Katie gave an obligatory glance out the window. "Mmm, that is pretty. We haven't had much snow this year."

Daria rose from the table and deposited her coffee mug in the sink. "Are you working today?" It was Christmas vacation, and she knew Katie was hoping to get in a lot of hours to increase her college money.

"Yeah, but I don't go in until ten."

"Lucky you. I've got to be there at eight. Well, drink some 7-Up; that usually helps. There's still some in the fridge."

"Thanks. See you there,"came Katie's distant reply.

In her bedroom Daria finished dressing. Rick's motionless form sprawled over the bed, his belly hanging out of his t-shirt, and his mouth sagging open. The sight was familiar. This was the way he always looked after a night of hard drinking with his buddies.

Daria thought to herself: *If there's a God up in heaven, please let my Katie girl's life turn out better than mine.*

8

❋

KATIE ARRIVED AT WORK shortly before ten. She was feeling much better, physically. She could not shake the hopeless feeling, though, that had grown inside her ever since she and Eric broke up. Nothing seemed to matter anymore, and loneliness was sad company to keep. Maybe her mom had been right all along. Maybe it was better to be with the wrong person than to be alone. As difficult as it was to shut the door on her hopes and dreams, Katie knew a person could avoid reality for only so long and still maintain their sanity. It was time for her to face the truth: she would end up just like her mother.

Katie's eyes glistened as she mindlessly scanned the next customer's items: $.89 for eggs, $1.29 for apple juice, $2.99 for ground chuck. She wondered: what value would her life ring up if it were scanned on the computer? As the probable answer came to her, the tears threatened to spill over. The last thing Katie wanted was a big emotional scene at work. She turned her head slightly in the hopes of avoiding the customer and dabbed at her eyes.

A gentle voice broke into Katie's determined masquerade. "Are you all right, honey?"

Katie looked up into the sweetest blue eyes she had ever seen. She nodded her head and swallowed down the little sob pushing for release from its prison.

"Well," came the gentle voice once again, "sometimes these prices make me want to weep, too." The delicate-looking older lady broke into a broad smile. A small giggle rose up inside Katie and began to do battle with the sob to see which would get free first. To

Katie's delight, the giggle won out. As it escaped she smiled. "Thanks I needed a pick-me-up."

"You know, we all need a pick-me-up from time to time." The smile was replaced by a visage that was serious yet remarkably soft and friendly. "I don't profess to know what's troubling you today, but I imagine that with a little time, things won't look as bad as all that. The good Lord has seen me through my share of heartaches, and He's always been faithful to keep me going." She fished for something in her purse while Katie resumed scanning the few remaining items.

"That's $42.56. Would you like paper or plastic, ma'am?"

"Plastic would be fine, dear. And it's so nice to hear a young person say *ma'am*. I was beginning to think this new generation found such terms outdated."

Katie bagged the groceries. "Well, I've wondered recently if I fit in with this generation at all." Katie surprised herself with this admission, and to a total stranger at that.

"It's hard trying to figure out where you belong in this world, especially when you're young. But, I'll tell you this: the Lord always puts us where we are for a reason. So you keep searching and asking, and you'll find the answers. I'm as sure of that as I am that there's a God up in heaven." Her countenance once again displayed a beautiful smile. "And rest assured, I know there is a God in heaven, and I know He cares about you just as much as He cares about me."

Katie had finished the bagging. Now she was struggling to understand what had just been told to her. Silently she reached out to receive the money the lady was handing her. On top of the stack of bills was a little card that said, "Cast all your anxiety on him because he cares for you. (1 Peter 5:7)"

"What's this?" Katie stared at the card, puzzled.

"Just something I want you to keep. Pull it out and read it when you're having a tough time." She paused as if considering what she should say next. Then she looked directly into Katie's eyes. "Don't you ever stop asking the questions. Search and search until you have your answers; then you'll be fine." She smiled again. "And when you read that card, think of a funny old lady in your grocery line who thought you were a really nice person."

Flabbergasted, Katie handed the lady her change. "I will, ma'am. Thank you for coming through my line. Do you want some help out with those bags?" She felt the words sounded lame.

"No, thanks. I think I can get it myself." She began pushing her cart but then stopped and turned back to face Katie.

"What is your name, dear?"

"Uh . . . My name is Katie."

"Good," she said. "If possible, I always like to know the names of the people I pray for." Then she was gone.

Stunned, Katie had the feeling the strange, sweet little lady had been able to see right through to her very heart. Katie almost bolted after her. She found a little consolation in the fact that no one was waiting in her line at the moment. She had a few minutes to replay in her head the strange encounter. She looked again at the little business-size card. "Cast all your anxiety on him because he cares for you." She mumbled to herself, "Could this really be true?" She was still contemplating the possibility when she heard her mother's voice.

"Hey, Katie. How's it going down here on aisle #3?"

Broken from her rumination, Katie responded, "It's okay. How about up there on aisle #10?"

"Oh, work's work and a paycheck's a paycheck. I won't complain—at least not today," she added with a mocking grin. Daria knew she wasn't known for having a cheery disposition.

"Have you ever noticed a sweet-looking old lady here before?"

"Only every day! Tons of sweet little ladies shop here."

"I know, but this one seemed kinda special. She had whitish gray hair pulled up in a bun and wire-rimmed glasses that sat low on her nose. She had a twinkle in her eyes and the kindest smile I've ever seen. Here, she gave me this."

Daria read the card then frowned and handed it back. "That's sweet, Katie, but it's just emotional hogwash. It may make you feel good for a moment; but it doesn't help out much in the real world." Seeing the disappointment on her daughter's face, she added, "You don't believe that stuff, do you?"

Katie paused a second. "No, of course not. I'm sure it's just religious propaganda, like you said."

"Oooo! Such a big word! You're learning more at school than I ever did." Daria's tone was light, and Katie knew the subject of the little old lady had been dropped. Oddly, this made her sad. She found comfort in knowing someone would be praying for her. So what if God didn't really exist. At least someone thought enough about her to think of her once in a while. That alone was worth something, wasn't it? She squeezed the little card and shoved it into her pocket. She would keep it no matter what her mom said. Katie was good at hiding things from her mom. She'd been doing it for years.

"Honey, the reason I came over here is to tell you I just talked to Rick on the phone. He needs his car today after all, so I'm gonna have to take it home to him. He'll drop me off back here, but since you get off work before me, you'll have to come back and get me at five. I hope that doesn't mess you up."

Katie shook her head and sighed. "No, it's no big deal. I don't have any plans anyway."

"I knew I could count on you. And don't forget, Rick and I are going out tonight, so you're on your own for dinner."

"I didn't forget. That's fine."

"Well, I gotta go take the car to Rick. Mr. Brinker said I could take my break now if I hurry, so I'm off."

Katie was reminded that she was seeing her future every time she laid eyes on her mom. But a customer with a cart piled with groceries was heading her way, and she didn't have time to dwell on the thought. She put her hand to the pocket and patted the card from the strange lady. With a smile she said, "Would you like paper or plastic, ma'am?"

9

KATIE WORKED HARD to convince her mom she liked the make-up kit
she had bought her for Christmas; and as far as make-up kits went,
it was a nice one: ten colors of eye shadows, three shades of blush,
an assortment of brushes, eye liners, lip pencils, and even pressed
powders. Katie figured it to be the Cadillac of cosmetic essentials. The
only problem was she didn't care anything about cosmetics. What little
she used, she picked up at the grocery store.

"Oh, Mama, you shouldn't have gotten me something so
extravagant! This must have cost a small fortune."

Daria smiled. "I wanted you to have it—something to make
you feel special and beautiful."

Katie figured as much. She knew her mom had been concerned
about her ever since her split with Eric, and to Daria's way of thinking,
nothing could cheer a body up faster than cosmetics. Try as she might,
Katie couldn't stop the little smile forming on her face. Even if she
didn't particularly like the gift, she did appreciate how her mom was
trying to make this a nice Christmas for her.

"Thanks, Mama." Katie gave her mom a heartfelt hug. "And,
now I want to give you your present." She crossed the living room
and pulled a package from under the tiny tree standing in the corner.
Katie was the one who usually insisted on having a tree. But this time
it was Daria who dragged the artificial tree out of the closet, set it up,
and decorated it, all in an attempt to brighten Katie's holiday. Katie
felt ashamed of the bad attitude she'd had lately. It wasn't her mom's
fault that her life had fallen apart a month earlier. And seeing all the

measures Daria had taken to ensure that it was a nice Christmas only made Katie grimace. Now she could add guilt to her already long list of raging emotions. She determined to straighten up her act. When she turned to face her mom, she was all smiles.

"Here, Mama. Merry Christmas."

"Oh, sweetie, you didn't have to get me anything." Daria's eyes glimmered. "But I sure am glad you did! And look how pretty the wrapping is. Katie, you have such a way of making things look nice. Did you see this, Rick?"

Daria held up the box so her boyfriend could see. "Huh? Oh, yeah, that sure is . . . uh . . . pretty . . . you did a real fine job on that there wrapping, Katie girl, real fine."

It was obvious to Katie that her mom must have had a talk with Rick and somehow managed to get him to promise to be on his best behavior. As best she could tell, he hadn't had a drink all day. And even though it was only 11:00 in the morning, that was saying a lot for Rick McBride.

"Well, what are you waiting for, baby? Open it up. Let's see what that little girl of yours got you."

"Okay, I think I will." She opened the package carefully so as not to damage the meticulous wrapping. "Katie, this is wonderful!" Daria pulled out a beautiful hand-knit cable sweater in a soft peach color with pale blue roses woven along the neckline. Holding it up against her torso, Daria ran her hands over it. "It's the softest thing I've ever felt. I absolutely love it! Rick, isn't this beautiful?"

"I think that's the prettiest sweater I've ever seen. You done good, Katie, real good."

Katie giggled at Rick's discomfort in having to play the "nice guy." She could only imagine what he would rather be doing. *Well, serves him right*, she thought. It had not gone unnoticed by her that Rick hadn't bought a single gift for Daria. She did have to concede, however, that so far this had been a pleasant Christmas.

"I'll tell you what I'm going to do," exclaimed Daria. "I am going to put on my new, beautiful sweater and then fix us some omelets. How does that sound?"

"Oh, baby, now you're talking! I was beginning to think you two were never gonna mention food!"

Daria laughed as if that had been a really funny comment. "How 'bout you, Katie? Want me to fix you one?"

"Thanks, but I think I'll pass."

"Is your stomach still upset?" Daria looked worried.

"Just a little. It kind of comes and goes. It's not too bad right now, but I don't feel much like eating."

"Okay, but if you change your mind, let me know."

"Sure, Mama. I think I'm gonna take a short nap. It's nice to have a day off from school and work."

After Katie left, Daria stared at the bedroom door.

"You okay, Dare?" asked Rick. "I thought you was gonna make us some omelets."

"Yeah. I was just thinking that Katie works way too hard for someone her age."

"C'mon, you know Katie likes all that book stuff; and she works because she wants to, not because she really has to. Besides, that's one thing I like best about being with you."

"What are you talking about?"

"The fact that Katie is so good at taking care of herself. She's not always gettin' in the way of you and me. I've dated women with kids before, and it was a mess. They'd always be hangin' around needin' their mama for one thing or another. And when I met you, I admit I was a bit concerned that you had a daughter, but so far it's worked out better than I expected. And now with her about to graduate, well, that'll give you even more time to spend with me."

"I never knew you felt this way."

"Well, I never felt the need to mention it, 'cause like I said, Katie's always taken care of herself. I guess what I'm tryin' to say is don't go worryin' about your daughter now. She's practically grown up and can make her own decisions. If she wants to work and study all the time, that's her business."

Daria knew she should defend Katie to Rick. Instead, she walked to the refrigerator and pulled out a carton of eggs.

Late that night, Daria stood in the kitchen gathering the courage to talk to her daughter about what was on her mind, but half trying to talk herself out of it. Rick's words kept popping into her head. Had she really ignored Katie as much as Rick had made it sound? She quickly rationalized that Katie seemed to be a very well-adjusted young lady. Still, it seemed cruel that Rick would be counting the days until Katie graduated so she would no longer be any trouble at all. In all honesty, Daria hoped Katie would stick around after high school. Daria couldn't imagine not having this constant and steadying presence.

Daria knew she would have to act fast. Rick wouldn't be gone much longer. It was already 11:00 on Christmas night. Katie had kept to herself most of the day, sleeping away a good portion of it, but now she was in her room reading. Daria could see the light shining under the door. She took a deep breath and knocked.

"Katie? Can I come in?"

"Sure," came her daughter's weary response.

Daria opened the door and saw the scene she could have predicted: Katie propped up in bed trying her best to keep her eyes open in order to finish the latest book she was reading. Daria grinned. She often wondered where her daughter got her love for books. It certainly wasn't from her, and she didn't recall T.J. ever being a big reader. But then he did have that ability to write some of the most beautiful lyrics she had ever heard, so she figured the two must be connected somehow.

"You're still up, I see," commented Daria as she made her way over to her daughter's mattress and sat down.

"Yeah, I'm tired, but I'm at a really good part and just have to keep reading to see what's going to happen."

Daria chuckled. "I can't imagine reading for pleasure! In fact, I can't think of anything worse!"

"Oh, Mama, you really should give it a chance. I bet you'd enjoy reading as much as I do. After all, I'm your daughter, and I must get my love of books from someone."

Daria was astonished that Katie had verbalized her very thoughts. She would have commented along those lines but was afraid it would lead to a discussion of T.J.. Remembering Thanksgiving, Daria smiled wryly. Holidays and painful conversations seemed to go hand-in-hand. Maybe, with a little luck, the ensuing conversation would not be as bad as Daria feared, and this Christmas would end on a good note.

Taking a deep breath, Daria began. "I'm glad you're enjoying your book, but that's not why I came in here. I, uh, wanted to talk to you . . . I mean . . . there's something I was wondering about, but I don't know . . . uh . . . I don't quite know how to say it."

"Mama, what's the matter?"

"It's kind of a . . . you know, a personal thing." Daria kept wringing her hands.

Katie sat up straighter in her bed. "You're scaring me, Mama . . . what is it?"

"I've been worried about you lately. I've assumed it was the break up with Eric and your falling out with Kristin—"

"You mean betrayal, don't you?"

"Yes, I know, sweetie, and I didn't mean to make light of it. Anyway, that's not what I wanted to talk about. I guess these past few weeks I've attributed your listlessness and lack of appetite to everything that happened around Thanksgiving. That wasn't a good time for any of us, I suppose. But lately, well I've been wondering if something else is going on. You keep mentioning that your stomach is upset and, well—"

"Yeah, but that comes and goes; I don't think it's anything serious. I appreciate your concern, but I'm okay. I've been working a lot, and you're right, this hasn't exactly been the happiest time of my life. I'm sorry I've worried you."

"Oh, Katie, don't apologize. You've done nothing wrong. I'm your mother, not a very good one I know, but—"

"Don't say that! I hate it when you put yourself down."

"Oh boy, I'm botching this whole thing. Look, I was just wondering if maybe it was possible that you might be . . . well . . . if you might be pregnant."

A few seconds passed, then Katie's eyes grew wide. "Why would you ask that? Why would you even think that?"

"Now Katie, don't be upset with me. I just remember how I felt when I was first carrying you, and you seem to have a lot of the same symptoms. You know: being tired, queasy some of the time. I don't know, it made sense to me. I mean you always have so much energy, but lately—"

"I told you I've been working a lot of long hours on my feet all day. Can't a girl be tired once in a while without her mother thinking she's pregnant?"

"Katie, please don't be upset with me. I just want to talk to you about this, if you'll listen to me for a minute—"

"No! You listen to me, Mama. I can't believe you're accusing me of this. Do you really think I'd be that stupid?"

"Katie, you don't have to be stupid to get pregnant."

"Oh, don't worry, Mama. I know all too well. I know you got pregnant without meaning to and I also know you're sorry you ever had me!" Tears formed in her eyes.

"Please, don't say that. You don't understand at all what it was like for me and why I did the things I did."

"Do you really think I'm that naïve, Mama? I know you had me so your boyfriend—my father—would marry you." She laughed a haughty laugh. "But it backfired and he left and you were stuck with me! So do you think I'd really be dumb enough to get myself into the same fix?"

"Katie, I don't know what to say. I'm not very good at these kinds of discussions."

"Yeah, I've heard that excuse . . . let's see . . . how many times? Whenever I want to talk about my father you brush me off because the whole thing makes you uncomfortable. Did you ever stop to think that maybe I need to talk about it, that maybe I need to know?"

Daria suddenly felt weary all over. "I never knew what to say. It was easier to just . . . to just forget, I guess."

"But that's just it. You never forgot, did you? Every time you look at me, you're reminded of the mistake you made, aren't you?"

Daria paused. She had to choose her words carefully. Her daughter understood a lot more than she had given her credit for. And, of course, there was Rick. He would be back any minute so it wouldn't do to get involved in a lengthy, emotional discussion now.

"Katie, I'm not denying everything you just said, and I am willing to talk about it. I never should have left you in the dark all these years. But I do think there's something more important to discuss right now, and that's you. So, even though I've never given you a reason to trust me, I'm gonna ask that just this once, you will. We'll sit down and talk about all of this, soon, I promise. Okay?"

"Why should I believe you?" Only a tinge of animosity remained in Katie's voice.

Daria sighed in relief. "Because I give you my word."

Katie stared deep into her mom's questioning brown eyes. Meekly she answered, "Okay, we'll do it your way. But I want us to talk soon. I have so many questions."

Daria awkwardly touched her daughter's hand. "I know, baby." Actually, she dreaded the present discussion even more. She closed her eyes in an attempt to gather both wisdom and strength.

"Katie, do you think it's possible that you might be pregnant? I mean, weren't you and Eric sleeping together?

Daria had always had live-in boyfriends, and what went on between a man and a woman had never been a big mystery to Katie. But now she appeared uncomfortable.

"Yeah, we slept together for about two months, I guess—but never without protection," Katie hastened to add. "Eric was as adamant about that as I was."

"Well, that's good to know. But accidents do happen. I suppose the big question is, have you missed your period?" Daria dreaded the response.

Katie gulped. "Um . . . I guess so, but . . . I've always been so irregular. I never get alarmed if I'm late."

Daria knew her daughter was more than late. Some things were hard to hide when you shared a bathroom. "How long has it been since your last period?"

Katie did some quick mental calculations. "Probably about seven weeks. I haven't thought anything about it with all the other stuff going on."

Daria had a desire to go grab one of those bottles she and Rick kept stashed under the kitchen sink. Alcohol always brought some measure of relief, even if only temporary. She closed her eyes and tried to push away the temptation and concentrate on the situation at hand. She pressed her palm to her forehead and whispered, "Oh, Katie, Katie."

"Just because I'm late doesn't mean anything, Mama. Why are you so sure I'm pregnant?"

"Maybe it has something to do with mother's intuition."

Katie looked dubious. "I thought women threw up and stuff when they first find out they're pregnant. I haven't done that even once."

"No, not all women. I think it's different for everybody. I never threw up, but I remember being tired all of the time, at first. I'd practically fall asleep while driving down the road! And Katie, let's face it: you have been exhausted lately. And even though you're working a lot, you've always juggled both school and a job. I don't think you can blame it on work. And the queasiness is a sure sign. If it was a virus or bug, you'd be over it by now. But it doesn't go away, does it?"

Katie's head moved slowly from side to side. She met Daria's gaze without trying to hide the tears that had gathered again. "So what do we do?" came the spiritless question.

"Well, we've got to find out for sure. I can pick up a pregnancy test kit tomorrow at work and you can take it when you get home—"

"No, not at work, Mama. You know someone would notice and think it was for one of us. I'd absolutely die if I had to answer a bunch of questions."

Daria was used to being the confused one while Katie was always the strong one. Her daughter looked so vulnerable.

"Okay, okay. I'll run over to the drug store across the street on my lunch hour." Daria didn't miss the look of relief that flashed across her daughter's face.

"Yeah, that would be better." Katie attempted a laugh. "Look, Mama, I apologize for being so much trouble."

"Oh, Katie, don't say that. Besides, maybe, just maybe, this will all be for nothing, and we'll find out you're not pregnant after all. I definitely wouldn't mind being wrong this time." Even to her own ears, Daria didn't sound convincing. She stood to leave.

"Mama," came Katie's whisper-soft petition, "if I am pregnant, will it change how you feel about me?"

Daria looked down at her daughter. She couldn't help thinking what a beautiful girl she was, and how much she looked like her father. "No, Katie, of course not." Daria liked to think she would have stayed and said more, but right then she heard the front door open and knew Rick was home. Ashamed at the relief she felt, she knew she should offer some kind of reassurance to Katie, but all she could manage was a swift kiss on the forehead and a "good-night" and a "Merry Christmas" before she was out the door.

10

✳

KATIE STARED STRAIGHT AHEAD seeing nothing. The dingy-white bathroom tile glared back at her with coldness steeling into her bones. She shuddered. In an instant Katie Montgomery knew her life would never be the same.

Slowly, starting at the soles of her feet, she began to shake. The involuntary movement made its way up her calves to her knees, up her thighs until it reached her stomach. At that point the shaking gave way to small convulsions. Her torso shook while her throat mechanically choked out sobs that were forming themselves somewhere in the hidden recesses of her being. Katie's body had taken over; it was in control. And for all of her outward quaking, Katie knew this was not a physical reaction she was experiencing. This was borne from deep inside of her, from places even Katie hadn't known existed. But, as alien and frightening as this was, it was a good thing. It was coming from her soul; her soul was breaking free and crying out.

She shook her head in amazement, still wondering at this sudden turn of events. She knew she wasn't free from her problems; she was pregnant and didn't want to be. But for the first time she could remember, she felt free to indulge her questioning heart, free to let the subterranean recesses of her untouched soul lead her to where she needed to go. No worrying about pleasing her mother or fitting in with the kids at school or what the future held in store for her. All of that was pushed aside to make room for this monumental milestone in her life. Even though she did not want to go through this trial, something told her not to shrink back from it, but to experience it

78

to the fullest.

So she did. She sat and let her mind go and was amazed at
the things that popped into her head, things totally unrelated to her
present circumstance. Her consciousness was consumed with thoughts
ranging anywhere from the dashing and debonair Cary Grant to the
graceful form of a gliding figure skater to the majesty held within the
vast, deep blue waters of the ocean. Her mind lingered on that one.
She had never seen the ocean, but liked to imagine it holding treasures
reserved for road-weary travelers—those who yearn to be cleansed
from the dust and debris that work their way under a person's skin
and stubbornly refuse to be washed away. Surely something as big
and powerful as the ocean could cleanse one tiny, insignificant speck
of humanity.

In her private dream world Katie was transported beyond the
pain and hopelessness of the recent occurrences in her life. When she
closed her eyes, she could vividly see her body being buoyed by the
strong, unseen hands that controlled the tides while simultaneously
housing millions of life forms, some yet to be discovered. She sat
in awe of this vast oceanic force pulsating with life and filled with
beauty as well as potential for violence and destruction. She had seen
footage of tidal waves and hurricanes. Beauty always has a downside,
a malevolence brewing just under the surface to ensure proper respect
and homage. You couldn't have one without the other. They went
together and perhaps they were what they were because of the other.
In an odd way, Katie found comfort in this. How she longed to
indulge this philosophical preoccupation and refuse to allow either
time or reason to encroach upon the sweet taste of freedom she was
now enjoying.

But, even in her present euphoric state, reason did find its way
in. Katie fought hard to keep the questions and doubts at bay, but
they wrestled and wrangled until the inner war was too much for the
frightened eighteen-year-old. She had no choice but to confront the
thoughts now taking over her mind and stripping away any wake of

peace that was left.

"No!" she cried, railing against the steady stream of fears crowding their way into her tired mind. "No, I want to float just a little bit longer! Please! She wanted the peaceful, cleansing blue water to remain.

But it was gone. As swiftly and gently as it had come, it now departed leaving Katie to wonder. She looked around. There was no ocean, no beauty, no peace, no power—just the bathroom, and there was certainly nothing supernatural or spiritual about it.

"Well, that settles it. I must be going crazy," she moaned. "As if being pregnant isn't enough, now I'm looking for oceans in my bathroom and even talking to myself!" She would have simply passed off the experience as more of her fanciful notions except for the wrinkled little card in her hand. She had frantically reached for the card as she was about to begin the test her mother had bought her. She had thought holding it close might bring solace. Now she gently smoothed it and once again read the words: "Cast all your anxiety on him because he cares for you."

As much as she wanted to dismiss the Bible verse and the little old lady who had given it to her as religious propaganda like her mama said, Katie was compelled to wonder if there was a connection between them and the strange peace she just encountered. Imagined or not, she knew it to be the sweetest and purest experience she'd ever had. Katie sat stone-still for a while longer, hoping the feeling would return. She felt silly sitting there, but sometimes one little thread of hope is enough to make a person do strange things.

After a time Katie pulled herself up from the cold, hard floor and made her way to her bedroom. She carefully placed the wrinkled Bible verse card on her nightstand before climbing into bed and turning off the lamp. In the darkness she kept thinking, *Lady, whoever you are, I hope you're praying for me now.* But as much as Katie wanted to believe prayer might somehow help, the relentless doubts in her mind assailed in full force as sleep claimed her. And Katie knew that when the light of morning dawned, she would still be very, very pregnant.

❊ ❊ ❊

Listening for any sign or sound of life, Daria pressed her ear to Katie's bedroom door. When she heard nothing and saw the light go out, she breathed a sigh of relief. *At least I don't have to deal with it until tomorrow.* What she really wanted to do was run—fast and far. That was always a comfortable way for her to handle life's more difficult moments. And if she couldn't physically escape, there were always those bottles under the sink. On this particular night they were more and more enticing. *No, not this time. I'm gonna face this one head on if it kills me. I can't let Katie go through what I did.*

So intent was she on her own foreboding thoughts that Daria didn't hear Rick steal up behind her. He put his arms around her and kissed the side of her neck.

"Rick, not now," came Daria's hollow refusal.

"Why not now? Seems like as good a time as any." He kept kissing until she wrangled free.

"Stop it! I said not right now." She started toward the bedroom but then thought better of it. By the time she gained the living room, Rick was right on her heels.

Grabbing his girlfriend's shoulders, Rick spun her around to face him. "What do you mean puttin' me off like that? What's with you anyway? You've been actin' strange."

Daria pondered how much to tell Rick. "Nothin's wrong, not with me anyway. It's Katie. I'm a little worried, I guess. She's got some problems and I wanna help, but . . . I don't know how. In fact, I feel completely helpless." Daria plopped down on the sofa.

"She still pinin' away over that Eric kid?"

Daria had to stop herself from saying something insulting. She hadn't realized how little Rick knew about what was going on in her daughter's life. *Why am I so surprised? He barely knows what's going on in mine.* It was probably better that way.

"Yeah, pretty much. I think she's feeling really alone right now." Daria released a disheartened sigh.

Rick shook his head. "It won't do you no good to worry, baby. I mean teenage girls—whew! They're a breed all to themselves!" He laughed. "I'll tell you what she needs though. She needs to get out more. In fact one of the guys down at the garage—you know Sheldon, don't you?—well anyway, I bet he'd love to spend a little time with our Katie girl."

Daria's stomach turned at the lurid glint in Rick's eyes. "Rick! That's my baby you're talking about. You sound like you're willing to auction her off to the highest bidder."

Sidling closer to her, Rick rubbed his hand up and down Daria's arm. "You know, Dare, your baby ain't no baby no more. She's eighteen years old and a fine looker. You were saying just the other night you thought she worked too much and didn't have enough fun. All I'm doing is tellin' you 'bout someone who'd like to show her a little of that fun you think she's missin'. Katie's old enough to handle it."

Daria couldn't argue with his last point. Katie wouldn't be in this predicament if she wasn't "old enough."

"I don't think that's what Katie needs right now, Rick, but thanks for trying to help."

"Well, then, what do you think she needs? I mean, I can't think of anything better than a good night out on the town. And, besides, that Sheldon guy is quite the ladies' man. He's always got some little thing hanging all over him. Charm, I suppose. But whatever, Sheldon seems to have more than his fair share of it."

It was like talking to a brick wall. But for her daughter's sake, Daria was going to hold her ground this time. "Like I said, thanks for thinking of her, Rick, but maybe another time. Katie needs something more personal right now. She's hurtin' down deep on the inside. Besides, I want more for her than a bunch of one-night stands."

"Well, she had that with Eric, but it didn't work out." Rick was clearly annoyed that Daria wasn't agreeing with him, and he was ready for the discussion to be over.

"I know, but I always got the feeling Katie never really cared for Eric. I don't understand it. He seemed to be totally in love with her, but she never felt strongly for him, I don't think. Maybe she needs more time." *If only it could be that simple,* thought Daria.

Rick stood up. There was no missing the irritation on his face. "Look, Dare, I appreciate your concern for your daughter and all, but if you're gonna stay up all night worryin', I'm gonna head to Mickey's Grill and drum up a little fun."

It would be so easy to tell him to go, so why can't I do it? Daria knew the answer. Even though Rick McBride wasn't much of a catch, at least she had managed to hold on to him for over two years now. She'd had so many failures in her life that she couldn't stand the thought of having to admit yet one more. But she hated the thought of her daughter living the same kind of life.

She resolved right then to talk to Katie first thing in the morning, and she knew exactly what to tell her. Sometimes you had to be tough. It was for Katie's own good. Daria may not be able to do much for her daughter, but she could protect her from a hopeless future filled with regret.

"You're right, Rick. Worryin' ain't gonna change nothin'." She reached for his hand. "Let's go to bed."

Katie was walking through a long and cramped corridor. The light was so dim she had to squint to see where she was stepping. She wasn't afraid; apprehensive would be the better way to describe it. The ever-tightening knot in her stomach was a constant reminder that this was a critical journey.

Somewhere in the distance Katie saw a faint light. It was all the encouragement she needed; the darkness was beginning to take its toll as ominous thoughts crept into her mind. *If I can just make it to the light, I'll be all right,* she reasoned to herself. She carefully inched her way forward, each step more tentative than the last. Finally she saw the light becoming brighter and brighter until the darkness was nothing but a few obscure shadows behind her.

Again Katie squinted her eyes, this time because the brightness was so intense it hurt after being in that caliginous tunnel for so long. She could barely make out the outline of a form coming toward her. Not knowing if it was friend or foe, Katie decided to keep her watchful position and let the stranger approach her. It probably would have been harder to stand still and wait if she hadn't had the notion this was not an enemy. She felt certain all was going to be well.

Katie was more than a little surprised when she saw a beautiful silver-gray wolf taking shape before her eyes as it neared the place of her vigil. When it came close, Katie reached out and hesitantly touched the creature's head. She was amazed at the softness of the fur that greeted her hand.

"Well, of all the things I might have expected, you are certainly not one of them! Where'd you come from, boy? You sure are a handsome fellow." Kneeling, she scratched the wolf's head.

The animal turned to walk away then looked back at his new friend.

"Oh, am I supposed to come with you?" asked Katie. "Okay." They walked side by side until they reached another long corridor, only this one was not darkened like the previous one. Instead, it had several doors, all closed. The wolf nodded his head in the direction of the doors.

"Which one am I supposed to go through, Kaleo?" Katie started. She had called the animal by name. How did she know his name?

"So, which do I choose?"

Kaleo shook his head and pointed his nose back at Katie.

"So, you're not going to help me at all, are ya' boy?" Katie wasn't put out. She was grateful to have Kaleo's company.

At that moment Katie heard a soft tapping sound behind her and whirled around to look.

"Katie, are you awake yet? Can I come in?"

Katie jerked at the sound of her mother's voice.

"Katie?" came the request again.

"Uh . . . yeah, Mama . . . I'm awake now, thanks to you." There was no malice in the voice. Daria opened the door.

"Sorry to wake you, but I've got to get to work in a little while, and I need to talk with you. Rick's still asleep."

Katie rubbed her eyes, trying to clear her head. She vaguely recalled something about a wolf named Kaleo and a bunch of doors. "I must have been dreaming."

"Do you remember what it was about?"

"Not really. I've just got snippets in my head that don't make much sense."

"Yeah, most of my dreams never make any sense either." Daria's smirk made Katie laugh. "It's good to see my little girl smiling."

"It's strange; I don't feel like crying. Mostly I'm confused."

"I figured that last night when you locked yourself in the bathroom. I hope you know I wanted to help you, Katie, but it seemed the best thing to do was to leave you alone."

"Yeah, thanks. It probably was good for me to not have to talk about it right away. I just sat in there and thought about a bunch of different things." There was no way Katie was going to share with her mom what had really taken place. She would dismiss it as nothing but emotions run amuck.

"So, do you want to talk now?"

"Sure, whatever. It's got to be done, I suppose."

"Well, have you decided what you're gonna do?"

Katie shook her head. "No. It seems too monumental to decide so quickly, you know?"

"Truthfully, I think it's a pretty easy one."

"What do you mean? How can this be easy?"

"Look, sweetie, I know this may sound harsh; but I only see one option for you. I think you need to have an abortion."

Katie caught her breath. Just hearing her mother say the word was a shock. It wasn't that Katie was opposed to abortion. In all honesty she had never thought much about it. She'd seen some demonstrations on T.V. where a bunch of religious fanatics were all up in arms about abortion, saying it was murder, but Katie never gave them much credence. But now that they were talking about *her*, she didn't feel so nonchalant about it. She managed, with some difficulty, to make her voice sound normal.

"Why do you think that, Mama?"

Daria reached over and cupped her daughter's chin. "Because you have so much potential." There was no missing the admiration in her voice. "I know you and I don't always agree, Katie, but I think you are so smart and pretty and so full of promise that I can't imagine seeing you saddled with a little kid on your hip."

"But you didn't choose to have an . . . an abortion."

"You're right, I didn't. But it's not the same, Katie, believe me. I had no future; I barely graduated high school. I had no clue what I wanted to do with my life. At that time all I wanted was to be near your father. He was everything to me, and I foolishly thought I was everything to him. Now I know that was crazy, but you couldn't have convinced me back then. I could just picture it in my head, you know, the three of us together in a little house with a little yard. I didn't care one whit about money or responsibility. I wanted the dream—that feeling I'd get when I was in his arms. I wanted it to last forever." She shook her head as if to clear out the memories.

"But you, on the other hand, are a completely different story, Katie. I think we both know you don't care about Eric, so that's not a consideration. You do have plans for college; and that's gonna be hard enough for you to afford without having to take care of a baby as well."

She spontaneously reached over and grabbed her daughter's hands. With desperation in her voice she continued. "Don't mess this up, please. I have never been sorry I had you, Katie; but I didn't have anything else. You do. I needed you so I wouldn't be alone." She sobbed. "I know in some twisted kind of way I've blamed you for T.J.'s leaving, but it wasn't your fault. He wouldn't have stayed no matter what. It was easier to blame you than to admit the truth to myself. He didn't reject you, Katie. How could he? He didn't even know you. It was me he rejected. He knew me and he didn't want me." She let herself give in to the sobs.

Katie put her arms around her mother. This role she could handle. She'd been taking care of her mother for years, and now she knew why. Daria Montgomery was nothing but a frightened, lonely girl in a woman's body. The two women rocked back and forth to the soft sounds of weeping.

After what seemed an eternity Daria lifted her head. "Katie, you've kept me going all these years. If I hadn't had you, I don't know what I would have done. Maybe I was meant to be a mother since I couldn't do anything else."

"You make it sound like only imbeciles should be mothers."

"I didn't mean it to sound that way, but let's face it: I'm not qualified to do anything besides working at a grocery store. And I'm fine with that, Katie, but you wouldn't be. You've always got your head in the clouds dreaming some fancy dream; and I know I put you down a lot for it, but the truth is that I want you to go after those dreams. I want you to catch them and make them come true."

Katie couldn't believe what she was hearing. She had always thought her mom was disappointed in her because they were so different from each other. But now . . . now her mom was insisting she be the total opposite. Katie's head swam, trying to assimilate all of this new information.

"Katie, I want you to know I won't support any other decision. I refuse to stand by and watch you throw away everything you've been working toward and dreaming about."

Katie's eyes expressed her shock.

"I know that sounds harsh, but this has to be the way it is. I don't have the means or the desire to help you with a baby should you choose to keep it, and I think it would be downright foolish to put yourself through the trial of a pregnancy just to give it away in the end."

Katie meekly spoke up. "But the choice is mine, right?"

"I suppose that's what it comes down to in the end. After all, you're the one who made your bed; now you have to lie in it. I can only tell you my feelings on the matter. You need to know up front where I stand. Now that I've done that, I can wash my hands of the matter."

"That sounds so cold, Mama."

Daria winced, but quickly recovered her unusually-determined countenance and steady voice. "I hope someday in the distant future you have a child of your own. Then maybe you'll be able to understand why I'm saying this to you now. Nobody's gonna help you through this, kiddo. You've got to take control of your own life. I'm trying to help you by being tough on you even if it seems cruel. What's that old saying? 'You have to be cruel to be kind.'" Daria chuckled. "Whoever wrote that must have been a parent."

Katie didn't know what to say; so she said nothing.

"Well, I've got to get to work. Let me know what you decide; but I wouldn't take too long if I were you. I hear these things get tougher the longer you wait." And with that she was gone.

And Katie was alone.

11

❧

KATIE FACED THE GRAY brick building.

How did this happen? One minute I'm trying to decide whether or not to break up with my boyfriend, and the next I'm standing in front of an abortion clinic. She couldn't decide if she felt like an adult making a mature decision or a little girl thrust too soon into a grown-up world.

Standing there, she felt that anyone who looked at her could tell exactly what she was thinking. This brought to mind a book she had read in school: *The Scarlet Letter. That's what I am. I'm Hester Prynne bearing my shame for all the world to see.*

But if she didn't have the abortion, wouldn't she still bear that shame, only then in the form of a protruding belly followed by a wrinkled, squalling baby? At least this way it stayed hidden from all but a few people and it could be wiped away never to be thought of again. Katie thought if she could endure the agony for a little while, she could get on with her life. And even though she hated the idea of an abortion, she wouldn't have traded the pride she felt when her mama had said she knew Katie could make something of herself. She had longed for words like those for so long.

Then out of nowhere she remembered that Bible verse, the only one she knew. It sounded good in theory, but exactly how did one go about casting a pregnancy on God? That didn't make sense. She reasoned this was more than an "anxiety" she could give to God. This was major. Anxieties were things like what to do about a test you hadn't studied for or what outfit to wear or which college to go to.

She liked the idea that God would care about such things. But this was huge. It far surpassed a mere anxiety and went into the realm of the monumental, earth-shaking, something that would determine the future direction of her life. She had to trust her mother this time. Taking a deep breath she walked in.

It took a few moments for Katie to size up her surroundings. She hadn't been in many doctor's offices, but she assumed this is what most of them looked like. Grateful the waiting room wasn't crowded, she headed to the window where she figured she was to sign in or something.

Since no one was there at the moment she stood and waited and tried to look nonchalant. Suddenly a face popped up in the window. Katie jumped.

"Can I help you with something?" came the question from the other side of the half-opened glass.

"Uh, yeah," stammered Katie. "I needed to talk to someone to see . . . to see if this is . . . where I need to be." She couldn't make herself say the word.

The girl, in her mid-twenties, seemed unconcerned about Katie's stammering. "You'd like to speak to a nurse?"

With a sigh of relief, Katie breathed out the word "Yes."

"Do you have an appointment?"

"Um . . . no . . . I'm sorry, I didn't know I'd need one. I just wanted to talk to someone, that's all." Katie felt more and more like that little girl being forced to handle adult things.

"You don't have to have an appointment, but it goes quicker if you do. If you decide you want to have the abortion, then you will need an appointment. But now you can sign in on the 'Walk-in' list and wait for the first available nurse. Okay?"

"Okay." Katie even managed a smile, grateful the receptionist hadn't made her feel like a complete idiot.

"All right, let me get a few forms for you to fill out, and then we'll get someone to speak with you. You're lucky; we're not crowded today. It shouldn't be long at all." With a faint smile she disappeared. Abruptly, she returned. "Here, fill these out and bring them back to me. And I need you to sign your name here and the time." She handed her a clipboard. "Take a seat anywhere, and then when you've finished you can bring them back up here. I'll need you to pay the $10.00 consulting fee, that includes the required pregnancy test. We don't accept personal checks, but credit cards are fine." She spoke as if reading from a script.

"Uh, thank you." Katie took the proffered clipboard, made her way to a maroon-colored chair and sat down. She stared at the forms in her hands, wanting to look up and see what the other girls there were doing. She imagined they were staring holes right through her. That thought kept her eyes riveted to the clipboard in her lap. Grabbing the pen she tackled the questions. Mostly they wanted medical information; this was easy since she'd always been extremely healthy.

So engrossed was she that Katie jerked when the girl at the desk called out, "Gina Hardemon, you can come on back."

Katie let herself look up just in time to see a girl a few years older than herself disappear through a heavy wooden door. *Is this the same door from the dream? It certainly looks like it.* Katie's imagination began to run wild. What's going to happen to that girl named Gina? Is she going in there to have an abortion right now? Could it actually be taking place in the very next room while all these other girls sit out here in their comfortable chairs leafing through magazines? A chill ran up Katie's spine. She braced herself for the scream she was sure she was going to hear from the other side of that wooden door.

It never came.

Slowly, she began to relax, chastising herself for letting her imagination get the better of her. She willed her muscles to return to their normal state. *Maybe this abortion thing is not that bad after all.* She desperately wanted to believe this.

She re-focused her attention to the forms. She gave a slight gasp followed by a chuckle when she read the last question: "How did you hear about us?" Here she was facing the biggest decision in her life thus far, and they wanted to know how she had heard about them! Leaving the line blank, Katie rose to turn in the forms and pay her fee.

After what seemed an eternity of skimming through beauty magazines and watching girl after girl go through that door, Katie heard her own name called. Now it was her turn to see what lay behind the big, wooden door. Actually, everything looked big here— maybe because Katie felt so small.

"Are you Katie Montgomery?" asked the woman standing in the doorway, who seemed to be in her late forties, not ugly, not pretty. *Nondescript* was the word.

"Yes, that's me."

"Come on in and have a seat, please."

Katie did as she was told, noticing the counseling room was outfitted with nothing more than a simple desk and two chairs. The woman followed her, Katie's forms in her hand.

"Well, you certainly are a healthy young lady."

"Yes, ma'am. I've never really been sick except for the occasional cold or flu."

"That's good." She smiled. "I'm Margaret Kilgore. I understand you wanted to speak with a counselor."

"Yes, ma'am. I had some questions about . . . my options."

"First, we need to verify that you're pregnant. Your chart says you believe you're about six weeks along?"

"That's right."

"Well, let's have you take this pregnancy test, so we'll know for sure, and then we can talk about what can be done. If you'll just go right in there, we'll get this test out of the way."

Katie did as she was told and found herself back in the counseling room in a matter of minutes.

Margaret Kilgore settled herself across from Katie, folded her hands on top of the desk and looked Katie right in the eye. "Why don't you tell me a little about your situation."

Katie swallowed, hoping her voice sounded normal. "Well, I was dating this guy, we broke up, and then I found out I was pregnant." Katie was embarrassed that something so devastating could be summed up in a few simple clauses. But there it was.

"Your boyfriend isn't a consideration in your decision?"

Katie shook her head. "No, he's definitely not interested in being a dad. He's not interested in anything but himself."

"And you're not interested in having a baby at this time either?" Margaret Kilgore was slowly moving her head from side to side, almost as if she were telling the story herself.

"Well, I think I want kids someday, but definitely not now. I'm a senior this year and hoping to go to college next year. I don't think I could do that and have a baby, too. Besides, I don't know anything about babies." Katie blushed. "My mom thinks this would be the best solution for me, and I can't find a good reason to disagree, so here I am." Katie felt stupid.

"I'm inclined to agree with your mother. Katie, do you realize how lucky you are to live in an age where you have options? You can still go to college and do all the things you want to do. A pregnancy doesn't have to change anything."

Katie couldn't help but think it had already changed everything.

"We do abortions up to eighteen weeks, Katie; however, the cost does increase the longer you wait because the procedure gets a bit more involved." The nurse wrinkled her brow and spoke matter-of-factly. "It's much simpler and cheaper if you abort in the first trimester."

"What kind of cost are we talking about?" Katie was suddenly aware that her palms were sweaty.

The nurse pulled a sheet of paper out of one of the desk drawers. "Here's a price sheet for you. It tells the different costs for the different services we offer."

Oh, how convenient, a price sheet. The counseling room suddenly felt cold. She glanced at the sheet. "You mean there's different kinds of abortions?" For someone who made almost straight As, Katie realized she knew nothing about this topic.

Margaret Kilgore smiled at Katie's embarrassment. "Really, a first trimester abortion is all very simple and virtually painless. If you'll look at the sheet, you'll see that the cost up until twelve weeks is $250.00. That's with a local anesthetic which means you'd be awake during the procedure. If you prefer to be asleep, the cost is $285.00. Both methods are safe and painless. The choice is yours." The nurse lowered her voice, adding a more sympathetic tone. "And don't be embarrassed if cost is a consideration. It is for most of our clients. Many girls choose the local because it's the cheapest."

None of this comforted Katie, but she appreciated the nurse's sensitivity. "Well, as a matter of fact, cost is a big consideration. I'm trying to save my money for college, but I'm gonna have to dip into it for this." Katie added, "What exactly happens when you have it done?" She feared the answer.

"I commend you for wanting to get all the facts." She smiled warmly. "When you come in, a nurse will give you the anesthesia. Then the doctor will perform what's called a vacuum aspiration. That simply means he inserts a tube into the uterus and cleans out the pregnancy tissue. It takes five minutes; then you're moved to recovery which doesn't usually take long at all. Most are out of here in about an hour."

"What about after you leave? Is there anything I need to know? I mean, I've never been in the hospital or anything so I guess I'm a little nervous. Isn't this a surgical procedure?"

"Technically, yes, but it's as simple as having your wisdom teeth pulled. Most women feel perfectly fine when they leave. There may be a small amount of cramping and bleeding, but nothing that interferes with your normal routine. Many women return to work the same day, but some prefer to take it easy. It's a matter of what you're comfortable with."

It sounded neat and efficient. Katie had expected a longer, more complicated process. She was strangely disappointed. She should have a whole list of questions to ask, but all she could come up with was, "Wow, it seems so simple."

Nurse Kilgore smiled again. "It really is. Women have this done every day, Katie, if that makes you feel any better." It didn't, but Margaret Kilgore didn't seem to notice. "Look, I can tell you're struggling; I want to help you get through it."

"Thanks, I am a little unsure, I guess. My mom made it sound so simple, and now you're making it sound easy. People always accuse me of making mountains out of mole hills."

"Well, it's wise for you to think this through. After all, it's your body we're talking about."

Katie knew what she was wrestling with inside but didn't know if she had the courage to articulate it. She was afraid of what the answer might be. But she had to know.

"Mrs. Kilgore, is this . . . well, some people say it's a life inside; but you called it 'pregnancy tissue'; I just wonder . . . is this a baby?" Katie unwittingly patted her stomach.

The smile seemed forced this time. "People have different opinions on that. The main issue here is that once you give birth, then you definitely have a baby. At this point, you have the potential to have a baby if you choose to let the pregnancy continue, and you have the legal option to terminate the pregnancy. You have to decide if you are ready to be a mother."

Katie stared down at her hands and slowly shook her head. In a quiet voice she said, "I'm not ready." She was surprised how it grieved her to say this. She felt unfit.

"Then let me ask you a question, Katie. Why would you want to bring a child into the world when you know you're not ready or willing to take care of it? The world has enough unwanted children. Just turn on the local news to verify that fact. So why add to an already staggering number?"

How could Katie argue with this? She didn't want a baby right now. She had dreams and goals. She'd worked hard in high school to make good grades. Why throw it all away on a child she didn't want? Meekly, she gave her response. "I don't know. I suppose that would be irresponsible."

The warm smile returned to Margaret Kilgore's face. "Another thing that would be irresponsible is throwing away the potential you have. You said you want to go to college, and you're working hard to get there. You deserve that chance, Katie. You can have children in the future when you're ready. And I'm sure it will be a wonderful experience for you. I have kids of my own, so I know."

Margaret Kilgore placed her hand on Katie's trembling one and looked squarely into the girl's eyes. "You know, all I can see sitting in front of me right now is a beautiful young lady with so much to offer the world. It would make me sad to see you throw that potential away."

Katie was stunned at the passion in this woman's voice and was almost afraid to look fully into her face. "Boy, you sure sound convinced about your position on this. I admire that."

"Well, I'll tell you this. I wouldn't be doing this job if I didn't believe it was important. I am so grateful that women can come to a place like this and find help for their problems. Katie, you're lucky you weren't around when women didn't have the privilege you have today. But I was around; and I do remember; and it wasn't pretty." She closed her eyes and shook her head as if to block out a painful memory. When she opened her eyes again, they were still flashing, but this time with hope and pride. "But, thankfully, it's not like that anymore. Now a girl in your position can still finish school, go to college, do whatever you want without being inconvenienced by an unwanted pregnancy. Now you and others like you can reap the benefits of a long, hard-fought battle." Suddenly Margaret Kilgore laughed. "Well, I didn't mean to get on my soapbox and preach! But sometimes I can't help myself."

"Oh, it's okay. You feel strongly about your beliefs." Katie longed to have her mind settled so firmly.

"I do feel strongly about this, because I don't want to see anybody forced into a life they're not ready for—especially when it's so easy and legal to fix a problem pregnancy. Even the Supreme Court agrees this is a good choice for women. And remember, Katie, this is your body we're talking about. People are finally beginning to understand that a woman has the right to do what she wants with her own body." Margaret Kilgore smiled triumphantly.

The woman made a lot of sense.

"I sure do thank you for your time, ma'am, and I'll think about everything you said."

"If you'd like, we could go ahead and schedule you in. School will be starting back soon, so it would probably be easier for you to do it this week."

"Yeah, thanks, but I'd rather wait and think about it a little bit longer if that's okay. I'm not a very impulsive person. Could I just call and schedule over the phone?"

"Certainly. I was merely trying to save you some time, that's all. And don't forget we're also open on Saturdays."

"Okay. Thanks. I appreciate all the information."

"Oh, don't think twice about it. Part of my job is to inform people." She stood up, and Katie did likewise. "I know you'll make the right decision. You seem like a really smart young lady who knows what she wants in life."

Katie couldn't help thinking how wrong Margaret Kilgore was about that. If she knew the questions and doubts . . . But she thanked the nurse again and headed for the door.

Outside, Katie realized how tightly she was gripping the price sheet and how tense she felt. Surprisingly, it hadn't been a bad experience, not like she had been dreading. An unmistakable sense of relief accompanied her as she drove home. An abortion was not nearly as big a deal as she had thought.

Why then couldn't she make herself schedule that appointment?

* * *

Daria Montgomery closed the door behind her, leaned against it, closed her eyes, and breathed in deeply. The aroma greeting her brought an instant smile to her face. "Oh, Katie, please tell me this is what I think it is!"

"It is!" came her daughter's sing-song reply.

"Well, if you weren't a saint before, I'd say you certainly qualify now!" On her way to the kitchen, Daria shed her coat and gloves. She hugged her daughter from the back. Katie was stirring something in a large pot. She smiled as her mom's hand came around her side to try and sneak a taste.

Laughing, Katie gently slapped the hand away. "None of that till it's ready. Mama, you're worse than a five-year-old!"

"But, sweetie, I've had a hard day at work." She exaggerated a pout. "Besides, I've never been able to resist your spaghetti sauce. I don't know how you do it."

"Well, it's absolutely the only thing I know how to make that tastes anything remotely like food!"

"Now you're being too hard on yourself. But I will admit, nothing is quite as good as your spaghetti." She tried again to pilfer a taste, this time successfully. Sinking into a kitchen chair, she closed her eyes to savor the perfect blend of herbs and spices that even an Italian grandmother would be proud to claim. "This might be your best batch yet."

Katie beamed.

"Are you gonna freeze some?"

"Yeah. School starts back next week, and it'll be nice to have some on hand. Life's gonna get hectic again."

"Yeah, I know. It sure has been nice having you around during the holidays, and seeing you at work during the day."

"I've enjoyed that, too."

"You know what, kiddo. I think I'm gonna go change into something more comfortable and then the two of us can have a nice dinner together. When should it be ready?"

"I just have to throw the salad together and warm the bread, so maybe fifteen minutes. Isn't Rick coming home tonight?"

"Not until later. He's meeting some of his buddies. I think it's a bachelor party for Chuck. He said not to expect him 'til late." Daria headed toward her bedroom to change. With a playful smirk, she called over her shoulder, "You can wipe that grin off of your face, Katie."

Katie only grinned bigger.

❋ ❋ ❋

Katie watched her mom take the last drink of her soda. If Rick were here Daria would be drinking beer or something harder. Daria was a different person when Rick wasn't there: more playful, less uptight. But it must be exhausting work trying to keep someone happy all the time. Katie knew a little about that herself.

"Katie girl, that was delicious. It was so wonderful to come home and smell that sauce cooking, I wanted to go out and come back in again just to experience it once more."

"Mama, you're exaggerating."

"Absolutely not! When I say my daughter makes the best spaghetti in the entire state of Wisconsin, I mean it!" When Katie blushed she added. "I haven't given you a lot of praise over the years, have I?"

"What are you talking about? Of course you have. It's not your fault I don't know how to take a compliment."

"Now don't go trying to take the blame for this, Katie Sue Montgomery." Daria ran her fingertip around the rim of her glass. "I should have built you up more; you know, told you when you were doing things right and all."

"Oh, Mama—"

"I know what you're gonna say, and I don't want you to. You've had a tough couple of days what with finding out . . . well, you know. I guess I'm trying to say I'm proud of you and how you're handling this whole thing." She hesitated, choosing her words. "You went down to the clinic today?"

Katie nodded.

"Was it okay? You seem to be in a good mood."

"Yeah, it actually went better than I expected. The nurse was very professional and encouraging." Katie conveniently left out the fact that she had declined to schedule an appointment for the abortion. "She kept telling me how fortunate I was since everything is legal now. She didn't say, but I got the feeling maybe she had a really hard time in the past. Maybe she wanted an abortion and couldn't get one, I don't know. But she definitely agreed it would be wise for me since I want to go to college. Actually, she sounded a lot like you."

"Really. Hmm. Imagine that." Daria was pleased.

Katie paused. Daria's eyes questioned. "It went well?"

"Oh, it did. I was just thinking. I asked the nurse if what was inside me was a baby yet."

Daria's brow furrowed. "And what did she say?"

"Well, she said people have different opinions on that. Apparently she thinks it's not a real baby until it's born. She kept saying I should be concerned with my future and my potential instead of someone who's not even born yet."

"That makes perfectly good sense. Don't you agree?"

"I agree it makes sense." Again she paused.

"But?"

"But I was wondering what other people would say, you know, those who disagree with the nurse."

"Oh, Katie girl. You're always afraid of disappointing someone. There's always gonna be people waiting to find fault with what you do. And yeah, abortion is a touchy subject. I've seen some stuff on

TV. But when it all comes down, you've got to do what's best for you. When you lay your head on your pillow at night, there's not gonna be anybody but you to answer to. So don't go borrowing trouble from people who don't know you or your situation but still think they have the right to judge you. Nobody should have that right unless you break the law. And the last time I checked, abortion was legal. Can't nobody condemn you for doing what the Supreme Court says is okay."

For the second time that day Katie found it hard to argue with what sounded like good logic. "You're right, Mama. It's just whenever I start thinking too much, I get all confused."

Daria thought a moment. "Well, I suppose that's what's good about abortion. Once it's done, it's done. If you gave it up for adoption, you'd spend your life wondering where it was and if it was okay. I can't see how that would give a person any peace. Especially someone like you with such a big heart."

Katie sighed. "How come things always make perfect sense when someone else is talking about it?"

Daria reached over and gave her daughter's hand a gentle squeeze. "I know this is tough on you and you want to do the right thing. You never have been the kind to jump head first into anything." She chuckled. "I remember trying to teach you to swim. Barry, the guy I was dating, kept telling me to throw you in. I was tempted, but I couldn't do it. I'd take one look at your scared face, and I'd just keep coaxing you and telling you it was gonna be all right and that I would be right beside you."

Katie was curious. "So what made me finally get in?"

"I think it had something to do with the fact that you were the only kid not in the pool having a good time. You sat on the side all sad and lonely. Finally, it got the better of you and you slowly climbed down the steps until you were all the way in. Then you started splashing around and laughing. I remember thinking, 'Now that's how my daughter's life ought to be, carefree.' I had enough heartache and misery for the both of us. I didn't want you carrying around the same load I had. Maybe that's why I'm so sure an abortion is right for you."

"I've lost you; what do you mean?"

"I mean that if you have a baby, you're gonna be right back on the edge of that pool watching everybody else having fun, living life. Katie, I want you to dive right in. Look what happened when you finally conquered your fear of the water and jumped in: you became an excellent swimmer and you loved it! I wouldn't trade anything for the joy I saw on your face that day when you realized how much fun swimming could be. Even though you were only three or four years old, I think you regretted wasting time on the side. You were too young for regrets then, and you're too young for them now."

"Like I said, it makes sense when you explain it."

Daria cocked her head and grinned. "Don't you think that should be telling you something?"

Katie had to laugh at that one. Her mom was right; it was really very simple. She was the one making it difficult. She got up and circled the table to give her mom a quick hug.

"Thanks, Mama. I needed that."

"Anytime, sweetie." Daria patted the hand resting on her shoulder. "I'll tell you what: not only will I help you solve all your problems, but I'll also clean up the kitchen. Rumor has it there's a figure skating competition on TV tonight."

Katie's eyes sparkled. "You wouldn't mind?"

"After that meal, I might even clean the entire apartment!"

Another hug was bestowed upon Daria as well as a kiss on the cheek. "Thanks, Mama, you're the best."

12

KATIE HAD NEVER FELT SO LIGHT or so beautiful. She vaguely recalled something was wrong, but she couldn't place what. She just concentrated on the smoothness of the ice and the rhythmic swish of the skates. She was a champion on the ice. Sit spins, triple jumps, spirals—nothing was out of her reach or her ability. It was intoxicating; the sweet taste of success.

Katie skated on, more and more comfortable in her new role. She couldn't even tell where the tip of her blade ended and the ice began. It was wholeness like she had never experienced before. It didn't make sense to her; she felt warm and secure when she should have been cold and scared. The freezing, hard surface of the ice should have brought chills with it; but instead it brought security and purpose. Katie drank it in.

In the audience Daria waved as her daughter skated past. Daria looked so beautiful and soft. Then Katie knew why. *She's proud of me.* Katie skated harder and harder, taking more and more risks. Her jumps were higher; her spins were faster. With each revolution her graceful body made she breathed out a promise to the woman sitting in the stands. *I will make you proud, Mama, I will, I will, I will, I—*

Coming out of her spin, Katie saw him. Standing on the edge of the ice was Kaleo beckoning her to follow him.

No, I won't go. She fervently whispered, trying not to notice the wolf's gentle eyes. *This is where I belong, here on the ice performing for all these people. I won't go.*

Her thoughts drawn elsewhere, Katie lost her balance and fell doing a single axle. The crowd gasped. Katie was mortified. Her moment of glory was over—and it was Kaleo's fault.

"I thought you were my friend!" Katie bellowed. "Why would you do this to me? Leave me alone!"

Kaleo only let out a slow, mournful howl.

❄ ❄ ❄

Katie tried to shake off the disturbing dream. It was the first day back at school, and her sociology teacher would be walking in any minute. This was an elective course; but Katie still wanted to do well in it. Besides, she enjoyed the class.

Her teacher, Mr. Lassiter, made it enjoyable. He was a eccentric guy, in his mid-thirties, Katie guessed. He always wore cardigan sweaters and plaid trousers as if he had stepped out of another decade. Gold, wire-rimmed glasses completed the ensemble and gave him the look of a highly-educated man—certainly too educated to be teaching high school. The students had affectionately dubbed him "Professor," a title which seemed to please him.

Even though Mr. Lassiter left himself open to ridicule dressing the way he did, the fashion-and-image-conscious teenagers who filled the seats in his classroom never laughed at him. These kids knew Mr. Lassiter cared about them and wanted them to learn. In turn, they cared about him and even tried to learn a thing or two. Actually, it wasn't that hard with the way he taught. He had learned a long time ago that teenagers were hungry to be heard, so he purposely ran his classroom with a discussion-style method of teaching. The kids adored him, and Katie was no exception.

Mr. Lassiter stepped to the front of the room after quickly dispensing with the "housekeeping" duties, as he less-than-affectionately dubbed the duties of roll call, signing absentee excuses, etc. On this particular Monday morning Mr. Lassiter had a gleam in his eyes.

"Well, class, I hope you all had good holidays."

A boy from the back called out, "They were good, but they

were too short!"

A chorus of "You bet" and "That's right" followed.

Mr. Lassiter only smiled.

"What's that smile for, Professor? What have you got up your sleeve?"asked a girl on the front row. The class was silent now, all curious about the day's lesson.

"Let's just say," Mr. Lassiter offered while rubbing his chin with his hand, "I think you're going to find it was worth coming back to school today."

"Come on, stop teasing us!" whined the same girl from the front row. "Tell us what's going on."

Katie was silent during all of this. Playful bantering didn't hold as much allure and merriment when you found yourself pregnant. Still, she was curious about the day's lesson.

"Okay, okay." Mr. Lassiter held his hand up for silence. When every eye was trained on him, he spoke. "We are beginning a new section today. And I'll tell you right up front that we have to treat this as adults if we're going to continue in the discussion format. Agreed?" His eyes swept the room.

"Agreed." The students' voices rose in unison.

"All right then. Today we begin our study of human sexuality." He paused here as if waiting for the inevitable. From various places around the room there erupted giggles, whispers, and from some of the boys, "All right, now you're talking," and "Now that's what I call an education." One boy boldly shouted, "Finally, a good use for our tax dollars!"

Mr. Lassiter chuckled. He held up his hand to quiet the class. "So much for acting like adults!" He laughed and the students knew they weren't in trouble. "One thing we do have to keep in mind is that this is a sociology class, so we need to focus on the societal ramifications of human sexuality."

"What does that mean?" a voice called out.

"Why don't you tell me. Who'll take a stab at it?" The professor's eyes rested on a cute dark-haired girl in the second row. A good student, well-liked by the other kids, she usually had pretty strong opinions. "How 'bout you, Janie. What do I mean by 'the societal ramifications of human sexuality'?"

The girl cocked her head to one side and chewed on her bottom lip for a second. Then she ventured, "I guess it means the way we deal with the whole issue of how sex affects the way our society is run."

"That's right. Now, give me some specific examples."

Again, the head cocked. "Well, for instance: If people believe homosexuality is okay, then it will eventually become an accepted part of society. Maybe teenage sexuality as well."

"How so?"

"If society deems it okay for teenagers to have sex, then the entire morality of the nation changes. Some would say it's a good change, while others would say it's bad."

"Tell us what you mean by good and bad changes," prompted the teacher.

"Well, if you thought it was a normal part of growing up for teenagers to have sex, then you'd think it would be good to have condoms distributed in school. And abortion rates would go up because wherever you have sex, naturally pregnancy is gonna happen."

"And if you were opposed to teenager's having sex?"

A boy in the back couldn't resist a little good-natured ribbing. "Okay, everybody brace yourself for a sermon!"

Katie stiffened, expecting an argument.

Janie Matheson turned around and flashed a big smile at the boy in the back. "You heard the professor, Shane. I have to answer the question or I might get in trouble."

Shane grinned and tipped an imaginary hat to the girl. Katie was astonished. She didn't know Janie Matheson, but she had seen her around school. She was popular, but not in an uppity way. The one attribute you couldn't help noticing about the girl who stood maybe five-foot-two was her smile. Every time you saw her, she was grinning from ear to ear. And it wasn't a fake smile like when you have to smile for your school picture and feel like a total idiot. No, this seemed genuine, and Katie admired that. She also admired how she didn't seem to mind being ridiculed in front of the class, even if it was all in good humor. She waited to see what the perky girl's response would be.

"Well, my belief is that teenagers shouldn't be having sex." A concert of groans filled the room, but she continued undaunted. "So, decisions to pass out condoms and teach 'safe sex' in public high schools would be decisions I would consider to be detrimental to society—"

"Yeah, but Janie," interrupted a girl named Wendy, "just because you don't agree doesn't mean it's not the best thing for society. I mean, kids are gonna have sex, so shouldn't we at least equip them with birth control and educate them so they won't get diseases or get pregnant?"

Katie unconsciously sank lower in her seat. She knew that education and condoms weren't the solution. She had a positive pregnancy test that told otherwise.

Janie shook her head. "Just because everyone is doing something doesn't make it right. Society shouldn't lower the standard just so people won't feel guilty about their choices."

Mr. Lassiter intervened at this point. He settled himself on the edge of his desk and leaned slightly forward. "Let's look at where our society is today concerning teenage sexuality. Talk to me about the choices that teenagers face."

A boy Katie didn't know spoke up. "Well, you have the choice to have sex or not to have sex; no matter what the laws are, it's still up to the individual."

"So, Craig, you're saying society can't make a person's choices for them, right?" questioned Mr. Lassiter.

The boy answered. "Yeah. I mean, if Janie believes it's wrong to have sex before she's married, then she doesn't have to do it. It's not a law. It's her choice."

"That's what I think, too," piped up a girl near the back. She twirled her blond hair around her finger as she spoke. "It really bugs me when people try to tell you how to live your life. Like with abortion. I've seen bumper stickers that say, 'If you're against abortion, then don't have one.' And I agree. I don't think anyone should be forced to have one if they're against it, but I also don't think anyone should say you can't have one. It should be the individual's choice, like it is now. I mean, the laws have been passed to make it legal, but people still try to say it's wrong. That doesn't make sense to me."

"I agree."

"Me too."

"It's a personal issue."

Katie could scarcely breathe. She was hearing much of the same rhetoric she'd heard from her mom and at the clinic.

"But, the issue here is the effect that all of this has on society," rebutted Janie. "And if you leave people to their own devices totally, you'll most likely lose all respect for life. Then what will happen to society?"

"Yeah, but who gives you the right to decide what's right and wrong?" questioned the blond girl vehemently.

"There has to be reverence for life or we'll be reduced to . . . to . . . a nation who would rather kill anything or anyone we deem a burden. And I'm not just talking about unborn babies; what about old people or handicapped people? What if we decide foreigners should be terminated? What then? We'll be no better than Hitler! Isn't that right, Professor?"

Mr. Lassiter looked around the room, but no one else had a thought-out answer, so he said, "Please, continue, Janie."

"Well, there has to be a standard. Look at fashion. Just because someone somewhere who is considered an expert in fashion says we should wear potato sacks, before you know it we'd all rush out and buy potato sacks!"

This brought a roar of laughter from the students that eased the tension building in the classroom.

"Oh, come on, you guys!" There was that ear-to-ear smile again. "You know it's true. We'd all get in line to buy the sacks, never mind the fact that we'd all look stupid in them. Just look at bell bottoms; need I say more?"

Janie paused while the room filled with more laughter. Then she plunged ahead. "Fashion rules change all the time, but if we try to change moral laws, look what happens: all the abortions taking place and the number of AIDS cases rising, not to mention all the other diseases out there. There are a lot of side effects to teenage sex."

Deathly quiet settled on the class for a few seconds. Then again Craig spoke up. "Yeah, that may be all well and good, Janie; but just think how many unwanted babies there would be if we didn't have abortion." A chorus of agreement followed.

"If a girl who didn't want a baby didn't have sex, there would be no baby to abort. Don't you see? I'm against abortion, that's true. I think it's terribly cruel. But maybe it's just a symptom of a deeper problem."

"And what would that be, preacher girl?" asked Shane.

"A nation that does what's right in its own eyes instead of God's," came the calm, matter-of-fact reply.

Mr. Lassiter stood up and quieted the class. With a smile he said, "I told you we would have to handle this like adults. And I commend you all. You've done a good job of keeping emotions under control. This is a difficult subject. Our discussion today proves there are no easy answers. We have to think through all sides of the issues. Many of you seem to disagree with Janie's stance; and that's okay. But she did raise some valid points to ponder."

Groans rippled across the room. Whenever the Professor used the phrase "points to ponder," it meant homework.

The teacher grinned. "I see you know where I'm going with

this. What I'd like you to do is simply get out a sheet of paper and begin to write the pros and cons of active teenage sexuality. Write out a few paragraphs explaining the conclusion you come to. You may certainly include the points mentioned today, but think hard about it for yourselves and see what other ones you come up with. Chapter Ten in your textbook may help as well. I want you to spend the remainder of the class working on this, and if you don't complete it then . . ." He waited for the class to finish his statement.

They did, as one synchronized voice: "You must complete the assignment for homework."

"Excellent, excellent. It's good to see you didn't forget everything over the holidays!"

Scarcely hearing the shuffling of papers and murmurs all around her, Katie took a sheet of paper from her notebook and stared blankly at it. What in the world would she write?

Katie made her way into the school cafeteria, her mind still reeling from her morning sociology class. The timing of the lesson was too coincidental. And then that girl, Janie Matheson, vocalizing some of Katie's very own thoughts! It was obvious the majority of the class disagreed with the vivacious little brunette, but it didn't seem to faze her one bit—nor did it diminish anyone's opinion of her. Katie had watched, flabbergasted, as the petite girl left the classroom laughing and joking with some of the very same students who had challenged her only moments before!

The whole ordeal was still fresh in Katie's mind as she carried her lunch tray and searched the cafeteria for a quiet place to sit. She used to sit with Kristin, but they hadn't shared a meal together since Thanksgiving. These days Katie opted for a secluded spot wherever she could find it; she'd either study or read or just sit and pretend to be content. She had a feeling any of those would be extremely difficult to do convincingly today. And that's when she saw her.

Sitting alone at a table in the far corner of the crowded cafeteria was Janie Matheson. Usually she was surrounded by a cluster of Stoughton High's best and brightest; but today she sat by herself, her head buried in a notebook and what looked like a half-eaten tuna sandwich. Before she realized what she was doing, Katie was standing directly in front of the girl who had never left her thoughts since sociology class.

"Hi," spoke Katie in an almost apologetic voice, "is it okay if I sit here? I mean, if it's not already taken."

Janie looked with a warm, inviting smile. "Sure." She quickly moved her belongings to make more room.

Katie sat down. "Thanks. I didn't see anywhere else to sit that wasn't swarming with people."

"I know what you mean. I didn't feel like being in the middle of a crowd either." She inclined her head toward a table off to the right. "I told my friends not to bother me today, that I had too much stuff to do."

"Oh, I'm sorry. I'll just scoot down a couple of seats." She began gathering up her books and tray to move.

"No, wait! I didn't mean I didn't want you to sit here! Wow, that really must have sounded rude. I'm sorry." Janie flashed Katie another smile, her eyes entreating her to stay.

"Okay. I promise I'll be quiet." Katie grinned. This was met with a chuckle from Janie.

"Well, I'm glad we got that out of the way! . . . Um, I know we have a class together; isn't your name Katie?"

"Yeah, sociology class. Your name's Janie, right?"

"That's me." Janie glanced at Katie's lunch tray. "Looks like you're braver than me to eat the school's lunch."

"Well, I usually bring a sandwich from home; but I was running behind this morning and didn't have time to fix one."

"I guess I'm kind of spoiled." Janie lowered her voice to a confidential tone. "It's embarrassing to admit, but my mom still makes my lunch every morning."

"Don't be embarrassed about that. It sounds good to have a mom willing to do that for you. In fact, I didn't know moms like that still existed."

She didn't notice Janie's nonplussed look.

Katie asked, "What's that you're working on?" indicating the small notebook in front of Janie. It didn't look like a school notebook.

"Oh, this is my prayer journal. I'm trying to update it and put in some new requests."

"Oh," replied Katie. She had no idea what a prayer journal was, but briefly wondered whether the little old lady at the grocery store had one. "Could I ask you a question?"

"Sure, anything," replied Janie as if she had nothing in the world to hide. Katie felt a moment of envy.

"I've been thinking about what you said in class."

"Yeah?" Janie asked, almost too quickly.

"Well, I was wondering how you know all that stuff."

Janie gave a little mirthless laugh. "I wish I could take the credit and say I'm just smart, but that would be a lie. The truth is we've studied a lot of current topics like abortion at church in my youth group. Our youth pastor really makes us think hard about things like that. He doesn't want us to just recite what our parents believe or what he believes." She shook her head and let out a sigh. "I have to admit it was a shock to walk into class and find out what the topic was. It was like God was saying to me 'Okay, Janie, here's your chance to stand up for what you've been saying you believe. Are you ready?' I just thought, 'Okay, Lord, here we go!' And I did it. I opened my mouth and all of a sudden I was explaining my position, and it felt great! I really didn't care what anybody thought because I knew I was stating the truth." She took a deep breath. "And I'm glad I had the opportunity. You always wonder if you'll have the guts to stand up for the truth in the middle of opposition, and today I proved to myself I could. I felt like God was proud of me."

Katie sat there bewildered. This was not the explanation she had expected. In fact, she was a little disappointed. She was hoping this girl who seemed to know so much could give her some concrete examples as to why abortion might be wrong. Instead, she just chattered on about God being proud of her. Unintentionally, Katie let out her breath rather loudly and her disillusionment showed clearly on her face.

Janie stared at her. "Katie, are you okay?"

"Uuuh . . . yeah, I'm fine. You just caught me off guard with what you said, that's all."

"Well, do you agree or disagree with my position?"

"What position?" asked Katie genuinely confused.

"Well, how do you feel about abortion?"

"I don't know. I've never thought much about it before, until now, that is. I guess I've always assumed it was okay, but I don't know why I thought that. I just accepted it; but now I'm not sure what to think. Ever since class let out, I've been panicked about what to write on our homework assignment."

Janie glanced at the clock on the wall. "Hey, if you'd like, I wouldn't mind sitting down and explaining to you why I believe the way I do. I mean if you think it might help."

In that instant Katie felt fear. "Oh, no . . . I don't think that's necessary. I'll come up with something. But I appreciate the offer." The last thing she wanted was some kind of intense religious discussion. She needed practical answers and she needed them fast.

"Well, I will tell you this, Katie. There's an organization called Care Net that can give you all kinds of information, not just on abortion, but on all those things we talked about in class. A lady from our church works there, and she's the one who supplies our youth group with information."

"Oh, okay, maybe I'll check with them. It's just a silly homework assignment. I don't know why I'm making such a big deal about it." Katie was having a difficult time disguising the embarrassment she was feeling. She was afraid her face had betrayed her and revealed more than she had intended.

Right then the bell rang, and both girls began to rise. Janie leaned over and touched Katie's arm. "I'm glad you sat with me today. It was nice talking to you."

"Yeah, me too. Well, see you around. I gotta go. Bye."

When Katie left, even though Janie had to get to her biology class, she sank back into the cafeteria chair and put her face in her hands.

13

※

SNOW HAD THREATENED all day, but not a flake had appeared. The man behind the driver's wheel studied the sky above as he sat unmoving in rush-hour traffic. Darkness was fast descending upon the city of Madison. Being an astute observer of his surroundings, the man noted that tempers within the stalled cars were rising as fast as the dim sunlight was setting. He grinned to himself thinking how nice it would be to get home to his family. The post-holiday time was always a rough one. Trying to get back into the routine of work and traffic was not very appealing after the comfortableness of spending so much uninterrupted time in front of a cozy fireplace with his wife of nearly thirty years or sitting at the head of his table surrounded by his five children and dish after dish of scrumptious holiday delights.

"Oh, Lord," he sighed out loud, "I thank You for the time You gave us over the holidays to be together. But now, Lord, I ask You to help us, help me, have a good attitude about going back to work and saying good-bye to the holidays." He thought of how much he'd enjoyed having his oldest two daughters home for the past couple of weeks. Saying good-bye to them two days ago had been bittersweet.

Everett Matheson supposed it went this way with all fathers. You work so hard to get your children ready to go out into the world and then you want to hold on to them when they're ready to fly. He was thankful he still had three more kids at home; he knew his heart wasn't ready for an empty nest. "And help me, Father, do and say only that which will be spiritually profitable for preparing my children for service in Your kingdom." He wasn't sure why he was prompted to pray that prayer right then, but he obeyed the subtle voice inside him. He'd find his answers soon enough. Traffic was beginning to resume its normal speed. Everett Matheson only smiled and whispered, "Thank You, Lord."

The woman in the kitchen had no idea Everett was watching her or that he was thinking she was the most beautiful woman in the world. Actually, this was a little ritual of his that his wife knew nothing about. For as long as they had been married, Everett delighted in sneaking peeks at his unsuspecting wife. This was his favorite time to do it—when she was putting the finishing touches on the evening meal. She always had a smug look on her face, one that said *I know my family is going to love this dinner.* Lydia Matheson was a woman who reveled in pleasing her family. And Everett loved that about his wife.

Everett and Lydia had married right out of high school. Most people said it wouldn't last, that they were too young. Not that it hadn't been hard over the years, but sometimes you just knew when something was right and good. Especially when you believed God had intended for the marriage to take place, that it was all a part of His plan from the beginning.

Everett smiled. Lydia was humming now. He tried to make out the tune. She loved music and he loved the joy it brought to her, so he'd never had the heart to tell her she couldn't carry a tune to save her life. But there was no mistaking the tune this time; even his precious Lydia couldn't botch "What a Friend We Have in Jesus."

He stole up behind her and joined his deep voice to her soft one: "O what peace we often forfeit, O what needless pain we bear, All because we do not carry Ev'rything to God in prayer." He bent and kissed Lydia's cheek. "So it's been a rough day, I take it, my love." It was a statement, not a question. Everett knew his wife only sang that song when she'd spent a lot of time crying out to her Savior, relishing closeness with the God of the universe.

Lydia looked at her husband. "You know me too well, don't you? You'd think I'd get used to it by now, but I don't. I hate seeing everybody leave." She mindlessly stirred a pot on the stove. "Janie was the last to leave for school this morning, and I just broke down and cried when she walked out the door."

Everett stared down at his diminutive wife. She was incredibly beautiful to him even after all these years. "My dear," he said sweetly with just a tinge of humor, "you are what is commonly referred to as 'a mother.'"

"Well, a lot of help you are!" She laughed as she gently pushed him away and dabbed at her eyes with the corner of her apron. "Thank goodness God doesn't treat me the way you do! At least He knows how to comfort me!"

Her husband nodded and stole a piece of bread from the basket on the counter. "And exactly how did God comfort you today?"

Lydia smiled. "By gently reminding me that my job as a mother is to prepare my children for the good works He has planned for them. And if I kept them here with me, they couldn't fully serve Him." She sighed and grabbed a potholder from a nearby drawer. "I just hoped it would get easier as time went on, but I don't think it ever will."

Everett nodded.

She shook her head. "It's a lesson I have to keep learning over and over again. I'm thankful God is patient with me." She sighed once again and smiled at her husband. "It feels good to confess my selfishness and to once again turn my kids, all five of them, over to the Lord's care. If God could let His child go, I have to be willing to let mine go as well."

"May I ask you a question, Lydia Matheson?"

"Well, of course, dear," she replied while bending over to pull a casserole dish out of the oven. "What is it?"

"Will you marry me?"

She spun around and saw the merriment in her husband's blue eyes. "What are you talking about?"

"All I'm trying to clumsily say is that I am so glad you are my wife. It amazes me how often we have the same thoughts. Besides, I can't imagine a better mother for our children or a better wife for me or . . ." the glint in his eyes grew brighter, "a better cook for my dinner." He hungrily took another bite of bread before giving Lydia another kiss on the cheek. "Seriously, you do know I love the way you love the Lord. You always teach me so much about trusting Him."

"I 've heard you say that before, but I find it difficult to believe."

"Well, you do, constantly." Now it was his turn to shake his head. "I confess I've had a little difficulty today as well. It's not just mothers who miss their kids. I tried and tried to focus on building plans today, but I kept seeing Johanna and Kendall's faces in the middle of the blueprints. Hard to get any work done that way."

Lydia gave her husband a quick hug. Then, handing him the bread basket, she playfully said, "Well, the good news is we still have three kids here to eat us out of house and home. So, if you would kindly stop stuffing your face and call them to the table, we can eat this food I slaved over all day while you sat in your office and accomplished nothing!" She feigned exhaustion as she winked at her husband.

Everett gave her his most charming smile, deposited the bread basket on the table, and headed for the stairs to call the kids for dinner.

❄ ❄ ❄

"Would you please pass me some more roast?"

No response.

"Well, then could I have some potato casserole?"

Again, silence.

"Ahem! Could I please have something to eat? I'll take any-thing." The voice had purposely taken on a pitiful, pleading quality.

But still there was no response. Dexter caught his brother's eye and grinned. "What do you suppose she's thinking about?"

Lydia shot a warning look at her two sons; she knew what was coming. Even at eighteen and twenty-two, Brady and Dexter Matheson still teased their little sister like they did back in grammar school. Even attending the University of Wisconsin hadn't matured Dex in that regard.

Brady stared at his sister for a minute. "I'm not sure, but I'll bet it has something to do with some guy."

"Yeah, you're probably right. You know how Janie is, in love with a different boy every week." Dex waited for his sister to respond, knowing full well she was anything but boy crazy. When she didn't oblige him with a clever comeback, he tried a less-than-subtle approach. "So, Sis, who does the lucky guy look like this time? Bullwinkle, Scooby Doo, what?"

Nothing. Not even a sharp look.

"Maybe he's more the Jughead type," chimed in Brady.

Everett stared at his daughter now. He, too, was curious as to what had his youngest child so preoccupied. She never let a chance to banter with Dex slip by. The two were uncommonly close. "Janie, aren't you gonna answer? Who does the guy look like?"

"Huh? Did you say something, Dad?" Janie looked up with that deer-caught-in-the-headlights look in her dark eyes.

The whole table erupted in laughter at this—with the exception of a very confused sixteen year old girl.

"The boys have been trying to get your attention for a while now," Lydia offered in the way of an explanation. "You seemed to be miles away."

"Is everything all right?" questioned Everett. He knew his youngest daughter usually preferred to be in the middle of everything.

"I was thinking about something that happened at school today."

"Well, now that the mystery's solved, do you think I could have some more roast, please?" Dexter shot another pathetic look at his sister. "I really am still hungry."

Janie, looking a bit confused, passed the meat.

Dexter Matheson accepted the proffered platter and put a slice of roast on his plate. "So, are you gonna tell us what happened?" His gentle voice conveyed his concern.

"Yeah, what's up?" echoed Brady. "It's not like you to ever be quiet."

"Well, we started this new unit in sociology today, and it was all about human sexuality."

"And you're afraid you're gonna fail the class, right?" jested Brady with eyes twinkling.

"No, nothing like that."

The two brothers looked at each other with brows raised, as did Everett and Lydia. It was evident to all that whatever happened was weighing heavily on the high school sophomore. She would never let an insult like that go by without a friendly fight. Although she was the smallest and the youngest, she could hold her own with anybody.

"Do you not want to talk about it? 'Cause if you don't, we'll be sure and leave you alone, won't we, boys?" Everett stared intently at his two sons. They both nodded.

"No, I don't mind talking about it."

"Well, why don't you tell us what happened in class," suggested Lydia.

Janie took a long drink of her iced tea. She set the glass down. "Mr. Lassiter asked me what I thought about some things. And, well, you know me. I dove right in and gave my opinion. I didn't talk about the Bible outright, but I gave my position pretty clearly, at least I think I did."

"How did the class respond?" asked Dex, interested.

"No one got mad or anything, but most of the kids disagreed with me." She paused and wrinkled her brow. "That's not what's bothering me, though."

"What is then, dear?" Lydia could hardly stand the suspense.

"Well, this girl came up to me during lunch. I was sitting alone because I wanted to write in my prayer journal about the opportunity God gave me to speak out in class. Anyway, she's a real quiet kind of girl. I don't know her at all; she keeps to herself a lot." Janie cocked her head. "I'm ashamed to say I've never even spoken to her before. She's really nice and pretty, but I guess I've kind of ignored her. I think she used to date this cute guy named Eric, but they broke up not too long ago. Since then, she's just stayed to herself. I guess that's one reason I was shocked when she sat with me today. It was totally uncharacteristic on her part; but then again, it's pretty uncharacteristic for me to sit by myself. So I keep thinking maybe God orchestrated the whole thing."

Everyone at the table breathed an inaudible sigh of relief. Now this was the old Janie, talking incessantly.

"What did you two talk about?" inquired Dex.

"Well, for homework we're supposed to write a pros and cons essay about teenagers having sex. She said she was stumped and didn't know what to write and was wondering how I knew all the stuff I did about it and, well, I told her I'd learned it at church. I just kept saying how glad I was that I had the guts to speak out . . . and . . ." Her eyes welled with tears and she turned to look into her mother's eyes. "I did exactly what I've been praying I wouldn't do. I talked and talked and never gave her a chance to say anything! I am so ashamed! Oh, Mom, once again my mouth took over."

"Sweetheart, how do you know you said the wrong things?" asked Lydia.

The tears spilled over now. "If you could have seen her face when I started talking about God and church. A brick wall went up, but did that stop me? No way! Not Janie Big-mouth Matheson! I was on such a high about how I had taken a stand in class. She must think I'm the most egotistical person she's ever met! And I was talking about God! I am so ashamed!"

Everett, who was sitting to Janie's left, reached over to comfort her. "How did the conversation end?"

Janie looked up and into the faces of her family. She sniffed and delicately blew her nose into her cloth napkin. "By the time I realized I had spent the whole time talking about me, lunch was almost over. I panicked and clumsily tried to tell her I wanted to spend some more time talking about all that stuff with her, but she shook her head and said there was no need. I blew it. I pushed too hard. Instead of listening and asking questions to put her at ease like we've been learning in youth group, I did what I always do and dominated the conversation. Now she'll probably never speak to me again! She probably thinks I'm some kind of wacko religious fanatic or something." She tried to hold back the tears, but to no avail.

"You know, little sister," said Dex sympathetically, "all is not lost. Even if this girl never speaks to you again, you can still pray for her."

Everett's strong yet gentle voice filled the room. "I say we all should pray right now for Janie and this girl."

"Oh, Dad, can we? That would make me feel better."

"You bet," replied Everett, encouraged to see his daughter's eyes twinkling again.

The family immediately took hands, being no strangers to praying together. Lydia said, "Since we're going to pray for this girl, Janie, it might be nice to know her name."

Janie giggled already feeling much lighter. "I guess that does make sense. Her name is Katie."

In unison the family bowed their heads and beseeched their heavenly Father to take care of the girl named Katie, to open her eyes to the truth, and to give Janie another opportunity to reach out to her.

14

KATIE STARED AT THE ALL-TOO-FAMILIAR CEILING of her bedroom. Nothing had changed. She still found no answers there. The only difference was now it irritated her. She kept thinking about Janie's words from class earlier that day. A nation that does what's right in its own eyes instead of God's. What exactly did that mean? Katie wondered if there actually could be a God who held right and wrong within His own hands. Or was it up to each person to decide what was acceptable?

She closed her eyes and tried to drown out the sound of her mom and Rick arguing in the next room. Apparently Rick wanted Daria to go out, and she wasn't in the mood. Katie wanted to fling the door open and shout at them to shut up! Didn't they know there were more important things in life than partying? Didn't they understand that she had a really important decision to make? Were they ever going to grow up like she was having to do? She rolled to her side and let the tears fall.

After what seemed an eternity, Katie balled her hands into fists and pressed them against her eyes. She could still hear the argument raging. Slowly she moved her hands away from her eyes to her ears trying once again to block out the slurred, demanding voice of Rick McBride and the pathetic pleading tones of her mother.

It took a moment for Katie's eyes to adjust to the light of the room after being veiled by her fists for so long. They finally focused on something in front of her. It was a rumpled card on the nightstand. She picked it up and stared at it. She expected it to hold as much insight as the ceiling had, but surprisingly she felt a lightness about her.

She pulled herself up, propped her back against the wall, and pulled her knees in front of her. She wondered what Janie Matheson would say about 1 Peter 5:7. She also wondered what Janie would say if she knew the girl she had eaten lunch with was pregnant.

This last thought made Katie sink back down on the bed, as if to hide herself from unscrupulous stares. She glanced down at her abdomen and breathed a sigh of relief upon seeing once again that it was still flat and trim. She shook her head at her silliness.

"Get a grip, girl." Her mind was playing tricks on her. Or was it some other part of her—maybe her soul? She had thought she heard her soul speaking to her as she sat on the bathroom floor staring at the positive pregnancy test.

Frustrated, Katie mumbled, "Why does this have to be so hard? Why can't I just have this abortion and be done with it and get on with my life like Mama and that nurse said."

Something inside Katie warned that it wasn't as easy as all that. But what was the "something"? And how could Katie listen to the voice of a God she wasn't even sure existed?

Suddenly she remembered the little old lady who had given her this card, her only source of comfort. She had said something about always searching until you had your answers. Was that what Katie was supposed to be doing now? Searching? But for what? The knowledge of a universal right and wrong? Katie didn't know if there was such a thing. *But Janie Matheson is obviously convinced there is.* For the first time that day, Katie felt like she had a purpose.

Rising from her bed Katie listened at her door. The argument had passed. She didn't know who had finally won, and she didn't care. She just wanted peace and quiet.

Tiptoeing into the kitchen she heard faint sobs coming from her mom's bedroom off to the left. So Rick had won the argument and had left the apartment. Katie glanced to the living room on the right and saw the phone on the nightstand. She surreptitiously retrieved it. On her way back to her bedroom she stopped and shuffled through a kitchen cabinet in search of the phone book, being careful not to disturb her mom. What she was about to do was better kept a secret. Then she scurried back to the privacy of her room.

It didn't take long to find the Abortion Alternatives listing in the yellow pages. With trembling hands Katie punched in the number of the nearest Pregnancy Information Center.

Dexter Matheson climbed the staircase leading to the second floor of his family's home. How he loved this house, not so much for its architectural beauty, but for the warmth of the people who occupied it, not the least of which was his younger sister. He still remembered the day his parents had brought Janie home from the hospital. From his six-year-old perspective, the tiny bundle wrapped in pink resembled a peanut. He had said as much, and the whole family had laughed. The memory made Dex smile as he peered into his sister's room. "Peanut" had her back to the door and hadn't heard him approach. She wasn't his baby sister anymore, although he suspected he would always view her that way.

Janie had the ability to wrap Dex around her little finger. And she knew it. But—and Dex had always admired this about her—she never abused that power. The two of them had an unspoken agreement that each would always champion the other. She was the encourager; he, the protector. He supposed that was what brought him to her room on this particular evening. He had seen her face at dinner and knew she had been deeply affected by the events that transpired at school, especially this girl named Katie.

Stealthily Dex grabbed a pillow off the bed and carefully aimed it at the back of his sister's head. Just as he was about to release it—

"Throw that pillow and you die!"

Naturally, he threw it anyway. But the now-moving target ducked a fraction of a second before contact, and the pillow fell to the floor uselessly. Dex groaned.

Janie, quick as a flash, grabbed one of her cologne bottles from the dressing table where she was sitting and whirled around to face her brother, the bottle thrust out before her. Her finger was poised, ready to shoot out a stream of flowery-smelling mist. "Okay, big brother, you were warned!" Her eyes at once flashed a threat and twinkled with delight. She slowly moved toward the tall, handsome man in front of her. "You know, I've always thought you were a sweet guy, for a brother and all, I mean. So I figured it was time you started smelling that way." She kept coming, very slowly, calculating the most advantageous time to strike.

She waited too long.

With one long stride Dexter reached his little sister and grabbed her wrist, twisting it just in time to see the sweet mist shoot out to the side, missing its intended target by about the same margin the pillow had missed Janie's head.

"What do you say to a truce? We're both obviously terrible at this warfare stuff." Dex spoke in a low voice.

"How do I know I can trust you?" Five-foot-two-inch Janie glanced warily upward at her six-foot-one-inch brother who had inherited their father's height and build.

"You don't know." His eyebrows moved up and down. "That's what faith is all about."

"I think I'll keep my faith in God and not in you, if you don't mind," the feisty brunette snapped in reply.

Dex laughed. "How can I argue with that? Now, I'm going to let go of your wrist, and I want you to promise you'll put down your weapon. I don't want to have to hurt you."

"Okay, deal." Janie smiled innocently.

Guardedly Dex released Janie's wrist and stepped back, not sure what to expect next. One second later he regretted his action as he was squirted squarely on the chest.

"That's it," Dex growled. "This is war!" He lunged forward, grabbed his sister around the waist and flung her onto the bed.

He then commenced the single lowest form of torture known to womankind—tickling. He showed no mercy. Not until he witnessed tears streaming down Janie's face did he even consider letting up. "Give?" he asked his victim.

"Yes, yes, please. I give. I'm sorry. I'll be your slave for life, just stop, please!"

Dex grinned at his prisoner. "Slave for life, you say? Hmm, that's pretty tempting." He loosened his hold on her so she could sit up. He pulled his face into a very serious, contemplative countenance. "I guess I'm in a generous mood tonight because I'm only gonna give you one order. We'll forget all about the 'for life' stuff."

"I knew you couldn't resist my charm and good looks."

"Yeah, well, you and I both know charm is deceptive and beauty is fleeting, so that's not it." Dex chucked his sister under the chin. "I think it has more to do with the fact that a woman who fears the Lord is to be praised. And you proved to me tonight at dinner that you definitely fear the Lord. I'm proud of you, Janie."

Janie beamed, unable once again to contain her tears. Only this time they were tears of joy. "Oh, Dex, thanks. I really needed to hear that right now."

"I kind of thought you might."

"So, what's my one order?"

"Simple. I want to know why you were so upset about what happened at school.

"I told you at dinner."

"Yeah, but I know you pretty well, little sister. This is really weighing heavy on you. You've always had a tender heart, but come on, you were in tears over someone you don't even know."

Janie sighed. "There was just something so vulnerable about this girl. It was in her eyes." Janie shook her head as she relived the brief encounter. "I still can't believe I babbled on like I did, when she was obviously in pain of some kind."

Dex ruffled her hair. "You're not perfect, peanut. But sometimes

I think you try to be."

Janie exhaled loudly and rolled her eyes. "I know; that's just one more of my problems. I'm a babbler and a perfectionist." She slumped slightly, then looked up at her brother. "I really wanted to help her. She didn't come right out and say it, but I got the feeling she has a bad home life, like nobody's there for her."

"It's hard sometimes to remember, not everybody has a place to come home to like we do."

"Boy, you're telling me! I wanted to ask her about it, but she changed the subject and asked me about that stuff from class and I began my one-woman show. By the time I finished my little speech, I noticed the clock on the wall and got in a hurry. I must have scared her off. I truly believe if I'd had more time I could have gotten her to open up."

Dex's look was gentle. "You don't know that, Janie. At least you broke the ice with her. First meetings are always awkward, so don't give up. Besides, God knows you truly care about this Katie girl."

Janie cocked her head and was silent for a moment. "Dex, promise me you'll pray about this?"

Dex couldn't help but smile. "You bet, peanut. But only if you promise to keep me posted."

Janie beamed. "Promise."

"Now, if you'll excuse me, I have to go change shirts seeing as how the stench of this one is about to make me sick." Dex comically crossed his eyes.

"Oh, um, sorry about that."

"Yeah, I'll bet you are." Dex laughed.

15

�֍

KATIE FELT EXACTLY THE SAME WAY she had the previous week when she stood outside the abortion clinic. This time, instead of staring at a medical building, she gazed up at a professional building with a myriad of offices. There was a dentist, a travel agency, a lawyer, and a realtor, among others. Smack dab in the middle of it all, on the second floor, was a sign that said "Pregnancy Information Center." Katie stared at it, toying with the idea of leaving. After all, it wasn't like she had an appointment. When she'd called the previous night, an answering machine had told her walk-ins were always welcome. Nobody inside the office even knew Katie Montgomery existed, much less that she was pregnant and looking for help. Turning around and driving back home would be so easy.

She stepped to the railing, peered over the edge, and stared down at the parking lot. For a fleeting moment she thought about jumping, but then laughed. *Oh, that's a good one, Katie. It's not far enough down to kill yourself, so you'd just wind up in the hospital with a bunch of broken bones and a stack of medical bills a mile high.* Still, she might lose the baby in the process.

She leaned back and looked at the awning overhead. She shuddered. Thinking about abortion was one thing, but deliberately trying to induce a miscarriage seemed so barbaric. Katie didn't know she was capable of such thoughts. Maybe she should go inside after all.

Katie heard the sound of laughter and turned her head. Two ladies were coming toward her, all smiles. One was probably in her mid-forties and on the tall side, while the other looked to be in her early to mid twenties. They were carrying sodas and bags of chips. Katie remembered seeing snack machines in the stairwell.

"Hi, were you waiting on us?"

Katie whirled around at the sound of the older woman's voice. "Huh? Oh, no, I . . . I wasn't waiting on anybody."

A look of relief passed over the women's faces. "Oh, good. Memphis and I ran down to the print shop on the first floor to iron out a big mess with some fliers we're having printed up. After we got down there, we realized we forgot to put the 'back in five minutes' sign up." As she spoke she unlocked the door to the Pregnancy Information Center. "I hate to think someone had to wait for us."

"I didn't even know the door was locked."

The younger girl held the door open for a second before saying with a bright smile, "Well, we're back, if you need us."

Katie desperately wanted to flee but couldn't get those words out of her head: *Keep searching and asking.* So far, she had taken other people's word for things. She owed it to herself to be confident of her decision. Though she was almost positive she knew what she wanted, a small seed of doubt lurked in her mind.

Katie swallowed hard and spoke through the still-open doorway. "If you're sure you're not too busy—"

"Not at all." Another bright smile from the girl named Memphis. "Come on in where it's warm. Here, let me close that door behind you so we don't lose all our heat."

Katie glanced at her surroundings. This place looked homey. Even though it was set up like a professional office space, someone had obviously taken great pains to make it comfortable and inviting. The walls were painted a soft mauve color with a pretty floral wallpaper border. The four chairs in the lobby area were noticeably old but had been recovered with a cheerful, rose-patterned fabric.

"So what can we do for you today?"

Katie was surprised to see that no glass partition separated her from the young woman speaking. Memphis was standing behind a simple brown desk adorned with a phone, some papers, and an arrangement of pastel-colored silk flowers. Katie thought it looked sweet, like something you might see in a little girl's room.

"Well," stammered Katie, "I . . .I, um, got your name from this girl at school. She said you have lots of information about abor—. . . about pregnancy and stuff. I was wondering if I could find . . . if you could tell me some things . . ." She let her voice trail off and fought with everything inside of her to keep the tears at bay. She felt totally humiliated.

Memphis watched her closely. "Do you think you're pregnant?" She asked gently.

Katie nodded and looked at the floor.

"Well, then, I'm certainly glad you came to see us. My name is Memphis Blue." She paused waiting to see the young girl's reaction. "I know it's a strange name, but my mom was a big fan of Elvis Presley. When I was born she didn't have a name picked out, so she called me the first thing that popped into her head. It happened to be Memphis because she was listening to an Elvis record at the time. You'll really laugh when you hear what my middle name is."

Katie could hardly believe this conversation. She just told the girl she had an unplanned pregnancy, and now she was chattering on about the history of her unusual name. Still, Katie couldn't deny that she was curious. She turned inquisitive eyes to Memphis.

"Believe it or not, it's Tennessee! My full name is Memphis Tennessee Blue. No comma between the first and middle name." At Katie's perplexed look, she added, "Sorry, that's my little joke. No one thinks it's funny except me!" She laughed.

Katie smiled thinking this was the weirdest conversation she'd ever had. On second thought, she'd been having lots of strange conversations lately—with the lady at the grocery store, with Janie Matheson, and now here. She wondered what it all meant.

"I'll tell you what—oh, I'm sorry, I didn't get your name."

"My name's Katie. Katie Montgomery."

"It's nice to meet you, Katie." She handed her a clipboard from the desk and gestured toward the four pretty chairs. "You can have a seat over there. And if you would, just fill this out and hand it to me when you're finished."

"Sure, thanks." Inwardly, Katie cringed at the thought of having to fill out more forms, with a lot of personal and, frankly, embarrassing questions. Settling herself into one of the chairs, she took a deep breath and began. Surprisingly, only one sheet was attached to the clipboard, and the questions were straightforward and easy. Nothing too personal and nothing too medical. Maybe this was not so bad after all. Soft, soothing music played through a speaker mounted on the wall. She felt herself begin to relax.

She finished the brief form and handed it to Memphis who told her Carolyn would be with her soon.

"That's fine, thanks," replied Katie in a near-whisper. She returned to her seat and looked around. A large bucket of toys sat in the corner. There was a hallway around the corner with several doors opening off of it. Katie's mind raced to her dream. There had been a long hallway with many doors. Perhaps this was it. Katie closed her eyes trying to wipe away the unbidden thoughts. *It was just a dream, a stupid old dream. It means nothing.*

A small Bible lay on one of the end tables as well as several brochures on prenatal care. She was tempted to pick one up but thought better of it at the last second. On the adjacent wall, above the two chairs was a framed print of a mother and child. In soft colors, it had an ethereal quality. While pondering what the little girl in the picture must have said to make her mother smile in such a gentle way, Katie found it difficult not to smile herself.

"That's a pretty picture, isn't it?"

Startled, Katie looked up to see the older woman. "Oh, yeah . . . I like it." Katie hated how breathy her voice sounded.

"Even though I see it practically everyday, I never get tired of it.

There's something powerful in the purity of it, I think." She smiled.

Katie just nodded her head.

"I'm Carolyn Grady, the director here." She was holding Katie's chart. "And you're Katie?"

"Yes, ma'am."

Carolyn's brows shot up, as if surprised to hear such manners in a teenaged girl. Gently, she said, "Why don't you follow me back here, Katie." She ushered her into a small bathroom. "If you'll put a urine sample in this cup and place it right here," she indicated a small sliding wooden door with a ledge, "we'll see what kind of results we get, and then we can discuss what you're going through and how you're feeling about all this. Okay?"

"Yes, ma'am. But I've already taken a home test and then another at the . . . at the clinic."

"And they were both positive?"

"Yes, ma'am." Katie was about to cry.

Carolyn reached over and gave her a hug. Katie stiffened at first, but then relaxed into the embrace. After a moment Carolyn pulled back to look into Katie's eyes.

"Nobody *wants* to experience an unplanned pregnancy, Katie. I know what you're going through; I've been there myself. You will get through this, and I'm going to do everything I can to help you."

Katie nodded, feeling as though this woman meant what she said and could be trusted.

"I'll be waiting for you right outside. Are you going to be okay?"

Again Katie nodded and closed the bathroom door.

✳ ✳ ✳

Seated in a small room on a sofa, Katie tried to keep from fidgeting, but it didn't do any good. She had the feeling Carolyn Grady knew everything going on inside her.

Carolyn came in and settled into a chair next to the sofa. She looked right at Katie and patted her on the knee. "Well, our test came back positive also. So let's see what we can do, Katie." Glancing at Katie's form, Carolyn spoke. "Based on the first day of your last period, you would be about seven weeks along." Carolyn pulled out a strange looking chart shaped like a wheel. "Well, according to this chart, that would make your due date the second of August."

Katie looked up surprised. She had never even thought about a "due date." That's something you thought about when you wanted the baby. Up until now her thoughts had been consumed with how to get rid of it, not when it would be born. She decided not to comment.

"I want you to know, Katie, that I care about your unborn baby, but I also care about you. You are just as important to me. And I think there's a way both you and your baby can have a life."

Katie stared down at her hands, desperately willing them to stop shaking.

"The first thing I'd like for you to do is to watch a short video." She rose from her chair and headed to the TV. "It chronicles a reporter's research of the abortion issue. I'll leave you in private to watch it and then we can talk about how you're feeling. Okay?"

Katie merely nodded and Carolyn patted her hand. The video began and Carolyn slipped quietly from the room.

❋ ❋ ❋

Katie could only stare at the screen in front of her. An abortion was actually being performed! It was obscene; it was ugly. Yet it was all very neat and clinical. Nothing seemed to fit together. A doctor being interviewed said it was strictly fetal tissue, that it wasn't a moral or ethical issue, but a medical one and a private choice. Then another doctor said exactly the opposite. It was so confusing; Katie wanted to scream. *All I want is answers! I'm so tired of debates and confusion.*

The video concluded that the fetal tissue everyone was so concerned about was indeed a baby. Maybe the reporter she had just seen didn't have a mother telling her to get an abortion or else. The reporter wasn't even pregnant. All that mattered to her was writing some stupid article which had nothing to do with real life. Katie's anger grew.

The video was over, and Katie still had no answers.

The door opened and Carolyn walked in and turned the VCR and television off. She looked at Katie's face.

"It's a lot to think about, isn't it?"

Katie's reply was barely audible. "Yes, ma'am."

"Katie, why don't you want to have the baby you're carrying?"

The bluntness of the question stunned Katie. No one had asked her that before. Not her mother and not the abortion nurse. They both assumed it would be better not to have it. But now Katie was being asked to think for herself.

Her eyes filled with tears. She struggled to find an intelligent answer. "I . . . I don't see how I can have a baby and go to school at the same time." The response sounded inadequate, and Katie took little comfort in the fact that it was the truth.

"You're in high school, right? A senior?"

"Yes, I want to go to college next year and I've been saving my money for two years. I work at a grocery store part time. See, I'm gonna have to pay my own way to college, which means I have to work. There's no way I could take care of a baby, work, and go to school all at the same time. It would be too much."

Carolyn nodded her head. "Yes, that is a lot to take on. What about the baby's father? Do you think he'd be willing to help?"

Katie stifled a laugh. "Eric? No way. The last thing he wants right now is to be a father."

"Well, what about your parents? Won't they help?"

Katie swiftly shook her head. "My mom's already told me she can't afford to put me through school. She barely makes ends meet as it is. And she's definitely not interested in having another kid around to raise." Quietly she added, "Besides, she's been through enough in her life already."

"Well, then, what about your dad?"

Katie's shoulders slumped. "He left when I was a couple months old. He never even knew me." She dropped her head and started fidgeting again.

"You've never even met him?"

"No, ma'am. He told my mom he didn't want anything to do with kids. He didn't know she was pregnant because he had been on the road with his band. When he got back to town, he found out about me." Katie gave a soft, mirthless laugh. "He wasn't exactly thrilled with the news. He left and never came back. My mom's heart was broken." Katie's voice became wistful. "She's never gotten over him."

"How does your mom feel about the baby you're carrying?"

Katie exhaled a laugh. "She's the one who told me to get an abortion."

"And yet she chose to keep you; she didn't abort you."

For the first time Katie looked straight into Carolyn Grady's eyes. For a moment time stood still.

"I think that was the biggest mistake of my mom's life."

Silence filled the room to a deafening decibel.

Then out of Carolyn's mouth came words that had comforted countless people countless times before.

For you created my inmost being; you knit me together in my mother's womb. I praise you because I am fearfully and wonderfully made; your works are wonderful, I know that full well. My frame was not hidden from you when I was made in the secret place. When I was woven together in the depths of the earth, your eyes saw my unformed body.

Carolyn looked into Katie's eyes and continued in a gentle voice.

All the days ordained for me were written in your book before one of them came to be. How precious to me are your thoughts, O God! How vast is the sum of them! Were

I to count them, they would outnumber the grains of sand.
When I awake, I am still with you.

Carolyn's eyes were now closed and a small smile was framed on her face. Katie studied her hands.

Opening her eyes Carolyn looked with compassion at Katie. She reached over in a motherly fashion and squeezed her trembling hand. "You see, Katie, you were one of God's thoughts. Before you were even conceived, God thought of you and wanted you to be formed. You were no accident and neither is your baby."

"Well, obviously my father didn't share your opinion."

Katie's cynical retort was not met with the expected defensiveness. The same peaceful smile lighted on Carolyn's face and she began quoting again.

Sing to God, sing praise to his name, extol him who rides on
the clouds—his name is the Lord—and rejoice before him.
A father to the fatherless, a defender of widows, is God in
his holy dwelling.

Down Katie's cheeks slid tears of confusion and longing. Why did this lady speak in riddles?

"Have you never thought of God as a Father?"

Katie managed to shake her head.

"Have you ever been to church or read the Bible?" asked Carolyn gently.

"No, ma'am."

"Then you probably don't know much about God, huh?"

"What's to know?"

Carolyn didn't seem to mind the harshness of Katie's reply. "What's to know? Only . . . only everything. Within God is life and meaning and fulfillment and joy and hope. Everything lies with Him. But the good news is that He freely gives it all away to those who seek Him with sincere hearts. For He chose us in Him before the creation of the world to be holy and blameless in His sight.'"

"No offense, ma'am, but I'm hardly holy or blameless. If I were I wouldn't be in this mess, now would I?" Katie was surprised at the anger in her own voice.

Pressing on, Carolyn said, "None of us is righteous, not me, not you, not Memphis, nobody. It's only in the person of Jesus Christ that we can find acceptance from God. You see, God allows us to be His children; He adopts us when we believe in His Son, Jesus Christ. He died on the cross for our sins, however big or small they may be in man's eyes. Believing in Him gives you peace with God."

This intrigued Katie. Peace was something she had craved for a long time. Her anger evaporated. "Right now I'd settle for being at peace with myself. Since this whole thing started, I've been in knots about what I should do. Everyone makes it sound like abortion is the only way. But I've never felt good about it, you know?"

"Oh, yes, I know, Katie. The only true peace comes from God. It's the kind of peace that allows you to be calm and serene when everything and everybody else is spinning out of control. The beautiful thing is that you were created to have that peace."

"I don't understand. If I were created to have it, then why don't I have it?"

Carolyn took an audible breath. "Let me try and explain it for you. In the beginning, God created the heaven and the earth. And He created everything else you see as well. But when He created man and woman, He gave them a hunger and a longing to have fellowship with God. And they did for a while. But all that changed when they sinned. Have you heard the story of Adam and Eve?"

"Yeah, I guess everybody's heard that at some time or another."

"I guess you're right," Carolyn chuckled. "But the thing is—that story is true."

"I don't see what any of this has to do with me."

"It has everything to do with you and with me. See, when Adam and Eve sinned, their fellowship with God was broken. And we inherited that brokenness when we were born. It's like our spirit, the place deep within each of us that we can't see, is crying out for God. But we seldom listen, unless we get in a jam. Then we cry out for help. Like you're doing now. You want to do what's right, but you're not sure what that is because a sinful world has distorted the truth." Carolyn shook her head sadly.

Katie's head shot up. "This girl at school said we've become a nation that does what is right in their own eyes."

"Exactly." This seemed to encourage Carolyn to continue. "We think we can do whatever we want without suffering consequences."

"Like getting pregnant, you mean." Katie's discomfort increased.

"Well, yes; but not just that. It can be something as simple as eating an entire three-layer cake and then getting mad because we gain weight. Whether it's a big or little issue, the fact of the matter remains that God is the one who sets the standard. We can either live according to His rules or our own. But, when we live according to our own, we don't have the peace we naturally crave, because we were created in God's image. Something is missing from our lives."

Katie looked away. She was well-acquainted with that hunger and longing. It was a millstone tied around her neck pulling her deeper and deeper into dark waters. Better not to think about it.

"Katie, God will do whatever it takes to reach you. Here, let me give you this." From the table she picked up a small booklet. "It explains how we have a void inside of us because of sin and our lack of fellowship with God. But, look on this page," she pointed to the booklet. "Jesus Christ can fill that void for you. 'For God so loved the world that he gave his one and only Son, that whoever believes in Him shall not perish but have eternal life. For God did not send his Son into the world to condemn the world, but to save the world through Him.' That's John 3:16 and 17. God let His Son die on the cross to forgive you and me."

"Why would God do that?"

"Because God loves you and is longing for a relationship with you. When we can't stand the emptiness anymore and turn to Him to fill it, we finally have peace in our lives."

It sounded good and sweet, but how did this help an eighteen-year-old girl with an unplanned pregnancy? Katie asked as much.

Carolyn hesitated, seeming to grope for the right words. "When we trust Christ, Katie, He sends us His Spirit to live inside us. The Holy Spirit gives us strength to do things and handle situations we can't even fathom. Like being a single mother while going to school. Like providing money for bills when we don't know where it's going to come from. The Spirit comforts us and teaches us what He wants us to do. He causes everything to work together for our good, even if it makes no sense to us. He never forsakes His children, and more than anything, Katie, He wants you to be His child."

Katie was perplexed. She didn't know why everyone wanted to talk about God instead of her present circumstance; first Janie Matheson, and now Carolyn Grady. All she wanted was a solution to her problem that would make everyone happy: her, her mom, and God if He existed. And so far, Katie wasn't convinced that He did.

"It's not that I disagree with you or anything, Mrs. Grady, but I'm more interested in the child I'm carrying than in being God's child right now."

Carolyn gave a sympathetic smile. "So you do agree that it is a child and not just fetal tissue?"

Katie sighed heavily. "No, I'm still not sure. There's a lot of argument the other way."

"You're right, there is. But before you make up your mind, I want you to have a look at this." She took another brochure off the table. "Here, Katie. Turn to the second page."

Katie did as she was told.

"Now, this is a picture of a seven-week-old embryo. Katie, this is what's inside of you right now."

The picture was a little alien inside a bubble. But it was distinctively human in shape, if not in proportion. The head looked two sizes too big for the body. Stubby appendages stuck out where the arms and legs were supposed to be.

"Katie, by the time the baby is seven weeks old, the brain, spinal cord and nervous system are already formed. The heart has begun to beat and is pumping blood through the circulatory system. Brain waves can already be detected and five fingers are visible on each of the tiny hands."

Katie stared at the page in silence. Carolyn continued. "Right now, Katie, during the seventh week, your baby's jaw and teeth buds are forming. Eyelids are forming to protect the eyes. Your baby's eyes will close and not reopen until about the seventh month. God knows the precise moment when it's safe for those little light-sensitive eyes to open back up.

"All of this is taking place inside you right now in a little human body barely more than an inch long. By next week, Katie, your baby will have everything that a fully-developed adult has. So, this is why I have a hard time accepting that what you are carrying in your womb is just a blob of tissue. Simply put: it's life, God-ordained life."

Katie stared at the picture of the little embryo and felt the weight of Carolyn Grady's words. Who was right? She or Margaret Kilgore? They were both passionate women who had spent a lot of time thinking through their positions. So had Janie Matheson. Now it was Katie's turn. Nurse Kilgore had said it was wise to get all the facts.

"It sure is a lot to think about."

"Yes, Katie, it is. And I'm going to give you one more thing to think about." Carolyn took a deep breath and leveled her gaze on Katie. "This is what it all boils down to: Do you think you can live with yourself if you kill your baby?"

A chill ran down Katie's spine and she involuntarily stopped breathing. Her eyes grew rounder and she licked her lips. Slowly, she shrugged her shoulders, afraid to meet the older woman's eyes.

"That picture you were looking at is what will be taken out

of you. And they won't do it gently. In early pregnancies like yours they suction out the baby. But what they don't tell you is that it literally pulls off the arms and legs, separates the head from the body and—depending on the size of the head—the doctor may have to use another instrument to crush the skull before suctioning it out. Then the body pieces are thrown away, discarded like garbage."

Katie went white.

"I'm not saying these things to shock you, Katie, but so you'll know what is going to happen if you have an abortion. It's not as neat and simple as women are usually led to believe. And there can be side effects and complications. I have files in my office of people who have died from botched abortions and infections caused by body parts being left inside the womb. And research is being done on the link between abortions and breast cancer. Not to mention the shock your body will go through. See, Katie, your body is getting ready to have a baby. It's stopped your menstrual cycle, it's producing more and more blood, it's nourishing your baby to sustain it. Abortion will instantly stop that process. A foreign object will enter your body and rip out what your body is working to protect."

Katie was afraid she might embarrass herself by becoming sick. "I . . . I . . . I never thought about it like that."

"Nobody wants you to think about it like that, Katie. Remember what we said about doing things God's way or the world's way? The world is working hard to make abortion seem like a perfectly natural alternative to motherhood when it couldn't be farther from the truth. Abortion is simply a way of controlling our own lives instead of submitting to almighty, sovereign God. And even though the medical profession is getting better and better at performing 'neat and tidy' abortions, the psychological effects can't be ignored."

"I don't know what to say," Katie whispered.

Carolyn reached for Katie's hands and continued in a gentler voice. "I know I must seem cruel to put all of this on you. But I want you to know all the facts, not just part of them. Whatever you decide, you have to live with it for the rest of your life. It's a tough decision, and I believe the only answers lie with God Himself." She paused. "Can I ask you one more question?"

Katie was afraid of what that question might be, but she was more afraid of not knowing. She nodded her head.

"What are you most afraid of concerning this baby of yours?"

Katie thought for a minute. "I . . . I don't know."

"I want you to think about that, and when you have your answer, ask yourself if it's worth sacrificing the life of a child. Okay?"

Again, all Katie could do was nod, her face deathly pale.

Still holding Katie's hands, Carolyn asked if she could pray with her. "This is such a tough choice for you that I think we need to ask God for guidance."

Katie had never prayed with anyone before. She wasn't sure she would know what to do. But before her fears took root, Carolyn was already beseeching the Lord on her behalf.

"Heavenly Father, I thank You for bringing Katie to this place today. I know there are no accidents with you, Lord. I ask that You protect Katie and the life of her baby. Help her to find her way to You, Lord. Give her wisdom to know how to handle whatever situations arise with her mom or friends or anyone else in her life. May the words spoken to her here today not return void, Lord. May all be done to Your glory, and Yours alone. Amen."

"Thank you," breathed Katie.

Carolyn smiled. "You're welcome." She stood and handed Katie the brochure with the embryo pictures in it. "Take this home with you and read it. And I have one more thing I'd like to give you. Wait just a minute please." She was out the door and back in a flash. "This is a copy of the New Testament of the Bible as well as the Psalms and Proverbs. I pray you find some comfort there and wisdom concerning the decision you have to make."

Katie nodded dumbly.

Carolyn hugged her again and patted her on the back. "If you need anything or have any questions, you call here. Okay? We only want to help you, no matter what choice you make—or if you just need someone to talk to. We love you, Katie; don't ever forget that."

"Thank you. . . . for everything," squeaked Katie. She was ready to leave; the emotions were getting too intense.

Carolyn walked her to the outer office.

"Good-bye, Katie. I'm glad you came," said Memphis.

"Yeah, thanks. Bye." Katie waved and walked out.

Memphis gave Carolyn a hug. "So? How'd it go?"

"So much guilt bottled up in such a fragile, pretty package. Many times I've quoted Psalm 139, trying to help pregnant women see that their unborn children are precious. But this is the first time I've used it to try to convince the mother that her own life was God-ordained and worthwhile." Carolyn shook her head. "I'm afraid she's going to have an abortion, and she's going to spend the rest of her life paying for it. We just have to pray. All we can do is pray."

16

✳

KATIE LAY MOTIONLESS in the engulfing blackness. For the first time she was glad her room had no windows. Darkness provided safety; light was the enemy. She tried to keep her mind in the dark as well. Like her mama said: things only tended to get complicated when she thought about them too much. If she would act instead of thinking, she would probably be a lot happier and maybe even find a little of that ever-elusive peace she so desperately craved.

Katie heaved a long sigh. In the darkened room she closed her eyes wishing she could get away from herself and her indecision. Neither her mom nor Kristin would have spent all this time dwelling on an unwanted pregnancy. They would've had an abortion and gone on with their lives. But Katie wasn't cut out that way. She supposed that's why she kept having those disturbing dreams, like last night.

Kaleo once again beckoned her off the ice. In previous dreams she had refused to go with him and the dreams ended with his sorrowful howl. But ever since visiting the Pregnancy Information Center three days ago, the nightly dream went further. Instead of falling into a sobbing heap on the ice, Katie would swallow her pride and embarrassment and follow the wolf out of the arena. She could hear the audience calling for her to return and telling her they would give her another chance. But something compelled her onward; not even her mother's pleas could sway her. She had to follow Kaleo.

The wolf led her through a dark tunnel and into the same long corridor of doors as her first dream. From the outside all the doors looked identical, so Katie was helpless to know which one to choose.

She knew each door was a gateway to her future, determined by the decision she was now being asked to make. Katie looked to Kaleo, pleading with him for counsel. But although his eyes seemed to will her to choose a particular door, Katie, try as she might, could not ascertain which door it was. In frustration she sobbed and sank to the floor longing to return to the ice and recapture her few moments of glory. Kaleo rubbed his soft, furry head against her arm, reassuring her that he cared. Yet Katie didn't want him to just care; she wanted him to tell her what to do.

She also wanted to pull the covers up over her head and let the world pass by, but that was not a plausible solution. For all her confusion, she remained a very logical, level-headed girl. Right then she cursed that quality. She pushed herself into a sitting position and stared into the chasm that was her room. "I just want this to be over with. I'm so tired of trying to ponder all the deep mysteries of the universe. I just want to be a normal eighteen-year-old girl!"

With that quiet outburst, she let herself fall back into the softness of her pillow. Tears welled in her eyes. She wanted to believe God was there, but so far He had done nothing to help. So she called out to someone more tangible. "Oh, Kaleo, show me what to do. I know I want to have an abortion and be done with it; but I'm scared. Something is holding me back!" Her desperation rose. "Just show me a sign—anything—to let me know that if I walk through this door, everything will be all right. Please!"

She lay there quietly for a while, waiting for the sign. It never came. The only sign she received was her alarm clock reminding her life must go on. Katie dragged herself out of bed to get ready for one more monotonous day at school.

❋ ❋ ❋

Katie stared at page 112 of her textbook, but couldn't concentrate on the words to save her life. She had a quiz on chapter nine in her third period Spanish class and was hoping to use her second period study

hall to do just that—study. But she had to go to the bathroom so
badly she could do nothing but sit there with her legs crossed praying
the pressure would go away. Her teacher, Mrs. Stuckey, hated to give
out bathroom passes, being certain the students abused the privilege
and engaged in all kinds of inappropriate behavior while supposedly
answering nature's call.

This is ridiculous! thought Katie. *I've heard that pregnant women
have to go to the bathroom a lot, but it's too early in my pregnancy for that!*
Still, she wasn't getting any studying done. So she decided to endure
the inevitable "Stuckey glare" and ask for a pass.

At the teacher's desk she timidly gave her request.

"You know how I feel about kids being excused from class."
The teacher glared; no friendliness or understanding.

"I know, ma'am, but this is an emergency. I'm trying to study,
but I have to go so badly that I can't even think straight! Please."
Sometimes you had to swallow your pride and beg.

Mrs. Stuckey looked carefully at quiet Katie, one of the few
who actually used study hall for studying. The glare softened a bit, but
the tone was dubious. "Okay, just this once." She filled out the pass.

"But you'd better make it quick." Leaning closer to Katie, she
spoke in a conspiratorial whisper. "And don't let anyone find out about
this; okay? I've worked hard for twenty-five years to get my reputation
as a battle-axe."

Katie wasn't positive, but she thought she saw Battle-Axe
Stuckey wink at her! Stifling a chuckle, Katie heartily thanked her
teacher and quickly exited the room.

Standing in the bathroom stall watching the water swirl down
the commode, Katie savored the euphoric feeling of relief. *That's better!*
As she buckled her belt, she heard voices. One of them sounded like
the pretty blonde girl from her sociology class.

"Really there's nothing to it. I've had two already."

"You're kidding!" responded a less-familiar voice. "You've really
had two? I had no idea, Heather!"

"Don't look so surprised, Felicia. It's no big deal. You just make an appointment and it's done in a couple of hours. Nobody even has to know."

Katie was struck motionless. *Could they be talking about what I think they are?* She dared not make a sound.

Felicia sounded hopeful. "So it doesn't hurt?"

"No, not much. There's a little cramping, but that's about it." She sounded exasperated. "What are you so worried about? You don't want a baby and you know it. So there's really no other option. You'd have to give up cheerleading; and besides, Mark would never let you keep it anyway."

"But shouldn't I at least tell him?"

Heather laughed loudly. "Not if you want to keep him as your boyfriend. He'd run so fast the other way if he knew. Guys are like that. They can't handle serious stuff very well."

Katie peeked through the crack of the stall door. She saw the blonde from her class and a pretty redhead who looked pale with doubt. She watched as Heather grabbed the other girl by the shoulders and looked her straight in the eyes.

"Felicia, you're being silly. Now you've got to do this! Nobody has to know but me. I'll go with you to the clinic. Heck, I'll call the clinic for you and set it all up." She grinned cryptically. "They practically know me by name down there anyway! Maybe they'll even offer a discount for referrals." She laughed again.

She sobered, however, upon seeing her friend's doubt. Putting her arm around Felicia's shoulders, Heather tried to comfort her. "It'll be fine. Think of it as a club. You'll be joining the secret ranks of thousands of women who have had abortions and gone on with their lives. Like I said, it's no big deal. Just stay clear of that religious wacko, Janie Matheson." Heather primped in front of the mirror. "She's straight out of the dark ages! I don't know where she gets off thinking a girl shouldn't be able to do whatever she wants with her own body." She frowned. "She'd have us spend the rest of our lives paying for one little accident—well, in my case, two."

"So you don't believe any of that stuff she says about God and right and wrong?"

"No way!" Heather shot an angry look at Felicia. "She's totally clueless. She lives in a shell and has no idea what the real world is like. She comes from some kind of Beaver Cleaver family—they're probably the last ones in existence."

"Well, you know I trust you, Heather. I always have. If you're sure I should do this, then I will."

Heather's eyes shone with a triumphant gleam. "Good. We'll call the clinic this afternoon and get it all set up. I can even lend you the money if you need it."

"Wow, thanks!"

Heather put her arm around her friend. "No problem." She grinned. "Maybe I should check and see if they have a credit card for frequent clients." She laughed and their voices trailed off.

Katie heard the door close. She didn't think she'd taken a breath during the entire conversation. Slowly, she left the stall, washed her hands, and headed back to study hall, thinking, *Thank you, Kaleo, for giving me the sign I needed.*

As she passed the window in the hall she noticed the sun shining brightly; she paused for a moment savoring the warmth as it flooded her body. For the first time in weeks, she craved light.

Katie consciously slowed her pace as she neared room 103. Since study hall she had attacked her schoolwork with a renewed sense of vigor and purpose, something she hadn't done since learning about her pregnancy. But now the lightheartedness she had gained during her covert eavesdropping session was rapidly waning. And she knew why. This was her sociology class. This is where she would see Janie Matheson.

Katie wasn't sure why she was nervous. How could someone

so small and sweet as Janie be so threatening? She supposed it had something to do with what Heather had said about Janie being a religious wacko. But, truth be told, Janie had been nothing but nice to Katie since their encounter in the lunchroom four days earlier. Much to her surprise, Janie had not once tried to shove any of her beliefs down Katie's throat. In fact, she had only spoken to Katie of trivial things like clothes or the weather. Katie felt like Janie had the potential to be a really good friend. Nonetheless, upon entering the classroom, she determined to avoid the little brunette. Her current state of peace and assurance had come at a high emotional price, and she wasn't about to do anything to jeopardize it, even if it meant not talking to the nicest girl she had ever met.

Dex watched his little sister, Janie, uncharacteristically wrinkle her brow.

"I don't know, Dex. It's like she didn't even see me or something. I mean, all week long, we've spoken or at least smiled to each other in passing. But then today, it was like she had blinders on." Janie grabbed a throw pillow from the couch where she was sitting and hugged it tightly.

Dex was tempted to reach over and ruffle his sister's hair, but he thought better of it at the last minute. That might make her feel like he was trivializing her emotions. And, since he'd promised to pray for this girl named Katie, he knew he needed to treat the incident with the proper amount of importance.

"I don't know what to say, Sis. But I do think you made a wise move in not pushing her with things she's obviously not ready for."

"But, Dex, how can you be so sure?" wailed Janie. "Maybe I should have just laid the gospel out for her while I had a chance."

Dex cleared his throat. "Well, from my point of view, you did the right thing. You let her know you were available to talk about God and the Bible, so it's really up to her. You can't push her into being ready. In the meantime you can offer her your friendship; and if she doesn't accept it—well, that's her choice." His sister looked disappointed at those words.

"Look, peanut, you don't know what's going on with this girl. You said you didn't think she had a very good home life. There's nothing you can do beyond what you're already doing: praying and being friendly."

Janie rested her head on the sofa back and blew all the air out of her lungs. Dex knew his sister's nature was one that hated to let go of things. She was like their dad in that.

"I know you're right, Dex. I've got to trust God to take care of her and to use me in her life if and when He wants to." She smiled up at her brother. "Why is that so much easier said than done?"

Dex grinned. "That one's a no-brainer. It goes all the way back to the Garden of Eden."

"So, you're saying I'm just like Eve, trying to be like God?"

"Something like that, little sister, but you're definitely not alone. We all do it. We all want to play God and solve everyone's problems according to our own understanding. But you and I both know that won't get us anywhere, at least not anywhere worthwhile."

Janie frowned. "I know."

"And, there's one more thing to remember."

Janie's eyes grew large with hopefulness. "What?"

Dex closed his eyes for a second trying to figure out how to put his thoughts into words. "We're not fighting against flesh and blood, Janie. Satan is alive and active. He wants to distort everything you do and say in the name of Christ."

"I don't follow you," said Janie in a confused tone.

"Satan wants to keep Katie in the dark every bit as much as you want to introduce her to the light."

"Is this supposed to be encouraging? It's not working."

Dex smiled. "No, I'm just trying to remind you that it's not a matter of what words you use or don't use. At Bible study the other day, Andy said the devil roams around waiting to steal, kill and destroy, not just lives, but words and good deeds as well. We plant seeds, and he comes along and tries to pluck them out."

"So what can we do? I want to help her, Dex!"

"I know, peanut. Maybe just keep praying and smiling." Dex had often thought a person might actually come to believe in Christ just by witnessing Janie's smile in full force.

"Yeah, but *doing* is so much easier than trusting."

"I know." Checking his watch he gave a low whistle. "And I've got to go do something now myself. I'm supposed to pick up Ally in less than an hour, so I'd better go shower and change."

Janie's eyes lit up. "So, Dex, is it serious?"

Dex flashed an enigmatic grin. "And why would I tell you that, little sister?"

"Because you love me, and you know I hate not knowing important things. Besides, Ally Hoffmann has been in love with you for years, and everyone has known it but you!" Janie shrugged. "I suppose I just want to know what made you finally notice her."

Instead of giving his sister the expected witty retort, Dex just smiled. "I guess I am a little slow when it comes to some things, aren't I?" He winked at Janie and then turned to exit the room.

❄ ❄ ❄

Dex's response caught Janie completely off guard. She laughed in bewilderment. It would seem that her brother, her champion and best friend, was in love with Ally Hoffmann!

Ally was a nice enough girl to be sure. But Janie had a hard time picturing her and Dex together. Dex was special, and Janie felt he needed someone who would recognize his sensitivity and tender heart. And Ally Hoffmann tended to be a bit bossy at times.

Janie tried her best to return her focus to the cross-stitch project she was working on but was unable to shake the sadness that had taken residence in her chest. She didn't know if it was caused by Katie

Montgomery's avoidance of her or Dex's surprising revelation. With a sigh she concluded it was a little bit of both.

※　※　※

Katie looked across the breakfast table at Daria, who asked, "Are you sure you don't want me to go with you this afternoon?"

Katie knew her mom was making an effort to be supportive. She also knew Rick would get suspicious if her mom went along.

"Really, Mama, it's okay." Katie smiled. "Just knowing you're willing to go means a lot."

"Well, if you change your mind, just call me at work. Connie owes me a favor; I could get her to cover for me."

"Don't keep tempting me! I may take you up on it!" Katie strove to put a lighthearted tone in her voice. With all of her heart she wanted her mom to accompany her; but the one thing she could boast about concerning her relationship with her mom was that she had never been any trouble. And besides, Katie was the one who'd gotten herself into this mess; she should be the one to get herself out. She shook her head, strengthening her resolve.

"No, Mama; I'll be fine. Besides, it's supposed to be a simple procedure. They do thousands of these everyday all over the country. No big deal." She ducked her head to hide her doubts.

"Oh, I know, Katie. It's just that . . . well . . . oh, I don't know. I feel like a good mom would be there for you. And I would; I mean I want to, but . . . Rick would want to know where I was and it's a lot simpler the less he knows."

Katie understood. She rose to put her cereal bowl into the sink. "Don't think twice about it. I'll be fine."

"I know. You sure make being a mother easy." Daria attempted a smile. "I do wish you could have gotten in on Saturday, though, so you'd have more time to recuperate."

"They were all booked up, and I didn't want to wait another week. Now that I'm ready to do it, I want to get it over with and get on with my life."

Daria rose from her chair and gave her daughter a hug. "And you will, sweetie, you will. You'll see." She looked into her daughter's eyes. "I'm sure of it." After a swift kiss on the cheek, Daria rushed to get dressed for work; and Katie never saw her tears.

Simultaneously, Katie hid her own tears as she turned toward the bathroom to brush her teeth.

17

❋

"Isn't Margaret Kilgore here?"

"No, she's off today," came the disinterested reply from behind
the glass window. "Helen Simmons is the nurse in charge today."

"Oh." Katie turned back toward the waiting room, eyes down-
cast, and selected a seat in the corner as far away from the others as
possible. She slumped in the chair. *I can't believe Margaret Kilgore isn't
here. She practically talked me into this.*

Katie had called the clinic after deciding to go ahead and have
the abortion. She had asked to speak with Mrs. Kilgore and was
delighted to find the nurse remembered her. She was so pleased Katie
was going to have the abortion. Katie had felt special to have the nurse
take such an interest in her.

Now she felt like a number, a statistic lumped in with all the
other girls in the waiting room. From this moment on she would
merely be a part of all the reports that came out saying how many
abortions had occurred during the year. She would be a faceless
statistic brutally and carelessly thrown around to help some stranger
make his point during a heated debate about the morality and legality
of a woman's right to abort. Katie felt cold and alone. She slumped
further in her chair and tried to block out the conversations taking
place around her.

❋ ❋ ❋

"Okay . . . uh, what was your name again?"

"Katie; my name is Katie," came the weary response.

"Yes, that's right. It's hard to keep all you girls straight. Well, Katie, if you'll just get out of your clothes and put on this gown, we'll get going on this thing. I'll check with you in a few minutes. You can have a seat on the table there."

"Okay; thanks. Um, how long will this take?"

Nurse Simmons never heard the question. She was out the door before Katie even realized she was leaving.

Katie began removing her clothing, meticulously folding each garment before laying it aside. She gazed down at her flat abdomen. Unconsciously, she placed her hand upon her stomach. Silent tears slid down her cheeks.

She whispered, "Is anybody in there?" There was only silence. Katie hadn't realized until that moment how badly she wanted there to be an answer, an answer that spoke of life and purpose and hope and a future. But there was only the deafening silence.

Sighing, Katie picked up the clinic gown and put it on. A despair enveloped her, one that screamed at her that she was sealing her fate in this lifeless room. Nothing good would ever come from Katie Montgomery. The weight of the thought almost drove Katie to her knees, but then a knock sounded at the door.

"Are you dressed yet?"

"Uh . . . yeah," Katie stammered while hurriedly wiping any remaining tears away. She threw herself up on the table in an attempt to make it look as if she'd been sitting there for hours, bored.

Helen Simmons came into the room. She was of average height, just the slightest bit overweight, and wore her hair pulled back into a bun. Katie guessed her to be in her late thirties, but she thought the severe hairstyle made her look older—that and the way she never smiled. She seemed duty-bound. Katie longed for the passion that had so obviously burned in Margaret Kilgore. But all she got were instructions barked out by Helen Simmons.

"Go ahead and lie back, please. I need to get a few vital signs before we begin. It won't take long at all." She thrust a thermometer into Katie's mouth.

Katie had no idea how long she lay on the table, waiting. But then, Katie didn't have anything to do to occupy the time except think. And that was what she didn't want to do right now, especially in a place like this, alone and cold. Every so often Helen Simmons poked her head in to ask a question or bring Katie a paper to sign. She even had to verify that Katie had paid! It was enough to make Katie laugh. But she didn't.

The tiny room was strictly clinical. No prints on the walls, no furniture. Nothing except equipment; and Katie didn't want to spend too much time looking at that. It was like going to the dentist. As long as you didn't see the drill, it wasn't so bad. But if you got just one look, that was it. The fear would set in. So Katie wisely avoided any close scrutiny of the medical tools, telling herself that any pain she might feel would last only for a short while. She tried to take in the rest of her surroundings as best she could, knowing this little room would mark a milestone in her life. She knew from now on her life would be categorized by two eras: pre-abortion and post-abortion. It saddened her that the room she was in was less than memorable.

Suddenly the door burst open and nurse Simmons appeared, followed by a large, burly man.

"Katie, this is Dr. Goldman. He'll be performing your abortion."

"Hello, Katie. Helen says you're in fine health and all your vitals look good, so we should have you out of here in no time." His deep voice echoed in the small room.

Katie nodded. She didn't know what to make of this big man who now had his back to her, scrubbing his hands.

Probably to get off the blood of someone else's baby. The thought shook Katie. She was glad both doctor and nurse had their backs to her. She closed her eyes and pressed her lips together as tightly as she could. *Don't think about anything. Let your mind go blank.*

But thoughts rushed in on Katie like the tide. In her mind

she saw Janie Matheson saying abortion was terribly cruel; she saw the little old lady from the grocery store saying God would always be there; she saw Heather in the bathroom at school saying there was nothing to an abortion; she saw Carloyn Grady praying; and she saw her mother saying all of Katie's dreams were going to come true.

The nurse interrupted Katie's thoughts. "All right, Katie, let's get your feet up in these stirrups."

Katie wanted to die. It was so degrading. She stared at the ceiling knowing she had turned a deep shade of red.

Dr. Goldman didn't seem to notice. "Katie, you're going to feel a little stinging for a few moments, but that's normal."

"Yes, sir."

She tensed at the stinging, but it wasn't unbearable. She allowed herself to breathe, even managing to look between her upraised legs and see the top of the balding head of her doctor. He raised up enough so she could see some of his face. He had beads of perspiration on his wide forehead, and Katie thought he looked tired. *Well, it is 4:30. He's probably been doing this all day.* The thought turned her stomach.

"How many more do we have today, Helen?"

"Just two after this one; we'll have a fairly early night."

Dr. Goldman chuckled lightly. "That's good. Marion's been on my case about the late nights. I've missed several of Ben's basketball games and Marly's beginning to think she doesn't have a dad."

Katie wanted to scream. *Hey, what about me? Does anybody remember me? Sorry to be such an inconvenience, but I'm having an abortion here!* She felt her anger rise; and she grabbed the sides of the bed as an emotional outlet.

Helen Simmons asked, "Are you okay?"

Embarrassed, Katie let go of the bed. "Yeah, I'm fine." *You liar.* Then in an attempt to placate her conscience, she added softly, "I guess I'm a little nervous."

"Oh, well, that's to be expected."

Oh, well, in that case, I feel much better now. How she longed for

Margaret Kilgore. She would have understood.

Dr. Goldman's voice broke through her thoughts. "Katie, I've opened up the cervix, so now I'm going to insert the aspirator and we'll be done with this."

"Um . . . is it gonna hurt?"

Dr. Goldman never stopped what he was doing. "No, the local should keep any pain away. There might be a pulling feeling, but that's about it."

Dr. Goldman had the fattest fingers Katie had ever seen. He was a large man. Not huge. But his hands! She had always thought of a doctor as having small hands so as to unobtrusively reach inside another human being to offer life-giving assistance. But then again, reasoned Katie, an abortion isn't exactly life-giving, is it? She would remember those fingers for the rest of her life.

All at once the room filled with a whirring sound, like that of a vacuum cleaner. Katie's eyes flew open wide. This is the machine Carolyn Grady was talking about! The one that shows no mercy. Katie steeled herself and tried to block out the noise, but it filled every cavity of the little room.

Katie's heart cried out. *Please, somebody help me; tell me not to do this!* In her mind she imagined her mother rushing in and saying she had been all wrong, that Katie should have the baby. Katie even managed to glance at the door, willing it to open; but it didn't. Her mom never came.

Katie then imagined Eric rushing in and saying he would be a good father if only she would have the baby. Katie knew she wasn't thinking rationally; but the thoughts kept coming, unbidden.

This time in her mind she saw Janie, Carolyn, Memphis, and the little old lady from the grocery store—they were rushing in to rescue her at the last second. But every time Katie looked up, all she saw was nurse Simmons and Dr. Goldman. And all she could hear was the aspirator searching for its prey. With every irrational thought, the machine got louder and louder, blocking out all else.

Then, amidst the roar of the aspirator, Katie thought she detected the faraway, mournful howl of a wolf. Kaleo hadn't abandoned her.

But before Katie could decipher the meaning of the wolf's presence, she felt a jerking on her insides, like she herself might be sucked off the table and into the machine. Instinctively, she grabbed the sides of the bed and held on for dear life. *Yes, life is dear, isn't it?* But the realization was too late. Unstoppable forces had already been set in motion. She closed her eyes tightly. Her knuckles were white.

And then she heard it. The machine stalled for a split second and then jerked again. No one had to tell Katie what had happened. She knew that whatever had been inside her giving her a positive pregnancy test was now gone. It had gone through that tube and could never be brought back.

It was finished.

Katie's vision blurred and everything began to move in slow motion as if she were underwater. An eerie silence pounded in her ears as she lifted her head just in time to see Helen Simmons exiting the room with a small sack in her hand. Part of herself was in that sack. Helen Simmons was carrying Katie's soul to the trash heap. Katie longed to scream, but all she could do was silently watch as the woman in white disappeared around the corner. Then a man's voice broke through the mire of her tangled thoughts.

"Now, that wasn't so bad, was it?" Dr. Goldman's loud voice startled Katie out of her silence.

"Huh? . . . Oh, no, it didn't hurt at all."

"Good, good! You came through like a trooper. I wish all my patients could be as compliant and healthy as you. It would make my job a lot easier."

Katie did not consider this to be a compliment, so she declined the expected thank you.

Dr. Goldman cleared his throat and began removing his rubber gloves. "Helen will be right back to check on you. Lie still and don't try to get up yet. All right?"

Katie nodded and squeaked, "Yes, sir."

Without another word, the man who had changed her life forever left the room and didn't look back. Katie closed her eyes and rolled her head away from the door. There wasn't even a window to provide a view. In fact, nothing in the room indicated life in any way. All Katie could see around her was the sterility of death. She thought she could even smell it's repugnant odor.

"Well, how are we doing?"

She hadn't heard the nurse return. "Fine. A little tired, I guess."

"That's totally normal. Here, I've brought you some juice and cookies. You need to eat these to keep from getting lightheaded or passing out. That's why you're not allowed to get up yet. If you do, it'll make your recovery time longer."

"We don't want that, do we?" snapped Katie. Noticing nurse Simmons's sharp look, Katie half-heartedly attempted an apologetic smile. But she wasn't sorry for the acerbic remark. Abortions must make you do strange things.

Without smiling, nurse Simmons handed Katie the little cup and napkin with the cookies. "I'll be back to check on you in a little while."

Katie tried to manage a softer tone. "Thank you."

Alone again, Katie nibbled the cookies and drank the juice. All she really wanted to do was go home, take a shower, and go to sleep. She had purposefully finished all her homework at school so she could spend the evening resting. Now she just wanted to fall into a deep and dreamless sleep.

Half an hour later, having been given the go-ahead to get dressed and leave, Katie found herself behind the wheel of her mom's car. She dreaded returning home and having to pretend everything was okay. Usually she could do this with no problem; in fact, it had become second nature to her. But today she felt fragile enough to crack. She glanced down at the literature she'd been given promoting safe sex. For the first time since arriving, Katie laughed. She put the car into reverse, backed out of the parking space, and pulled up to a garbage can. She shoved the brochures and free condoms into the gaping mouth of the receptacle, vowing to leave that place and never return.

❋ ❋ ❋

Katie heard the noise before she had even brought the car to a complete stop. *Please, no! Don't let it be coming from our apartment.* But it was. She parked and climbed out of the vehicle. Her anger grew with each step. She opened the door.

"Hey, Katie, come on in!" slurred Rick. He was holding a beer, obviously not his first. "Join the party! We're just getting pumped up for the big Packer's game on ESPN." He grinned luridly and tried to wink. "Sheldon's here, too."

Katie rolled her eyes as she took in the sight: five guys and three women packed into the tiny apartment. Most of them she recognized from the garage where Rick worked as a mechanic; but a couple were strangers to her. Over the crowd Katie saw her mom in the kitchen pouring salsa into several small bowls. She made her way through the noisy bodies, hearing a few off-color remarks about her backside along the way, until she stood face to face with Daria Montgomery.

"Baby, I'm sorry. I didn't know Rick was inviting people over. I told him you weren't feeling well, but what else could I do?"

"You could have said no to him for once in your life! You could have done it for me, Mama." The tears were falling freely now; and Katie could only speak between sobs. "Mama, how could you do this to me. . . . today of all days."

Daria grabbed Katie, held her close, and whispered in her ear. "Katie, I'm really sorry. But you didn't want me to tell Rick the truth, did you?"

"No." Katie buried her face in Daria's thick dark hair.

"I said you were having female trouble, but he didn't consider that a worthy excuse to cancel a party." She pulled back to look at her daughter's face. "Then all these people showed up and there was nothing I could do. I'm really sorry."

"I'm sure you are, Mama." Katie rubbed her face with her hands. She tried to quiet the anger in her heart, but it was stronger than she was. "You're always sorry for things, but you never do anything about them. You just go on doing what you want, and to hell with everybody else!" Katie startled herself and could see she had shocked her mom, but the anger was like an avalanche in her soul and refused to be stopped. She lowered her voice to a hiss. "Your daughter's having an abortion, and you're hosting a football party! Oh, that's a good one, Mama, that's a real good one. I'll just have to nominate you for mother of the year, won't I?"

Katie knew she had gone too far but was still surprised by the quickness of her mother's hand as it flew at her, slapping her left cheek hard. The room went deathly quiet, save the announcer of the pre-game show on the television droning on about the weaknesses in the Packer's defensive line.

"Katie, I didn't mean to do that." Daria reached for her daughter, but Katie was too quick for her.

"Don't worry about me, Mama. I'll get out of your way so you can enjoy your party." She turned to leave, grateful she hadn't taken her coat off. As she headed for the door, a hand reached out and grabbed her.

"What's goin' on with you, girl?"

Katie wheeled around to find herself staring into the eyes of Rick McBride. In her present state she was liable to say something she'd really regret later. Completely giving in to her simmering rage was tempting; but she stifled it. Her mother's blow had knocked some of the steam out of her. She answered him in a tired voice.

"Rick, just let me go. I need to get out of here."

With every eye in the place on him, Rick tried to speak without garbling his words. "I think you prob'ly owe your mama an apology.

Whatever you said to her must not 'a been too nice."

"Rick, let her go. It was nothin'."

Katie glanced over and met Daria's gaze. She tried to feel compassion for the woman; but pity was all she could grab hold of at that particular moment.

Daria tried again with a little more urgency. "Rick, please let her go and forget it ever happened. I'm fine, really."

Rick looked from mother to daughter and back to mother again. "Whatever you want, Dare. She's your kid." He released Katie.

"Thanks, Mama." She didn't smile, but she did try to convey her appreciation with her eyes. "I gotta go." She made for the door and welcomed the silence and anonymity of the stairwell. Too tired to fight, Katie sank down on the steps and let the tears fall. She buried her head in her arms and tried to block out every crashing thought.

Daria came out and found her there a while later. Without a word, she slipped her arms around her daughter and gently rocked her, vowing to continue until Katie decided it was time to stop.

Katie wasn't sure when her mother's arms came around her, but she was grateful for the warmth that accompanied them. She wished she could stay in her mother's arms forever. Finally, she lifted her head.

Daria's heart broke. In that moment she saw her beautiful baby girl as she used to be—the one who thought the world was coming to an end because she had scraped her knee. Katie never had been able to stomach the sight of blood. *And you let her go and get an abortion all by herself. Daria, what were you thinking?* She closed her eyes and squeezed Katie harder.

"Was it just awful?" Daria gently asked, trying to contain her self-loathing.

Katie found a wrinkled tissue stuffed in the pocket of her jacket and wiped her nose. She shrugged her shoulders. "I don't really know how to answer that."

"What do you mean?"

Katie stared out into the evening air. It was almost completely dark, but a last glimmering remnant of light remained. "I feel the way the sky looks right now—all dark and sad. But I also know I did what I had to do to get my life back to normal. That small truth is the only light that's keeping me going right now. I keep saying it over and over. When it starts getting too dark inside my head, I reach for that light."

"So you're saying you feel okay physically, but it's kind of hard emotionally?" She spoke slowly.

Katie shook her head, not sure how much she could reveal to her mom. She wasn't even sure of her feelings herself; but she did know her mom couldn't handle emotional things very well. That was why she drank when life got too tough. Sniffing again, she spoke with forced resolve. "I think it's gonna take some time to get used to the idea that I could be pregnant one minute and not the next."

"But that should make you happy because you didn't want to be pregnant in the first place."

"I know; it sounds crazy even to me." She kept thinking about what Carolyn Grady had said about the body being all ready to nurture and care for a baby and then being shocked by an abortion. Even though Katie wasn't too sure about all the God stuff Carolyn had talked about, the physiological stuff made sense. "I think maybe my body is in shock right now. It needs time to get used to the idea that it's not pregnant anymore, that there's no ba—" Katie couldn't bring herself to say the word "baby." It was too condemning. "It has to get used to the change, I guess. And until it does, I probably won't feel like myself." She sighed, trying to sound nonchalant. "At least that's what I've heard."

"So it's normal to feel this way?"

Katie gulped. "I think so." She managed a smile as she looked at her mother. "This is all new to me, Mama."

"Well, you've always been so strong, I'm sure you'll bounce back in no time." She gave her another quick squeeze and a kiss on the cheek. "I'm real proud of you."

"Even after what I said to you in there?"

"Oh, Katie, I deserved that. I should have insisted on going with you today or at least that Rick not bring his buddies here. And . . ." She hesitated. "And I'm sorry about slapping you. I don't know what came over me. I guess I was feeling so guilty that I took it out on you. It's unforgivable."

Katie lay her head on Daria's shoulder. "Mama, I know you didn't mean it. And I didn't mean what I said either."

This made Daria laugh. "You and I both know I'm not exactly 'Mother of the Year' material, now am I?"

Now it was Katie's turn to chuckle. "I guess we've both got a lot of learning to do, huh?"

"I suppose you're right. And we can help each other along the way, how 'bout that?"

Katie smiled. "I'd like that; I'd like that a lot."

"Is there anything I can do to help you now?"

Katie shook her head. "Nothing other than what you're doing. I felt so lonely after it was over. It's nice to know you're here."

"I am, sweetie. But it's cold out here."

Katie noticed her mom had come out without a coat on. "Oh, Mama, you must be freezing to death! I'm sorry."

"It's all right, baby. You're worth it. But I do think I need to get back in there before my fingers turn to icicles. Why don't you come inside, too?"

"I couldn't, Mama. I'm too embarrassed at how I acted."

"Oh, everybody'll probably be too drunk in a little while to even remember what happened."

Looking straight into her mother's eyes, Katie asked, "And what about you? Are you gonna get drunk, too?"

Daria drew in a long, deep breath and leveled her gaze at her daughter. "No, Katie, I'm not. I won't check out on you this time. I'll be here, and I'll be sober."

"Thanks," was all Katie could say. Knowing her mom was willing to sacrifice the booze for her sent a warmth through her cold body.

"So, let's go in, okay?"

"I don't think so; but don't worry, I'll be okay."

"Where you gonna go?"

Katie had no idea. A couple of months ago she would have gone to Kristin's; but that was out of the question now. And Eric . . . she could forget that! Then an image of Janie Matheson flashed across her mind. She longed to see that bright smile, but didn't know how to get in touch with her.

"I think I'll probably just drive around for a while, maybe go to the library or the mall.'

"Are you sure? I can see to it nobody in there bothers you—"

"Thanks, but no. I couldn't handle all the noise right now. I'll be fine."

"Okay, but you come back soon, promise?"

"Promise."

Both mother and daughter got up to go their separate ways. At the apartment door, Daria turned toward Katie and added a whim, "Katie, do you want me to go with you? I could, you know."

Katie stopped dead in her tracks. She'd dreamed of this many times. Her mother had never offered to walk away from Rick before. "I don't think Rick would like that."

"You're probably right; but he'd get over it."

Katie examined her mother's face and was pleased to see the offer was genuine. And that was enough for her. She ran over and hugged Daria tightly. "I love you, Mama!"

"I . . . I love you, too, Katie."

"I don't mind going alone, really. Just knowing you'd go is enough for me. I don't want to cause any trouble between you and Rick."

"You never have before, Katie, so I think it would be okay this one time. Really."

Katie pulled back and shook her head adamantly. "No. The last thing we need right now is more trouble . . . of any kind. So, you go back inside and I'll be back soon."

"Okay, but you take care of yourself."

Katie was already headed down the stairs as she called out, "I will!" Halfway down she stopped. "Mama!"

Daria stuck her head over the rail and looked down at her daughter. "Yeah?"

"Thanks for coming out after me."

Daria's face lit up in a smile. "You're welcome!"

Daria watched as Katie got into the car and drove away. When she could no longer see the taillights, she headed back to the party. A heaviness settled over her right before she opened the door. She didn't understand why the thought of going in there was so depressing. It never had been before.

18

✳

KATIE DROVE AROUND MADISON with no particular destination in mind. She found herself circling the campus of the University of Wisconsin. She supposed she had been lured there by the hope of a now-attainable future. Staring at the U.W. Memorial Student Union, she tried to imagine what it would be like to actually belong to a place like this, to feel a kinship with the other students and the campus as well. For as long as Katie could remember she had desired to fit in somewhere, to really and truly belong. Ever since the ninth grade, she had dreamed of being a student at the university. This was how she planned to break the dysfunctional cycle choking the life out of her mother.

But on this night the place offered no comfort. Her pregnancy had threatened her plans; but now she had taken care of all that. So why couldn't she shake the melancholy? She had many times fancied herself sitting on the terrace overlooking Lake Mendota, studying and eating a sack lunch only to be interrupted by an incredibly handsome upper classman asking if he could join her. Now all she could imagine was telling him about her abortion. She grimaced. If he walked away, she couldn't blame him; if it didn't bother him, she'd have to wonder how he could be so uncaring. Either way, she wound up the loser.

She drove mindlessly until she found herself parked in front of the Pregnancy Information Center. *What would Carolyn Grady think of me now?* Katie wondered.

Katie glanced at her watch. It was 8:15 p.m. and she hadn't eaten since those couple of cookies at the clinic. Remembering the snack machine in the stairwell of the office building, Katie fished through her purse hoping to find enough change to buy a pack of crackers and a soda.

"Yes! Just enough!" Katie exclaimed. She made her way to the vending machine and was just retrieving her purchase when she heard someone say, "Don't I know you?"

She whirled around and found herself face to face with Memphis Blue.

"Um . . . I don't know . . . I mean . . ." Katie's voice trailed off. She felt her face flush.

"Now don't tell me. I pride myself on never forgetting anybody." She paused and looked at Katie. "I've got it! You're name is Katie! You came in a couple weeks ago."

Backed into this corner Katie had no choice but to agree. "Yeah, that's right. And you're Memphis."

"So you do remember!"

"It's hard to forget a name like yours." Katie stated.

Memphis giggled. "I guess you're right about that."

Katie studied the older girl for a moment and surmised that the strange name fit her perfectly. It suited her outgoing personality, as did her naturally-curly hairstyle.

"So what brings you out here at this hour?"

"Hunger, I guess." Katie held up the crackers and soda. "I was driving by and remembered the vending machine." Would a sharp girl like Memphis buy such a lame story?

"Yeah, me and this machine have spent a lot of quality time together. My waistline hates it though!"

Katie perused the girl's figure and didn't see anything to complain about. Everything about Memphis seemed ethereal: the long hair, the flowing skirt, the gracefully tall frame. Even the way she moved was pure poetry. Katie wished she had half the style of the girl standing in front of her. She gazed down at her own jeans and tennis shoes and felt about ten years old.

"I know it's none of my business," said Memphis, "but I'm wondering what you decided."

Katie looked away.

"You had the abortion?"

Katie was stunned. She slowly nodded her head. *Why did I have to come here of all places?*

Memphis briefly looked down, but Katie saw the disappointment on her face. In a soft voice Memphis asked, "So how are you doing?"

"I don't know . . . I'm not sure what I'm feeling."

"When did you have it done?"

Katie swallowed. "This afternoon," she whispered.

"Whoa, that's gotta be tough on you. I'm surprised you're out and about. Why don't we go back up to the office where we can talk and you can eat. In fact, why don't I take you out to get something. Were you planning on making those crackers your dinner?"

Embarrassed, Katie nodded in the affirmative.

"You really should eat something more substantial than that." Before Katie could reply, she was being pulled toward a white Volkswagon Cabriolet. "Come on, get in."

"No, I can't, I've gotta get home."

Her objections rolled right off of Memphis. "We're not gonna sit down to a five course meal or anything! It'll only take a few minutes. There's a Burger King right down the street. Carolyn and I go there a lot."

"Where's Carolyn tonight?" Katie tried to keep the panic from her voice.

"Oh, she left early."

Relieved, Katie didn't know what else to say. She had expected condemnation, but Memphis acted like it was no big deal that Katie had rejected all their advice. This was an enigma to Katie. But, there was something about the willowy girl that drew Katie.

Memphis had pulled into the parking lot. "Would you like to

go inside or to the drive-thru?"

"Whatever. You really don't have to do this."

"I know, but I'm going to anyway. Besides, I liked you the minute you walked into the clinic. So, what would you like?"

"Anything's fine."

Memphis spoke into the microphone ordering a burger and fries for Katie and a milkshake for herself. She smiled at Katie. "I know. Everybody thinks I'm crazy for drinking milkshakes in the dead of winter; but I'm addicted."

Katie gave a small laugh. She felt comfortable with this girl. She reminded her of Janie Matheson. They were both squeezing every ounce of joy they could out of life.

Memphis drove up to the small window and paid the clerk. "Wow, it's cold out there!" She grabbed the food and quickly rolled the window back up. "Here you go." She took her milkshake and handed the sack to Katie.

"Thanks. This is really nice of you."

"Don't mention it. I feel bad barging into your business the way I did. But that's my personality, I guess. Sorry."

"It's okay. I'm just a little embarrassed, that's all."

Memphis shook her head. "Don't be. I got into this ministry because I care about girls like you, not because I want to point the finger at you. And if I've guessed correctly, you're probably beating yourself up much harder than I ever could."

Katie looked out the window. Memphis reached over and touched her arm. "I could tell the day you came into the office that you were a sensitive person."

"I feel so empty inside. I certainly didn't want to have a baby right now, but I've felt . . . incomplete ever since this afternoon."

"That's to be expected. You lost a part of yourself."

"How do you know so much about it? Have you ever had an abortion?"

Memphis shifted in her seat and looked Katie square in the

face. "No, I've never had an abortion; but I have been aborted."

Several seconds passed as Katie tried to make sense of what she thought she had heard. "I don't understand."

Memphis took a deep breath. "See, when my mother was pregnant with me, she waited until real late to have the abortion. When the baby's too large to suction out, they do what's called a saline abortion. That means they inject a saline solution into the womb. It burns the baby. Then they induce labor, and a still birth occurs. In the case of my mother, it didn't work. I came out alive."

Katie was tempted to believe Memphis had made up this story; but something in the older girl's eyes and voice told her it was true.

Katie stammered over her words. "I don't . . . I mean . . . I didn't know that could happen."

"Yeah, most people don't. But I'm physical proof. That's why I'm so involved with the Care Net Organization. I like their approach. I don't want to condemn or harass anybody, just help them. My mother wasn't a bad person. She was lonely and frightened."

"Where is she now, if you don't mind my asking?"

"She died a couple years ago. But it's all right, because I know she's in heaven. Having me come out alive literally put the fear of God into her!"

"But how could it not have worked? I know I sound stupid—"

"No, everybody asks that question. Usually, when a baby comes out alive, it's ignored; not fed, held, or anything. They just wait for it to stop breathing." Memphis closed her eyes and shook her head.

Katie exhaled loudly. "This is so incredible."

Memphis turned a sympathetic face to the younger girl. "You know, I've spent a lot of time wondering why my life was spared. For some reason, the nurse tending to me just couldn't leave me alone to die. She took me to my mother and told her I was alive and seemed to be healthy. My mother took one look at me and broke down. God works in mysterious ways, Katie, and all I can say is that God wanted me to come out alive so I could testify of His awesome glory and power."

"Do you ever get accused of making up the story just to change people's minds about abortion?" Katie asked timidly.

"Yeah, sure; but they usually quiet down when I show them this." She pulled her sweater up to reveal an ugly burn running down the right side of her torso. Katie was afraid to ask how far it went, but Memphis offered, "It goes almost up to my clavicle bone and almost down to my hip bone." She smiled. "It makes it a little awkward wearing a bathing suit, but a modest one-piece hides most of it."

Katie couldn't imagine how Memphis could be so nonchalant about having a mom who wanted to abort her and a terrible scar as a reminder. "I don't know what to say."

"You don't have to say anything. It doesn't bother me anymore. In fact, the scar has faded a lot over the years. And through lots of prayer I've come to look at it as a gift that can help people better understand what abortion is really all about. I've still got a lot to learn about counseling, though. That's why I'm grateful to Carolyn for taking me under her wing. Her love for people never ends." Memphis leveled her gaze at Katie. "She started loving you and praying for you the day you came into the center."

Katie grunted. "Well, I guess she'll change her mind after she hears I went ahead and did it."

"No, she won't. In fact, she'll probably pray for you harder, because now you've got a whole new battle on your hands. Now you've got to heal. It's like any wound—if it heals properly, it won't cause you any problems in the future; but if it doesn't heal properly, it'll keep rearing its ugly head and bringing pain into your life."

Katie thought that the pain had already started.

"Here, let me give you this." Memphis shuffled through her glove box until she pulled out a card and a brochure. "Here take one of these. We do a lot of post-abortion counseling. We have seminars, group sessions, or one-on-one counseling. Please call us, Katie, if you feel like you need some help with this. Every woman is different, so

I don't know what you're going to go through; but I do know I'd
like to help."

Katie took the card and thanked Memphis. This talk about
healing was too much. She said, "I think I'd better get going. My
mom'll be wondering where I am."

"Okay, I'll take you back to your car. I'm glad you agreed to
eat with me."

Katie's face warmed again. "I didn't really have a choice, did I?
You practically kidnapped me and threw me into your little car!" Her
levity relaxed the situation.

"I guess I did do that, didn't I?" Memphis made a funny face.
"Sorry. I'm not the most subtle person."

Katie couldn't help but like this odd girl with the strange name
and the ugly scar. But yes, she was rather direct and it was almost too
much to take right now.

In a matter of minutes Memphis was pulling back into the
professional building's parking lot.

"Well, we're back. Which car is yours?"

"The little blue one over there."

Memphis pulled up to the place Katie indicated. "I'll be praying
for you. Call if you need anything or just want to talk. That's what
we're here for."

Impulsively, Katie reached over and gave the girl a quick hug.
Memphis returned it fervently. She whispered in Katie's ear, "God
loves you. Don't ever forget that."

"Bye."

"Good-bye, Katie." Memphis waited until Katie was safely in
her car and on her way, then drove away herself with a sad, serious
look on her face.

❄ ❄ ❄

Katie slipped into the shower and let the water cascade over her tired
body. Physically, she felt fine. There had been little bleeding and only

a hint of cramping. She felt lucky. But she thought, *It should hurt or something! If everything Carolyn and Memphis said was true, then why doesn't it hurt? Why is it so easy for me to do this?*

Katie had no reason to believe Carolyn or Memphis would lie to her, but to accept everything they said would mean that she had . . . had . . . It was too scary to contemplate. She couldn't even make herself think the words.

As much as she wanted to stand under the running water indefinitely, she didn't have that luxury. The living room full of inebriated football fans would put the small apartment's only bathroom in great demand. They'd soon be banging on the door.

Retreating to her bedroom Katie double checked the lock on the door and tried to muffle the intrusive party sounds with her hair dryer. The warm air felt good. She had a chill.

Mindlessly winding the dryer cord Katie's thoughts were filled with one solitary mantra: *Now you've got to heal, now you've got to heal.* How could she heal when there were no scars or pain? If she had been left with a huge, ugly scar like Memphis had, then she could see a need to heal. But she bore no signs of the surgical procedure that had only hours earlier ripped into her uterus and cleaned out all the unwanted tissue. She was healthy and whole.

"But why does that make me sad?" she whispered into the air. "Shouldn't I be rejoicing that it's all over?" She knew that's what Margaret Kilgore would want her to do. "Or shouldn't I be writhing in guilt and regret?" She knew that is what Carolyn Grady would expect of her. So why didn't she feel anything at all? Only emptiness.

As Katie reached over to return the dryer to the drawer, her eye caught sight of a little rumpled card. She picked it up and smiled wryly. *Cast all your anxiety on him because he cares for you.*

"Yeah, right." Just as Katie was about to toss the card into the trash can, she was startled by a knock on her door, so she quickly thrust the card back into the drawer along with the hair dryer.

"Who is it?"

"Katie, it's me," said her mom. "Can I come in?"

She hesitated for a second. "Sure." She got up and unlocked the door. Daria came in and squatted on her daughter's mattress, wrapping her arms around her raised knees.

"So, how are you doing?"

"I think I'm gonna be okay." It was the safest response she could think of.

"I never doubted that for a minute." Daria waited for Katie to return her smile, but her daughter didn't oblige. Trying to sound nonchalant, she pressed on. "So, where'd you end up going?"

Katie shrugged her shoulders. She wasn't about to tell her mom about Memphis and the ugly scar. "I just drove around." Katie attempted a little laugh. "Like always, I ended up at the campus."

"Let me guess. You went to the terrace on the lake?"

Katie grinned. "You know me too well." Her mother didn't really know her at all. But it was better that way.

"Katie, you're gonna go to the university, sit on that terrace and study and meet new friends next fall. Just like you've always wanted. You may even meet Mr. Right there."

Katie blushed a little. "Well, Mama, I admit, I have fantasized about that more than a few times."

"What, my ever-practical daughter has had a romantic fantasy? Are you positive you're Katie Montgomery?"

"Now, Mama, don't be cruel or I'll regret I told you!"

"Okay," Daria held up her hands in surrender, laughing. "I'm just glad to know you think about these things."

"I do, but it's still not the most important thing to me."

"So tell me what is."

"You already know. I want to go to college and get a good education so I can make something of myself someday."

"And not end up like me, right?"

Katie closed her eyes. "Mama, it's not that . . . it's just —"

"It's okay. I don't blame you. I don't want you to turn out like me, either. But it scares me when I see you thinking college is the answer to everything. Sure it's part of it, but not everything. It may open doors; but it's not going to guarantee your happiness. People like us can't hope for too much."

"Well, it's all I've got, isn't it?"

"Sweetheart, I don't want to fight with you. It's just that I've noticed that ever since this all happened, you've cut yourself off from people. You've never been real social, but now you don't have anybody in your life. I know Kristin and Eric hurt you, and lord knows I'd like to wring both their necks, but that doesn't mean you should stop dating or trying to make new friends."

"And end up with somebody like Eric again, or Rick, or even someone like my own dad, who's gonna run out on me anyway?"

Daria stood up with a sigh.

Tears filled Katie's eyes. Barely above a whisper, she spoke, "I'm sorry. I didn't mean to hurt you."

Daria brushed her apology aside. "It doesn't matter. I just came in to tell you that the ball game's over and they're taking the party down to some bar. I'm staying here, though. I told Rick you weren't feeling well, and I needed to stay." With that she turned to leave.

"Mama?"

"Yeah?"

"Thanks. For staying, I mean."

"You're welcome, Katie. You look tired; you should try to get some rest. I know it wasn't an easy day for you."

"Yeah, you're right about that. Good night."

"Good night, baby. Sleep well."

❄ ❄ ❄

"Well, Daria," she said to herself as she walked toward the kitchen sink, "you just never have gotten the hang of this mothering gig, have you? Even when your intentions are good, you manage somehow to botch it up." She stooped to retrieve the bottle stashed behind the garbage can and cleaners. "Katie'd be a lot better off without you butting into her life." She clutched a glass and half filled it with the amber liquid. Grabbing an open coke can from the counter, she filled the remainder of the glass.

Daria slouched at the table by the window. With undisguised hopelessness in her eyes, she lifted the glass into the air, whispering, "Well, T.J., the biggest crisis of our daughter's life, thus far, and you've missed it, and I've screwed it up. We're quite a pair, aren't we? Here's to us."

In one swift motion, Daria threw her head back and drained the glass. So intent was she on refilling it that she never noticed her daughter watching her, tears silently rolling down her cheeks. Nor did she hear the muffled sobs that finally carried Katie Montgomery into a much-longed-for slumber.

❄ ❄ ❄

"Katie, could I see you for a minute before class begins?"

Katie looked up from the seat she was slumped into. "Uh, sure, Professor." She made her way up to Mr. Lassiter's desk, grateful for this unexpected reprieve from her thoughts. She was having difficulty focusing on anything today except the memory of Kaleo from her dream the night before.

She had lain on her bed asleep when she was awakened by the smell of smoke. She was trapped in her tiny bedroom, the doorway encased in raging flames. With no escape, she had fallen back on the bed into a pool of her own tears. That was when the extraordinary wolf had appeared. He grabbed her hand in his mouth pulling her toward the door, toward the fire. Katie could not believe the wolf actually wanted her to go through the fire. She would never survive. She concluded the wolf must not be a friend after all and it was her time to perish. How grateful she was to finally wake up and realize it had been just a dream.

"Katie? Are you okay? You look a little pale."

Embarrassed, Katie quickly answered Mr. Lassiter. "Oh, yeah, I'm fine. Just a little distracted, I guess. What did you want to see me about?"

"Well, I'm averaging grades for this quarter, and I was surprised to see your grade was not up to your normal standards. You missed a lot of homework assignments and scored lower on your tests than usual. Is there something going on that you need to talk about?"

Katie felt her skin warm. Never had her grades been questioned before, and certainly not in a "slide" class like sociology. She took a deep breath.

"No, everything's okay now." How she wished she believed her own words. "I mean, yeah, I had some personal stuff going on, but it's all passed now; so I think my grades will be coming back up." She didn't tell him that the reason they would be coming up was because they had finally finished the section on human sexuality.

"Well, that's good to hear. This was so unlike you. I know it's an elective course, but you should be doing better."

"Yes, sir, I will. I promise."

Professor Lassiter's eyes showed concern. "Katie, I hope you can find your way out of whatever difficulty you might be facing."

"I will."

He smiled. "Well, good, I look forward to having the old Katie back—and the old Katie's grades."

"Um, Professor, how bad is my grade?"

"Let's just put it this way: you'll pass, but that's about it. High grades during the other quarters will help. This class should be a breeze for a smart girl like you."

"Thanks." She murmured. Heading back to her seat, Katie thought, *Okay, girl, that's it. This whole mess has got to end. Your grades have suffered enough. Right or wrong, this abortion thing is over and done with; nothing can change the fact that you did it. So, you'd better get on with the business of living or you'll ruin the very future you tried to ensure.*

Katie had to smile at the irony of it all. Yes, this grade would be her wake-up call back to the land of the living. All guilt ended here and now. And she determined also to put Kaleo far from her mind. Whatever message he had for her was not worth the turmoil he put her through. No, indeed, life was too short to be lived that way.

Katie looked up then and saw Janie Matheson walk into the class and take her seat. Katie, in her new-found resolution to move on, almost smiled and spoke to the perky brunette, but opted at the last minute to move to a seat next to the beautiful, blonde Heather. Even though Katie would take her abortion secret to the grave, she gained confidence knowing that the girl next to her would only applaud the decision she had made.

"Hey, Heather, isn't it?"

The startled blonde twisted in her seat and looked at the usually-quiet loner.

"Yeah, that's my name. And you're Katie, aren't you?"

"Mm hmm." Katie smiled. "Would you mind if I sit here? I heard that we were gonna be doing some group work this quarter, and I thought, if it was okay, I could be in your group. I usually sit over against the wall by myself, but, if you wouldn't mind—"

"Sure, sit down," returned Heather with a wave of her hand. "You know, I've been wondering whatever happened between you and that cute hunk you used to date."

Katie forced a smile. Pretending was something she was expert at. "Let's just say that Eric and I didn't have the same goals in life. There was no future in the relationship."

19

�֍

Seven months later

STANDING IN FRONT OF the admissions building and holding the final forms she had to fill out before beginning her life as a part-time student at the University of Wisconsin, Katie looked at the warm August sky. She filled her lungs with the balmy air. She giggled and whispered, "I'm gonna do it. As silly as it may be, I'm gonna do it." She turned toward the student union, shaking her head at her own giddiness. She could easily fill out the forms in the stuffy admissions office. But something was pulling her away. She supposed it was the pent-up excitement at finally realizing the fruition of her dream.

Even though she wasn't a full-fledged student yet, and classes didn't start for a few more weeks, she could at least make one dream come true now. She could go and complete her paperwork at the Memorial Union terrace on the shore of Lake Mendota surrounded by other University of Wisconsin students. Maybe she'd meet some other incoming freshman girl and strike up an instant friendship. Or perhaps she'd meet that special guy. The thought made her smile. It really was okay to dream, after all.

She mentally chided herself for having wasted so much time brooding about past mistakes. Life truly was worth living once you gave it a chance. Katie had spent a lifetime trying to make life what she thought it should be; now, slowly, she was learning to take it as it came and to make the best of what it gave. And she was finished trying to live up to some archaic moral code that was unachievable in a modern world and only left pain and confusion in its wake anyway.

By following her newly-formed resolutions, Katie's senior year turned out to be more than merely biding her time until college rolled around. By doing extra credit work in her sociology class, Katie pulled her semester average to an eighty-five percent. Professor Lassiter seemed genuinely proud of her.

Getting together with Heather was a stroke of genius. Katie had been careful not to confide in Heather like she had Kristin; once burned was enough. But she enjoyed the gorgeous blonde's friendship.

Katie hadn't become a party animal, but she did loosen up a bit. Daria had never been more pleased. Katie thought her mom might burst with pride when she told her she had accepted a date to the senior prom with a really nice looking, shy fellow senior. Katie even let her mom talk her into curling her hair and wearing what Katie referred to as a garish amount of make-up.

Katie's date hadn't seemed to mind. He'd brought her flowers and treated her like royalty—even rented a limousine for the special night! Eric never even thought about pampering her like that.

Eric. Katie slowed her pace as she thought of her former boyfriend, the father of her aborted child. She supposed the only downside to her new carefree lifestyle occurred whenever she encountered Eric. Heather said it was good to flaunt yourself in front of an old boyfriend, just to remind him what he was missing. Katie wondered when the feeling of satisfaction was going to come. Her run-ins with Eric usually left her feeling hollow inside. They never spoke, just casually nodded and went their separate ways.

But Katie always sensed a sadness in his dark eyes. She felt responsible for that sadness. Once in a while Katie allowed herself to wonder what Eric's eyes would do if she told him about her choice to abort the child he hadn't even known she was carrying. But, she always concurred with her original assumption that he could not have handled such a difficult and serious decision. She silently congratulated herself for having the sensitivity to spare him what would have been certain upheaval in his immature life. Knowing she had helped protect him so he could stay in his cocoon made it easier to quell any doubts that dared to raise their ugly heads.

And really, those doubts hardly ever came anymore. In fact, Katie even entertained the idea of looking up Margaret Kilgore to thank her for helping make up her mind about having the abortion. Only a last small remaining ember of resentment at Margaret's absence from the abortion kept Katie from following through with the idea.

On that same note, fleeting yet impassioned moments of justice and the need to champion the cause of scared young girls everywhere would occasionally fill Katie with the desire to re-visit the Pregnancy Information Center, this time not as a client but as a voice for the pro-choice cause. She imagined herself calmly and intelligently telling Carolyn Grady and Memphis Blue that their ministry, although gentle and loving, was simply not helping girls make the best choice for themselves. Katie never considered herself political, but she felt the legislating of morality wasn't the way to go about helping people. It smacked of oppression. No matter how much Katie admired Carolyn and Memphis, she came to the conclusion that, in spite of their misguided passion, they were simply wrong.

Just as her thoughts were winding down, Katie arrived at her destination: the picturesque terrace overlooking Lake Mendota. She lifted her face to the summer breeze and scoped the perfect place to sit to make her long dreamed-about vision become a reality.

This is where it all begins for me. Everything in my life has been leading up to this moment. She settled herself at a little table for two, close to the railing. When the breeze blew just right she felt a fine mist waft across her face, refreshingly cool on such a humid day.

A young woman was taking a kayaking lesson down by the pier; and from the looks of things, she was having difficulty mastering the art of the roll. Katie smiled and glanced toward the right where a group of four guys were heading out for deeper waters in a sporty speed boat. Her gaze lingered on the scene. What would she do if one of those handsome college guys noticed her? She laughed at her own foolishness; but it was good to finally be here.

You were right, Mama. You said all my dreams would come true, and it's actually happening. I wish you could see me right now! Katie had long since ceased to cry over Daria's choices in life. That ended with her own self-liberation. Her abortion freed her from more than an unwanted pregnancy. It taught her to focus on herself and her own problems instead of trying to take care of everybody else. Oh, Katie still loved her mother and wanted to see her free herself from her continuing cycle of loser boyfriends, alcohol, and past memories; but those had all been Daria's choices. She was still with Rick, still afraid to be alone, and still checking groceries at the Pic-n-Save. Just because Daria's life was headed in a downward spiral didn't mean her daughter had to be dragged down with her.

Indulging in a last look around the surrounding campus, she finally focused on the forms in front of her, eager to begin the final step of her entry into her new life.

Katie carefully printed her name and address on the top of the first page. As she finished filling in the date, she was surprised by a high-pitched crying sound. Looking around, she saw a young woman, probably close to her own age, sitting at a table behind her and lifting a small baby from an obviously well-used stroller. Katie couldn't hear the soft words of comfort being offered to the howling infant, but she could see the girl's lips moving as she raised the pink bundle to her shoulder and began a gentle rocking motion.

The girl closed her eyes and appeared to be singing to the baby. Katie noticed the backpack propped next to the girl's chair and the book and notebook spread open on the tabletop.

Katie's thoughts sped through her brain like a cavalcade in true military fashion. Could this girl be a student at the university? Could she be an unwed mother? How could she study and take care of her baby at the same time? How was she paying tuition? Did she have a family to help her financially?

Into Katie's mind streamed the words Carolyn Grady had spoken months before: "When we trust Christ, Katie, He gives us strength to do things and handle situations we can't even fathom. Like being a single mother while going to school. Like providing money for bills when we don't know where it's going to come from. He causes everything to work together for our good, even if it makes no sense to us. We just have to trust that He will take care of us."

But Katie hadn't trusted. She had done what was right in her own eyes. She had convinced herself for the past seven months that she had made the right choice. So why did it hurt so much now as she heard this baby crying? The pain wrenched Katie's heart. She struggled to hold back the tears. That could have been her sitting there rocking that baby. Would it have been so terrible? The girl appeared happy and content, smiling at her child. What seemed so insurmountable in January now seemed natural and desirable.

Katie sat motionless. She felt all the happiness and peace of the past seven months drain out of her heart. Simultaneously, into the vacated space an unseen hand poured misery and longing. This pain was deeper and colder than what she had experienced last winter.

What have I done? What have I done? Her soundless cry resonated in her head keeping perfect time with the rhythm of her pou9*nding heart. *I have to get out of here. . . . I have to get out of here.* She grabbed her purse and attempted to gather the scattered forms that had fallen from her grasp in the midst of her silent torture. She didn't know where she was going, but she had to get away from that crying baby. As she reached to retrieve the last paper, her own handwriting leapt off the page at her: *August 2.*

Katie froze. This was the day she was supposed to give birth to her baby. Would it have been a boy or a girl? But now, where there should have been life, there was only death—a cold dark sepulchre that used to be Katie's heart.

In that same instant Katie knew Memphis Blue had been right. Now she was going to have to heal. But Katie didn't want to heal. To heal would mean to journey into that dark grave. No, Katie did not want to heal. She wanted to lock her heart up tight and run.

Part Two

20

❀

Four years later

KATIE DOUBLE-CHECKED THE FOLDED NEWSPAPER. The address in the ad matched the one on the door in front of her. "This must be it," she whispered, glancing around. The fairly new office plaza called The Depot was located in one of the more picturesque and fast-growing business districts in Madison. It was close enough to the University; making it to evening classes wouldn't be a problem.

But it could be a problem trying to fit into a place like this. With the high-priced landscaping and the stylishly modern lines of the architecture, it was a far cry from the uncomely grocery store where Katie had frittered away the last four years. The Pic-n-Save was safe and familiar; this place was strange and out of Katie's element. *I don't belong in a place like this.* But it was now or never. She took a deep breath and entered the door that said DesignLink, Inc.

Inside, Katie tucked the newspaper into her shoulder bag, unsure what to do next. The front office was empty, so she perched on the edge of one of the two chairs and waited in the tan and green room. She surmised DesignLink must be a predominantly male business, since most women would have opted for lighter, brighter colors.

"Can I help you?"

The voice startled her and Katie jerked. She stammered, "Uh, yeah . . . I have an appointment with Dexter Matheson. I'm answering the ad from the paper." She hoped she looked calmer than she felt. She'd been on what seemed like dozens of interviews the last few weeks, but it never got any easier.

"Oh, okay. I'll tell him you're here. I'm Kevin Holland, by the way, Dex's partner." He extended his hand. "I didn't catch your name." The large, curly-haired guy smiled warmly.

Katie reached for Kevin's hand and replied, "I'm Katie Montgomery and my appointment is for 1:15."

"Well, now you see why we need some office help around here. I didn't know anything about it. In fact, if I hadn't needed a cup of coffee, you might've been sitting out here for hours!" He chuckled apologetically. "I'll tell Dex you're here." He grabbed a fresh mug and poured the dark liquid, then raised the full cup toward Katie. "Care for some?"

"What? Oh, no, but thanks anyway."

"All righty. Hey, do you know how to make a decent pot of coffee?"

"Sure, I guess as good as anybody." She'd made it all the time for her mom.

"Well, then, I'll put in a good word for you. The stuff I make is barely fit to drink. And Dex's is worse than mine! But don't tell him I said that. He might fire me!" With that, he exited the room.

Katie sighed. Kevin seemed nice, younger than she had expected for a partner in a business like this. But she wasn't so sure about the Matheson guy. She didn't know if Kevin was joking about the firing bit. Maybe Dexter Matheson was a monster to work for and she should leave now before finding out. But what if he wasn't?

"You must be Katie Montgomery."

For the second time that afternoon Katie was startled out of her self-talk. This time the culprit was a man about the same age as Kevin Holland but taller and much leaner.

"Yes, yes I am. Are you Mr. Matheson?" Katie stood up.

"Yeah, but most people call me Dex." He smiled, and Katie couldn't help but notice how attractive he was. "Why don't you come on back to my office. But I'm afraid you'll have to excuse the mess. Kev and I are like two bachelors living together. Whatever you do, don't open the refrigerator. There's no telling what you'll find in there."

This wasn't like any of the other interviews. But most of those had been for big corporations with impersonal personnel departments. She didn't know what to make of these two enterprising young men who had time to smile and make jokes and who seemed intent on making sure she felt comfortable.

"Just have a seat right there, Katie. I'm kind of new at this interviewing thing, so why don't I just tell you a little about our company and the job position, and you can tell me if you're still interested in working here, okay?"

"Okay, sounds good."

"Our company is called DesignLink, and we offer personalized architectural designs for residential and small commercial properties. We specialize in computerized design, so we can customize each individual job before even drawing up a blueprint. Most of our work is done right here in the office as opposed to a job site. Kevin and I prefer to spend our time on the designs instead of the office work, but we do want the place to appear a little more efficient and welcoming than it does now. When a client comes in, it would be nice to have someone greet them and so forth." He grinned sheepishly.

Katie smiled.

"So basically we're looking for someone to act as a receptionist, secretary, do light bookwork and office cleaning. I know that last part isn't very glamorous, but it's got to be done. You can see for yourself it's not getting done now." He leaned back in his chair and gave Katie a crooked grin. "So, there you have it, or at least a quick rundown of it. Are you still interested?"

This guy was really charming in a genuine sort of way, so she felt the need to be honest. She forced herself to make eye contact. "I need to tell you I've never done office work before. I've only worked at a grocery store, so mostly I've been interviewing with big companies who have entry level positions. I doubt I'm qualified to do the books, and my computer experience is elementary."

"If you aren't interested, I understand. But if you are interested, I'd certainly like to look over your resume."

Katie fumbled with her shoulder bag and retrieved her resume. "I also have a letter of recommendation from my boss."

"He's anxious to get rid of you, huh?"

Katie felt her face turn several shades redder.

"Sorry, bad joke. I'm used to scrapping with my sister, who's probably about your age. Forgive me?"

"Huh? Oh, sure. I've worked for Mr. Brinker five years."

"You must have been a good worker."

"I don't know." Katie tried to hide her embarrassment at his compliment. "Grocery checking is all I've done since my junior year in high school. I want a job with more future, but you know how it is when you get stuck in a rut with something comfortable."

Dex's face clouded and he looked down. He seemed to be studying the resume in front of him.

"I see you've been taking some classes at the University. And you've got an impressive GPA. What are you studying?"

"Just my basic courses. I got kind of a late start. I need a full time job to pay the bills and the tuition, so that doesn't leave much time for studies. I'm hoping to get through with school before I'm thirty." She attempted a light laugh to cover her embarrassment over revealing so much personal information to a complete stranger.

"So you're paying your own way through school?"

"Yeah, it's the only way I can go, and I've always dreamed of graduating. I'll probably get a business degree. That's why I'd like to work in a business environment, to get some experience."

"Well, we're just a small business; but I'm sure we could teach you a little about how an office runs. On second thought, though, maybe you'd be teaching us! We haven't done a very good job of running things so far." He smiled.

This time Katie effortlessly returned the smile.

"Look, Katie, maybe you would be better off in a big corporation. They might have more to offer than we do, but I think you could handle this job. It's a learn-as-you-go thing. We're not even sure what all we need yet. Only been up and running for a year and a half. But the company's going well, and I know we can pay better than an entry-level position. We also have a decent benefits package. Here." He swirled around and pulled a folder out of a file cabinet. "This sheet explains the benefits, and here's the salary we can offer right now as well as a semi-annual pay raise with holiday bonus. The work day starts at 8:00, but we could be flexible with quitting time, so you could schedule late afternoon classes at the University."

"Wow, that sounds really good."

"Why don't you take this home, read it and think about it, and then call tomorrow and tell me what you decide."

"Okay, thanks." Katie stood up and began to put the papers into her bag. Unsure, she asked, "So the job is mine if I want it?"

"Yeah. Your resume looked great, grades looked great, recommendation was more than flattering, and my instinct is telling me it would work out—that is if this is what you want. Think it over and call me or Kevin and let us know what you decide."

"Okay, I will. Thank you, Mr. Matheson." Katie reached to shake his hand, proud of herself for remembering good etiquette.

Dexter gladly took the small hand in his. "It's Dex. Here, let me get that." He jumped in front of her and opened the door to the lobby. "I'll walk you out."

❄ ❄ ❄

While Dex stood at the door watching Katie leave, Kevin sauntered up beside him. "You hired her, didn't you, buddy?"

Dex grinned. "That girl would be lost and out of place in a big company." He didn't tell his partner that something in the girl's quiet voice and pensive ways just melted his heart.

"I knew you should have let me handle the interviewing. One pretty face and you're wiped out!" He slapped his friend on the back.

"Do you think she'll decide to take it?"

Dex shrugged. "She's gonna let us know tomorrow."

❅ ❅ ❅

Katie stared at the papers in front of her. The benefits weren't as great as a large company could offer, but they were certainly adequate. The salary was more than most entry-level positions, so that was definitely a plus. The atmosphere was much more pleasant than other companies where she had interviewed. And, of course, DesignLink was the only company that had actually offered her a position.

She picked up the phone and dialed.

"Hello."

"Hey, Lou. It's Katie. Is my mom there?"

"Sure, hold on a second. I'll get her."

"Thanks." Katie smiled to herself. She had been upset when her mom first told her she was moving to the other side of Madison to live with Lou Duffy. But as it turned out, Lou was a far cry better than Rick McBride. At least Lou treated her decently, paid his own bills, and ran with a somewhat nicer class of friends.

"Hello, Katie?"

"Hey, Mom, how are you?"

"I'm good, you know, same old stuff—work, work, and more work. But I'm not complaining; it pays the bills."

"But you're doing okay financially?"

"Oh, yeah, I'm fine. Don't you go worryin' about me. . . . So, have you had any more interviews?"

"Well, that's why I called. I had an interview today with a small business in Madison called DesignLink. They offered me the position, and I think I'm gonna take it."

"Honey, that's great! I knew you didn't belong behind a check-out desk like me. When do you start?"

"I'm not sure. I think they were ready for someone yesterday."

"Are you excited, nervous, or what?"

"Nervous. I've never done this kind of work."

"I know you can do it. And they're lucky to have you."

"Thanks, Mom. I needed to hear that right now."

"Well, I'm proud of you. Call me and let me know when you start. Hey, how's the old apartment?"

Katie glanced around the room and smiled at the changes she had made. "It looks great. You should really try to get over here. I've done a lot since the last time you saw it."

"Yeah? Like what?"

"Well, I talked Old Man Carraway into letting me paint the walls. The living room is a pale yellow color, and I stenciled some ivy around the door. And I've started the bedroom. It's going to be a light green. You wouldn't believe how much a little paint changes the whole look of the place. And I picked up a few small pieces of furniture at the second-hand store that I'm gonna re-do. I even recovered that old blue plaid sofa you left here when you moved. It actually looks decent now! I picked up some fabric on a discount counter and checked out a book on how to upholster furniture." Katie couldn't hide the pride that had crept into her voice. "It's really pretty, Mama. It has big light pink cabbage roses on it and looks kind of Victorian." Katie paused, surprising herself with her next thought. "I'm starting to feel like this is my own home instead of an old apartment."

"It sounds beautiful, sweetie. You've always had a knack for that sort of thing. Goodness knows I don't!"

"You've just never tried, Mama."

"Yeah, I guess I never felt the need to make a home since I've never had anybody to share it with."

Katie closed her eyes, hurting for her mother. She spoke softly into the receiver. "You've had me."

"Oh, Katie, I didn't mean that like it sounded. Of course I've always had you. If I hadn't, I don't know what I would have done. But look, we're not talking about me. This is your moment to shine—new job, new look for your apartment. Sounds like things are looking up."

"Maybe so, Mama, maybe so. Well, I'll let you go now. I'll call you after I start my new job. I love you."

"I love you, too. Congratulations again. Bye."

"Bye." Katie hung up. *Please let Mama be right. Please let things be looking brighter for a change.* Did she dare resurrect hope? It had been a long time since she had given breath to any of her old dreams.

※ ※ ※

Three weeks later, Dex smiled at his new secretary. "Well, Katie, you've been here for a little over two weeks. What do you think so far?"

"I'm glad I took this job. It's so different from the Pic--Save! I mean, I knew it would be, but I wasn't sure if I'd fit in or not."

"And now you feel confident that you do?"

A flicker of worry crept across Katie's face. "Um, well, I think so," she answered.

Dex grinned but inwardly kicked himself. He hadn't learned a lot about Katie Montgomery in the short time she'd been there, but he had learned confidence was not a strong trait for her. And he'd just blundered in and forced her on the spot about that very issue.

"Well, let me put your mind at ease, then. Not only do you fit in perfectly, but I don't know how we ever got along without you." He saw her physically relax.

"Thank you. I'm glad you think so."

"Look, the reason I called you into my office is to say you're doing a terrific job, but I did want to mention one thing." Dex paused, not knowing quite how to proceed. "See . . . well, it's my fault, really. I never took the time to inform you about our dress code." Immediately, he saw Katie's face redden as she looked down at her hands. With the exception of only a couple of days, she had been wearing the same black skirt and blouse she had interviewed in.

"I know my wardrobe lacks a lot, and I'm sorry. I was just waiting for my first paycheck so I could go and buy some appropriate office clothes. I was able to wear jeans and really casual clothes at the grocery store, so that's what I mostly have." She looked down at her hands again. "I'm sorry."

Dex didn't even try to hide his distress as he rubbed his hands over his face. "Boy, I've sure made a mess of this, haven't I? I think Kevin's right. From now on, I'm gonna let him handle all the personnel matters." He leveled his gaze on his employee. "Katie, I apologize."

"I don't understand." Katie dared to meet his eyes.

"What I've been trying to say is that we run a really informal office around here. And while you've looked beautiful everyday you've walked in, I don't want you thinking you have to dress up so much. Please, don't go spending all your paycheck on fancy business clothes, unless, of course, you want to." He smiled. "I'm certainly not opposed to it, but it's not necessary. Kevin and I, I'm sure you've noticed, very rarely wear ties—only if we're having a big meeting or something. Khakis, sweaters, that kind of thing works for us, so it's only fair it should apply to you as well."

"Oh, am I ever glad! I'm so tired of having to wash this skirt and blouse!"

Dex laughed, intrigued at how her face lit up when she was happy. "You know, Katie, it's obvious I don't know what I'm doing. Oh, I can design buildings and things, but running a company's a whole 'nother ballgame. Why don't we just go ahead and establish a line of open communication right now. You're doing a great job for us, and I hate to think you might be stressing out over something because I was too ignorant to outline it for you. So, why don't we make one of your primary duties that of keeping Kevin and me from making big idiots out of ourselves, okay?"

"Oh, you guys are great to work for!"

Again her smile caught Dex off guard. "Then let's put it this way: If there's anything you're not sure about, please come and ask Kevin or me. And if you have any ideas about how to make the office run smoother, speak up. We need your input!"

"Do you mean that?"

"Sure. Why? Do you have some ideas?"

"Kind of. I was thinking since a lot of women clients come in, sprucing up the lobby might be wise. It's small, so it shouldn't take much money, but I think it could be much more inviting."

Dex was shaking his head while listening. "You know, you're absolutely right. In fact, Kevin and I talked about that very thing when we started DesignLink. This used to be an insurance agency, so they really hadn't done much in the way of decorating. But, you know how it is, you get busy doing other things and forget. What did you have in mind?"

"Oh, I don't really have any experience. Maybe some plants or flowers would help. Painting the walls would certainly brighten it up. That brown paneling is a little dreary. People are coming here because they want their homes or businesses to have a fresh new look and layout. It might make them feel better about the company they've hired if it had a new look as well."

"See, I knew you'd be an asset to this business. If you'd like to tackle the project, I'll see what we can do in the way of beginning an Office Improvement Fund. We don't have a lot of cash to spare, but we'll try and come up with something."

"Oh, that's fine. I like the challenge of seeing how far I can stretch a dollar. . . . If that's what you want."

"Great! I say you get started on it right away. Take an extra long lunch break, look around and get some ideas, and we'll discuss them before you leave today. Sound good?"

"Yeah, sounds great." She stood up and started to exit. She paused at the door and turned around. "Dex?"

Dex looked up from his desk. "Yeah."

"Thanks."

"Sure, no problem." He wasn't sure why she was thanking him, but it didn't really matter. All that seemed important was that Katie was happy.

21

❋

"YES, SIR, can I help you?" Katie smiled at the man who had just entered the office.

"Oh, I just popped in to say hello to my son."

"Let me guess." Katie studied the gentleman for a moment, then said, "You've got to be Dex's father."

"What gave me away?"

"I think it's the eyes. And the smile." The older man had a huskier build, but his face was a carbon copy of Dex's.

"Well, I always told Dex he got his good looks from me, but he always insisted it was from his mother."

Katie giggled before noticing Dex's phone light was still lit. "It looks like your son is still on the phone. If you'd like to have a seat, I'd be happy to get you a cup of coffee." She gracefully motioned toward the sitting area.

"I'll take you up on that. I've been running around today. Sounds good to sit for awhile. But . . ." He held his hand up to stop Katie. "Don't you go waiting on me hand and foot. I can get my own coffee." He smiled and headed toward the refreshment center. Katie had set up a small table, two chairs, and kept a fresh supply of pastries from Fosdahl's Bakery.

"You know, this place looks great! Lydia—that's my wife—kept saying Dex and Kevin needed to lighten it up a bit. I'm glad to see they finally did." He noticed the smile Katie was trying hard to hide. "Let me guess, my son didn't have anything to do with the decorating, did he?"

"Well, that's a fine way to talk about someone when he's not in the room to defend himself."

Dexter stood in the doorway to his office.

"Oh, come on, Son, lighten up. You know how you and Kevin are when you start working on your layouts. You don't have time for anything else. I'm glad to see you finally had the good sense to hire someone to bring a little class to this place. Not to mention beauty." He grinned and looked toward Katie. "My son tells me he's finally hired a secretary, but he neglects to mention she's beautiful as well."

"What did you expect, Dad? With Kevin's ugly mug around here, I needed someone to help balance things out."

"Hey, I heard that! I'd come out and defend myself if I didn't have to get this project done. I mean, since you're having a family reunion, somebody's got to do the work!"

"Yeah, yeah, quit your belly-achin', partner, or I may not let you have that time off for your wedding and honeymoon this November."

"Point well taken. Rachel would not be thrilled if we had to cancel the honeymoon. But if I've got to do all the work, the least you guys can do is keep it down a little."

"You got it, Kevin. I'll do my best to keep this wayward son of mine in line. In fact, I may even get him out of your hair for a while. Nice talking to you again."

"You too, Mr. Matheson."

"So, Dad, what brings you to this part of town?"

"I had to deliver some plans to Burney Construction right down the road. Thought I'd pop in and see if I could take you to lunch."

"A free meal? You don't have to ask twice about that!" Dex turned to his secretary. "Katie, could you file this for me and call and schedule that appointment with Phil Carmichael for sometime next week, please? His number's on my desk."

"Sure. Enjoy your lunch," replied Katie as she took the file from her boss's hand.

"Yeah, I will. And if I'm not back in time, go on and take your break. You know how older people are when they get to talking." He winked at Katie.

"Disrespect toward your elders just might cost you the price of a good, hot lunch!" Mr. Matheson winked this time.

"Yeah, I've heard that before. You'd never let me pay. Must be some kind of pride thing with you older folks."

Katie headed to Dex's office to get Phil Carmichael's number, listening to the banter of the two Mathesons as they exited the office. She shook her head. *I didn't know people like that really existed. A father and son who actually like each other!* She leaned across Dex's large desk for the slip of paper. As she did so, the file she was holding in her hand fell and the contents spilled onto the desk.

"Oh, man! I can't believe I did that!" Frustrated, Katie moved to the other side of the desk and began gathering the papers. "I wonder if these were in any special order," she murmured as she tried to sort them out. She sat down in her boss's chair trying to make heads or tails out of the mess.

Returning the last sheet in what she thought might be the right order, she decided to write Dex a note alerting him to the fact that the file might be a jumbled mess. Looking around for a post-it note, she realized she had never been on this side of the desk before. She felt like an intruder, but she did allow herself a brief look around.

A small framed quotation sat on the right-hand corner of the massive desk. It was cross-stitched in threads of vivid colors. Katie reached for a closer look. It was then she read the quotation, scarcely believing her eyes.

"Dex's sister made that for him when he was first thinking about starting his own company." Katie looked up to see Kevin standing in the doorway.

"It's really pretty. I didn't mean to be nosy; it just caught my eye." She carefully set it back in the exact spot where she had found it. Remembering to grab Phil Carmichael's number, Katie stood to leave. "Hey, Kevin?"

"Yeah."

"I was just wondering, why did his sister stitch that particular quote for him? Do you know?"

"Yeah. That was a really tough time in Dex's life—going through a lot of changes and decisions."

"And one little Bible verse helped him know what to do?"

"Well, not just that verse, but what it stands for. See, Dex had to trust that God cared about all his problems and that He would work it out for him in the way that was best. That's hard to do. Usually we want to figure out what's best."

"But I don't see how that's wrong. Shouldn't you do what you think is best? I mean, what more can a person do?" Katie grimly thought of a certain decision she had made.

Kevin scratched his head. "I guess it depends on how you view God. If He's real to you, you want to do what He wants. If He's not real to you, you tend to do whatever you want to do. For Dex, there was only one choice: to trust God and do what He said to do."

"So, God just spoke and told Dex to start DesignLink? I'm supposed to believe that?"

Kevin laughed lightly. "I guess it might sound strange. Dex never heard a voice or anything; but He did feel led to change his plans. See, Dex never wanted to simply punch a time clock; he wanted to feel like he was making a difference. That's why he gets involved helping to design and build facilities for churches or charities. Having his own company allows him the freedom to pursue these ministry projects.

"You see, Katie, God's plans for us are a lot better than anything we could come up with on our own. But they're usually a little scarier, too. The tricky part is getting to the point where we can let go of our own ideas and start trusting that God knows best."

Katie was intrigued. "So, what was Dex gonna do instead of starting DesignLink?"

Kevin thought a moment. "Dex would probably be the one to ask about that. I will say, though, that I'm glad it worked out the way it did. I think Dex is really happy now."

"Do you believe the same way he does about God?"

Kevin didn't hesitate. "Yeah, I do."

"Thanks for telling me all that. I was just curious."

"Hey, no problem. If you want to go ahead and take your lunch break now instead of waiting for Dex to get back, that's fine. I can answer the phones and all."

"Thanks, I am getting kind of hungry. I'll just schedule this appointment and then head out. See ya'."

"Yeah, see ya'."

Katie thought of the crumpled card buried in her bedside table drawer. She had almost thrown it away several times, but had felt compelled to keep it. She was glad. It was comforting to know that something so meaningful to her also held significance for her boss.

※　※　※

Everett looked at his son across the lunch table. "So your new secretary's working out okay?"

"Katie? Yeah, she's great." Dex took another drink of his cola before continuing. "I just had this feeling I was supposed to hire her. It didn't make much sense at the time, and I guess it still doesn't."

"What do you mean?"

"Well, she didn't have any office experience. I suppose the wiser move would have been to hire someone who would have immediately known how to set up an efficient office. Now instead of two people feeling their way, we've got three."

Everett Matheson leaned back in his chair and looked carefully at his son. "But you're glad you hired her?"

"I've got no complaints."

"Well, she did a great job on the reception area."

"It did look a little shabby before, didn't it?" Dex grinned at his father. "Katie picked out the paint, the plants, the furnishings. She got it all at great prices, too—bought the table and chairs at a second-hand store and refinished them at her house over the weekend. The whole bit cost very little. I'm gonna compensate her for the time she worked at home, though she said she didn't want me to because she enjoyed it."

"It's unusual in this day and age to find someone willing to work for nothing."

"Yeah, that's what I thought, too. Especially when I know she can use the money. She's paying for her own apartment and for evening classes at the university."

"Sounds like a very independent young lady."

"You'd think so, wouldn't you?"

"What, you don't think she is?"

Dex sighed and leaned back in his chair as well. "I'm not sure what to think, Dad. She's an enigma to me: capable and efficient, good ideas for the office; but for all that, I still look at her like a little lost puppy. It doesn't make sense."

"Did you hire her because you wanted to rescue her?"

Dex laughed. "Boy, you're intuitive today, aren't you? Maybe I did. From the moment she told me she was planning to work for some large corporation, I had a desire to protect her for some reason. Sounds totally insane, doesn't it?"

"No, not totally, just a little." Everett leaned forward, grinning and eyeing Dex closely. "Are you falling for her? It would be understandable. She's a beautiful girl, and she's with you almost every day."

Dex rubbed his chin. "I'm not sure how I feel. Of course I noticed how attractive she is; but I don't think that's why I hired her. I just want her to succeed." He twirled his fork. "I think she's had a tough life and could use a break."

"You said yourself she's doing a good job. I'm just thinking that you haven't had feelings for anyone since—"

"Since Ally, I know."

Everett saw his son's expression change. "Look, Son, I don't mean to bring up anything painful." He chuckled softly. "I'm probably gonna risk sounding like your mother when I say this; but I don't want to see you get hurt."

Dex set the fork down and stared back at his father. "Thanks, Dad. I don't think I'm ready to leap into a relationship or anything right now. But I am having feelings I haven't felt in a long time. I know you're worried about me getting hurt; but I'm more afraid of hurting someone else. I'd hate for that 'someone else' to be Katie. She's a really sweet girl."

"All I can do is pray for you."

"And I appreciate it." Dex reached for his wallet. "Look, I know you won't let me pay for lunch; so at least let me leave the tip, okay?"

"Deal."

"And, Dad, one more thing."

"What's that?"

"I'd kind of like to keep this quiet. I mean, about Katie. I don't think she's a believer, so that would definitely be a problem. And I don't want people asking questions."

Everett nodded. "Sure, I won't say a thing, and I won't bring it up again unless you do. You have my word on that."

"Thanks. But now I do need to get back to the office. Dennis Grayson's coming by at two for a meeting."

Both men stood. "Dennis? Wow, I haven't seen him in ages! Are you doing some work for his downtown project?"

"Yeah, they're renovating an old warehouse. The ministry's growing by leaps and bounds." Dex grinned. "Hey, you'd probably have some good input for us on this type of work."

"Be sure and tell the old rascal I said hi. And let me know if I can help with materials, labor . . . Just ask."

"Will do, Dad. Hey, thanks for lunch."

Everett put his arm around his son's shoulders as they walked out. "Maybe we can do this more often, Dex."

22

*

DEXTER GLANCED DOWN AT THE ADDRESS scribbled on the paper in front of him. "This must be it," he muttered, marveling that he was there at all. When Katie had called in sick that morning, he'd been quick to reassure her they could carry on fine without her. Then he started thinking about her alone in that apartment with no one to take care of her. He wasn't a worrier; but then again, he always had a mom or older sister looking out for him when he was sick. Katie had nobody.

Dex parked his Jeep Cherokee on the side of the street and stepped out. The neighborhood wasn't a bad one by any means, but it lacked eye appeal. He felt Katie deserved prettier surroundings. He climbed the stairs to the third floor but hesitated before knocking. *She's gonna think I'm some kind of wacko for doing this.* Either that or she'd see right through him and know how he was beginning to feel about her. He wasn't sure which was worse.

But since he'd come this far already, he knocked and gently called out, "Katie, it's Dex."

* * *

Katie's eyes bugged. She clicked off the TV and called out, "Just a minute!" She had on gray gym shorts, an old T-shirt sporting the Nike logo, and white sweat socks. Her hair was pulled up in a pony tail. She grimaced. *Not one of my better moments.* She was not thrilled that her very attractive boss, who always looked like he just stepped out of the pages of a catalog, was going to see her like this.

She opened the door. "Hey, come on in."

204

✳ ✳ ✳

Dex entered the apartment but found it difficult to take his eyes off his secretary. Even though she was obviously sick, he thought she had never looked more adorable. He cleared his throat and held up the two bags in his hands.

"Care packages. I thought maybe you could use a little pampering. You sounded bad on the phone this morning."

"Really, I'm not that bad off." At that moment she was seized with a coughing spell. Dex grinned at her.

"Yeah, I think you ought to go on into the office and at least get half a day's work done. Don't you agree?"

Behind a smile, Katie mumbled about overbearing, do-gooder bosses. She went back to the couch and motioned for Dex to sit down as well. He chose the chair next to the sofa.

"So, Dr. Matheson, what's in the bag?"

Dex grinned again. "Well, since I wasn't exactly sure what was wrong, I brought a little of everything." He began pulling items out one by one. "We've got cough syrup, tylenol, throat lozenges, tea bags ... You name it, it's in here." By the time he finished, Katie's coffee table was overflowing with medicines and treatments. "And this bag contains whatever you need to fight boredom: let's see, a puzzle book, some magazines, and some movies. I hope you like Cary Grant."

"He's my favorite! How did you know?"

"I've got a mother and three sisters. They're all Cary Grant fanatics. What is it with the guy anyway?"

Katie looked dreamy-eyed. "He's just so suave! It's impossible not to like him. He's such a gentleman!" As soon as she said it, she turned crimson, and Dex was pretty sure it wasn't from fever. "I can't believe I said that. You must think I'm some kind of romantic nut!"

"Not at all." Dex was thoroughly enjoying this side of his secretary. The office didn't lend itself to conversations like this. "In fact, I think there's a definite place for romance in this world. I just didn't know old-fashioned guys like Cary Grant still held appeal."

Katie blushed again, her voice whisper-like. "I'm not so sure I'm a modern girl. I think I've always preferred the old-fashioned way of doing things."

Dex hoped he hadn't caused the sudden sadness in her voice.

"Well, I'm not exactly a knight in shining armor, but at least I can try to make one damsel in distress a little more comfortable. I'm gonna make you some hot tea." He stood up. "And don't tell me you don't want any; I see you drinking it at work." He headed to the kitchen. "Mind if I just rummage around until I find what I need?"

"No, that's fine." Katie began thumbing through a decorating magazine Dex had brought.

From the kitchen he noticed which magazine she had picked. "I thought you might get some more office-decorating ideas. I could sure use some help in my office. Kevin, too. We'd pay you extra."

"You don't have to do that. I think it's fun, but I don't really know what I'm doing. You should hire a professional."

"Why would I do that when I've got you? People comment all the time on how nice the lobby looks—even decorators. Face it, you've got a flair for it." He glanced around the apartment. "Your place looks great, too. I'll bet you did most of this yourself, didn't you?"

Sheepishly, Katie answered, "Yeah, I did all of it, but this is simple stuff. Mostly I just copy what I see in magazines or books."

"As long as the end product looks good at an affordable price, I guess it doesn't matter where you get the idea."

"Are you serious about wanting me to help with your office, or are you just being nice since I'm under the weather?"

"Absolutely serious. I'm sure you've noticed my office needs a facelift. What do you say?"

Katie started to answer when another coughing spell took hold of her. Finally, she caught her breath and replied. "Sorry about that. Sure, I'd love to help. Just say when."

Dex returned with a steaming cup of tea in his hand. "Well,

certainly not today. In fact, I think we've had enough shop talk for one day. Here, drink this." He handed her the cup and grabbed an afghan off the chair. "You might want to put this around you, too. Looks like you're shivering."

"Thanks. One minute I'm hot and the next I'm cold."

"Katie, I don't mean to pry, but isn't there someone who could come over and help look after you?"

Katie giggled.

"Oh, that hurt! My throat is sore so don't make me laugh anymore, okay?"

"I'm serious. You don't need to be alone when you're sick."

"Dex, I'm not a baby. I'll be fine."

Dex sat back down. "Look, you've got to understand. I come from a family where we all look out for each other. It's in my nature to want to pamper someone if they're sick."

Katie looked at him over her cup's rim. "Sounds like you've got a real nice family. But I've been taking care of myself a long time."

"Don't you have anybody?"

Katie set the cup on the table and pulled the afghan up under her chin as if it were a shield. "Sure, I do. My mom lives on the other side of Madison. If I needed her, she'd come. But it's only a cold or a mild case of the flu. It's no big deal. I don't understand why you're making a federal case out of it."

"You know, Katie," Dex sighed, "you could always go to the doctor. You've got insurance; that's what it's for."

"No way! I hate going to the doctor, so you can just save your breath! It's just an annoying cold—nothing more." There was a fierceness and finality in her voice as she spoke.

Dex stared at his hands, wondering why she was angry. "I didn't mean to sound like I was attacking you. But . . . well, I'd like to think we're friends as well as boss and employee. I only wanted to help."

Katie closed her eyes and leaned her head back. Letting out a sigh, she slowly opened her eyes. "I'm sorry, too. I didn't mean to overreact. I'm not used to all this attention. But I do appreciate what you've done." She glanced at the overflowing coffee table. "It really was sweet of you."

"I probably should have called first. You just sounded so pitiful on the phone, I wanted to do something to help."

"Well, you did, and I thank you for it. Nobody's ever gone to such trouble for me before."

"It was nothing. But be prepared the next time you get sick 'cause I'll probably do exactly the same thing."

"You make a great knight in shining armor, Dexter Matheson." Then Katie groaned. "I can't believe I said that."

Dex laughed. "Maybe you're delirious from the fever."

"Yeah, we'll say that's what it is." She glanced at the clock. "Don't you have to get back to work or something? Or do you plan on staying here and humiliating me all day?"

"I'm going, I'm going. You probably just want to kick me out of here so you can be alone with Cary Grant."

Katie grinned. "Now that's not a bad idea!"

Dex rolled his eyes. "You women are all alike!" He grabbed one of the movies and put it in the VCR.

Katie snuggled down into the sofa. "*Charade*! One of my favorites! This is great, Dex. Thanks."

"Sure, no problem. But I want you to call me if you need anything, or even if you just get lonely and want some company. I'll be at the office until about 6:00 this evening, then I'll head home. Here's my home phone. And you already know my cell number." He jotted something down on a scrap piece of paper and left it on the coffee table. He stood to leave.

"Hope you get to feeling better."

"Thanks, me too. I'm sure I'll see you tomorrow at work." Katie's eyes were focused on the TV.

"Don't rush it. Take another day off if you need it."

"I'll be fine."

As Dex closed the door behind him, he faintly heard Katie say in a breathy voice, "Oh, he is so good looking." He just didn't know whether she meant him or the ever-so-suave Cary Grant.

❋ ❋ ❋

"Hey, peanut. How are your new classes going?"

At Dex's words, Janie's head, which had been buried in a biology textbook, jerked upright, and the petite girl leaped from her chair. She embraced her brother melodramatically. "Thank you for rescuing me from all of these amoebic, parasitic, bacteria-causing, germ-like life forms!"

"That's no way to talk about your professors, little Sis."

Janie crinkled her nose. "Very funny! You know science never came easy for me. I wouldn't take it if it weren't required."

"I'll try to help if you need it. I might remember a thing or two from my college days."

"I may take you up on that."

"So, how does it feel to be a sophomore?" Dex plopped down into an overstuffed chair.

"I suppose it doesn't feel much different than being a freshman. I still have tons of homework, thousands of pages to read, and endless papers to write." She cocked her head. "But you know I love it! I can't wait until I get to start observing in a classroom somewhere. Then I'll feel like I'm actually working toward my goal of being a teacher."

Dex grinned. "They use all those basic courses to weed people out. You gotta suffer through it like everyone else."

"I know, I know, and I will. I just want to complain a little if that's okay with you."

"Fine, fine. Go ahead. Use me as a venting machine for all your frustrations."

"You know I would never do that!"

"Yeah, right."

Janie laughed out loud. "Just like you'd never come here to get a free, home-cooked meal, right?"

"Hey, it's tough on a guy living all by himself. Especially one who likes to eat as much as I do."

Janie looked thoughtful for a moment. "Actually, I'm surprised you don't come around more often. I wish you did."

Dex smiled at his sister. "Yeah, I wish I did, too. But work is so good right now that it keeps me pretty busy. And I'm certainly not gonna complain about that. Besides, now's the best time for me to be busy, I suppose."

"Why's that?"

"Well, since I don't have a family of my own, it doesn't matter if I put in a lot of late nights. Kevin's gonna have to cut back when he gets married in a couple months."

"I guess you've got a point there. But I like it when you come around. Kind of like old times. Remember all the talks we'd have and how you'd always help me solve all of my earth-shattering problems?" She comically rolled her eyes.

"I remember, Janie." He thought of Katie living alone and convincing herself she was happy that way. "Actually, Janie," Dex began tentatively, "I kind of wanted to talk to you about something, if you've got the time."

Janie recognized the serious look on her brother's face and quickly closed her textbook. "Sure, Dex. What is it?"

"Well, it's more of a favor, I guess."

"Let's have it. You know I'll help if I can."

"It's about the girl I hired to be our secretary at work."

Janie's eyes grew round. "Oh, yeah, Dad said he met her and she was really pretty." Dex gave her a reproving look. "Oh, and he also said she was very efficient at her job."

Dex couldn't keep from laughing. "You really are incorrigible, little sister; did you know that?"

"Yes, I know!"

"But truthfully, that's what made me think of you for this.

You're such a fun person and you're great with people. If anybody could help me, it would be you."

"So, what is it you want me to do?"

"Katie—that's my secretary's name—was sick the other day. And to make a long story short, I found out she doesn't really have any family or friends to speak of. Her mom's on the other side of Madison, but I don't know how often they see each other. Katie works and takes a few evening classes, but that's about it. She studies a lot, but a person's got to have time to unwind and be with people. I find it hard to believe she's happy living that way."

Janie cocked her head. "Dex, is there something you want to tell me about this girl?"

"You want to know if I'm interested in her, don't you?"

"Well, now that you bring it up, yes."

"Can I trust you to keep a confidence?"

Janie looked offended. "You know you can! I may talk a lot, but I can be trusted, Dex, especially with you!"

He laughed. "I know. I just want to be sure of my feelings before admitting to anything. Rushing has never gotten me any-where." He gave her a sad look.

"Oh, Dex, I'm sorry. But I still think you'd make such a great husband. I can't understand why God hasn't brought you together with somebody yet."

A chuckle escaped Dex's lips. "I suppose I've asked God the same question a million times. But, for a while there, I didn't even have the desire to meet anybody, much less get serious. But now . . . now that I've met Katie . . . I'm not so sure what I should do. It's a little complicated."

"How come? I mean, if you like her—"

"I don't think she's a believer." He paused and then added, "No, I know she's not a believer. Kevin had a chance to talk to her about it a little bit. So, you see, it's not a simple matter of just asking her out. A lot of other stuff needs to be addressed first."

"And you think I can help with that?"

"Yeah. Katie doesn't let people get close to her. She keeps them at arm's length. If I tried to initiate a relationship, I think she'd see it as just a way to go out with her. And I don't want that to happen. Besides, I'm not sure I could keep my motives pure anyway. I'd start out doing it for her own good, but I'd most likely end up doing it for my own benefit. But you, that would be a different story."

"What is it you want me to do exactly?"

"Come by the office and strike up a friendship with her."

"It's not that easy, you know!"

"Hey, don't laugh at me. You know what I'm talking about. Just come down there and do what you do best. Make her feel good, make her feel like you like her and put her at ease. Maybe she'll respond to you. Most people do."

"Dex, I'll do what I can, but I can't make any promises. You can't force her."

"You're right, and I know that. But I think it's at least worth a try. Maybe some time next week?"

"Let me think . . . I only have one class on Tuesday morning, so I could come by after that, around 11:00."

Dex felt confident that if anyone could break through Katie's shield, it was his little sister. "Great! I knew I could count on you. Now . . ." He stood up, rubbing his hands together. "I'm gonna go see what Mom's cooking in the kitchen. Sure smells good."

"It's chicken enchiladas."

"You know, you were right, peanut. I should come over more often." He squeezed his sister's shoulder.

23

"PLEASE COME OUT, Katie. You've been in there for so long; It's time for you to come out."

Katie refused to open the door. The voice sounded friendly, but she was still apprehensive. "Who are you?"

The gentle reply floated through the air. "You know who it is, Katie."

"No, I don't. And I won't open the door." Katie frantically tried to keep her emotions at bay. The voice belonged to the gray wolf Kaleo. "Just go away and leave me alone."

"I can't go away, Katie. I love you."

Katie was shocked by the wolf's response. He had never been so personal with her before, and this was the first time he had ever spoken. He usually did no more than gently nudge her or rub against her leg or howl when she disappointed him. Why start talking now? And why say things like "I love you?" Trying to figure it out was too taxing. She could only plead with him. "If you really love me, then, please, just go away!"

Katie jerked up in bed. *Oh no, not again.* Although the gray wolf had consumed her dreams for several months during her senior year, she hadn't thought of him since graduation.

"After all this time. Why now when life is going so well for me?" Katie's voice echoed in her empty bedroom. That Kaleo could so suddenly return to her life and be so intimate with her was unsettling. Katie didn't like to get close to anybody—not even imaginary animals. She ran her hands over her face, then turned to glance at her alarm clock. Almost 5:00 a.m. She never woke this early.

She sat up and threw her legs over the side of her bed. She wanted to blame her restlessness on the medications she had taken but knew that was inaccurate. It had taken several days for her to start feeling normal again, but she was fine now, physically.

Katie did something she hadn't done for a long time. She closed her eyes and whispered, "God, if you're there at all, please don't let me keep having these dreams." She opened her eyes, discouraged that nothing seemed different. She still felt uneasy and nervous. The dream had to be some kind of portentous prophecy. Katie wanted to cry.

"No, not this time," grunted Katie. "I eluded you once before, Kaleo, and I'll do it again." With a fierce resolve, she stalked to the bathroom and turned on the shower.

❁ ❁ ❁

"Hello! Anybody here?" called Janie.

"Come on in." Dex answered at the front desk.

"I thought you hired a secretary for this kind of thing."

"I did, but she's helping Kevin organize files."

"So you get to play receptionist. Is that how it works?"

"You think that's funny, huh? I'll have you know I'd make an excellent receptionist. In fact, if I ever get tired of this architecture stuff, I just may do it!" He tried to look sincere, but it was useless. "Actually, I came up here to get some phone numbers out of Katie's rolodex. I have a way of always misplacing the number I need."

Janie giggled. "Then I guess you'd better stick to being an architect because you'd make a lousy secretary."

"Touche'!" Then, "Hey, thanks for coming by."

Janie stretched to her full almost five-foot-two-inch height. "I always keep my word, no matter how awkward it may be." Then she lowered her voice. "To be honest with you, I'm kind of excited about meeting this girl. If she's turned your head, she must be special."

"Well, that much is true."

Janie glanced around the office. "Wow, this place does look great, like Dad said."

"Yeah, we're tackling my office next. She's already started working up some ideas. Here, come on back with me." He motioned for his sister to follow him to his office.

As they made their way down the small hallway, Janie peeked into Kevin's office and stopped dead in her tracks. She only had a profile view of the pretty girl hunched over the stack of files, but there was no mistaking who it was. She hovered in the doorway for a few seconds longer then burst into her brother's office closing the door behind her.

"Dex, you're not gonna believe this!"

Dexter looked up and noticed the expression on his sister's face. "What are you talking about?"

"Your secretary, the one in there with Kevin?"

"Yeah, what about her?"

"That's Katie!"

"Janie, I already know that. I hired her, remember?"

"I mean that's *Katie*—from my high school! Her hair's a little shorter, but it's the same girl. I'm sure of it!"

Janie saw that none of this was making any sense to her brother. "Think back to when I was a . . . a sophomore, I think. I asked you to pray for a girl I had met briefly. I told you there was something about her that made me want to help her, but I could tell she was uncomfortable with the whole 'God thing,' so you recommended I just try and be her friend. Well I did, but it was like she shut herself off from everybody. Then, when she finally opened up, she chose this other girl to hang around with. She never had anything to say to me after that."

Dex's face still registered confusion. He slumped in his chair. "So you're saying the girl in the next room, my secretary, is the same Katie we prayed for four years ago?"

"That's what I'm saying! It's unreal, isn't it?"

Dex just kept nodding his head. "Seems like I can remember Dad praying for her at the dinner table."

Janie's eyes lit up. "Yes! I remember that, too."

"Yeah, we prayed God would use you in her life." He exhaled loudly. "And now, I've asked you to reach out to her, not even knowing it was the same person. This is incredible!"

"I don't even know what to think."

"Well, one thing's pretty obvious, little sister."

Janie cocked her head. "What's that?"

Dex leveled his gaze on his sister. "God wants you to be connected to this girl in some way."

"So I guess it's no accident that I'm here today, is it?"

Dex smiled. "You know as well as I do there are no accidents with God. He's in control whether we understand it or not." He stood up and began pacing. "No, this is no accident at all. Janie, from the time I laid eyes on Katie, I've felt compelled to help her in some way. And now, knowing who she is just confirms that we're supposed to be doing this."

Janie cast a thoughtful look toward her brother. "It would seem God has finally answered our prayers."

"Well, you always say you need to learn patience."

"I guess you're right." Janie frowned. "I feel so bad, Dex. I mean, after Katie graduated I made myself forget about her, and I stopped praying. It seemed so useless, but I should have remembered that all things are possible with God."

Dex sat down. "Don't beat yourself up too bad about this, peanut. Be grateful that Katie's back in your life."

"Yeah, it's like He's giving me another chance." She took a deep breath. "But this is all so weird, Dex. How am I supposed to act when I go out there to talk to her? I don't want to make her feel uncomfortable."

Dex folded his hands on his desktop. "Why don't we do what we did back then."

Janie nodded, and both brother and sister bowed their heads to pray for the girl named Katie.

❋ ❋ ❋

"Dex," called Kevin from the hallway, "I'm heading to lunch. I'll probably be gone a while. Rachel's meeting me at the caterer so we can sample wedding cakes."

Janie piped up, "That sounds like the perfect job for you, Kevin!"

"Hey, Janie! I didn't hear you come in." He walked into Dex's office and gave Janie a big hug. "How long has it been since I've seen you, squirt?"

"Too long!" smiled Janie. "I'm not a little kid anymore, you know. I just started my second year of college."

"Yeah, Dex keeps me pretty well informed, but you know you'll always be a little squirt to me!"

"Comments like that just might make me change my mind about getting you a wedding present." Janie feigned a hurt look.

"You win. I apologize, but I do have to run or there may not be a wedding. You girls take all this stuff so seriously. It's just cake for crying out loud! Why the big deal?"

Dex laughed. "I never thought I'd see you complaining about having to eat cake!"

Heading back down the hall, Kevin called over his shoulder, "You just wait, Dexter Matheson. You'll be going through this some-day and you'll come crying to me for sympathy; but you are not, I repeat not, going to get it." He laughed.

Watching Kevin leave, Dex said to his sister, "That guy needs to hurry up and get married. I don't know how much more of this wedding stuff he's gonna be able to take."

At that moment Dex saw Katie step out of Kevin's office. "Hey, Katie, come here for a minute. I want you to meet my sister." He briefly glanced at Janie and smiled. Katie was in his office in a matter of seconds.

"Katie, this is my little sister, Janie, or 'peanut' as I like to call her. Janie, this is my secretary Katie." He watched as the two girls eyed each other and then as Janie's face broke into a huge smile. He knew this was going to go well.

"I know you! We went to high school together, didn't we? This is so weird that you're working for my brother!"

Katie was stunned. In one split second she was transported back to Stoughton High and was struggling with the biggest decision of her life. And high school was the last thing she wanted to think about these days. In fact, she had expended a lot of energy trying to forget the entire experience. Katie forced herself to look at the girl in front of her. There was that smile that had warmed her heart four years ago.

Katie stammered. "Yeah . . . we had a class together, I think. I didn't know Dex was your brother."

"Janie doesn't like to talk about me much. She must be ashamed of me." Dex smiled at his little sister.

"That is so not true!" retorted Janie. She turned her attention back to Katie. "And I am so glad to see you again, Katie! I'm sorry we didn't have more time to get to know each other in school."

Katie looked down for a moment.

Janie quickly added, "But then you were a couple years ahead of me and had different classes mostly."

Katie knew she was being let off the hook by the still-smiling Janie Matheson. She was very aware she had snubbed the younger girl. And she remembered exactly why she had done it. Katie once again forced herself to make eye contact with her. "Well . . . um . . . I was kind of a loner in high school. I . . . uh . . . didn't hang out much with the other kids. I worked and that took up most of my time."

Dex spoke up. "Yeah, we tried and tried to get Janie to go to work and start earning her keep, but she wouldn't do it. In fact, she still won't. She just goes to school and then comes down here and pesters me, keeping me from working. Just what is it you have against work, Janie?"

Janie laughed, her eyes twinkling. "Actually, big brother, I'm working right now. I'm not supposed to tell, but I am being paid a rather large sum of money to come down here and spy on you!" She winked at Katie and spoke in a conspiratorial tone. "See, our parents wanted me to make sure Dex really does have his own company. They never could trust him; he always was a wayward kind of guy, getting into all kinds of trouble. Boy, don't get me started!"

"Katie, don't believe a word she's saying! She makes up outlandish stories like this all the time. That's really why she can't get a job. Nobody can trust her to tell the truth and then there's her habit of—"

"Okay, okay! Enough! You win, Dex. I can't keep up with you. Besides, what is Katie gonna think of our family now!"

Katie put a shocked expression on her face. She added amusement to it. It would seem her boss got on as well with his sister as he did with his father. She shook her head in disbelief. "Maybe I should go and let you two battle this out in private." She started backing toward the door.

"No!" exclaimed Dex and Janie at the same time.

"We didn't mean to run you out of here. In fact, Janie came by to ask me to go to lunch with her; but since Kevin's gone, I'm gonna have to stay. Hey, why don't the two of you go?"

"Yeah, that's a great idea! What do you say, Katie?"

Katie swallowed. "No, I don't think so. Besides, Dex, I can stay so you can go with your sister. I don't mind."

"That's sweet, Katie, but I've got to get some plans done before 2:00 this afternoon. A guy's coming by to pick them up, so I'm gonna have to hustle to finish. In fact," he grinned at Katie, "you'd be doing me a favor by taking this kid off my hands." He gestured toward Janie. "I'll never get anything accomplished with her around!"

Twenty minutes later Katie found herself seated across from Janie Matheson in a local restaurant wondering how she had gotten there. She had the sneaking suspicion that she never stood a chance against the dynamic brother/sister duo. She felt awkward when Janie insisted on paying; but after looking around the nice surroundings, Katie conceded this was much better than a peanut butter sandwich and a candy bar.

❄ ❄ ❄

Once back at DesignLink Janie was pulled into her brother's office. Katie had quickly run down to the post office. "So, how'd it go?"

The urgency in Dex's eyes caught Janie by surprise. *For somebody who acted so in control around Katie, he's totally smitten with her! If only she could see him now!* She tried to keep her voice normal. "It went great. I had a good time." Janie plopped down. "She's still real quiet and shy, but she's nice as she can be." She paused for a moment and looked at her brother. "It's funny; even after all these years, she still affects me the same way. I still want to break through her shell and help her. The only problem is that I . . . I—"

"You don't know what's wrong."

"Exactly!"

"But you take one look at her eyes, and you know something is going on behind them."

"Yeah," agreed Janie, "they're so vulnerable looking. They say the eyes are the window to the soul."

"Unfortunately, Katie's got the blinds drawn and the curtains closed." Dex sighed. "It's gonna take some time to see inside, I think."

"But I'm pretty confident I made a good start today."

Dex looked anxious. "How can you be so sure?"

"Because we're going shopping together this Saturday."

24
❊

THE ROAD WAS FLANKED on both sides by trees. Branches formed an arch overhead as if awaiting the procession of a radiant bride. Katie indulged the fantasy and tried to invision herself as that bride cascading down the aisle to a smiling, eager groom. Her boss's handsome face flashed across her mind.

What are you thinking, girl? Snap out of it. A guy like Dexter Matheson would never be interested in someone like you.

But Dex had been nothing but nice. He encouraged her to do more decorating around the office, he was more than flexible about her quitting time so she could get to class, not to mention his "doctor" routine when she was sick. And just last week he gave her his old computer when he discovered she was going to the library to write her research papers.

Dex's manner puzzled her. Sure, Kevin treated her great as well, but Dex was different. She couldn't quite place her finger on it as she navigated the winding road that would take her to her boss's parents' home. Dex accidentally left his briefcase there the previous night and realized too late that it contained some papers he needed for a meeting that afternoon. Knowing he had an appointment scheduled for the morning as well, he asked Katie if she would go out to get it during her lunch hour. And, of course, he'd pay her the mileage.

"What did I ever do to deserve such a wonderful job?" Katie asked herself out loud, not for the first time. A small, but forceful voice answered Katie from the recesses of her mind. *Nothing. You deserve nothing, and you know it.*

Katie's thoughts strayed to all the people who had treated her as nothing more than an object: Eric, Kristin, her own father, and even her own mother. As painful as it was, Katie knew in her heart that her mama would sacrifice her in order to have a man in her life. The only time Daria had chosen Katie over a man was the time T.J. Nichols, her only true love, had walked out of her life.

Guilt was a heavy load to bear. Katie had to keep it from getting the upper hand. She determined that Dexter Matheson and his sister Janie would not learn anything about her that might make them turn away. *I don't belong with people like them, people who have it all together.* But the alternative was so lonely.

She spoke aloud this time. "I'll make myself fit in. The less they know, the better it will be."

Then she saw a sign that read Lake Wingra. "This must be where I turn." She maneuvered her old Toyota Corolla around the corner and was astounded by the beauty of her surroundings. "How did they ever find this spot back here buried in the woods!" At the end of the street she pulled into a driveway leading to a two-story brick home. "Wouldn't mind having a place like this of my own!" she muttered, getting out of the car.

The manicured yard served as a pleasing welcome to the Matheson home. Dark pink begonias lined the winding walkway. The front porch ran almost the entire length of the house. Two wooden rocking chairs with a table and potted plant provided an inviting entrance. Katie rang the door bell.

A petite, auburn-haired lady with an uncanny resemblance to Janie opened the door.

"Yes?"

"Hi, I'm Katie Montgomery, Dexter's secretary."

"Oh, of course. Dex phoned and said you'd be coming by. Please come in." She stepped back so Katie could enter. "I'm Lydia, Dex's mother."

Katie smiled. "It's nice to meet you." Her eyes quickly scanned the foyer. "You have a beautiful home."

"Thank you. The Lord has indeed blessed us with this place. Come on back to the sun porch. You can see the lake from the window. It's my favorite room in the entire house." She motioned Katie through a spacious kitchen area with an adjoining family room and into the sunroom. "Miss Ellie and I were just about to have lunch." An elderly lady sat in a sage-colored print chair with her feet propped on an ottoman.

"Oh, I . . . uh . . . I didn't mean to interrupt. I'll just get . . . um . . . Dex's brief case and be out of your way."

"Nonsense! Dex said you were coming on your lunch hour, so the least I can do is feed you! That son of mine should know better than to make you work during lunch."

"Really, I don't mind. I don't want to be in the way."

"You'd better give up and give in, dear. When Lydia sets her mind to something, not much stops her." The older woman smiled sweetly at Katie.

"Now, Miss Ellie." Lydia grinned. "Don't go telling tales on me." She turned back to Katie. "Katie, this is my mother-in-law, Eleanor Matheson. But everybody calls her Miss Ellie. And don't let her fool you; she's ten times more stubborn than I could ever dream of being!"

Miss Ellie offered a frail hand to Katie. "It's nice to meet you, dear. Please sit down." She motioned toward a sage colored sofa in a coordinating checkered fabric. "And Lydia's right. I am more stubborn than she is, and I insist you stay for lunch." She leaned closer to Katie and spoke in a conspiratorial tone, but loud enough for Lydia, now in the kitchen, to hear. "Lydia is making chicken salad. That's the main reason I moved in here with them—to get Lydia's chicken salad recipe. She's a real snoot about it, won't tell anybody how she makes it. But I'll get it out of her one way or another."

Katie laughed. "Somehow, I think you will!" She shook her head. "I can see where Dex and Janie get their personalities. Every

Matheson I've met so far is a kidder!"

Lydia was coming into the sunroom with a tray in her hands. "Well, don't hold that against us, please. We really are a nice family. Maybe a little warped at times—"

"Speak for yourself, dear," commented Miss Ellie as she accepted a napkin from Lydia and spread it on her lap. "Actually, Katie, my husband was the worst kidder of all! He died a while back." A wistful look passed over the elderly lady's soft features, then she grinned again. "You never knew if the man was being serious or not—and usually he was not!"

Katie smiled. "I wish I could have met him. I've never had a grandfather or grandmother."

Miss Ellie looked intently at their guest. "How is it that you don't have grandparents, Katie—if I may ask?"

Katie cleared her throat. "I never knew my father so I don't even know if his parents are still alive. And my mother is not on speaking terms with her folks, so it's always just been my mom and me." She looked down at her hands. She wasn't sorry she had told them; after all it was the truth. But she didn't want them feeling sorry for her.

Lydia cleared the coffee table, a rustic-looking pine chest, and began setting out the food. "Well, Katie," said Lydia, "Miss Ellie has always said a person can't have too many grandkids. So if you ever need a grandmother, you won't have to look far." She winked at her mother-in-law.

Katie felt the older Mrs. Matheson studying her intently but discreetly. "There, I think that's all we'll need for lunch," spoke Lydia as her eyes canvassed the table. "I hope you like chicken, Katie."

"Oh, yes, ma'am, I do. It's just that, well, I . . . I still kind of feel like I'm intruding."

Lydia, without looking up, replied, "Don't be silly! Now, would you like a wheat roll or a white roll?"

Miss Ellie laughed. "I told you, Katie, you didn't stand a chance!" She laughed again.

Katie shook her head. "I think you were right, Miss Ellie." She turned toward Lydia. "Wheat's fine, thank you."

❄ ❄ ❄

Lydia closed the front door and went back to the kitchen to clear the lunch dishes.

"So what did you think?"

"About what, Miss Ellie?" asked Lydia casually.

"About Katie, that's what!"

"I'm not sure I know what you mean.

Eleanor Matheson stared back at her daughter-in-law. She twisted the bottom of her blouse between her fingers as her eyes took on a distant gleam. Slowly she spoke. "She's a real special girl, I think."

Lydia smiled. This was not the first time Eleanor had taken an instant liking to someone. She possessed a rare gift for perceiving the needs of others. Her mouth curved into a small smile. She laid the dishtowel down and came near her mother-in-law. "And what is so special about her?"

Eleanor rested her white head on the overstuffed chair and closed her eyes. When she spoke it was in a searching tone. "She has a gentleness about her. Having her here just seemed right." The longer she talked, the more confident Miss Ellie became with her own thoughts. "Yes, she definitely is a gentle soul, but wounded, I think. She rather reminds me of a lost kitten out in a storm. She's searching for a shelter but doesn't know where to look—at least not yet."

Lydia made herself comfortable, sitting in the exact spot Katie had vacated minutes earlier, content to wait on Miss Ellie while she prayed. Her mother-in-law always began her prayers with a deep breath, almost as if it could cleanse and purify her soul, making it ready to commune with the Father.

After several moments of silence, Eleanor raised her head and stared into her daughter-in-law's eyes. "Lydia, if something happens to me, promise me you'll look after Katie."

Lydia was flabbergasted. "But . . . but . . . Miss Ellie, I think Katie already has a mother. And we just met her. She doesn't need me to look—"

"You're the one, Lydia, you're the one."

"But, I don't even know her! She works for my son, that's all. She . . . she's a friend of my daughter's. I don't understand what you think I should do."

Miss Ellie smiled. "You just have to invite her."

"Invite her to what, Miss Ellie?"

"Well, I can't rightly say I know the answer to that one." She looked sheepishly at her daughter-in-law.

Lydia exhaled and chuckled at the same time. "Then how am I supposed to accomplish this!"

"You'll know when you need to know. Just promise me you'll take care of her. She's going to need you, Lydia." Miss Ellie reached over to gently grasp the hand of her son's wife. "And I don't think I'm going to be around much longer to help. That's why God told me to tell you to do it. You know, just tying up lose ends before I go on my journey."

Miss Ellie had always referred to life as a journey. Lately she spoke more and more about the final leg of her journey—the one that would take her to meet her Savior face to face. "Oh, Miss Ellie, I don't know if we're ready to let you go. I know I'm not; I still need you." She pulled the frail hand to her cheek. "And Janie will be lost without you."

"My dear sweet Lydia." Eleanor returned the caress. "You still see Janie as that red-faced peanut-shaped baby you brought home from the hospital. But she's not a baby anymore. She is a faithful servant of the Lord, and He has work for both of you to do, whether I'm here or not." Her voice held both tenderness and determination.

Tears streaked Lydia's cheeks, but she smiled, knowing her mother-in-law would want her to be strong. "Then, teach us, Miss

Ellie, teach us everything you can before you go."

❋ ❋ ❋

Janie Matheson had her head stuck in a rack of clothing, searching for "the perfect sweater." Every so often her dark hair popped up and she asked a question or made a comment. But, like a machine, she never stopped shopping.

"So you liked my mother and Miss Ellie?"

Katie stifled a laugh. "Yeah, it was a great lunch. They insisted I stay. I couldn't have gotten out of it if I'd wanted to."

The head popped up again—this time long enough to smile at Katie. "Yeah, they're both great. I was named for Miss Ellie, you know." The head disappeared again.

"But you're name is Janie, not Ellie."

"Well, my full name is Eleanor Jane Matheson. But since Miss Ellie already went by the name Ellie, my mom thought it would be a lot less confusing if I went by Jane. Then everyone started calling me Janie because it seemed to fit a baby better than plain old Jane. Ooo! I love this sweater! What do you think?" She pulled out a carnelian-colored cowl-necked sweater and held it up for Katie's inspection.

"It's nice. It would look good with your dark hair."

Janie laid it on top of the rack and continued her frenzied search. "Well, anyway, like I was saying, the name Janie seemed to stick, and that's what I'm still called." She looked up and smiled, and then the head was gone again. "When I was only hours old, Miss Ellie was holding me and she told my mom and dad I was gonna be exactly like her. She just knew it. Said God had told her. So that's when my parents decided to name me after her. We're all named for someone in the family." Janie's head popped up again. "I've looked at all the clothes on this rack. Let's go to that one over there. It has a sale sign on it." She was there in a flash. Katie followed

"Who was Dex named for?"

"Well, Dexter is my mother's maiden name. She was Lydia

Dexter before she became a Matheson."

Katie studied the perky young girl with her head stuck in the shopping rack. She wondered what it must be like to feel so connected to people, and to have a history. This was all new to Katie who had always felt like she was drifting through life with no heritage and no anchor. She sighed and pretended to be interested in a pink V-neck pullover. "I'm surprised you weren't named for your mother; you sure do look like her."

"Yeah, that's what everybody says, but that's okay because I've always thought she was pretty. So I take it as a compliment when people say we look alike. Hey! This would look nice on you." She pulled out an ecru cable-knit cropped sweater. "You have such a natural look; this would look really good! What do you think? It's on sale for forty percent off."

"It is?" Katie perked up and began inspecting it. "Maybe I could afford it." Katie hated to be such a penny-pincher. She was surprised, but relieved, when Janie suggested they come to a discount shop. Katie was grateful they had at least one quality in common—even though Katie's need for bargains was due to a lack of money while Janie seemed more interested in the thrill of the hunt.

Katie picked up the ecru sweater and looked it over again. "I do like this." She held it up against her to see if she thought it would fit.

Janie diligently searched another rack. "You should get it. It'll start turning cold before you know it. Now's the time to buy." She pulled out a blue cardigan and stared at it, then reconsidered and hung it back up. "I still kind of like the red one. What do you think, Katie? Should I get it?"

"Well, dramatic colors like that look good on you."

Janie cocked her head, contemplating whether to buy or not to buy. "You know, I probably need jeans worse than I do a sweater. But I hate shopping for pants." She rolled her eyes as she hung the red sweater back on the rack. "I can never find them short enough. I get so frustrated!" Janie assessed the body of her new friend. "You're such a good size, Katie. And you have a nice figure, too. I'll bet you don't have much trouble finding things that fit, do you?"

Katie shrugged. "Not too much. Jeans are usually too big in the waist, though."

Janie rolled her eyes again. "Oh, well, that's a terrible problem to have!" She laughed and grabbed Katie by the arm. "Let's go pay for your sweater and then get some ice cream! Since my waist will never be as tiny as yours, let's see if we can't fatten you up a bit!"

Katie smiled. She had learned one thing for sure in the past couple of days: it was impossible not to like Eleanor Jane Matheson—the grandmother or the granddaughter.

Katie blinked. She had read the same sentence about three times and still didn't have the faintest clue as to whether Getulio Vargas or Juan Domingo Peron had the more successful political regime for the Argentina peoples. She closed her history textbook with a thud. "Oh, who cares anyway?"

She wandered over to the cabinet and rummaged for a snack. Grabbing a bag of pretzels, she glanced out the kitchen window. Dull and gray. She saw no signs of life on the street below, only an occasional car going too fast. Katie slumped into one of her dinette chairs, mindlessly reaching for another handful of her favorite salty snack.

Why do people drive so fast? At least they're going somewhere. Here I sit staring out the window while life passes me by.

Life had become merely survival for Katie. Getting from one day to the next sometimes took all the energy she could muster. Katie's heart had become like a vault, tightly sealed. She wanted to believe something valuable was inside, something worth protecting, but she wasn't so sure anymore. And that was her problem. If she opened the vault, what would she find? What if it were truly empty? Sometimes

Katie was tempted to peek, just so she could finally know and put her mind at rest, but then the fear would creep up on her. She wasn't ready to face the possibility that she was drained of life and spirit at the age of twenty-three.

Katie's mind flashed back to that decisive day four and a half years ago. She distinctly remembered watching nurse Simmons disappear from the clinic room with a sack in her hand. Could that little sack be the key to Katie's vaulted heart? She recalled thinking how Dr. Goldman and Helen Simmons had used that terrible machine to pull her soul out of her body and then carelessly threw it away like yesterday's garbage. Katie shuddered and tried to reprimand herself for letting her mind dwell on past events that couldn't be altered. She'd snapped out of these reveries often enough before. In fact, she was getting to be an expert at it.

So why couldn't she do it now? Something deep inside her, probably the part that was locked up, wouldn't let Katie ignore it this time. It was a force compelling her not to just think about it, but relive it. Over and over again. This same force also invaded her dreams. Kaleo was never far away. Where he had wandered to all those years, Katie wasn't sure; but he was back now—and speaking to her as well. At least twice a week, usually when Katie was overly tired, he would show up with his regular mantra relentlessly entreating Katie to follow him, to trust him. "He doesn't know what he's asking," murmured Katie. Trusting was something Katie didn't know if she could do. Sometimes, when Kaleo would say he loved her, she would be tempted to follow him. But just as she would be about to move toward him, her body would start shaking and her feet would become rooted to where they were. She would cry, but she couldn't move. Something was weighting her down—something invisible. Then Kaleo would leave, and always he would look over his shoulder, always giving her one more chance to join him. But she never would.

Teary-eyed, Katie made her way to the sofa and plopped down. She was restless and bored, unable to study, unable to let herself search her own thoughts, and unable to move from where she was. Her tiny apartment had become a haven and a prison at the same time. Picking up the remote she thoughtlessly clicked through the channels hoping an old movie or an ice skating competition would be on. She wasn't surprised to find neither. "Just my luck," she growled at the TV as she vehemently turned it off and practically threw the remote back on the coffee table.

She thought about taking a nap but was afraid of what Kaleo might say to her. She had determined to face him only when absolutely necessary, and that meant at night when she had no choice but to sleep. A plastic bag lay on the sofa. She reached for it and pulled out the sweater she had bought the day before with Janie Matheson. She smiled as she recalled the pleasant shopping trip. She had laughed more in that one afternoon than the past four years.

Right then Katie decided to put on her new sweater and go for a walk around the neighborhood. It was still a little too warm for the heavy wool sweater, but she didn't care. The sweater made her feel safe and protected.

Katie glanced at her reflection in an antique hanging mirror she had picked up at a garage sale for five bucks. Making herself smile, she exited her apartment. In no time at all she was clipping along at a fast rate. If she couldn't chase the demons out of her head, maybe she could outrun them.

25

※

LYDIA RAN THE BRUSH through her auburn hair. In the mirror she saw her husband watching her from behind.

"Wow, you look great!" Everett exclaimed.

Lydia smiled at his reflection. "Thanks, but shouldn't you be getting dressed instead of gawking at me?"

"Maybe, but I'd rather keep doing what I'm doing."

"Well then, at least make yourself useful. Here, fasten this for me, would you?" She held a delicate diamond necklace.

Everett obliged, tenderly clasping the tiny gold chain, then resting his hands on her shoulders. His gaze took in the necklace sparkling against the emerald silk dress, then moved to her hair, her shoulders, and the soft curve of her hips.

"I ought to lose a few pounds," she said.

"I like your figure. Even after giving birth to five children, you're still the most beautiful woman I've ever seen."

"Everett! What has gotten into you?" beamed Lydia.

"Oh, I don't know," he answered carelessly. "Maybe all this talk about Kevin's wedding has put me in a romantic mood." He turned his wife and pulled her toward him.

Lydia smiled up at him. "Then maybe we should go to weddings more often," she lifted her face for a kiss.

"Mom, can I borrow your earrings, the gold ones with the diamond in the middle?" Janie came to an abrupt halt in the doorway. "Oh, sorry, Mom; sorry, Dad."

Everett stared gravely down at his daughter. He still held Lydia in his embrace. "You know, Janie, I don't think you really are sorry. Let's see," he began making a mental calculation. "How old are you now?"

Janie looked confused. "I'm almost twenty, why?"

Everett finally released Lydia and replied in a calm, even tone, "Because for the last almost twenty years you have been interrupting me when I'm trying to romanticize your mother. I have never met a kid with more impeccable timing!"

Janie laughed out loud. "Just call it a gift, Dad!"

"More like a curse," mumbled Everett as he dropped himself on the bed with a defeated look on his face.

"Oh, poor dear," spoke Lydia with mock sympathy. "You know, Everett, you should be thanking Janie."

"Thanking her! For what?"

Lydia leaned over and kissed him on the cheek. "Because you really do have to get ready to go or we're going to be late. And you know how I hate to start something without finishing it, so . . ."

"Mom!" laughed Janie with a hint of shock in her voice. "I can't believe you just said that—and right in front of me!"

"Said what, dear?" asked Lydia innocently.

"You know, about not starting something that you can't, you know . . . finish." Janie's face was blood red.

Everett and Lydia burst out laughing.

Janie, still blushing, tried to defend herself. "I don't know what you guys think is so funny. I'm not the one talking about sex in front of my kid!"

Lydia reached for her jewelry box. "No, but you are the one who entered the room without knocking." She held out her hand to her daughter. "Are these the earrings you want?"

Janie glanced at her dad who was trying to keep a straight face. Rolling her eyes she reached for the earrings. "Yeah, those are the ones. You don't mind if I borrow them? I mean, I wouldn't blame you if you didn't want someone as rude as me wearing your jewelry. It would be totally understandable. In fact, maybe I should give them back to you now 'cause . . ." She would have continued her monologue, but she was broad-sided by a flying pillow.

"Just go, peanut! Take the earrings and go!"

"Well, okay, Dad, if you're sure. 'Cause, really I wouldn't mind staying so we could talk about it some more. You know, it's healthy for families to talk their problems out instead of keeping them bottled up inside."

Everett flopped back on the bed with a defeated thud. "You win! I give up!"

Janie laughed. "It's about time, Dad. I don't think sparring with me is good for your health. You look a little flushed. Maybe you should take a cold shower."

Everett's hand shot out to grab his daughter, but she ducked too quickly and he missed her by an inch.

"Sorry, Dad, gotta go!" she called out merrily heading for the door. "I told Katie I'd pick her up at 5:30. Bye!"

Everett rolled onto his side. His wife shook her head.

"Someday you're going to learn that our youngest daughter refuses to be outdone by anybody, not even her loving father." Lydia walked to the closet and pulled out Everett's gray suit. She laid it on the bed beside him.

Everett fingered the fabric. He pulled himself to a sitting position. "Yeah, you're right about that. Janie has a way of getting what she wants."

Lydia looked thoughtful for a moment. "She's like the persistent widow in the book of Luke."

Everett nodded in agreement. "It still amazes me that Katie, of all people, is Dex's secretary. That's not coincidence; that's answered prayer."

"I agree. Janie prayed and prayed for that girl. She prayed she would be saved, that God would use her in her life, that she would be happy at home—anything she could think of, she prayed. And now she turns up after five years."

Everett spoke from the bathroom where he was getting dressed. "Maybe now Janie will have the pleasure of seeing some of her prayers answered. I hope so."

"Everett?"

"Yeah."

Lydia sat on the bed. "I told you what Miss Ellie said about Katie, about how I should look after her?"

"Yeah, Mom can be a little vague at times."

"Well," Lydia began tentatively. "I think maybe I know what she meant, at least part of it."

Everett stuck his head into the bedroom. "What is it?"

"Oh, Everett, I wish you could have heard her that first day when she came over here. I know she didn't mean to make me feel sorry for her, but I couldn't help but feel bad when she said she didn't know her grandparents and had never even met her father. She doesn't even know if he's alive!"

Everett emerged from the bathroom dressed in his suit. "I guess it's hard to imagine life any different than we know it. We've both been blessed with good, loving families, and now we're able to watch our kids grow up and have families of their own." His eyes twinkled. "With lots of grandkids!"

"That's exactly what I mean!" exclaimed Lydia.

"I'm afraid I don't follow you. What does all that have to do with Katie?" Before the mirror he straightened his tie.

"I prayed about what Miss Ellie said about inviting Katie and taking care of her. Then I read in Psalm 68 that God puts the lonely in families." She took a deep breath. "I think God wants Katie to be a part of our family."

"Brady's already married, and Dex is strictly her boss—"

"Oh, I know that, dear. I didn't mean she would literally become part of our family, but I thought maybe we could—or I should say, I could—start viewing her as a daughter."

"But doesn't she already have a mother?"

"She does, but I get the feeling it's not a good relationship."
Lydia stared vacantly out the window.

Everett sat next to his wife and reached for her hand. "You
know, I can't think of a better mother in all the world than you." He
lifted her hand to his lips and lightly kissed it.

Lydia laid her head on his shoulder. "Thank you."

"Honey, you've already got five kids, two grandkids and one on
the way. That's enough to keep you busy."

She shook her head. "I know, but I think God wants me to
be a little bit busier." She made her voice light, but she felt a little
frightened by the responsibility. "Maybe Katie won't have anything to
do with me. But I feel like I need to try to reach out to her and show
her what it's like to have people who love you unconditionally and
support you no matter what."

Everett put his arm around her. "Well, I'm not gonna argue
with you. And I'll do whatever I can. Pray, for starters."

Again Lydia sighed and closed her eyes in relief. Knowing her
husband supported her made all the difference in the world. "Thanks.
I really do love you, you know."

He kissed her temple. "I know. But what I don't know is how
you're going to go about this. Any ideas?"

Lydia straightened. "Well, since she's going to be at Kevin's
wedding today, I thought I'd try to find some time to talk with her
and invite her to Thanksgiving dinner. She may have plans with her
mother, but I can at least ask."

"Sounds good to me." He stood up. "Okay, how do I look?
Would you mind being seen with me?"

Lydia laughed and looked him over approvingly. "Everett
Matheson, you have never looked better!"

"Really!" He feigned surprise. "Then we'd better go now if I
look that good!" He grabbed his wife's hand. As they descended the
stairs Lydia silently prayed that God would give her success in reaching

out to Katie Montgomery.

❊ ❊ ❊

The sign read "Holland-Adams Wedding." Katie glanced at Janie as
she whipped her little red Honda Accord into an empty parking space.
Janie didn't drive recklessly, but she practically attacked the road, or so
it seemed to Katie who had always been a rather timid driver. Janie did
everything in her life with an overload of passion and energy.

"I think we made good time." Janie said, climbing out of the
car. "I hate to be late. I don't want to miss anything!"

Katie thought of how she'd been to only two weddings in her
entire life. One was when she was so little she barely remembered it,
and the other was for a co-worker at the grocery store. But that had
been a small affair in a backyard.

"Do you go to weddings a lot?" asked Katie trying to keep up
in her uncomfortable high heels. Her friend headed for the front doors
of the church. Katie wasn't sure if Janie was moving so fast because
she was just that excited or because it had turned surprisingly cold
that afternoon.

"Yeah," replied Janie not slowing down. "Every time I turn
around, somebody I know is getting married. In fact, I've already been
a bridesmaid three—no, four—times." Now she turned to wait for
Katie. "Don't you think weddings are about the most romantic thing
in the world?"

Katie grimaced. "I think I would find it a lot more romantic if
my feet weren't killing me!" Then she laughed.

The two young ladies reached the front doors of downtown
Madison's Grace Episcopal Church. Katie felt infinitesimally small
next to the massive oak double doors adorned by ivy wreaths laden
with rose-pink flowers. Katie thought Janie looked comical as she
wrestled open the mammoth wooden door. Much to Katie's surprise,
however, it swung open quite easily. They stepped into the church's
foyer and she instantly felt out of place. An air of formality enveloped

them. To Katie, it was stifling. Janie didn't seem to notice.

"Here, let's sign the guest book." Janie tugged on Katie's arm, and they each signed their name.

"Janie, hi, how are you?"

Katie and Janie both whirled around to see a tall girl with glasses smiling at them. Janie let out a small shriek and embraced the girl. Katie clumsily stepped back to make more room for the reunion.

"Oh, Micki! I didn't know you were going to be here! How did you get away from school?"

Micki grinned. "I'm only at Northwestern. It's not far!"

"Well, it seems like it is to me. I miss you! Maybe we can get together while you're here. When do you head back?"

Katie didn't hear the girl's response. She was too busy with the conversation in her own head. *Just calm down. Why are you so nervous because Janie's talking to someone else? You must have known she would have lots of friends here.* But none of that placated Katie's turbulent emotions. As long as she had Janie, she felt like she belonged. But if Janie weren't around, she would feel as if she were lost in a foreign country where she didn't speak the language.

"Katie, this is Micki, I mean Michelle Ferguson."

"What?" So intent was Katie on fighting her own demons of insecurity, she hadn't realized Janie was trying to introduce her to her friend. "Oh, nice to meet you."

Micki smiled. "Nice to meet you, too, Katie. Janie, I heard Dex was a groomsman."

Janie smiled. "Yeah, he's here somewhere, but I haven't seen him yet." She shrugged her shoulders and looked toward Katie. "I guess we should go ahead and get seated. Hey, Micki, why don't you sit with us?"

Micki looked disappointed. "I wish I could, but my family is saving me a seat. I just drove in so I haven't even seen them yet. Mom would never forgive me if I didn't sit with her. But we'll hook up at the reception, okay?"

Janie gave the tall girl another quick hug. "See ya'."

"Nice meeting you, Katie."

Janie made her way to the open doors that marked the entrance to the sanctuary, Katie following close behind.

"Bride or groom's side?"

"Dex! What are you doing ushering?" Janie smiled brightly. "Shouldn't you be in the back with Kevin?"

"That's exactly where I'm heading now. But, as I was passing through here, I saw the two prettiest girls I've ever seen, and I couldn't help myself. I had to stop." He grinned.

"Well, in that case, brother, get to work. We need really good seats on the groom's side, where we can see everything."

"I'll see what can be arranged." He perused the right side of the sanctuary, then held out his arm for his sister. They started down the aisle and Dex called softly over his shoulder. "You wait there, Katie. I'll come back for you."

Katie couldn't have moved if she'd wanted to. She knew her boss was attractive, but to see him in a black tuxedo! And he was coming back to escort her. Studying his retreating form, she thought maybe Janie was right. Weddings were romantic.

As soon as Dex began making his way back down the aisle, Katie averted her gaze. *Can't let him know what I was thinking. He'd laugh me out of this place.*

"You sure do look nice, Katie." Dex smiled and held out his arm just as he had for Janie.

"Thanks," replied Katie taking his arm and walking beside him. "So do you." She blushed as she said it.

"Well, thank you. I guess I can clean up, huh?"

Katie nodded. "Yeah, you should start wearing a tux at the office. You know, bring a little class to the place."

Dex grinned. "No, that's your job. And you're already doing it." Before Katie could think of a response, he announced, "Here you

239

go, right next to peanut. Now, I've gotta get back and try to keep the groom under control. He's gonna explode if we don't get this wedding over with soon."

"Bye, look for us at the reception," whispered Janie. She smiled to herself knowing Dex would never miss an opportunity to be with Katie in a social setting. But she kept her promise. She would not tell anyone of Dex's feelings for his secretary.

Katie had never been inside a church like this. Along each side wall were huge stained-glass windows in vivid colors, the carpet was a deep indigo, and the pews were sturdy oak, polished to a rich gloss. The light blue cushions looked scratchy, so she was grateful that her mid-calf-length vintage dress provided the back of her legs with protection from the menacing fibers. Unfortunately, she had no such guardian for the self-degrading thoughts assaulting her mind.

I don't belong in a place like this. These women are all so pristine with their matching shoes and handbags. And the men! They probably all own their own companies while their kids are spending all their money at out-of-state universities and joining the most prestigious fraternities and sororities.

The sanctuary reeked with the opposing scents of piety and wealth. Katie was trying to decipher which smell was stronger when the bridal party started down the aisle.

"Here comes Dex," whispered Janie. "He's escorting Trina Adams, Rachel's youngest sister."

"Oh," responded Katie dumbly. She didn't really care who the girl in the deep rose-hued taffeta dress was. She had eyes exclusively for her boss. The only time she did look away was when he passed her on his way up the aisle. She did, however, notice before she looked away that he smiled in her direction. He must have been smiling at his sister.

Katie didn't have time to ponder the situation. At that precise moment the organ music, which had been rather soft, was joined by a trio of trumpets and swelled to a resounding version of the wedding march. Katie rose to her feet with the rest of the crowd and turned to see the bride make her grand entrance on the arm of her beaming father.

"She's beautiful," breathed Katie.

Janie leaned forward to see beyond Katie as Rachel walked past. "I told you weddings were wonderful!"

Katie could not get over the transformation in Rachel Adams. She had come by the office on several occasions to see Kevin; and although Katie had considered her to be cute, nothing could have prepared her for this. Rachel was taller than average, on the slim side, and usually had her hair pulled back in a clip while sporting very tailored clothing. She always seemed to have a simple elegance and style about her, but nothing suggesting the grace and femininity she now exuded. Her gown had a translucent effect, making it almost shimmer in the light. The train cascading down the back gave her the illusion of being even taller, while the crown-like veil hinted that she must have royalty in her ancestry. Katie looked up in time to see Kevin's face reflecting the love and admiration he obviously felt for his bride.

Before she realized what was happening, Katie felt tears forming in her eyes. *Oh, great! The one time I wear mascara, it's gonna be running down my face!* Something soft touched her hands. Janie was offering her a tissue.

"I always come prepared with lots of these." Janie smiled and nodded her head, encouraging Katie to take it. "Trust me, I'll be needing one before long."

Katie was embarrassed by her show of emotions. Even though Janie didn't seem to think anything about it, Katie was sure this was not proper etiquette. She didn't even know Rachel Adams-soon-to-be-Holland. Why should she be so affected by the woman's wedding? And Kevin, he was just her boss. Though Katie got along well with him, she wouldn't go so far as to call him a friend, not a close one anyway.

The ceremony itself was rather brief with a lot of monologue Katie didn't understand—words about a marriage being an earthly illustration of Christ's love for the Church, the ring being a symbol of God's never-ending love for His people, and the candle lit by Kevin and Rachel being a reminder that their two separate hearts should now beat as one. It was all very poetic and beautiful, but it didn't seem practical for the 90s. At least not for someone coming from Katie's background where a man and woman usually hitched up to share expenses, to avoid being lonely, and to have someone readily available to satisfy their physical needs. Katie figured when all the flowers died, the dress was boxed up, and the guests went home, that's about what it would boil down to.

"I think I like weddings because they're so full of hope," said Janie. She dabbed at her eyes with a well-used tissue that had practically disintegrated in her hands. The last bridesmaid exited the sanctuary. She giggled. "See, I told you I'm a basket case at weddings."

Katie turned to look at her friend. "What did you mean about weddings being full of hope?"

Janie cocked her head. Her voice sounded dreamy. "Oh, you know. Sometimes, when you look at the world around you, it's easy to become bitter and lose hope. But then, when you come to a wedding and see two people pledge to love each other forever—well, it kind of restores your hope, I guess. Don't you think so?"

Katie frowned. "Yeah, but how many people actually make good on their vows to love each other forever? What's the divorce rate up to now? About 50% or something?" She shook her head. "That doesn't seem very hopeful."

Janie spoke tentatively. "Well, Katie, I don't believe real love is something two people can create all by themselves. It's . . . " she gestured with her hands, "it's bigger than that."

"Bigger than what?"

"Well, as much as I love weddings, I know that this," she gestured again with her hands, "is not what love is all about. The love celebrated here today began a long time ago."

"You mean when Kevin and Rachel met?"

"Well, . . . no, that's not what I mean. I mean that love began ages ago when God created mankind. God wanted someone to fellowship with, to talk to and spend time with. So he created Adam. But then He saw that Adam needed someone who was like him. God was Spirit, but Adam was flesh. So God created Eve. He made woman just for man, that the two would be together, love each other, and become one in flesh. Kevin and Rachel believe that." She closed her eyes for a moment. "It's always beautiful when two people are brought together in God's plan, and they can serve God together." She focused on Katie. "It really is a reason to celebrate, Katie. I know there's a lot of bad stuff in the world, but this is some of the good stuff."

Katie was thinking of someone else who had spoken similar words about four years earlier—Carolyn Grady at the Pregnancy Information Center. Katie hadn't bought it then and she wasn't buying it now. It was too idealistic for such a dirty society. She purposely put a sharp edge into her voice.

"So you really believe all of that stuff you just said—about God, I mean? Even with the world the way it is?"

"I do," she echoed the vows spoken earlier.

Such a simple declaration took Katie aback. "Oh, well, then . . . I guess that's good for you. If it helps you to cope, then why not?" She tried to sound nonchalant. But inwardly she craved what her friend had—not so much the "God stuff," but the conviction that came along with it. Margaret Kilgore at the clinic had that. Katie had been searching for it for four years now. But it always eluded her, mocked her.

Janie touched Katie's arm. "Katie, God does more than help me cope. He gives me life. Without Him I'd be existing from day to day with no purpose, no passion, nothing!"

Katie glanced around. "Looks like everyone's left, huh?"

"Sure does." With a forced smile, Janie grabbed her purse and stood up. "Let's head over to the reception before the cake's all gone. That's my second favorite part of weddings!"

Katie stood as well. "I'm not gonna argue about that. I didn't eat lunch, and I'm starved!"

The two young women walked down the corridor leading to the fellowship hall. Katie tried to convince herself she really did fit in.

26

Dex stared at the paint samples laid out on his desk. He was supposed to choose a paint color for his office, but all he could think about was the girl on the other side of his desk.

"I don't know, Katie. Which one do you like?"

Katie rolled her eyes. "It doesn't matter what I like. It's your office; you've got to choose."

Dex leaned back in his chair and clasped his hands behind his head. "You know, you really should consider studying interior decorating. You'd be good at it."

Katie laughed softly. "That's funny, Dex, real funny."

Dex leaned forward. "Why would you say that?"

Katie fumbled with the paint samples, apparently interested in the taupe-colored one. "I don't know. That kind of job isn't for someone like me."

"What do you mean, 'someone like you'?"

Katie finally plopped down in the chair opposite her boss and looked him in the eye. "I mean someone who comes from the kind of background I do. People who have money to hire decorators don't want someone like me telling them what their house should look like. They want someone like . . . like . . . well, like you or Janie or Kevin or Rachel." She waved her hand to make her point.

Dex turned his head to the side, partly to think of what to say and partly to avoid Katie's eyes. Hearing her talk like that literally made his heart hurt. He knew her confidence level was low, but he had no idea the reasons ran so deep. He cleared his throat and attempted a convincing tone.

"Well, that's a good theory, Katie, but it doesn't look like any of us are willing to play by your rules."

"I don't get what you mean."

"What I mean is that Kev and I are architects, not decorators, and—"

"Yeah, but it's the same thing. The clients who come in here are more than happy to deal with you or Kevin. You're all cut from the same cloth. You all fit in well together."

"And you don't think you fit in with us?"

Katie shrugged her shoulders and looked away. She crossed her arms in front of her and began tapping her foot.

Dex noticed her body language and decided to soften his approach. "Look, Katie, I just hate to think you have everybody pigeon-holed into certain categories. We've all been given gifts and talents in certain areas regardless of where we come from. Take Janie and Rachel for instance."

"Why should I? What's the point anyway?"

Dex smiled. "You're the one who brought them up."

Katie let out a frustrated sigh. "Yes, I remember." She waved her hand impatiently. "Go ahead."

"I was just going to say that Janie has no interest in working with high-paying clients or hob-nobbing with rich people. She wants to be a first or second grade teacher. And Rachel has a degree in social work. She's got a real heart for abused children. I wouldn't be surprised if she and Kevin ended up opening their home to foster kids."

Katie hung her head and spoke softly, all traces of hostility gone. "I had no right to suggest you were all shallow because you've had a different life than I have."

Dex had to strain to keep from reaching out and grabbing her hand. He'd been fighting that desire ever since the wedding five days earlier. Seeing her all dressed up like she'd been and then going out with her, Janie, and Micki afterwards was more than he thought his heart could take. And now, seeing how she saw their lives existing on two different planes, he wasn't sure how to proceed.

"It's okay. You're not the first person to jump to a wrong conclusion based on appearances. I just don't want you not using your talents because of some false notion you have about yourself that you're not good enough. Because that is simply not true."

Katie eyed her boss contemplatively. "You know, I think you're about the nicest guy I've ever met; and I'm not saying that because you're my boss. I mean it."

Dex wanted to keep the conversation going. "So, what kind of guys do you usually meet?" He'd never asked her such a personal question before.

Katie shrugged her shoulders. "Definitely not like you."

Dex figured this was the end of the discussion as far as Katie was concerned. He grinned at her, wishing he could read her mind. "Since I'm not sure what you mean by that, I'm gonna take it as a compliment."

She smiled. "Oh, it definitely is." She rose to leave.

"Katie, one more thing."

"Yeah?"

"I was wondering if you'd maybe reconsider about Thanksgiving. Mom really wants you to come. . . . That is if you don't already have other plans."

"I don't know, Dex, I don't think I'd feel comfortable—"

"Don't forget Janie'll be there. She really wants you to come. And Miss Ellie. She was asking about you on Sunday. She's hoping you'll change your mind and come." And praying for you, Dex wanted to add.

"Really? Miss Ellie asked about me?" Katie smiled.

"She sure did. She took an instant liking to you the day you went out there." Dex thought he saw Katie soften at the mention of his grandmother.

Katie leaned against the door frame. "Can I ask one question?"

"Sure."

"Why is it so important to all of you that I come? Your family doesn't even know me."

Dex leaned back in his chair. "That's just the way we are. Especially Mom. She loves to mother people. Why do you think she had so many kids! Besides, for the holidays we always have a house full of people. The more the merrier."

"Yeah, but I don't really like crowds.

"Then what are you going to do to celebrate?" Dex struggled to hide his frustration.

"Nothing. Thanksgiving never meant much in my household." Her last words were barely more than a whisper.

"Then it's time to make it a big deal. Won't you please come, Katie? I think you'd have a good time. You can bring your mother. We'd love to have her come, too."

"You would? . . . That's sweet, Dex, but Mama's going out of town with her boyfriend. You did know my mom lives with a guy, didn't you? In fact, she's lived with about four or five guys that I can remember. Probably more before that."

Dex answered matter of factly. "No, I don't think you've ever mentioned it before. In fact, you've never said much at all about your family or your life outside of work."

"There's not much to tell, at least not much you'd be interested in." Cynicism dripped from Katie's tongue.

"That's where you're wrong. If it concerns you, I'm interested. You don't have to push us away, Katie. We like you; it's that simple. Janie likes you, I like you, Miss Ellie, my mom, my dad, we all like you; and the rest of the family would too if you'd give them the chance." His face broke into a smile. "Face it, Katie, you're a likable girl."

"I was thinking I might call Mr. Brinker and try to work some over the holiday weekend."

"Work? You need the money that badly? I could give you an

advance or a loan. Are we paying you enough?"

"It's not that. See, when I quit I told Mr. Brinker I'd be available on holidays and busy days. The extra cash wouldn't hurt, but I'm making it okay financially."

"That's good." He relaxed again. "Look, I'm not gonna bother you about this anymore, but I want to make sure you know we all want you to come. I hope we haven't done anything to make you think you aren't welcome."

Katie walked back to the chair and plopped down. "Oh, Dex, I feel stupid making such a big deal out of this." She shook her head. "You've done nothing but be nice. I don't know why accepting your invitation is so difficult for me." She paused and licked her lips. "Holidays have never been anything more for me than either parties full of drunk people or being completely alone while my mom went off with her boyfriend. Neither one is desirable, but it's all I've ever known. I know how to handle that kind of situation and that kind of rejection. But a big family—even though I've always wanted to be part of one—would be unfamiliar. Saying 'No, I won't come,' is easier."

Dex felt like a knife was lodged in his chest and now was being twisted. "But is that what you *want* to say?" He hoped he had succeeded in disguising the pity he felt.

Katie looked up. "I'm not sure. It's like meeting your favorite movie star. It would be terribly exciting, but what if you were disappointed? I mean, what if he turned out to be a big jerk in real life? It would probably be better not to have met him and go on with the illusion that he was as nice as you always dreamed. Does any of this make sense to you?"

"I never told you why I hired you, did I?"

She shook her head.

"When I first met you, you commented that sometimes when you get stuck in a rut, it's hard to change—it's easier to just stay with what's comfortable. Remember?"

Katie laughed lightly. "I remember. I was so nervous."

Dex nodded. "I knew you were. And I admired the fact that you came anyway. You were right about what you said; it would have been easier to stay with the status quo, even if you didn't like it. But you chose to make a change. I respected that and wanted to help you accomplish your dream." He gave her his crooked grin. "Maybe I'm a romantic at heart."

Katie grinned back. "Maybe, but I think I had it right the first time. You are one of the few really nice guys left in the world." Katie took a deep breath. "And I'd love to come to your house for Thanksgiving—on two conditions."

Dex immediately brightened, yet he spoke with trepidation. "And what might those conditions be?"

"Well, first, you have to let me bring something." She held up her hand to ward off his protest. "No, that's how it has to be or I won't come. I want to contribute to the meal." She lowered her voice. "But I confess, I'm not a very good cook. All I know how to make is spaghetti. Maybe I could bring something really simple, like rolls."

Dex laughed, amazed at how light he felt now. "Yeah, you can never have too many of those!"

"Now, for the second condition."

"Let's have it."

"You have to promise you'll have a paint color picked out by the end of the day."

This time Dex groaned. "No, anything but that!"

"Too bad, buddy, but that's the deal. We'll just see how badly you really want me to come to Thanksgiving dinner."

"You're really sneaky, but you've got yourself a deal. I'll make a decision before you leave today."

"Good. Now, may I get back to work, or do we need to continue this therapy session a little longer?"

"No, no, that's all." He waved her out of the room. "But next time, I'm charging you for my counseling services."

Katie called over her shoulder, "I'll decorate that monstrosity of an office you've got, and we'll call it even."

"Deal!"

Dex never would have believed he would enjoy picking out paint samples. But he did.

❄ ❄ ❄

"Hey, Andy, got a few minutes to spare?" Dex addressed his pastor as the Thursday morning men's Bible study group was breaking up. The church usually cleared out quickly as the men headed to work. Since Dex owned his own company, he could take a few more liberties than those who were punching a time clock.

"Sure! As long as you don't rip apart my lesson!"

Dex grinned easily. "Not a chance. If anybody knows the book of Ephesians backwards and forwards, it's you. Besides, this is something entirely different."

He motioned Dex down the hall of the church until they were in front of his office. "Why don't we go in here and have a seat. We shouldn't be disturbed."

Dex sank into one of two navy blue leather chairs while Andy moved several books and papers out of the way and perched on the edge of his desk.

"Working on Sunday's sermon?" Dex nodded toward the open concordance and various commentaries.

Andy glanced at his disheveled desk and grinned. "No, actually I'm doing some research for a new series on the deity of Christ. It should be ready in a couple of weeks."

"I'll be looking forward to it."

"So, Dex, what's on your mind? I'm your pastor but I'm also your friend. You can ask me anything. Is it a theological question or a personal one?"

Dex leaned forward and rested his elbows on his knees, clasping his hands. "Definitely a personal problem. I need someone to commit to pray for me."

"Okay, you know I'll do that. What is it?"

"Well, it's about this girl I'm interested in. She's the secretary I hired at the office." Dex looked up at his pastor. "There's a lot of problems; I'm not gonna pretend there's not."

"I take it she's not a believer?"

Dex shook his head. "No, she's not a believer."

Andy pulled the wire-rimmed glasses off his face and rubbed his eyes. "Dex, I don't have to tell you there's no future for you with someone who doesn't share your faith."

Dex put his head in his hands. His voice was muffled. "I know, I know. But I can't seem to change how I feel. I've been begging God to lessen my feelings for Katie, but instead they grow in intensity whenever I'm around her. I almost lost it yesterday when I thought she was in financial trouble. I started offering her money!"

"Did she take it?"

"Huh? Take it?" Then understanding dawned. "No, she didn't take the money."

"Then you can thank God for that small grace. Somehow money has a way of complicating things for people."

"I suppose you're right, but I honestly think if I thought she needed it, I'd offer it again. I can't seem to help it. I practically forced her into having Thanksgiving dinner with my family. I didn't want to take no for an answer."

"She didn't want to come?"

"Well, she did, but she didn't. It's complicated." He launched into an explanation of how his receptionist had come into his life, how they'd discovered she was an acquaintance of Janie's, and how the entire Matheson clan seemed to have a burden for the pretty girl.

"Wow!"

"Yeah, my thoughts exactly. I keep thinking there's a bigger purpose going on here. That's why I asked Janie to try and strike up a friendship with her. I didn't trust myself to keep my thoughts and motives on the straight and narrow, if you know what I mean. I take one look at her and all I can think of is . . . well, stuff I shouldn't."

"So, she doesn't have any idea how you feel about her?"

"No, I don't think so. Janie's the only other person who knows, and she promised not to say anything. Dad knows something's going on, but he doesn't know how strong my feelings are. It's strange. I don't ever remember feeling this way about anybody."

"Not ever? Not even at some point with Ally?"

Dex focused his gaze on Andy. "No, this is completely different." Dex stood and began pacing in the small office. "This is nothing like that, Andy. I mean, that was all so serene and neat. This is messy." He turned toward his pastor. "But this is the most real thing I've ever felt." His tone was pleading, needing to be understood.

"Andy, you know I'm not the most feeling guy in the world. I tend to operate on facts. Emotions are Janie and Miss Ellie's department. They're always feeling how God is telling them what to do or think or say. I've never been like that. But I can almost hear God telling me to reach out to this girl. The more I pray about it, the stronger the feelings get. I'm not sure how much more I can take." He sank back down in the chair amazed at how much emotional energy he had exerted just talking about Katie Montgomery. "I haven't been so sure of anything since I changed all my plans and started my own company. And I know that was the right move."

Andy repositioned his glasses on his nose and ran his hand through his thinning blond hair. "Dex, I know more than anybody that your walk with the Lord is a sound one. So, I'm inclined to agree there's a reason this girl is in your life and that your family has taken an interest in her as well. What I'd like to do is first and foremost commit to praying about this like you asked. You know you can count on me for that. Now, my next suggestion might be a little uncomfortable for you, but I think it would be for the best."

Dex looked curious. "What are you thinking?"

"I think it would be wise if you had another man to keep you accountable. Because of your work situation, you have to spend a lot of time with her, which can be potentially dangerous. You do know it's not possible to pursue a relationship beyond friendship?"

"Yeah." Dex sounded disappointed but resigned.

Andy gazed sympathetically. "I counsel most people in your shoes to distance themselves from the person they're attracted to. But I won't do that with you because if anybody can handle this, it's you. I'm not saying it'll be easy; but I think you'll be able to keep from getting ahead of yourself."

"What do you suggest I do?"

Andy crossed his arms. "Just keep doing what you're doing. Be a friend and a light as well. Pray hard and continually. I'll call you twice a week, say on Mondays and Thursdays, to see how you're doing. I'll do my best to encourage you, but if I get the feeling she's pulling you away, I'll certainly confront you with it. And, of course, you can call me anytime. Do you think that plan will work for you?"

Dex nodded his head and pushed himself out of the chair. "Do I really have a choice?" he asked, grinning.

Andy grinned back. "No, not if you want my help."

"I really do appreciate this. I feel better knowing someone else is praying—not just for Katie's salvation, but for me as well. I think I'm gonna need it in the near future."

Andy opened the door so Dex could exit. As he followed the younger man into the lobby he offhandedly remarked, "I . . . uh . . . ran into Nan Hoffman the other day."

Dex stopped. "Yeah? Did she speak to you?"

"Just long enough to let me know Ally is engaged."

Dex let the news sink in. "Anybody we know?"

"I don't think so. Some guy originally from Detroit. He's on staff at Lakeside Christian, in charge of media."

"Was that awkward for you, running into her like that?"

"No, not too bad. She made it clear this guy was 'a wonderful young man who'll make a perfect son-in-law.'"

"I hope she's right, Andy. I hope she's right."

27

✻

"PLEASE, GOD, LET THESE ROLLS come out okay." Katie muttered as she kneaded the dough. The back of the box of hot roll mix said to pull the dough toward you folding it in half and then push on it with the heels of your hands, rotate it a quarter turn and do it all over again, continuing for five minutes.

"Seems like a lot of work. They better taste good!"

Even though her task of bringing bread was a small one, she determined these would be the best rolls the Mathesons had ever eaten. The last thing she wanted was to embarrass Dex for insisting she come. As she folded, pushed, and turned the dough, she thought, *I can't believe I let him talk me into this.*

But how could she refuse? Dex practically pleaded with her to come. She was sure it was out of pity, but why shouldn't he pity her? He had everything she had always wanted: a home, a real place to belong, plus lots of people to care about him and that he in turn cared about. Now, for some strange reason, he wanted to share it all with her, his secretary.

Dexter Matheson was nothing short of a mystery to Katie Montgomery. He was smart, handsome, funny, and on his way to being a successful businessman, yet he was the nicest guy she'd ever met. He wasn't stuck on himself like Eric Martin. Dex concerned himself with other people more than with himself. And lately, most of his concern was focused on her. Katie kneaded the dough with a little more ferocity. *It's just pity, that's all; pure and simple pity.*

So why didn't it ever feel like pity when she was talking to him? How come the expected condescension never came? And Katie certainly had waited for it. Her mama always said it would come if she'd just give it time. But how much time? She'd been working for Dex and Kevin six months.

Katie wanted to believe that what she thought—and hoped— she saw in Dex's eyes was really there. But she couldn't let herself. Betrayal hurt too much, and fantasies only left you disappointed. However, Katie didn't want to fall as deeply into cynicism as her mother. So she determined she would accept the friendship the Mathesons offered, including Dex. If she continued to keep her heart locked up tight, there would be no danger of having it stomped on.

The timer on Katie's oven went off signaling five minutes had passed. She grabbed the box and read that she was now supposed to separate the dough and form it into little round balls. After doing so, she laid a towel over the rolls to let them "rest" for another thirty minutes, whatever that meant. She reset the timer for the designated thirty minutes. Now would be a good time for her to grab a quick shower. If she used her time wisely, she should be ready to go well before Dex arrived to pick her up at 11:30. Apparently the Mathesons liked to eat around 1:30. Katie didn't want to make Dex wait on her and give him the idea she wasn't appreciative of the invitation or his offer to drive her.

Just as Katie was about to step into the shower, the phone rang. She half entertained the idea of not answering it, but what if it was Dex saying he wasn't coming or that they'd changed their minds and didn't want her joining them after all? It would be better to get it over with now.

Katie knew she was being silly, but doubt was Katie's constant companion, even in her dreams. Just last night she had almost allowed Kaleo to convince her to follow him through that strangely inviting yet foreign door. She touched the doorknob long enough to feel a warmth radiating from within. She couldn't tell if the comforting heat was coming from the other side of the door, from the gray wolf as he stood next to her urging her on, or from inside herself. But wherever it came from, it left the moment Katie removed her hand from the knob. Ice water invaded her veins. Kaleo slowly backed away.

"Please don't go, Kaleo!"

He had answered that he must go, that he had to pass through the door with or without her.

"But why? Why can't you stay here with me? I'm afraid, Kaleo, I'm afraid. Part of me wants to go, but what if it's not a good place?"

"That is a risk you have to take. You must have faith," came the wolf's mystifying response.

"I . . . I can't. Sometimes when you think something is good, it turns out to be terrible. I . . . I can't take that chance again. You ask too much of me."

Kaleo's eyes darkened. "Perhaps you ask too little. I must go now."

"But . . . will . . . will you come to me again?"

"Do you want me to?"

"Yes! I need to know you'll be back."

She watched Kaleo walk away, but she knew he would return. But this time that knowledge didn't distress her; it comforted her.

Now, as she wrapped a towel around her to head for the phone, she wondered why she was no longer afraid of the gray wolf. Was she beginning to trust him? Why? Was it because of that brief feeling of warmth she had experienced? It had been hard to let go of that knob; the enveloping heat had been very desirable. Or maybe it was the look on Kaleo's face, so hopeful, so sanguine.

"That's it!" exclaimed Katie aloud. The expression on Kaleo's face was a mirror image of the one on Dex's face when Katie finally agreed to come to his home for dinner. That's why it had comforted her. But Katie couldn't stop the negative thoughts from assaulting her mind. *I've seen that same look on lots of people's faces, people who in the end only let me down--Kristin, Eric, Margaret Kilgore, Mama. Why should Kaleo or Dex or even Janie be any different?*

As Katie reached the telephone, she concluded that her new friends, real and imaginary, were probably like all the others. But, at least she wouldn't have to be alone.

"Hello."

"Hi, Katie. Happy Thanksgiving."

"Hi, Mom. Happy Thanksgiving to you, too."

"Look, Katie," Daria pleaded. "I'm calling to see if you won't change your mind and come with me and Lou."

"Mama, I already told you—"

"We're gonna be leaving in about an hour, so that gives you time to get over here before we go. I can even stall Lou if you need more time."

"Mama, no! I've already told you I'm going to Janie and Dex's house. They invited me, and I accepted. I can't back out now!" A tone of irritation had crept into Katie's voice. They'd already had this conversation several times.

"But it won't be the same without you, sweetie."

"What do you mean, it won't be the same? Thanksgiving's never been a big deal for us before."

"I know, but you've always been there."

Enlightenment came to Katie. Daria didn't crave Katie's company so much as her reliability. This would be the first major holiday Daria would have to face without her. If Lou got drunk and left, if they had a fight, if Daria drifted into one of her somber moods, Katie wouldn't be there to pick up the pieces.

"I'm sorry, Mama, but I can't come." Daria was going to have to go it alone this year.

"But you always said Lou was an okay guy!"

"Yeah, Lou is, but not his brother. Vic's a lowlife! He drinks and gambles and thinks all his stupid jokes are funny. I can't believe he and Lou are even related!"

"It would be so much better for me if you were there!"

Don't do this to me now, Mama. I don't have time! Katie strained to fight off the compulsion to run to her mother's rescue. "Mama, you made the choice to go with Lou. You knew what it would be like."

"Yeah, but I never see you anymore. I miss you." Daria's voice had grown childlike and pathetic.

Katie steeled herself against the unbidden vision of her mother's plaintive face. "You decided to move across town. You knew I wasn't gonna go with you."

"But that shouldn't mean we never see each other. It's a holiday, for crying out loud, Katie!"

Ire raged within Katie's breast. She had always longed for her mother to care about holidays, like any normal family would. But Daria always chose her boyfriend's wishes over her own daughter's. And now she was trying to make Katie feel guilty? No way, not this time. Katie practically yelled into the phone. "Don't you dare make your misery my fault! All those years I was miserable, I never once blamed you! And I had just cause, Mama; I had more than just cause!"

"Katie," cried Daria, "why are you speaking to me like this? All I want is to see you. Is that a crime?"

Katie closed her eyes and took a deep breath. "Mama, I'm sorry I lost my temper, but can't you see? You're using me to block out the reality of what your life has come to be."

"What are you talking about? My life is just fine!"

"Then why are you so desperate for me to be there?"

"I . . . I'm not desperate! Why would you say that?"

"You're dreading this holiday just like you've always secretly dreaded any holiday. You've never liked your life, but you don't have the guts to change. Well . . . well, I do, Mama! I'm trying hard to change, to believe there's a better way to live. And you're not gonna stop me!" Katie contemplated hanging up on her mother but couldn't.

Daria sobbed. "If that's how you act when you're around your new high and mighty friends, maybe you ought to re-think the company you keep! You were a lot nicer before!"

Katie was pleasantly surprised at the calm she felt. "No, Mama, I wasn't nicer. I was just your doormat. Look, I've got to go so I won't be late." She glanced at the oven timer. "Mama, you know where I live. If you want to see me, you should come by sometime. I'm always inviting you, but it seems I'm the one who always has to travel to see you. It's a two-way street all the way from your house to mine. Think about it." With a shaking hand she hung up the receiver.

As she headed to the bathroom to take a lightning-fast shower, she clicked the radio on—loud. Anything to drown out the thought of her mother's face.

❄ ❄ ❄

"Is something bothering you?" inquired Dex of the quiet girl sitting beside him as they pulled onto the freeway.

"Hmm? Oh, no, I'm okay."

"Well, those rolls sure do smell good." Katie had been carefully placing them in a pretty basket when he'd arrived at her apartment. He was shocked at how comfortable he felt walking in and seeing Katie working in the kitchen. *Wouldn't mind coming home to that every night*, he thought and then quickly ducked his head lest Katie see his feelings.

Katie smiled. "I hope they taste as good as they smell. I've never done any like this before. I made sixteen. Do you think that will be enough?"

"Oh, sure. That'll be enough for me. Everybody else'll have to fend for themselves." He threw Katie a winsome grin.

She matched his smile with one of her own. "You ought to taste them before you make such claims, you know."

"No, food that smells that good can't be bad."

Katie turned toward her boss. "Do you really believe that, Dex?" Her tone was serious.

Dex looked at her quizzically while trying to maintain safe eye contact with the road in front of him. "Why do I get the feeling we're not talking about bread anymore?"

Katie sighed and leaned her head back against the tan leather headrest of the forest-green Jeep Cherokee. "Oh, I was just wondering if you really believed something had to be good because everything about it indicates it will be." She laughed softly. "That sounded pretty stupid, I'll bet, huh?"

"Not stupid at all." She looked like she had just stepped out of a Cover Girl ad with her faded denim jeans, neutral-colored sweater, and brown hiking boots. She echoed the simple beauty of nature. Yet Dexter Matheson thought nature's beauty was anything but simple. To fully understand it, one needed to appreciate the complexity of its order. So he purposed at that moment to listen with his heart and soul as well as with his mind and ears to what this girl was saying. Something was going on with Katie, and he knew it had to do with much more than hot rolls. "Sometimes you have to listen with your gut, regardless of how something may appear. God can give us the discernment to know if it's good or bad."

Katie looked thoughtful for a moment. "Hmm. I think I get what you're saying. You're talking about natural instinct, aren't you?"

"Kind of, I guess." *But it's so much more!* He added, "Are you having second thoughts about coming with me?"

Katie's head popped up from its relaxed position. "No, please don't think that." She actually reached out and touched his arm as if that might reassure him of her sincerity. She quickly pulled it back. She stared out the window. "I admit I was having second thoughts earlier today, but . . . but then I talked to my mom on the phone . . . and . . . well, I suddenly felt sure I was making the right choice."

Dex cast her a sidelong glance. "Was your mom upset with you for spending Thanksgiving with us instead of her?"

"Yeah, but she'll get over it. I think that's only the second time in my life when I've gone against her. The first was when she moved across town. She wanted me to move with her, but it seemed like another dead-end to me." She shrugged. "I figured I was old enough to live on my own."

"Are you glad you did?"

Katie paused before answering. "Yeah, I am. It felt right then, and it feels right now. Which is surprising. I've never been able to turn my back on my mom before. She's always needed me, and I always thought I had to be there for her. And most of the time I didn't mind. But for some reason I couldn't do it this time. Maybe I'm just tired of it all, I don't know."

Dex longed to reach out and touch her as she had touched him. Even though it had only been for a second, it had sent a veritable shock through him. "Maybe you've simply grown up." He smiled, then looked worried. "Look, Katie, I didn't mean to cause any trouble between you and your mom; I just wanted you to have a good Thanksgiving, that's all." He cringed at the thought of sweet, shy Katie being surrounded by a bunch of rowdy, hard-drinking, gambling lowlifes. He felt a measure of peace knowing Katie would be safe and secure at least for one day.

"I do believe you, Dex. I'm where I want to be. And perhaps you're right. Maybe this is all part of growing up. But still, I . . . I do love her. I don't want her to be . . ." Tears filled Katie's eyes.

This time Dex did reach over and gently squeezed her hand. "You still love her, Katie. And you always will. That's what family's all about." He released her hand and rested his hand on her shoulder. "You've got to remember, though, that you don't have to be miserable because she is. You can love her and still choose a different path for yourself." He removed his hand. "I'm glad you decided to come. And now that I know how hard it was for you, I'm honored as well."

"You're honored . . .to be with . . . someone like me?"

For the tiniest second, Dex thought he saw a longing in Katie's eyes. Or was he merely seeing what he wanted to see? He was sure of what he was feeling, though.

"Trust me, Katie, I am."

28

THE VIVACIOUS BRUNETTE THREW HER ARMS around her new friend. "Katie! You're here! Happy Thanksgiving!"

Katie laughed a little uneasily, aware of the scene they were making in the entryway to what the Mathesons called their family room. "Happy Thanksgiving to you, too, Janie."

Dex spoke from behind the two girls. "Peanut, you act like you haven't seen her in over a year."

"Oh, you!" She now threw herself at her brother. "I can't help it if I get excited during the holidays."

"Here, Janie, take these to the kitchen before I tear into them." Dex shoved the basket of rolls into his sister's hands. "I begged Katie to let me taste at least one, but she refused. It was pure torture having to smell them all the way here."

"Oh, poor baby!" Janie grabbed Katie's hand and pulled her toward the kitchen. "Come on, Katie, I'll introduce you to everybody. Miss Ellie will be so glad to see you."

Out of the corner of her eye Katie saw Dex watching her and smiling. Then Everett slapped his son on the back as he headed for the kitchen. "They keep shooing me out of there, but maybe they'll let me in this time to say hello to our new guest."

"Don't count on it, Everett," said Lydia from behind the kitchen island. She was wearing a blue checkered apron and brandishing a chopping knife in one hand and a potato in the other. "Every time you men come in here, you eat up the food as fast as we can cook it! At this rate, we won't have anything to put on the table!"

Everett held his hands up in mock surrender. "Okay, okay, you win. I promise not to set one foot beyond this line right here." He indicated the space dividing the kitchen from the casual dining area. He then caught Katie's eye and winked at her. "Hello, Katie. It's nice to see you again. I'm glad you could join us today."

"Thank you, sir. I'm glad I could come, too."

"You know, I'd give you a big hug, but I'm afraid my wife would cut off my hands with that wicked-looking knife she's waving around."

Lydia spoke matter-of-factly without even looking up from her cutting board. "It would serve you right, dear, flirting with pretty young girls right under my nose while I'm slaving away to fix you a nice Thanksgiving dinner."

"Well, I think I just might have to take my chances!" In the blink of an eye, he had rounded the island and was making his way toward Katie yelling, "Help me out, Janie! Block for me!"

Laughing, Janie grabbed her mom while Everett gave Katie a bear hug and a quick kiss on the cheek. Katie blushed.

"Sorry, Dad, but I can't hold her any longer!"

With that Everett tore out through the dining area with Lydia in hot pursuit. "Everett, you get back here! You owe me a hug, you big lug, and a kiss on the cheek!"

Janie grabbed Katie's hand and pulled her into the sunroom. "Come on. I'll introduce you to my brother Brady and his wife, Sasha and their little boy, Jake." She grinned. "I promise they're a little more sane than my parents."

Katie smiled weakly. "I'll believe that when I see it." The two elder Mathesons still ran through the house playing their friendly game of tag. This was going to be an interesting day. And she was fairly certain these people didn't even drink.

❉ ❉ ❉

"Where did you say the bathroom is?" whispered Katie into Janie's ear. They were sitting on the floor watching Jake attempt to build a house with his blocks. Everybody oohed and aahed, but Katie never saw anything that even slightly resembled a building.

"It's right through the family room, down the hall, second door on the left. I'll show you if you want."

"No, that's okay, I can find it, I think."

I've never been in a house this big, though. Katie thought, rounding the corner into the family room. She heard Dex's voice and stopped dead in her tracks. He was leaning over so his head was even with the slightly protruding belly of someone Katie surmised must be his pregnant sister Johanna.

"Hello, little one," he said, gently. "This is your Uncle Dex, remember me? We spoke last week. Anyway, I want to wish you a happy Thanksgiving. And just think, next year, you'll be out here where we can all see you and you can see us." At that moment Dex noticed Katie staring at them. "Oh, and I'd like you to meet a good friend of mine." He stood upright and motioned Katie to come closer. "Katie, this is my sister Johanna McKinnon."

"Hi, Katie, nice to meet you."

"Nice to meet you, too."

"And this," Dex said as he indicated Johanna's rounded stomach, "is my youngest niece or nephew." He cast a friendly scowl at his sister. "They refuse to find out if it's a boy or girl, so I have to keep referring to it as 'little one.' Johanna and Bruce say they want to be surprised, but I think knowing would make things a lot easier."

Johanna playfully swatted at her brother's arm. "You just wait, Dex, until it's your turn, I'll bet you'll want to be surprised, too."

Dex tried to deflect the assault but was too late. "Ow, that hurt!" He grabbed his tricep in mock pain and grinned at Katie. "Just like an older sister, huh? Always picking on younger siblings."

Katie nodded dumbly. "Um . . . I was just . . ." She motioned toward the hallway that Dex and his sister were blocking. "I needed to get . . . Janie said it was down the hall."

Johanna was the first to decipher Katie's jumbled message. "Oh, I'm sorry. Dex! We're blocking Katie's way." She grabbed her brother by the arm and pulled him to the side.

"What?" he said.

"I'll be right back," Katie darted past the two of them.

❊ ❊ ❊

Dex was bewildered. "What was that about?"

Johanna grinned. "Dex, don't you know anything? She had to go to the bathroom, and you were in her way."

"Well, why didn't she just say so?"

"She was embarrassed. It happens to all of us. Hey, would you mind going out and helping Bruce unload the van? We've got lots of food and I tell you what, going anywhere with a two year old is like packing for a journey half way around the world!"

"Yeah, I'll go help, sure." Dex headed toward the front door, wondering what was wrong with his secretary—certainly something more than mere embarrassment about having to use the bathroom. But for the life of him, he couldn't figure out what it might be.

❊ ❊ ❊

Katie locked the door behind her, not even noticing the beautiful guest bathroom. She rubbed her temples, trying to steady her throbbing pulse. But she couldn't erase from her mind the image of Dex talking to his sister's stomach. *He really believes there's a baby in there—his niece or his nephew. But it's not. It's not! It's just a mass of tissue, like Margaret Kilgore said.* But Katie knew that to these people it was much more than tissue. *No, everybody here today thinks it's a baby. What would they do if they knew . . . knew what I did?* Katie closed her eyes tightly. *They'd kick me out for sure. They'd send me where I belong, to Vic's house with Mom and Lou. That's where I belong anyway, not here, not with people like this.*

She felt the sobs coming and quickly turned the faucet on to

266

drown them out. *Why did I ever agree to come here?* She sank to the cold tile floor and longed to hide in the solitude of her own apartment. But had she ever really been able to hide? No, the pain followed her wherever she went. It slept with her, it worked with her, it ate with her. And it was apparently going to have Thanksgiving dinner with her. With a sigh, Katie rose and looked in the mirror.

"Great," she muttered. "Now, on top of everything else, I have red eyes." She quickly splashed water on her face and dabbed it with a towel. She tried to smile and see how she looked; but she gave up. Just the sight of her reflection made her sick and was a cruel reminder that she did not belong in this beautiful house. Everything in it seemed to reek of righteousness from the startlingly clean tile floors to the elegant furnishings to the comforting aromas emanating from the kitchen. Everything in it except for her, that is. The Matheson's purity only made her foulness stronger, and, she was sure, much more obvious. But how was she going to get out of this? Would it even be possible for her to leave? And if she did leave, how would she explain her departure? And then Katie remembered she hadn't even brought her own car.

"I'm trapped. I can't even leave!" she moaned. Closing her eyes again, she resigned herself to the situation. She decided she'd better use the bathroom facilities and then go out there and get it over with. One thing was sure. She would avoid Johanna and her growing stomach at all costs.

Dex stepped into the living room hoping to find Katie. He hadn't seen her since the hallway episode. She was there, looking at a display of family photos on a table by the front window. She made a striking figure standing with her head slightly lowered, the sun casting a warm glow around her. Sometimes when Dex looked at her, he saw pure sunshine; times like now, he sensed a dark storm lurking somewhere on the horizon. The problem was, he didn't know from what direction the storms came.

"So there you are. I was wondering what happened to you." He sauntered into the room and stood beside her.

She looked up at him sadly. "I'm sorry. I just passed by and the pictures caught my attention." *Actually, I was trying to escape.* The sadness in her face changed to worry. "Is it okay that I'm in here? I mean . . . I didn't ask or anything; I just—"

"Katie, it's okay." He glanced around at the room. "We don't come in here much. Sometimes we forget it's here. We spend most of our time in the family room or the sunroom."

"It's so beautiful." Her glance scanned the black marble fireplace with the whitewashed, carved mantle; then noted the rich tones of the Persian rug before traveling to the sophisticated sofa and chairs. Finally, Katie's gaze rested on a baby grand piano in one corner of the elegant room. "Do you play?"

"Me?" Dex gave her one of his famous crooked grins. "I'm afraid not. I tried to learn back when I was a kid but wasn't cut out for it. My mom plays, and so does Johanna. Mom used to play at church, but it always made her nervous. Now she only plays if they're really in a pinch." He noticed Katie had not yet averted her gaze. "Do you play, Katie? If you want to try it out, you're more than welcome."

Startled, Katie snorted softly. "Me, play? No way! I've never learned. I always wanted to, though. I like music, but Mama was always against me learning."

"Usually it's just the opposite—the parent wanting the child to learn while the child has no interest."

Katie turned to stare out the window. "I'm not sure, but I think it had to do with my father."

Dex drew a long breath. It was the first time Katie had ever mentioned her father except to say she'd never met him.

"Was he musical?"

Katie smiled lightly at her boss. Her voice was filled with longing. "Yeah, he was. He played in a band when Mama met him.

Sometimes when she drinks herself into a melancholy mood, she'll talk about him. She told me he used to write songs for her and serenade her. She always cries when she talks about it; the pain is still pretty intense for her."

Dex reached over and timidly pushed a strand of hair behind her ear. "Katie, do you know what happened to make your father leave?" He paused and then added, "You don't have to tell me if you don't want to."

Katie took a deep breath. "I don't mind telling you. From everything my mom has told me, I figure the main reason my dad walked out is because of me."

"Because of you? I thought you didn't even know him."

Katie grimaced and folded her arms in front of her. When she spoke, there was an edge to her voice. "I *don't* know him. In fact, he only saw me one time when I was still an infant. But that was all it took. He walked away and never looked back. I suppose he thought a kid would get in the way of his music career." She sighed.

Dex couldn't imagine a man turning away from his own flesh and blood, his own little daughter. "I'm sorry, Katie. I don't know what to say."

Katie's voice softened. "Of course you don't know what to say, Dex. How could you? You have a really great family."

"Are you sorry you agreed to come here today?"

"No, I'm not sorry at all about that." She glanced once again at the beautiful piano. "But I am sorry I'm in such a somber mood when it's supposed to be a holiday."

Dex smiled warmly. "Katie, holidays are times to be together with people you care about. You don't have to put on a front for anybody. If you're sad, that's okay. If you're happy, that's okay. We just want to know you—the good, the bad, and everything in between."

"That's sweet, Dex; but this is your family, not mine."

"Well, that may be so, but don't let Janie hear you say that. She's already adopted you as her sister."

Katie laughed, grateful for a change in the conversation. "I guess a person could do worse than have her for a sister."

Just then the youngest Matheson popped her head into the room. "So there you guys are! I've been hunting all over for you. Dinner's ready; Mom wants everyone to come to the table." Then, as quickly as she had appeared, she disappeared.

Dex looked at Katie. "Shall we go eat?"

"Yeah." As she walked past the piano she gingerly ran her hand over the glossy black surface. "It's so smooth."

Dex stepped up behind her and placed his hands on her shoulders. She seemed so small and fragile to him, not like his sisters that he always joked with. "I'm sorry you never got a chance to learn to play. It's not too late, though. You could still take lessons. Mom could teach you."

Whirling around she put a huge smile on her face and filled her voice with mock sarcasm. "Oh, sure, I could take lessons in all my spare time! You obviously haven't met my slave-driver boss Dexter Matheson!"

Dex grinned the crooked grin again. "He sounds like a bear. How do you stand working for him?"

"Well, he does work me to the bone, but he pays pretty well and he also promises a terrific Thanksgiving meal."

Dex grabbed her elbow and began ushering her toward the door. "Then we'd better go make sure your boss comes through with his promise." He looked down at her one last time. "And if he doesn't, he'll have to answer to me!"

❄ ❄ ❄

Dex had no trouble making good on his promise. Katie had never seen so much food in her life: turkey and stuffing, mashed potatoes with gravy, several different salads, an assortment of vegetables, every type of dessert known to mankind, and numerous baskets of breads and rolls. Katie was pleased to see her basket was nearly empty. She was aware that Dex had taken at least three. His compliments on their taste meant more to her than he could have imagined.

There was one tense moment right before the meal. The Mathesons had a custom of taking turns telling one thing they were thankful for. No one could eat until everybody had a turn. Katie listened as Everett and Lydia each were thankful for their family and friends; Johanna and Bruce for the new life they were expecting; little Emily for toys; and so it went. Janie was thankful for a loving and faithful God, while Dex spoke of God's provision at DesignLink. At Katie's turn, she took a deep breath and shyly expressed her thanks for her new job and her wonderful bosses. Miss Ellie was the last one to speak, saying she was grateful her life was nearing its end and that she would soon be joining her Lord and Savior and the ranks of all those who had gone before her. This unsettled Katie; she could see no reason why someone with such a wonderful life would be anxious for it to end. No one else seemed to think it an odd statement, though several of the women wiped tears from their eyes.

And then the meal began. Since so many people had gathered, some took their plates into the family room or the sunroom. Not everyone could fit around the impressive oak trestle table with the eight ladder back chairs. Katie tried inconspicuously to count everybody. This was no easy task since people were moving around all the time; but she judged fifteen people to be present: Miss Ellie, Everett, Lydia, Johanna, Bruce, little Emily, Kendall, Kendall's boyfriend Javier, his sister Selena, Dex, Brady, Sasha, little Jake, Janie, and finally Katie. She marveled that Lydia had enough matching dishes.

Everyone made Katie feel at ease, asking questions about her without prying too far into her personal life. She did, however, make a conscious effort to distance herself from Johanna. The sight of Dex's pregnant older sister reminded Katie that she didn't, and never would, belong there.

Kendall, on the other hand, fascinated Katie. Like Memphis down at the Pregnancy Information Center, Kendall had that confident air about her, the kind that commanded respect and attention yet wasn't pushy. It was the kind of personality Katie dreamed of but never possessed. Janie told Katie that Kendall worked at the downtown mission run by Dennis Grayson, the man for whom Dex was designing the House of Hope. Kendall worked as a teacher and mentor to underprivileged children. Katie could see she would be good at that.

Kendall had an earthy beauty which distinguished her from Johanna, who was small and feminine like Lydia. Kendall was taller and larger boned, but she was just as sophisticated as the other Matheson females. She wore her dark hair short with a hint of curl. Her almond shaped eyes seemed to twinkle non-stop. Katie concluded that Janie had inherited the best of both of her older sisters—Johanna's grace and femininity and Kendall's strength and enthusiasm. Katie wondered where she fell in the spectrum. Probably far short. She didn't seem to possess any of the Mathesons' qualities.

"Penny for your thoughts," Dex said.

"Oh, they're not worth nearly that much." Katie smiled.

"I'm not so sure about that. Did you get enough to eat?"

"Enough! I think I had way too much. I've never seen so much food in one place. And it's all delicious. Maybe I should take cooking lessons instead of piano lessons!"

Dex laughed. "Well, Mom could give you both. She's an excellent cook now, but I've heard stories about some pretty awful meals when she and Dad first got married. Mom always says if there was hope for her, there's hope for anybody."

"That's true," said Lydia, coming up behind the couple. "I hate to break up this conversation; but Dex, duty calls."

"Duty?" asked Katie. Did Dex have to leave?

Dex groaned. "But, Mom, I'm entertaining Katie. Surely that's more important than cleaning the kitchen."

Lydia turned to Katie. "Can you believe such a helpless man could be so successful in business?"

Katie laughed. "It is hard to imagine, isn't it?" Dex shot her a dirty look. She shrugged her shoulders before addressing Lydia once again. "I don't mind helping with the cleaning. After all, I only contributed one basket of rolls."

"Oh, don't feel bad about that. We have a tradition in this family. The women do the cooking and the men do the cleaning. I see no reason to change that now." She winked at Katie. "Besides, it'll do Dex some good to roll up his sleeves and do some manual labor."

"But Mom, I need to stay and keep Katie company—"

"That won't be necessary. Katie, Miss Ellie was feeling kind of tired, so she went to her room to rest. She said she'd really appreciate it if you'd come visit with her a while."

"She asked for me?"

"Yes, she did. Miss Ellie is anxious to get to know you, I think. She already knows everybody else here pretty well, so she'd rather spend her time with you. Will you come?"

"Uh . . . of course. Where's her room?"

"Just follow me."

Lydia led Katie down the same hallway as before. They stopped at the third door on the right. "She's in here. We gave her this room since it's on the lower level. Miss Ellie has trouble with stairs these days, don't you, Miss Ellie?"

The elderly woman was propped up on a chaise with a crocheted afghan thrown over her legs. She did look tired to Katie, but her eyes sparkled merrily.

"I'm an old lady; I have trouble with everything these days!" She motioned Katie to come close. "Hello Katie. Sit down and keep an old lady company."

"Yes, ma'am."

"I'll leave you two alone to visit." Lydia waved and closed the door behind her.

"So, have you had a good time today, Katie?"

"Oh, everybody's been so nice, and the food was fantastic!"

"Well, I'm glad for that. You're a nice girl." She speared Katie with her eyes. "But you're not always honest, are you?"

"I . . . don't know what you mean."

"Oh, I'm old and haven't got much time left! If I beat around the bush too long, I may not get all the way around it before the good Lord calls me home."

Katie tried to smile. "I still don't understand."

Miss Ellie patted Katie's hand. "I like you, Katie, but I'm not blind. We make you a bit nervous, don't we?"

"No, I'm not nervous . . . I've . . . I've had a great time." Katie knew full well she was stammering and didn't sound convincing. "But I guess I do feel a bit like I don't fit in." She shrugged her shoulders and looked out the window.

"Is it because of the money?"

Katie immediately began to deny it, but then she wondered why. Certainly that wasn't the only thing bothering her, but she had vowed to keep her other secrets to herself. "I suppose that's part of it. I don't feel comfortable around all this beautiful stuff."

"I know; it takes a little getting used to."

"What do you mean?"

"Oh, the Mathesons haven't always lived like this." Miss Ellie waved her arm to indicate the lovely furnishings and linens that adorned her room. "In fact, Everett is the first one to ever make any kind of money. The rest of the clan are struggling like everybody else, I suppose."

Katie's eyes widened. "I had no idea. I guess that explains why Janie was excited to find a good bargain."

"Oh yes!" laughed Miss Ellie. "It's ingrained in all of us Mathesons to search for bargains! My husband Leland was just a poor country preacher when I met him and a poor country preacher when he died three years ago. He never did give up his pulpit; well, not until he physically couldn't stand up there and preach. My other son is a small-town pastor right outside of Des Moines, and my daughter is married to a missionary serving in Romania. Everett was the only one who had any knowledge in the field of business."

A dreamy look passed over Miss Ellie's face. "Everett was always building things from the time he was able to crawl. As he got older, he wanted to know how things were put together and why tall buildings didn't fall down when a strong wind came." She laughed. "I thought that child would drive me crazy with all the questions he asked!" She shook her head at the memory. "No, it didn't take us long to figure out the good Lord had something else in mind for our youngest son. So we scrimped and saved to send him to college to study engineering. But it still wasn't enough. He had to work his way through. He was also bound and determined to marry Lydia right out of high school. Everyone told him he should wait, but they were too much in love." She gestured toward her bedside table. "That's their wedding picture right there."

Katie reached over and picked up the framed photo. She saw a younger version of the couple she knew staring back at her. She was captivated by the look in their eyes and the smiles on their faces. Katie swallowed as she felt a small sob rising in her chest. "They look like the happiest people in the world. I had no idea Everett worked his way through school." She delicately placed the antique-looking frame back on the table. "I'm having to pay my own way through college, too. I suppose I judged your family unfairly. I just assumed they had everything handed to them on a silver platter." She took one last look at the photograph. "They sure don't look like they're worried about money in this picture, though."

"They had their faith to get them through. They worked hard but never complained. And I'm certainly not gonna complain either. I couldn't ask for a finer daughter-in-law than Lydia. She's been a real blessing to me, especially since my own daughter lives halfway across the world."

"So Everett worked 'til he could afford this house?"

"Not exactly." Miss Ellie adjusted the afghan on her lap. "The land this house is built on was purchased by Leland's father years ago. He had always dreamed that one day the Mathesons would have a homestead, as he called it—a place for the entire family to gather and call home." Her eyes grew sad. "But he died before that became a reality, and the land was passed on to Leland. Oh, that husband of mine!" Miss Ellie did nothing to hide the tears glistening in her eyes. Katie thought they looked like diamonds. "He wanted so much to make his father's dream come true, but his congregation could barely support him as it was. And then when Everett wanted to go away to school . . . well, you know how it is, something always came up and the house never got built." Miss Ellie eyed Katie suspiciously. "Am I boring you, dear?"

"Oh, no, Miss Ellie, please go on with the story."

"Well," Miss Ellie continued, "Everett did very well for himself and was able to buy a nice, comfortable home in Stoughton. He talked with his father a lot about drawing up the plans for the dream house, but with five kids, something always came up. My husband understood all too well about that! Then when Leland got sick about six years ago, Everett decided he'd put it off too long. He went to his father and told him he was going to go ahead and draw up some plans and start building the house so Leland and I could spend our golden years there. But Leland said the only way he would agree is if Everett designed it specifically for his own family with lots of room for guests. At first Everett refused saying the design should be left up to Leland and me, but we finally persuaded him to see the foolishness in that. I mean, what would two old people like us do in a house this size? It was ridiculous! But I think Everett always felt a little guilty about the money we gave him for college and wanted to pay us back somehow. He knew we didn't have much to give, but we wanted him to have it; and we would do it the same all over again if we had the chance. People are more important than buildings, Katie; don't you ever think otherwise." She pointed her finger in Katie's direction to intensify her point. "But Everett really did want to be able to give his father the home he'd always dreamed of. But we wouldn't have wanted it to work out any different than it did. Besides, we've always been so proud of the way Everett uses his talents to glorify the Lord. He's always donating his time and materials to various churches and organizations. I think that meant more to Leland than any house ever could. And Dex is following right in the footsteps of his father, always using his skills and talents to help someone out." The older lady's face beamed with pride.

"Miss Ellie, did . . . did your husband get to see . . . see the finished house?"

The elderly woman looked at Katie and smiled. "No, dear. He died about two months before it was completed. But he saw all the plans, and he was happy, Katie. Really, he was. He knew he was going to a better place—a place where a glorious mansion was waiting for him."

"A mansion? I don't understand."

"I'm talking about heaven, child. The Bible says Jesus is preparing a mansion—a dwelling place—for each person who believes in Him. When we go to heaven, we'll finally be in the home we were meant to have. Leland knew that and took comfort in it. I guess it is sad to think that he got so close to seeing his dream home built; but when you compare it to heaven, this beautiful house on Lake Wingra pales in comparison. Don't you think so, dear?"

"I guess. But I wish he could have seen it."

"Oh, I'm sure he knows all about it. I wish you could have met him, Katie. He was a fine man! And he loved to flirt with pretty young ladies like you!" Seeing Katie's shock, Miss Ellie laughed. "He was a spitfire, that husband of mine. He would have taken a shine to you, just like I have."

Katie licked her lips. "Miss Ellie, I feel like I shouldn't be taking up your time. You probably would rather spend time with your own kids, grandkids and even great-grandkids."

Miss Ellie reached out and held Katie's hand. "I've had a

lifetime with my family, and I cherish them, every one. I couldn't love them any more if I tried. But when I look at you, I feel like I'm looking at the future."

"The future? What do you mean?"

"Perhaps I'm just a silly old woman rattling on about nothing. But I like to think in all my years of walking with the Lord, He and I have developed an especially close relationship. Sometimes I sense God telling me things, tasks I need to do before I go home. Recently He told me I should be close to you. So that's what I'm doing." Seeing the perplexity in Katie's expression, Miss Ellie laughed. "Well, if that didn't make any sense to you, will you just believe that I like you?"

Grinning, Katie replied, "Now you sound like Dex!"

"Well, that grandson of mine is pretty smart. You'd do well to listen to him. After all he is your boss!"

Katie laughed out loud. "You're right about that. And I thank you for sharing all this history of your family. I feel like I know them better now."

Miss Ellie's countenance and tone took on a maternal quality. "Oh, child, I hope you'll come to think of this place as your home. Leland would be so pleased if you would."

Katie's eyes filled with tears and she leaned over to hug the older woman. "Thank you, Miss Ellie, thank you."

"You're welcome, dear," she said as she gently patted Katie on the back, delighting in the show of affection. "There now," spoke Miss Ellie as Katie pushed herself into a standing position, "you'd better go join the others, or I'll never hear the end of it. They'll all be mad at me for keeping you to myself, especially Dex. Now, you run along. I need my rest."

"Yes, ma'am. Thank you again." Katie quietly left the room, thinking, *So that's what it's like to have a grandmother!*

Back in the family room most everybody had gathered to watch a football game. Janie made room for her on the sofa. Katie felt like maybe she could fit in this family—just maybe.

29

❀

"Brady," implored Sasha, her exotic eyes flashing mischievously. Her husband frantically searched for a new ballgame to watch. "Jake is crying and it's *your* turn to go check on him. Could you please tear yourself away from the TV long enough to do your fatherly duties—?"

"All right, all right! I'll go!" Brady tossed the remote control to Dex as he exited the room muttering something about three year olds not respecting the importance of football.

Dex grinned at his sister-in-law. "You know, Sasha, the only reason he agreed so easily is because the game was over."

"Why do you think I waited until now to remind him that Jake is his responsibility, too?" Sasha put a triumphant look on her face. "I've learned a thing or two in four years of marriage."

"Yeah, like how to manipulate your husband," said Everett from behind his newspaper. "You must be taking lessons from Lydia."

Everett was expecting the pillow that flew in his direction. He easily deflected it with one hand without even lowering his paper. "You are getting entirely too predictable, dear."

"Oh, am I?" Lydia asked as she rose from the rocking chair where she had been sitting with little Emily. She made her way to Everett's recliner and plopped his granddaughter down in his lap. "Since I've been giving lessons to Sasha, maybe you should do as Brady is doing and take care of Emily." Two year old Emily threw her arms around Everett's neck and cooed, "Gampa!"

Everett smiled at first and then wrinkled his nose. "Oh, that was low, Lydia, that was low, even for you!"

"I know, dear. Emily's diaper bag is in the sunroom."

Throwing a smirk toward his wife, Everett picked up his grand-daughter and headed for the sunroom. "Emily, looks like we've got some important business to tend to."

Katie smiled. She didn't particularly enjoy being around kids, but at least pregnant Johanna had gone to take a nap. And Katie never tired of the endless bantering the Mathesons engaged in.

"Dex," Lydia entreated, "see if anything is on besides football."

"But it's a tradition to watch football on Thanksgiving!"

"Well, some traditions are made to be broken."

Dex scowled. "You didn't feel that way about the guys doing clean-up duty."

"Of course not. But I think you'll notice now that Brady and your father have left the room, you are vastly outnumbered by the female members of this family."

"Yeah, Dex," cried Janie, Sasha, and Kendall in unison.

Dex turned to Katie. "And what about you? What's your vote? You're not tired of football are you? And don't forget I'm the man who signs your paycheck."

"Dex, that's not fair!" shouted Janie as she scrambled to pull the remote out of her brother's hand. "Hand it over!"

With Kendall's help, the two sisters were able to wrangle away the much-coveted control. Janie quickly flicked through the channels. An ice skating exhibition flashed across the screen. Katie spoke up.

"Oh. I love ice skating!"

Janie switched back to the show. "I enjoy watching skating, too, especially the exhibition performances when the skaters aren't so nervous and don't make as many mistakes."

"This will be a nice change of pace," said Lydia in a matter-of-fact-tone. "It's much better than watching grown men stumble all over each other to get a little brown ball."

Forty five minutes later, even the men conceded it had been a good show.

"Let's go for a walk," Dex exclaimed. Katie didn't seem to hear, but lingered on the sofa with a dreamy look on her face. Not until he grabbed her hand and began pulling her off the sofa did she seem to come back to reality.

"Hey, let's go for a walk," repeated Dex. "I'll take you down by the lake; then we can come back and have seconds on dessert." He dragged Katie toward the closet where they'd hung their coats. "It's pretty chilly, but the sun's still out so it shouldn't be too bad."

Katie laughed. "I can't believe you're thinking about eating again. I'm still positively stuffed!"

Dex helped her into her coat. "That's what the walk's for, silly! We walk off what we just ate to make room for more. It's what Thanksgiving's all about."

"I thought you said it was about being with people you care about and being thankful for the good things in your life."

"Oh, yeah, well that, too." He grinned that crooked grin.

Dex continued with his explanation of the meaning of the famous November holiday. "You have to understand, Katie, that one of the things I'm most thankful for is an abundance of food—and having a day where you can eat tons of it and not feel bad. I mean, it's just what you're supposed to do to celebrate. Make sense?"

"Whatever you say, boss. If you want to eat 'til you pop, go right ahead." Katie tried her best to sound condescending.

"Well, we'll see if you can resist Mom's chocolate pie or Johanna's cheesecake. It doesn't get any better than that!" He smacked his lips together to emphasize his point.

The two had reached a small pier. They walked to the edge and stared out at the glassy lake.

Katie nodded toward a little rowboat pulled onto the shore. "Do you fish out here in the summer?"

"Sometimes. Not so much anymore since I moved closer into town." Dex looked at Katie. "Do you like to fish?"

Katie shrugged her shoulders. "Don't know. I've never been. It

281

doesn't sound all that appealing to me."

"What about swimming?"

"Not on a day like today! But in the summer, I guess it's my favorite sport to participate in. Someday I'd love to swim in the ocean—or just see it, for that matter. I can't imagine what it must feel like to stand on the edge of all that water."

"You've never seen the ocean?" His tone betrayed surprise. His family had gone to the beach for vacations ever since he was a kid, usually once every other year. The years in between they would take a winter vacation and go skiing.

Katie didn't seem to take offense at his question. "No, I've never seen anything bigger than Lake Michigan, but that's pretty impressive in and of itself."

"Yeah, it is." Dex was having a hard time fighting the urge to hold her in his arms and tell her he would take her to see the ocean and anywhere else she wanted to go. But he couldn't do that. Perhaps in the future if God willed it to be so. But he would have to be patient—something that was becoming more and more difficult to do. He cleared his throat. "I didn't know you were such a fan of ice skating."

Katie blushed until her cheeks matched the red of her cold nose. "Yeah, I've liked watching it since I was a kid. I can't believe I blurted that out back there. I spoke up before I knew what I was doing."

Dex put his arm around her shoulders. "I'm glad you did, Katie. It showed that you were starting to feel at home."

Katie smiled up at him. "Miss Ellie did tell me to consider this my home. But, I didn't expect to do it so soon!"

"Well, good for Miss Ellie, and good for you!"

"She's the sweetest person I've ever met. She's so at peace with her life. But then all of you seem that way."

"And you're not?"

Katie shook her head. "No, I'm still waiting for the time when

I'll finally feel at home in my own skin, you know?"

"Yeah, I know what you mean, but I'm not so sure it ever happens this side of heaven. We're just passing through on this earth. Heaven's our real home."

Katie looked thoughtful. "That's what Miss Ellie said. But I guess I don't understand why it has to be so hard. Passing through or not, I'd prefer it to be a little easier."

Dex longed to cheer her up. "I think the tough times are designed to make us stronger, to make us more like God intended for us to be."

Katie looked down at the water. "I remember somebody else telling me something similar a long time ago."

"And did you believe it?"

Katie shook her head again. Dex's heart sank. "No, some tough times don't do anything but beat you down. At least that's how my life has been." She stared down at the water again. "Maybe that's why I like ice skating so much."

"I'm afraid I don't follow you."

Katie hesitated a moment. "I've always wanted to live my life like an ice skater—to go through life gracefully and beautifully. I'd like to not be afraid to take risks and jump higher. . . . higher than I ever thought I could. And then when I did fall, I'd like to get right back up and continue skating as if nothing had happened. I admire the way skaters do that. They fall with all the people watching. And usually the falls are anything but graceful—hands and feet all sprawled out on the ice. But instead of lying there, mortified and humiliated like I know I would, they get right back up and keep going as if the fall had never happened." She lowered her head. "I've never been able to do that. Sometimes you can't get back up and go on. The weight of the fall is like a noose around your neck." She looked at her boss. "I guess that's what separates the amateurs from the professionals."

Dex returned her look. His eyes showed concern. "And you're resigned to being an amateur?"

"That's pretty much the conclusion I've come to. But you, Dex, now you're a professional. Your whole family is."

Dex wanted to straighten out Katie's twisted thinking. How could he tell her that any strength and fortitude she saw in him or his family came from their trust in Jesus Christ. Would she accept it and understand it? He silently prayed, and when he felt like he had his answer, he took a deep breath.

"Katie," he spoke gently, "please don't think I go through life without making mistakes. I've taken some pretty bad falls that were anything but graceful."

"Yeah, but things always turn out okay for you."

"Sometimes the price for that is pretty steep. And in some ways, I suppose I'm still paying." His eyes clouded over.

"I don't know what you mean; but if you don't want to talk about it, it's okay."

"No, I want to tell you. Some mistakes stay with a person, as you said—like a noose around their neck. I've got things like that in my life. I know Jesus has forgiven me, but I still have to live with the consequences." Now Dex looked out over the lake, but he didn't see it. He continued speaking to Katie without looking at her. "I was engaged to be married a couple of years ago."

"You were?" Katie's voice registered her shock.

Now he did look directly into her eyes. "I was a fool, and I hurt a lot of people. The guilt of it still haunts me."

Guilt was something Katie understood, even though she never spoke of it. She reached out and touched the sleeve of her boss's leather jacket. "I'm sorry, Dex. Let's go back inside. We don't need to talk about this."

He turned and grasped both of her arms. "Yes, we do. It's important to me that you understand." Then he let go of her.

Katie pulled her coat more tightly around her. "Okay, if you really want to tell me, I'm listening."

He spoke as if he were giving a report. "Her name's Ally. We started dating about five years ago. We went to the same church. She'd had a crush on me for a while but I'd never noticed. I was too busy in school, I guess. But then, during my senior year of college it dawned on me what a great girl she was. I thought she had everything I wanted. She was pretty, smart, believed in God, came from a good family, and so on."

"Did you love her?"

Dex shifted his weight until he was half facing Katie while leaning on the pier rail. "I thought I did; but I know now I was never in love with her." He shook his head. "You know, I never even asked God if she was the right girl for me. I just jumped right in with both feet. The problem was that she really *did* love *me*."

"Why was that a problem?"

Dex closed his eyes before speaking. "Because three days before the wedding I called it off."

Katie gasped.

"Pretty rotten of me, huh?"

"I don't know what to say. It must've been really hard."

Straightening, Dex jammed his hands in his coat pockets. "Yeah, it was hard all right. We had a big wedding planned. Ally's very capable with that kind of thing." Dex smiled ruefully. "I think she had the wedding planned before I ever proposed. I'll never forget the expression on her face or the hurt in her eyes when I told her I didn't want to marry her." He shuddered. "It was a nightmare. All the gifts had to be sent back. Ally had bought an expensive, custom-made dress, all the groomsmen and bridesmaids had their tuxes and dresses, the honeymoon had been partially paid for—"

"But, if you weren't in love with her, wasn't it best to call it off before you got married?"

The realization that Katie wanted to comfort him made Dex smile. "Yeah, I'm sure it was the right thing to do. I'm just sorry it took me so long. If I'd been seeking God all along instead of doing what seemed right in my own eyes, I would have saved a lot of people a lot of grief, myself included."

"I remember Kevin telling me once that Janie cross-stitched that Bible verse—the one in your office—when you were going through a really tough time. Was it during this time?" Katie hoped he wouldn't be angry that she and Kevin had been talking about him.

He just chuckled and nodded. "Yeah, peanut did that for me. It's in First Peter: 'Cast all your anxiety on him because he cares for you.' Janie was pretty devastated to see me in such a depression. And you know Janie; she always has to do something to let people know how she feels." He crossed his arms over his chest. "Me and peanut, we've always been close. I don't know why, but we've always understood and trusted each other. In fact, I think Janie knew all along that Ally and I weren't right for each other."

"Kevin said that was the time you started DesignLink." She threw a saucy smile at him. "Maybe it's selfish, but I for one am glad you started your own company, or I'd probably still be checking groceries at the Pic-n-Save. Nobody else would hire me, you know."

Dex met her cheeky grin with one of his own. "Well, that's their loss. I have to admit that having you come to work for us is one of the brighter spots in the last few years of my life. I may even have to give you a raise."

"You'll get no complaints from me about that!" Katie was delighted that his mood was brightening. "What were you gonna do before you started your own business?"

Dex's smile faded as quickly as it had come. "Ally's dad is a partner in a very prestigious architectural firm in Madison. He pulled a lot of strings and secured me a position that nobody coming straight out of college should have. He trusted me, and I threw it all back in his face when I broke up with his daughter." He shrugged his shoulders. "I thought that's what I wanted. I mean, I went to school to be an architect so I naturally jumped at such an opportunity, again never bothering to ask God if that's what He wanted me to do."

"So how did you know you should start DesignLink?"

Dex rubbed the back of his neck. "I'm not sure how to explain it. I was in a pretty deep depression wondering what to do." He gave a self-incriminating laugh. "I've always admired the way my brother and my sisters knew what they wanted to do. But me—I've never been as settled. I mean, I knew I wanted to be an architect, but something about doing the expected, normal thing didn't sit well with me. I wanted more freedom, but I wasn't sure why I wanted it. I kept praying and praying, and the idea literally popped into my head to start my own company. I knew I'd be able to branch out and pursue a lot more ministry-type projects if I were on my own—like the thing I'm doing for Dennis Grayson's downtown mission. I wanted God to use my talents."

Dex noted the quizzical look on Katie's face. "For the first time, I had a real peace about what God wanted me to do. Since my Dad's in the engineering business, he knew a lot of contacts, so that helped me get started. When Kevin went in on it with me, that simplified the money aspect. God began blessing us with clients and it just took off." He reached over and gently tugged on Katie's hair. "Then God blessed us in the best way when He sent you to us!"

Katie laughed and swatted his hand away. "Oh, you call someone with no office experience a blessing! This God of yours must have a strange sense of humor!"

"Well, I won't argue with that! But it sure keeps life interesting." He grabbed her hand and pulled her down the pier. "It's cold. Let's walk a little, get the blood pumping."

Dex led Katie around the perimeter of the Mathesons' property giving her a little more history of the family. When they'd come back to the front of the house, Dex plopped down in one of the rockers on the porch. He knew the temperature was dropping and they probably needed to go inside; but he knew that once they did, he'd have to share Katie with everyone else. He wasn't quite ready to do that.

Katie sat in the other rocker and pulled her knees up to her chest to ward off the cold. "It's beautiful here. So peaceful and serene.

I can see why your great grandfather picked this land. The first time I came out here, I remember thinking how great it would be to live in a place like this."

"Yeah, it is pretty terrific. But I think I'd rather have a great family and live in a shack than a beautiful home and be alone. For some reason God saw fit to bless us with both."

"Miss Ellie said the same thing. She said never forget that people are more important than buildings."

"That grandmother of mine is a wise woman. I know what she's talking about. To have people stand with you through thick and thin can be the difference between sanity and insanity, I think."

"What makes you say that?"

"Well, when I broke up with Ally, it caused a big ruckus at the church. The Hoffmanns, that's Ally's family, had been at the church since the beginning, kind of like my family. They had the idea that my family and I should leave the church because of all the pain I caused them. I would have left, too, if it hadn't been for our pastor, Andy Powell. He tried to reason with them, but they wouldn't listen. He was counseling with me at the time and was convinced it would have been wrong for me to marry Ally. I apologized, or tried to, at least half a dozen times. I wrote letters saying how sorry I was and asking for forgiveness, but they couldn't bring themselves to give it. I can't really blame them except for the fact that the Bible commands us to forgive." He shuddered at the memory. "God knows I didn't mean to hurt Ally or anybody else."

"What happened then?"

He let out a loud sigh and leaned back in the rocker. "It caused a big split in the church. About seven families left. They were all close to the Hoffmanns and couldn't stand to see them hurting like they were. It was a big blow to our church. We're not that big of a congregation—about 300 people—and a lot of the ones that left were founding families. It was hard to see them go. I kept telling Andy I'd leave, but he kept assuring me we'd done everything we could to reconcile." He ran his hands through his hair. "So not only did I hurt the Hoffmanns, but the entire church as well! It was just awful, Katie. If my family, Andy and his family, and others in the congregation hadn't stuck with me, I don't think I would have made it. None of this," he gestured toward the Mathesons' property, "means anything if you don't have a strong support system. It's just brick, wood, and plaster. But what's inside is priceless."

Katie wiped a tear from her cheek. "I'm glad they were there for you, Dex."

"I'm really glad you came today, Katie. It's been nice getting to know you away from the office."

"Thanks for inviting me, and . . . thanks for telling me all of that. I know you didn't have to, and it's obviously still painful for you to talk about, so I'm glad you trusted me enough to confide in me."

"I should be thanking you for putting up with me and my sad stories." He grabbed her hand. "I hope you know we're not really all that different. We're both trying to make it through this life, and I like knowing we're on the same side." Technically, Dex knew he and Katie couldn't totally be on the same side until she trusted her life to Christ, but he did feel they'd become a lot closer that afternoon. "So, are you up for another helping of dessert?"

"Sure, but then I'm gonna have to get going. I told Mr. Brinker I'd work tomorrow and Saturday; I have to clock in at 8:00."

Dex tried to hide his disappointment. He hated the thought of her working a second job as well as taking evening classes, but he knew he had no right telling her what to do. "Then let's get to it. We'd better hurry before Brady and Bruce eat everything up."

A short time later, in Dex's Jeep, they neared the street where Katie lived—the street where he'd have to drop her off and say good-bye until Monday morning. He was dreading it, partially because he didn't want to say good-bye and partially because he knew it would be awkward. They hadn't actually been on a date, but it sure felt like one. He knew he wanted to treat it as such, but that was impossible at this point.

As he feverishly tried to figure out how to end the evening in a comfortable manner, Katie asked a question.

"Do you think I could ask a favor of you? You can say no if you want to."

His curiosity was piqued. "Sure, ask away."

"I need some help moving my mattress. I could do it myself, but it would be a lot easier if I had someone else."

"I'd be glad to help. Why do you need to move it?"

"I bought a new bed skirt the other day, and I'd like to put it on. Mr. Carraway, the man who owns the building, is usually available to help, but he's been out of town this week and won't be back until Sunday. I thought since you were here, maybe you wouldn't mind and I could get it taken care of." She smiled at him hopefully.

He pulled up in front of her apartment. "Then let's get to it. But hold on, I'll get the door for you." He got out and made his way to the other side of his Cherokee.

"Here we go." Dex held the door open. "Lead the way."

He followed her up the stairs and waited as she unlocked the door. He felt a little strange, but he'd already promised to help her.

Katie stepped inside and flipped on the light. The place was tidy and that didn't surprise him.

"Hey, you've done some more painting in here." He pointed toward a row of ivy stenciled on each cabinet door in the kitchen. "And the cabinets are white now. Didn't they use to be dark brown?"

"Yeah, I was ready for a change."

"It looks great. I guess I was in such a hurry this morning when I picked you up that I didn't even notice. It looks like a little cottage in here."

Katie smiled widely. "Do you really think so? Because that's exactly the look I was going for."

Dex's heart melted at the pride he saw on her face and heard reflected in her voice. If only she knew what she did to him! "Oh, yeah, this looks really good. I keep telling you, Katie, you've got a knack. You really should consider studying decorating." His eyes brightened as a thought struck him. "You know, Katie, you'd be a great asset down at the office if you were certified in interior design. Clients would be thrilled to get their architectural plans and their design plans all in one place. The larger firms do it all the time. I never considered before now that we could do that, too."

Katie looked doubtful. "Do you really mean that?"

"Sure I do. It's a great idea! We don't have the money right now to pay a decorator, but by the time you finish school, I bet we will. I'd have to run it by Kevin, of course, but I don't see why he wouldn't go for it."

Seating herself on a kitchen chair Katie slowly shook her head. "I've never even considered something like that."

"Now you sound like me when I first had the idea to start my own business. Just because it's a new idea doesn't mean it's a bad one."

"I suppose so." Katie scratched her head, clearly thinking through the possibility. "A business degree always seemed so safe to me; there'll always be jobs of some sort available in business. I don't know, Dex."

He sat down across from her at the little table. "You were the one telling me just this afternoon how you wanted to take risks, remember—the whole 'jumping higher' thing?"

She giggled. "I did say that, didn't I?"

"Yes."

"I will think about it, but now—"

"I know. You need my help moving a mattress. Take me to it!"

Katie laughed. "Follow me, it's right through here."

Dex felt he was invading Katie's privacy by being in her bedroom, and he certainly didn't like the direction his mind started moving when he saw her bed. However, he appreciated the opportunity to see more of Katie's handiwork. Her room was a clear reflection of her—clean, crisp, and fresh.

The quilt on the bed boasted large pale yellow and white stripes with dainty rows of ivy and delicate pink roses. Lots of fluffy white pillows adorned the simple white wicker headboard. Hanging on the wall above the bed was an old white window and shutters that Katie explained she found at a garage sale for ten dollars, brought home, cleaned and stuck on the wall. On each side of the window display was a whitewashed sconce with a fat pink candle on top and little candle rings of baby pink rosebuds. A cascade of white tulle hanging from the ceiling framed the bed on both sides of the headboard. Everything was beautifully set off by the pale green of the walls.

"This is beautiful—like something out of a magazine."

Her laughter filled the room. "That's because it is, silly! I told you that all I do is copy stuff I see in pictures. I change things here and there, but mostly I steal someone else's ideas."

Dex shook his head. "No, if it were that simple, everybody would have showcase houses. But they don't because it takes a certain kind of talent."

"Maybe so, but right now I'd settle for putting my new bed skirt on." She began pulling the pillows off the bed and on a whim threw one at Dex.

"Hey, what was that for!"

"Oh, I don't know. Everyone at your house is always throwing pillows at each other." She looked at him innocently. "Just thought I'd try it out."

"Yeah, and you were worried you wouldn't fit in with my family. Maybe you fit in too well! Now you'll be abusing me like all the other women in my life!"

"Oh, poor baby. I think your mom was right. You do need to do some manual labor."

Dex grabbed the quilt and began pulling it off the bed so he could more easily grab hold of the mattress. He continually muttered something about demanding and ungrateful females, but Katie saw the smile he was trying to hide.

As Dex put his jeep into drive and pulled out, he marveled at Janie's insight. She had said she thought this was going to be a special day. And it had been—from the way he'd opened up to Katie to all that he'd learned about her to the warm hug she'd given him just before he left her apartment. He especially liked that last part. But Dexter Matheson was no fool; he knew they had a long way to go before their relationship went beyond friendship. He also knew, even though it was Thanksgiving and he hated to bother his pastor at home, he desperately needed to talk to Andy Powell.

30

KATIE STARED INTO HER TEACUP as the morning sunlight flooded the table. Unfortunately, her mood didn't match the weather. She couldn't shake off last night's dream. She had learned to look forward to Kaleo's nocturnal visits; but nothing could have prepared her for the visions permeating her subconscious just hours earlier.

She had been sitting on a bench outside the university's student union building peacefully studying when she was disturbed by a soft moaning sound. Looking around, she saw nothing, but she could still hear the muffled plea for help. Deciding to investigate, she walked toward the sound. Then, just as she reached the shade of a large oak tree, a tiny baby suspended by a rope dropped down in front of her. That vision alone was unsettling; but the child was badly mangled, missing one of its arms and one of its legs. It was a little girl. Katie turned around and ran. She didn't make it very far before she almost ran over Kaleo.

"Oh, Kaleo, help me!" she cried. "Make it go away!"

The gray wolf shook his furry head from side to side. "I can't."

"But why? If you are my friend, you'll help me and keep that . . . that thing from haunting me! Please!"

"I can't. It's part of you." Kaleo then turned and left, abandoning Katie to her own self-discovery. Thankfully, Katie had awakened then and been able to postpone the inevitable meeting with the crying infant. But she knew the infant would be back.

After waking Katie hadn't dared try to go back to sleep. It chilled her to think of returning to the horrific nightmare. Even a steaming cup of tea wasn't enough to warm her. Katie recalled how her mom had always attempted to escape her sorrows in a brown liquid much more potent than earl grey tea. "Maybe there's something to that," muttered Katie; but even as she spoke the words, she knew her agony was inescapable. Drinking, running, denying—none of those defense mechanisms were strong enough to combat the force now relentlessly pursuing Katie Montgomery. It was the force of Truth, and Katie knew it. She shuddered.

As she washed her cup and breakfast plate and threw away the barely-eaten English muffin, she lamented the fact that it was Saturday. Rushing to work—and spending time with her handsome boss—would have provided a diversion from her tormenting thoughts.

But Katie and her mother were going shopping together, which they hadn't done in ages. Katie wished she had the kind of relationship that Dex and Janie had with God, if He existed. She could use some divine wisdom in her relationship with her mom.

The waitress brought the lunches Daria and Katie had ordered. Katie had insisted on taking her mom out to eat. It was Katie's form of peace offering, since she had declined to spend Thanksgiving with her. She selected a quaint little café. Katie figured it was time Daria was treated to something besides fast food.

"Oh, Katie, this looks delicious. You must be doing well at your job to bring me here!" bubbled Daria. Katie wondered at her mom's childlike reaction. Had no one ever treated her to a nice meal out? Probably not. *She's never had anyone make her feel special. That must be why she clings to the memory of my father. As awful as he was to her, at least he would write and sing songs for her. Nobody else has done anything except use her up.* The thought bothered Katie more than she wanted to admit, and she struggled to hide her emotions. She took a long, careful look at her mother and saw the familiar hardness. Hidden beneath the cynical eyes and heavy make-up, an attractive woman over forty desperately wanted to be loved, but Daria had given up on that dream. Katie wanted to cry.

Katie shook her head and determined this would not be the last time she took her mom out for lunch. Now, she tried to re-focus on her mom's chatter.

"—and I can't get over that apartment! You were right, Katie; I didn't even recognize it. I'm surprised Mr. Carraway agreed to let you do all that."

"Well, I had to promise to re-paint the walls when I move out, and I'll have to pay for the paint. But I figured it was worth it to make the apartment feel like my own home. Besides, I've had fun doing it."

"You sure have a knack for it," complimented Daria around a bite of vegetable lasagna.

"That's exactly what Dex said. In fact . . ." Katie hesitated. "He thinks I ought to study interior design."

Daria coughed and grabbed a drink of cola. "Whatever would you do that for? You'd have no future in that career."

"I don't know why you'd say that, Mama. I'm doing really well at the office now."

"Yeah, but that's clerical stuff. It has nothing to do with decorating." Daria slumped back in the soft booth. "You simply don't have the right pedigree to tell rich ladies how to fix up their fancy houses."

Katie looked uncomfortable and Daria quickly added, "It's nothing personal. I'm sure you'd do a great job. I'm just afraid nobody would give you a chance. People have radar. They sense where you come from. You might fool them for a while, but the truth catches up with you, kiddo."

"Maybe, you're right, Mama. But Dex thinks I'd do well at it, and he should know. He said that in a couple of years, after I got my degree, they could hire me at DesignLink."

Daria peered at her daughter. "Are you sleeping with him?"

Katie almost spit out the cola she had just sipped. "What!

Where did that question come from?"

"Don't look so mortified. I know how guys are. They'll tell you nice things like that when you're sleeping with them, but it's all a big game."

With her elbows on the table, Katie rested her head in her hands for a moment. Finally she straightened and looked her mother in the eyes. "Mama, you don't know Dex. He's not like that." She dared to add, "He's not like my father."

Daria's eyes darkened. "So you are sleeping with him?"

"No!" Katie almost shouted. She regained her composure and tried again to make her mother understand. "No, Mama, I'm not. Dex wouldn't do that to somebody. He's not that way; he's the . . . the . . . well, he's definitely the nicest guy I've ever met. And he treats me with so much respect. Nobody's ever done that before." Katie became lost in her own thoughts, almost unaware of her mother's presence. She had never articulated her feelings about her boss to anybody before. "When I'm with him I get the feeling he truly cares about me with no ulterior motive. He's not like Eric or Kristin, who only looked out for themselves. And his sister is different, too. She's the best friend I've ever had. I wish you wouldn't judge them." Katie looked down. "I judged them before I got to know them. But I was wrong, Mama, I was wrong." She looked up, her eyes pleading. "I believe in them; they've been nothing but good to me. I know they're not perfect. Dex went out of his way to prove that to me so I wouldn't think he was some kind of saint . . . but still . . . I've never met anybody like him or his family."

Daria reached over and awkwardly grabbed her daughter's hand. "My sweet little girl, you always did try to see the good in people. I'm just afraid you're gonna get hurt. Don't be a fool, sweetheart."

Katie stared at her mother's hand. She silently wondered how many grocery items those fingers had checked. There was nothing wrong with checking groceries for a living, if a person were content with that. But Katie knew she never would be, and she knew Daria wasn't, either. But Daria had convinced herself there was no hope for change; the risks involved were too great. Her heart couldn't stand another crushing disappointment. But Katie wasn't Daria. More and more she was beginning to realize this; now if she could just get her mother to realize it as well.

Katie gently pulled her hand away. "My choices have to be my choices, Mama."

"I know, sweetie, but you can learn from my mistakes."

"I feel more hopeful now than I have since . . . since . . . high school." Katie almost choked on the last few words.

"That's just my point. You made a lot of sacrifices to go to college and make a future for yourself. You worked and studied hard and . . . and . . . you . . ."

"I had an abortion."

Daria's head jerked up and she met her daughter's steely gaze. She spoke in monotone. "Yes, you did. You did all those things so you could go to school and get a business degree. It's what you said you always wanted."

"She would be four years old now. Did you know that?"

"Um . . . who . . . who are you talking about?"

Katie's face was deadpan. "My daughter."

"What . . . why would you say that? How . . . how do you know . . . you don't have a daughter."

"No, I don't. Not now. But I did."

"You're not making any sense, Katie." Daria smoothed the napkin on her lap. "If you're referring to your . . . to the . . . well, you know."

"Abortion, Mama. The word is abortion. We agreed that the best thing for me would be to get rid of my little girl so I could get a business degree."

Daria glanced around self-consciously. In a hushed voice, she asked, "Why do you keep calling it a little girl? You had your . . . you had it so early that the pregnancy hadn't even advanced to the point where it was a, a—"

"Baby. The word you're looking for now is baby. And I know—I'm not sure how, but I know—it was a little girl. She would be four years old."

"What's done is done. So why keep rehashing it?"

Defeat rested on Katie's face. "I don't know, Mama." She sounded tired. "I suppose it's been on my mind lately. Maybe considering changing my plans has made me go back and re-think the choices I've made in my life."

"You've made good choices. Don't torture yourself."

Katie locked eyes with her mother. "I'm not sure *all* of my choices have been good."

"Katie, it's natural to wonder 'what if this' or 'what if that,' but all that really matters is the here and now. If you want to chase some pipe dream concerning this decorating thing, then go ahead. But I hate to see you waste your hard-earned money on classes that may not work out for you. And I certainly don't want to see a man, no matter how nice he is, break your heart and cause you any pain. You deserve better."

"What about my daughter? Didn't she deserve a chance?"

"Katie, stop this! You'll have children someday."

"Maybe it's not about me, Mama. Maybe I shouldn't try to make the world revolve around me and my desires." Katie suddenly had the need to unburden her mind of all the nagging doubts and thoughts that had been building up for the past four years. "I keep thinking that maybe I'm trying so hard to control my life, when perhaps it's not mine to control."

"What are you talking about?"

Katie twisted her hands in her lap and searched the small café as if the right words to say might be suspended in mid-air. "I know it sounds crazy, but I've been thinking about God a lot lately. I know you've never put much stock in religion, but some people do. Some people base every decision they make on what they think God would have them do."

"Well," said Daria in a clipped tone, "I think it's a bunch of nonsense. I'm not saying there's not some power that made the earth and got the ball rolling. But I don't see how it has anything to do with you or me. I do know you've got a life to live, and there's no sense spending it looking over your shoulder to see if some god is happy with you or not."

"It does sound far-fetched, doesn't it?" She strove to put levity in her voice. "You know me, Mama. I've always had a melancholy streak. I'm sorry if I've spoiled our afternoon."

Daria reached over and patted her daughter's hand. "It's not spoiled at all. I say we put all of this behind us and go do some shopping! Maybe we could find you a new outfit."

"Okay." Katie pasted a smile on her face as the waitress brought their check. "I need to stop by the office for a minute, though. I left my history book there yesterday, and I want to do some studying this weekend. It's not far. Do you mind?"

Daria smiled brightly. "Not at all. It'll give me a chance to see where you work. I love telling the gals at the store that my little girl works at an architectural firm."

In no time at all Katie was unlocking the door to the Design-Link office. She flicked on the light in the waiting room. "Well, this is it!" She made a sweeping gesture around the small room.

"Oh, this is definitely more comfortable than a grocery store. Is this your desk?"

"Yeah. I like to call it command central." She laughed.

"Katie, is that you?"

"What? Dex? What are you doing here?"

There was Dex leaning against the wall and grinning. "Well, I own the place. What are you doing here?"

"Oh, I'm . . . um . . . I . . . left my history book here yesterday, so I just came by to pick it up."

"And you must be Katie's mother. I'm Dexter Matheson." He crossed the room in two long strides, extending his hand to Daria.

Katie mumbled an introduction.

Daria studied the handsome young man before her, sizing him up. Then she placed her hand in Dex's.

"Well, it's nice to meet you, Miss Montgomery. I must say your daughter is quite an asset to our little company here. I don't know how we ever managed without her."

"I certainly do thank you for giving my daughter the opportunity. I know she enjoys it."

"That's good to hear. So, what are you two ladies up to today?"

Daria raised her chin slightly. "Katie treated me to a wonderful lunch; I don't know when I've had better. But then, she's always been like that, doing nice things for everybody. I don't know what I ever did to deserve such a terrific kid."

"Mama," mumbled Katie.

Daria walked over to her daughter and put an arm around her. "Now, don't be embarrassed, Katie. I haven't seen you in a while, so you'll have to let me brag on you a little bit. I've missed you, that's all."

Katie lowered her head. She knew her mother was playing tug of war with Dex, and she was the rope. *Please, Mama, don't do or say anything foolish.*

"Miss Montgomery, I want to thank you for letting us have Katie on Thanksgiving. My family is extremely fond of her." He glanced at Katie. "I know it must have been difficult to be away from her."

Daria fumbled with the button on her coat. "Yes, well, Katie's a big girl now and can make her own decisions. But I did miss her."

Katie had to change the subject. "You never did tell me what you're doing here on a Saturday."

Dex waved his hand toward his office. "Oh, I'm working on some designs for Dennis Grayson, the guy with the mission downtown."

"Oh, yeah. How's it going?"

"Pretty well. Dennis has been working on getting donations. I think I've finally got an idea of how much money we have to work with." Dex suddenly snapped his fingers in the air. "Katie, there's something I've been meaning to show you. If you have a few minutes, could you come take a look?"

"Um . . . I don't know. We were just stopping by and—"

"I don't mind, Katie," interrupted Daria. "Maybe you could show me where the little girl's room is."

"Sure, it's right through that second door." Dex pointed.

Daria slipped past the two younger people. "If I get through before you, Katie, I'll just look around a little if that's all right."

"Sure, make yourself at home." Dex looked at Katie and nodded his head toward his office. "After you."

As soon as they were in his office and Katie knew her mother was in the restroom, she turned to Dex and began to apologize in a hushed voice. "Dex, I am so sorry for the way my mom behaved out there. She's still jealous that I went to your house for Thanksgiving, and she wanted to make sure you thought everything was wonderful between us, and . . ."

Dex walked over, squeezed her shoulders, and looked directly into her eyes. "It's okay, Katie. Really, it is. It's no big deal." He had a legitimate reason for asking her into his office. He motioned for her to come around to his side of the desk so she could see the layouts he had just printed. "Here, look at this." He pointed to the perimeter of the drawing. "This is the space we have to work with. Now, what I'm planning on doing is designing a wall that goes like this . . ."

He continued explaining his plans to Katie. So engrossed were the two of them that neither was aware of Daria standing in the hallway listening to every word.

"So what exactly do you want me to do?" asked Katie.

Dex leaned back in his chair and placed his hands behind his head. He looked up at Katie. "You're always telling me you're the queen of budget-decorating. Well, that's what we need here."

"What kind of look do you need?"

"This section right here is going to be a nursery for preschoolers. These kids get very little stimulation at home. Many of them are neglected. They need lots of bright colors and something cozy and inviting, so it feels like a home." Dex leaned back in his chair again. "Dennis really wants to avoid an institutional look. He's trying to convince these kids that even though they may not have much of a family at home, the House of Hope is the second-best thing."

Katie considered several options. "I think we'd need lots of soft materials: furry rugs, cloth toys. Pictures of animals, too. And plants. Living things that remind you that life goes on even when everything seems black and dark. And I think you're right about the bright colors. It's gotta be fun and energetic for kids that young."

Dex beamed. "So I take it you're interested in helping?"

She looked at him. Not until then did she realize how caught up she had been in her own thoughts. She laughed. "I guess so."

Dex sobered. "This is a ministry project. I'm not getting paid for it, which means you won't either."

Katie's eyes widened. "I want to help. I'll make time. I like the idea of being able to make a difference."

"Great! I was hoping you'd feel that way." He stood up. "I'll talk with you more about it on Monday, but you can go ahead and start putting some ideas together, or should I say looking through magazines and stealing ideas!"

Katie punched his arm. "Hey, you get what you pay for!"

Dex looked at her and grew serious. "Sometimes we get a lot more than we ever dreamed of. Thanks for agreeing to help."

"You're welcome," replied Katie softly, suddenly embarrassed.

"I'll bet your mom is waiting for you. I don't want to hold you two up any longer. I'll walk you out."

Daria darted back to the lobby and tried to act as if she had been there all along. She'd never seen Katie so intense. And the way Dex had been looking at her! He had such tenderness in his eyes! Could Katie have been right about him? Could he be different than other men Daria knew? The thought frightened her because it would mean she would have to re-think her entire life's philosophy. But wouldn't it be worth it if her daughter could actually be happy, really happy.

31

❊

"Katie?"

No response. Dex tried again, a little louder. "Katie?"

Still no response. His secretary was vacuuming the lobby, but she should have heard him that second time. Then he noticed the headphones covering her ears. She was softly singing along. He stopped to listen. She had a nice voice. *Maybe she takes after her father.* He reached out and gently touched her.

Katie jerked around. "Oh, Dex! You scared me!"

He held his hands up to plead innocence. "Sorry, I didn't mean to." But he couldn't stop the grin that was forming. "Wow, I didn't know a person's eyes could get that big!"

"Very funny!" Katie clicked the vacuum cleaner off. "Did you want something, or do you just get your kicks going around and frightening unsuspecting women?"

Dex looked guilty. "You caught me; what can I say?"

"You don't have to say anything, but I sure wish I had a pillow handy right about now. Then maybe I could get even with you!"

Dex laughed. "One afternoon with my family and a perfectly nice girl is corrupted forever!"

"Well, worse things could happen, I suppose," mumbled Katie as she began to wind up the vacuum cord.

"Were you finished? I just had a quick question."

"I was about through. Besides, I hate to vacuum."

"Is that why you had the radio on?"

Her face clouded. "Yeah, I guess so."

Dex smiled in sympathy. "Well, maybe before too long we'll have money in the budget to hire a cleaning crew."

Katie grinned. "That'd be nice, but really, I don't mind."

Dexter couldn't imagine why she blushed.

She changed the subject. "What did you need to ask me?"

"Oh, yeah. Kevin called. He's having lunch with Rachel. Anyway, they're going to pick up some tickets to a Wayne Watson concert. I mentioned a while back that I'd like to go, so he was calling to see how many tickets I wanted. Janie's going and her friend Micki—you know, the one we went out with after Kevin's wedding. Well, I was thinking that since you like music so much, maybe you'd like to go as well."

Katie looked at Dex uncomprehendingly. "Micki's going?"

"Yeah, she's a big Wayne Watson fan; and since it's a Friday night concert, she's gonna drive up from Northwestern."

"Then maybe I better not go."

"I don't understand." He was befuddled. "I'd really like you to come. I'll pay for your ticket if that's the problem."

"No, that's not a problem."

"But I want to; I don't mind." Dex spoke the words before realizing he had done so. He wasn't so sure Andy Powell would approve. This was sounding more and more like he was asking Katie for a date.

"It's not about money, Dex." Katie began twisting her hands and plopped down in one of the lobby chairs. "I think Micki might enjoy it better if I'm not there."

Dex wondered if he had cobwebs in his brain because none of this was making any sense to him. "I don't know why you'd say that. Janie's gonna be there."

Katie looked helplessly at her boss. "But Janie is your sister."

"So?"

"So, she's not a threat."

Slowly, understanding dawned on Dex's face. He carefully

asked, "You think Micki's interested in me?"

"Oh, Dex, if you could see your face right now! How is it that you can be so smart about business and so completely in the dark when it comes to relationships? . . . Dex, I didn't mean that. I'm . . . I'm sorry."

Dex hadn't missed the emotions rolling over Katie's face. He wanted to reach out and pull her to him and tell her it was okay. He wanted to tell her Micki was the farthest thing from his mind. He wanted to tell her that all the pain he went through with Ally would be worth it if he could just have her, Katie, in his life.

Instead, he said, "It's okay. You don't have to walk on eggshells around me." He chuckled in self-mockery. "When it comes to relationships, I am pretty slow. Ally had a crush on me for a long time before I ever noticed." He cocked his head toward his secretary. "So you really think Micki likes me?"

Katie nodded dumbly. "I picked up some pretty strong signals after the wedding." She continued tentatively. "She's an attractive girl. You two would look good together."

Dex closed his eyes and grimaced. When he opened them they were trained right on Katie. "Ally and I looked good together, too."

Katie stared down at her hands and mumbled another apology.

Dex slid into the chair next to hers. "Look, Katie, I'm not interested in Micki at all. She's nice, pretty, and smart. Maybe I should be, but I'm not. I just know that Janie called and invited her because she's a friend and because she's a Wayne Watson fan. I just know I was hoping you'd come. I think you'll enjoy it."

"Who is this guy anyway? I've never heard of him."

Dex didn't want to scare her off, but he didn't want to lie either. "He's a Christian recording artist. He plays the piano and guitar. Mostly he sings songs about his life experience as a believer, you know, how he sees the world and such. He's a real talented guy. I've seen him several times and never been disappointed." *But I will be this time if you don't agree to go.*

"When is the concert?"

"It's a week from Friday, 7:00 p.m. We'll probably leave straight from here, grab a bite to eat, and head for the church."

"Church? I thought this was a concert."

Dex's shoulders slumped. "It is, but it's held in a church, that's all. The church is in downtown Madison, which is why there probably wouldn't be time to go home and still make it to the concert before it starts. Besides, if we get there a little early we'll get better seats. And you know Janie, she's gonna want to be as close to the front as possible." He eyed her again. "Will you come?"

She smiled. "Yeah, I'll come. It might be fun."

Dex stood and helped Katie to her feet. "Great, I'll call Kevin and tell him to pick up an extra ticket." As he turned and walked away, Dex let a wide smile stretch over his mouth. He also let a prayer escape from his heart beseeching God to use the music and testimony of Wayne Watson to carefully and lovingly break through Katie's guarded heart.

❄ ❄ ❄

Daria sat in the café booth, studying the pictures on the wall, and trying to appear calm. *You can do this, girl.*

A small woman wearing a two-piece chocolate brown suit walked in and looked around. It had to be Lydia Matheson. Katie had described her as a petite, sophisticated woman with shining eyes. *I wonder how Katie would describe me. Certainly not petite or sophisticated. Maybe statuesque, voluptuous, daring, wild, sad, phony, hardened?* Daria didn't like the direction her thoughts were going. Suddenly she didn't like anything about herself or her life at all.

Daria took a deep breath and waved at the lovely lady standing by the door.

The lady smiled brightly and made her way to Daria's booth. "Hello, Daria. I'm Lydia. I'm so glad to meet you."

"Yeah, me, too." Daria shook the hand Lydia offered, hoping

her palm wasn't embarrassingly sweaty.

"I'm glad you called and suggested we get together. We adore your daughter. You've done one terrific job with her."

Daria looked down and began fingering the silverware. "Katie is a great kid, but I didn't have much to do with it. She practically raised herself."

Lydia studied the woman before her. "Well, God is pretty wise in putting people together. He must have known the two of you would make a good team." Lydia smiled and took a sip of water.

Daria was astounded. *Katie wasn't kidding, was she? This lady hasn't been here ten seconds and she's already brought God into the conversation.*

"Do you come here a lot, Daria?" inquired Lydia.

"What? Oh, no, this is only my second time. Katie brought me here for lunch last week." Somehow she didn't think she should call up someone like Lydia Matheson and say, "Hey, how about meeting me at McDonalds?"

"I'll bet that was nice. I've wanted to try this place."

"I'm glad you like it." Daria buried her nose in the menu.

"Daria, do you mind if I go ahead and ask you why you wanted to get together? Perhaps we could both relax and enjoy lunch together if we got it out in the open." She smiled.

Daria laid the menu aside. "I don't want my daughter hurt."

"I'm afraid I don't understand what you mean."

Daria spoke evenly, trying to keep the accusation out of her voice. "I don't want your son to hurt my daughter. Katie hasn't had an easy time. She likes to see the good in people; but she's been hurt before, and I don't want it to happen again."

"How could my son hurt Katie?"

In the face of Lydia Matheson Daria saw genuine confusion. Could it be that she wasn't aware of her son's feelings? From everything Katie had said, the Mathesons were a very close family—they did all those things that most families never do like talk to each other, pray together, celebrate holidays together. So how could this woman not know how her son felt about Katie?

Daria cleared her throat. "I am under the impression that Dex is interested in Katie. I saw them together myself on Saturday, and the look in his eyes was more than casual." Seeing the shock on Lydia's face, Daria quickly reassured her. "Oh, I know they're not really seeing each other or anything, but I do know Dexter has a lot of influence over my daughter."

"What are you worried about, then?"

"Oh, come on. We're both grown women. Katie's an attractive girl and your son is more than handsome. He's intelligent and on his way to a successful career. Somebody like that isn't gonna stay interested in someone like my daughter."

"Whatever you are accusing Dexter of, Miss Montgomery, it's totally unwarranted. He would never intentionally hurt anybody."

"Look, I've never gotten involved in my daughter's affairs before. Like I said, I haven't exactly been the best mother in the world. The only reason I'm meddling now is because I get the feeling Katie might do something rash." Tears formed in her eyes. "Katie deserves better than what she's always had. I . . . I can't stand to think of her . . . getting hurt." She choked out the last few words.

❋ ❋ ❋

Lydia reached for Daria's hand, and Daria gave in to the sobs that had been fighting their way to the surface. The waitress coming to take their order headed back to the kitchen.

"Please understand, my son was raised to put other people's needs ahead of his own. And I know he thinks the world of Katie."

Daria sniffed rather loudly. "Well, he might not mean to, but Katie's bound to fall for him. Can't you see that? He'll care for her for a while until somebody else comes along—somebody richer or prettier or from a better family. Katie'll just be a stone around his neck and he'll cut her loose. But by that time Katie will have fallen so hard for him it'll literally cut her to pieces when he breaks it off." The tears returned, but Daria kept going. "Her heart is gonna get stomped and she'll be all alone and frightened and feel like she has no reason for living."

Daria fervently clutched Lydia's hand. "Please don't let that happen. Please tell your son to leave her alone."

Lydia grasped the hand clutching hers. Lydia was at least ten years older than Daria. Her voice was motherly, soothing and filled with compassion.

"You must have been hurt terribly, Daria. I'm so sorry." Lydia rose and walked over to Daria's side of the booth and scooted next to her. She put her arm around her and simply rocked her, every once in a while offering a comforting word.

Finally Daria raised up and blew her nose on the napkin. "I'm sorry," she sniffed. "I don't know what came over me."

With a soft laugh, Lydia moved back to her side of the booth. "Don't apologize for being a mother! Parenting can bring on emotions you didn't even know you had!"

"Katie said you have five kids." Daria dabbed her eyes.

"Yes. But whether you have five or one, the feelings are the same. These little people come into your life, turn it upside down, and slowly break your heart into tiny little pieces. But God is good; He sustains us through the tough times, gives us wisdom in the doubting times, and comforts us in the scary times." Lydia laughed at herself. "Listen to me! I sound like I'm quoting from a book. I guess you can tell I've thought a lot about this subject, can't you? But I do know one thing. You've got a mother's eyes, Daria Montgomery. And I also know that anything you said today was out of love and concern for your daughter." She reached for Daria's hand one more time. "And I want you to know I'm on your side."

Daria studied the face of this older woman, so unlike her own. Within seconds she knew this woman could be trusted. Swallowing her pride, she confessed, "You were right. Somebody much like your son swept me off my feet over twenty years ago. He was tall and handsome with a head full of dreams. Unfortunately, I didn't fit into those dreams." Daria stared out the window for a moment. "I never have gotten over him." She chuckled in self-disdain. "That's pretty pitiful, isn't it? Here I am a woman over forty who hasn't come to terms with a break-up from twenty-some years ago." Daria rifled through her purse for a cigarette.

"You mind if I smoke?"

"No. Go ahead."

Daria did, blowing smoke out through her nose and mouth. "I needed that. I don't usually smoke, but I can't seem to talk about T.J. without some kind of controlled substance." She tried to laugh at herself, but it sounded phony. "I generally prefer alcohol to cigarettes, but since we're in a public place, I'll try and behave. Katie's always trying to get me to quit."

"Perhaps you've never had a good enough reason."

"I've had a daughter for twenty-three years. You'd think that would be reason enough." She took another drag on the cigarette.

"Children are wonderful, but they can't live your life for you. Mothers have to face their demons by themselves—not even a daughter as terrific as Katie can do that for you."

Daria was intrigued. This lady, despite the fancy outfit and expensive-smelling perfume, sounded like she understood. She wasn't condemning; she was offering an explanation.

"I think maybe I know what you mean. I've had a tough time since I moved to the other side of Madison. I've felt lost and . . . and . . . well, I guess defensive is the word. I've been mad at Katie for not moving with me. I know she's grown up, and it was bound to happen, but . . . I think I've always used her as my security blanket. I was afraid to face life without her." Daria laughed rather loudly. "Now that's funny, isn't it?"

"What do you mean?"

"My life wasn't all that great when Katie was still with me. She's tried to tell me that thousands of times, but I never listened. I'd just keep spouting my world-wise wisdom, trying my best to convince myself I was okay." She paused and stared out the window again. "But now that Katie's not there I don't have anyone to convince, which means I can't convince myself either." She searched around for an ash tray. "Don't tell me we're in the no smoking section."

Lydia slid her glass toward Daria. "Here, this should work."

Daria's eyes teared up again. "Thank you" was all she could manage to say. She let the cigarette fall into the water and watched it begin to disintegrate. Finally, she said, "Katie told me I shouldn't judge you or your family. She said you were really nice. She was right . . . again. Katie's always right."

Lydia smiled. "She's terrific. I've grown fond of her."

"Yeah, but you were right."

"About what, Daria?"

"About Katie not being reason enough for me to change. Here I sit, a middle-aged drinking, smoking grocery checker. Not a pretty picture, is it?"

Lydia leaned over the table. "I'm not nearly as concerned about your age or your compulsive habits as I am about your heart."

"My heart?"

"Because until you've had a change of heart, nothing else really matters. And nobody can do that for you—not your daughter, not a boyfriend, not a haunting memory . . . nothing."

Daria grunted her reply. "So there's no hope for me."

Lydia's eyes brightened. "Oh, I didn't say that; not at all. I merely said no *person* can help you. Your heart and soul need to be taken care of by the One who created them. We may have some control over our bodies and our minds; but our hearts, that's a different story. That's where healing begins."

"You're talking about God, aren't you?" Daria's shoulders slumped. "Katie said you were religious people. She's even been thinking about some of that stuff, too."

"I suppose some people would call it a religious thing."

"That's what it is, ain't it?"

Lydia cocked her head. "Well, *religion* makes it sound like something you do because you have to as opposed to something that is a part of your life, of your very existence. It's much deeper than a simple spiritual exercise."

"Well, that's good, 'cause I hate to exercise."

Lydia laughed heartily.

※ ※ ※

Lydia softly knocked on the office door, then gently pushed it open. Her husband's face broke into a grin as he motioned her in.

"Hi! Got a minute?"

"For you I've got at least two—maybe more if you've come bringing good news. If you're here to complain, I'm afraid I won't be able to help you."

Lydia looked sympathetic. "Bad day, huh?"

Everett leaned back in his chair and put his hands behind his head. "I guess you could say that. The problem is nobody wants to do anything on my timetable. I've been on the phone with builders, contractors, you name it. This project is way behind schedule and I'm gonna be left holding the bill." He grunted. "Please tell me you've got some good news."

Lydia smiled widely. "I can do better than that. I've got great news!" She sat in the chair opposite her husband. "I had lunch with Daria Montgomery, Katie's mother, and she professed to believe and trust Christ! Right in the restaurant!"

Everett's eyebrows shot up. "Really, just like that?"

"Oh, Everett. This poor woman has been carrying around grief and heartbreak for over twenty years. She was so ready to release it; she just didn't know anyone wanted to take it from her."

"So what made her open up to you?"

Lydia looked thoughtful for a moment. "I think she was afraid the same thing was going to happen to Katie, and that terrified her. She's convinced Katie's gonna fall for Dex and that he'll end up breaking her heart just like a guy named T.J. did with her."

Everett rubbed his chin thoughtfully.

"I told her Dex would never do anything like that; but she's a mother, and she's concerned. Maybe Katie has a crush on Dex."

Everett reached for his wife's hands. "I can't tell you how glad I am. You said you felt God calling you to do something in Katie's life. You've been faithful to that call. What better thing could happen to Katie than this, other than her own salvation?"

"You're right. But I'm gonna pray harder than ever for Katie."

Everett thought how interested his son would be in these recent events concerning the mother of his secretary. He thought about calling him right then but remembered that Dex was leaving the office early to go to a concert. The good news would have to wait.

32

✳

KATIE EYED HER BOSS surreptitiously. He looked great in his khaki pants and long-sleeved denim shirt. The more she got to know Dexter Matheson, the more handsome he became.

Katie glanced at her own outfit which she had bought on impulse two days before, a stylish black and maroon plaid skirt and cropped maroon sweater with black piping. The outfit was the type Memphis Blue would go for. Girls bought new clothes for dates all the time, but Katie kept reminding herself that tonight was not a date. Just friends.

By late afternoon Friday Katie couldn't help wondering if she'd made a mistake spending her hard-earned money on the not-exactly-cheap garments. Dex had not even casually mentioned that she looked nice. Katie turned back to the filing cabinet and tried to push the silly thoughts from her mind.

"So, are you looking forward to tonight?"

Katie spun round, face to face with the man who occupied her thoughts. "Oh, yeah. Thanks again for inviting me."

"No problem. I figure we can leave in an hour. Janie's gonna meet us at Ruby Tuesday's for an early dinner. I'll never make it through the concert if I don't eat something."

Katie grinned. "Yeah, I saw you pack it away on Thanksgiving. It's a wonder you don't weigh 400 pounds!"

Dex leaned on the filing cabinet. "High metabolism."

"Lucky you." Katie closed the file drawer. "I guess I'll just follow you to the restaurant."

Dex cleared his throat. "I've been thinking, Katie. Why don't you ride with me? I don't want you to have to drive by yourself; it'll be late by the time we're finished."

"I don't mind, really, as long as I have someone to follow. I hate driving to unfamiliar places at night."

"Well, that settles it. Since I know the way, you can ride with me. I can bring you back here to get your car after the concert. Then I'll follow you to your place just to make sure you get there okay."

"You don't have to do that. I drive home from school twice a week at night."

"It's Friday night, and I'd feel better if I followed you. Lots of people party on the weekends. No need to take any chances."

Katie smiled in acquiescence. "Guess I can't change your mind."

"Nope."

"Okay, we'll do it your way."

"All right, then." Dex slapped the top of the filing cabinet. "I'll just get a little more work done before we go."

"Dex?"

"Yeah?" He spun around.

"I was just wondering . . . is this . . . do I look okay for the concert? I wasn't sure what everybody would be wearing."

"You look great, Katie. Is that a new outfit?"

"Yeah. I forgot to ask if this was a dressy event or not. I thought this could go either way."

"It's really nice." His eyes swept her from head to toe in an appreciative manner. "Some people might be dressed up a little, but most will have on jeans, I'll bet. You'll fit in fine."

Dexter Matheson couldn't have known how sweet those words sounded to Katie.

❄ ❄ ❄

Katie found it difficult not to stare at her friend in the seat next to her.

Janie's eyes were closed and her head was tilted slightly upward. Her hands were spread open, palms facing upward and she was mouthing the words being sung by Wayne Watson: *Almighty, most holy God, faithful through the ages./Almighty, most holy Lord, glorious almighty God.*

Dex, sitting on the other side of Katie, casually dropped his arm behind her and whispered, "Janie worships like she does everything else—with complete abandon."

Katie turned to face her boss, feeling his nearness. She wondered what he meant by "worship."

"And what about you? How do you 'worship'?"

Dex pointed to his chest. "On the inside I do it the same way Janie does. But I'm a little too reserved to show it on the outside. Maybe someday I'll grow up and be like my little sister." He smiled and squeezed Katie's shoulder, then removed his arm.

Katie begrudgingly averted her attention back to the man sitting at the piano. She enjoyed the music but preferred talking to Dex. Mr. Watson told a humorous story about when he and his wife first got married. Katie laughed with the rest of the audience.

Katie enjoyed the evening. She found herself longing for a family like the one Mr. Watson spoke of. Many of the songs he wrote and sang were about his wife and two kids.

Midway through the concert, the lyrics and lilting melody of one of the songs brought about a strange sensation inside Katie. Her entire body tensed as her hands gripped the seat. She fought hard to keep the tears at bay, but she was fearful they would succeed in the end. She longed to close her eyes and give in to the stirrings of her heart, but she knew that, like Dex, she would be much too reserved to do so. Instead, she carefully listened to the words pouring into her soul.

> Smile, make them think you're happy.
> Lie, and say that things are fine.
> And hide that empty longing that you feel.
> Don't ever show it—

Just keep your heart concealed.

Why are the days so lonely?
Where can a heart go free?
And who will dry the tears that no one's seen?
There must be someone to share your silent dreams.

Caught like a leaf in the wind,
Looking for a friend—where can you turn?
Whisper the words of a prayer—
And you'll find him there
Arms open wide—Love in his eyes.

Jesus—He meets you where you are.
Jesus—He heals your secret scars.
All the love you're longing for is
Jesus—the friend of a wounded heart.

How did this Watson guy know about her silent dreams and her secret scars? She had kept her heart concealed, just like the song said. So how did this man know? She really was like a leaf caught in the wind searching for some place to land and grow.

❋ ❋ ❋

Dex watched Katie with concern; but he felt it was best to let her ride out her emotions. This powerful song had lost some of its intensity for him over the years. Now he tried to re-hear it from the ears of an unbeliever. And he knew then that Katie's heart was wounded somehow. He earnestly prayed for the girl he loved.

❋ ❋ ❋

"That was incredible!" gushed Janie as the concert ended.
Dex laughed and reached over to lightly pinch his sister's arm. "Peanut, you look like you've just finished running a marathon."
Janie sighed. "I know; music does that to me. My mind is exploding with all the thoughts going through it." She smiled in

childlike wonder. "God is so amazing, isn't He? I mean, He's interested in every facet of our lives—our relationships, our pain, our triumphs, our failures, our thoughts, our sins—yet He's bigger than all of those things put together! I needed to be reminded of that."

Micki tugged on her friend's sleeve. "I hate to interrupt your sermon, but let's go buy a CD before they're all gone."

Janie perked up. "Hey, if we hurry, I'll bet we can get him to sign it. He usually sticks around for a while."

With that, the two headed toward the lobby. Kevin and Rachel talked to some friends they spotted on the other side of the church. Once again Dex found himself alone with Katie.

"Did you enjoy the concert?" Dex asked.

Katie nodded. "That guy's really talented. He says a lot in his songs. His lyrics are really picturesque."

Dex agreed, pleased. "That's why I appreciate his music. Like Janie said, it makes you think. I've got pretty much all of his CD's if you'd like to borrow them sometime."

"I'm not sure my heart could take it," Katie blurted.

Dex leaned closer. "You don't have to keep your heart tucked away. I'm your friend—Janie and Kevin, too. Don't be afraid to let us into your life."

Katie lowered her eyes.

"I'm not trying to pressure you; I just thought maybe you could use someone to talk to. God created us to need each other, Katie. We need God, and He's always there for us; but He wants us to be there for each other as well. I've got people I lean on all the time."

"Really? Who?" She looked up.

"Janie, for one. And my dad. Then there's my pastor, Andy Powell. When I'm stressed about work, I usually go to Kevin." He smiled that crooked grin. "I have lots of problems so I have to have lots of different people."

Katie smiled.

"What about you, Katie? Who do you go to when you're

hurting?"

Katie shrugged and stared down at her skirt.

Dex pushed. "Don't you have someone to confide in?"

"Sure I do," Katie became defensive. "I have my mom. We don't always get along, but we talk on a regular basis."

"You're mad at me, aren't you?"

Katie's look matched her tone. "No!"

Dex couldn't help grinning. "It's okay to be mad at me. I know I'm being nosy. Just tell me to mind my own business."

She whispered, "I'm not sure I want you to."

Her quiet unsteadiness poured a balm on Dex's longing heart. Although he hated to see her so discontented, he knew sometimes, spiritually speaking, that was the best place to be. As Wayne Watson had sung, *Sometimes a rough and a rocky road/Can lead you to a beautiful place.* Dex found himself selfishly hoping that Katie's beautiful place included him. But what if it didn't?

❄ ❄ ❄

Katie snuggled a little farther into her bed, pulled the pillow closer, and hugged it tightly. She was exhausted but closing her eyes would have been like opening the last Christmas present under the tree—you couldn't wait to see what it was, but you knew that once it was open, the celebration was over.

After the concert the six of them had gone back to Dex's apartment for games and snacks. (Dex insisted it was time to eat again, even though nobody else was hungry.) Katie smiled as she thought of how Dex skillfully avoided Micki's subtle hints while managing to do nothing to hurt her feelings. Katie gathered that by the end of the evening Micki had figured out that Dexter Matheson was not interested in anything other than friendship with her. Katie chastised herself for the joy this information brought. After all, Dex was nothing more than a friend to her as well.

But still, merely being in his apartment caused stirrings in

Katie's heart. Even though six people were present, she felt an intimacy with her boss. His place was a perfect reflection of the man—classic and sophisticated but very comfortable. Dex joked that his mother had done all the decorating, but Katie knew he'd had a large hand in it. His signature was everywhere, from the warm hardwood floors to the cushiony tan and black pencil-striped sofa to the black wrought-iron accent pieces: extremely masculine but softly inviting. The fluffy throw pillows and chenille afghan made Katie feel cozy and warm while the tufted wool area rug softly squished under her toes. The fern colored walls suggested naturalness. There was nothing artificial about her boss.

Or his faith. She supposed she couldn't separate the man from the faith any longer. It permeated every aspect of his being. He apologized if he ever stepped out of line, he put others above himself, he gave God credit for the successes in his life, and he took responsibility for his mistakes. That last one stumped Katie the most. Dexter Matheson never claimed to be perfect; in fact, he was quick to point out his mistakes. But then he moved on. Just how did one do that?

Katie shook her head against the softness of her pillow and tried to think more lighthearted thoughts. She smiled as she remembered the fun they'd had playing *Pictionary* and how Dex complimented her artistic, albeit silly, drawings. Katie laughed and joked with all five of her companions. She couldn't remember when she'd had such an enjoyable evening.

The only damper on the night came when she recalled those lyrics about the wounded heart and the strange tension washed over her again. Katie closed her eyes, pushing it from her mind, determined to have sweet dreams for the first time in a long time.

It didn't happen. Kaleo was back, and so was the mangled baby. It was calling to her, begging her for help. But Katie ran as fast as she could the other way.

She woke up Saturday morning with tears in her eyes.

33

❀

DEX STARED AT THE SMALL, ranch-style house in front of him. The address matched the one Daria Montgomery had given him over the phone. He still got chills when he remembered his father's words that morning: "Your mother led Daria Montgomery to Christ yesterday."

"What?" Dex had exclaimed.

"Just what I said, Son. Apparently Daria called and wanted to speak with your mom about Katie's future."

"Why would she call Mom about that?"

"Well, from what I gather, when Daria met you a couple weeks ago, she sensed that you had feelings for her daughter. She convinced herself Katie was gonna make the same mistake she did years ago and would be left with a broken heart. I guess she figured your mother had some influence over you and could tell you to back off from Katie."

"She saw how I felt about Katie?" Dex rubbed the back of his neck with his free hand and clutched the phone with the other.

Everett laughed softly. "It would appear so."

"Is it that obvious, Dad?"

"Well, maybe to everybody but your mother. I don't think she realizes you're ready to move on."

"What did she think?"

"I'm not sure they got around to talking about it. Apparently that's when Daria broke down and told your mom all about her past; and one thing led to another and Lydia told her Jesus could heal her broken heart. And Daria accepted Jesus there in the restaurant."

"That's incredible! It's also strange, because last night at the concert I know Katie was affected by one of the songs dealing with that same issue. But she wouldn't talk about it."

Then Dex concluded that he needed to go and meet with Daria face to face. At least he would be able to converse with her as a fellow believer. If nothing else, perhaps he could ease her mind about her daughter, assuring her he would do everything in his power to see that she wasn't hurt. And beyond that, he would appeal to One far more powerful than he to protect and guide Katie Montgomery.

Dex had gone to the office and looked in Katie's personnel file to get her mother's phone number. He remembered Katie saying that her mom lived with her boyfriend so that explained why he couldn't find her listed in the phone book. After placing the call, he had been more than relieved to find Daria eager to meet with him. With a prayer for the meeting to go smoothly, Dex set out to chat with his new sister in Christ.

At the front door, Daria looked him up and down appreciatively but cautiously. "Hello. Come on in, please." She stepped back so he could enter. "Lou's out for a while; we have the place to ourselves. Can I get you a drink?"

"Water's fine, thanks."

"Okay, make yourself at home. I'll be right back."

He chose a rather stiff, uncomfortable chair. *This is obviously just a place to hang your hat at the end of the day.* Nothing suggested family warmth. Dex suddenly felt a protectiveness toward this woman he barely knew. She was now a believer; and she was Katie's mother.

"Here you go." Daria was handing Dex a tall glass of ice water.

"Thanks." He took a quick drink.

"Wouldn't you like to take your coat off?"

"Huh, what?"

Daria smiled and pointed toward his jacket. "Your coat. Would you like to take it off while you're inside?"

Now Dex smiled. "I didn't even notice I still had it on. I guess you can tell I'm a little nervous."

Daria watched him as he shed the brown leather jacket and placed it on the back of his chair. "Well, I admit I'm kind of surprised that I'm not nervous," she said. "Normally, I would be. I sure was yesterday when I met with your mom. I thought more than once about canceling. Now I'm glad I didn't. I suppose she told you everything that happened?"

"Actually, I haven't talked to her. My dad gave me a quick rundown, but I wanted to talk with you myself." He hesitated. "I know you've been concerned about Katie."

Daria half turned and covered her cheek with her hand. "I admit I have been." After a moment she looked at Dex's open face. "I convinced myself you were gonna use her up and throw her aside. That wasn't fair, seeing as how I don't even know you; but it does happen, you know." She gazed intently into Dex's eyes. "I don't want my daughter to be like me."

Dex spoke kindly. "But you're not the same person anymore, are you?"

Daria's face broke into a huge smile. "No, I guess I'm not." Her eyes shone. "For the first time since I can remember, I feel happy, like I'm at peace with myself. But I don't know how I'm gonna explain this to Katie. She's mentioned God from time to time, and I've always put her off saying it was foolishness. And now . . . now . . ." She turned pleading eyes toward Dex. "Now, what do I tell her? How do I say, 'I was wrong all those times.' I think Katie has wanted to believe for quite a while, but she's been afraid to. I certainly didn't help her. But I . . ." Daria crossed her arms. "I really did think religion was pure foolishness. I was resigned to taking life as it came, never looking for a purpose, just surviving it. That's all I wanted—survival. But, Katie, now she's a different story. She always wants to know a reason for everything. She's real . . . oh what's the word?" Daria gestured in the air. "You know when you have to figure it all out."

"Analytical?"

"Yeah, that's it! Katie's real analytical. She weighs her options and thinks about them for days before acting. But not me; I'd just do something and move on never caring if it was right or wrong—as long as I kept moving. I thought if I sat still too long, the doubts would all catch up with me."

"But you're sitting still now, right?"

"Yes, I am. I know the past is taken care of; it can't hurt me now." She saw concern on Dex's face. "Oh, I know I'm gonna have to deal with some of the bad choices I made. And I admit, the one that scares me the most is having to face up to the kind of mother I've been. You just wouldn't believe some of the stunts I've pulled."

"Even so, Katie turned out well. You must have done something right, or I doubt I would have fallen in love with her."

"So you do love my daughter?"

Placing his hands on his thighs and leaning slightly forward Dex replied, "Yes, ma'am, I do—very much. That's why I give you my word I won't do anything to hurt her."

"I believe you." Daria's voice shook.

Dex admired how she readily trusted him when everything in her past would tell her to do otherwise. "I've never told Katie my feelings. I don't think I should, seeing as how she doesn't share my—" He corrected himself. "Seeing as how she doesn't share *our* faith."

"I think I understand what you mean. Your mom said God doesn't want someone who believes to hook up with someone who doesn't believe."

"That's exactly right." Dex thought his mom probably had not used the term "hook up," though.

"It doesn't seem fair that I should believe when Katie doesn't. I feel like I've betrayed her or something."

Dex moved to the sofa to sit next to Daria. "There's no reason for you to feel that way. All you've done is accept the gift God offered you. Katie can do the same if she only will."

"But I've always known Katie was interested in spiritual things, and I would tell her it was stupid and a waste of time. If it weren't for me, she might already be a believer now!"

"Please don't lessen your own salvation because of Katie's unbelief. The Bible tells us heaven rejoices whenever one sinner repents. The angels are having a party in your honor right now."

Tears now streamed down Daria's face. "It's all so hard to take in. Rejection I'm familiar with. But this—the idea that angels are happy about me—that's kind of hard to swallow."

"Someday, the angels are gonna rejoice over Katie."

Hope flashed across Daria's features. She grabbed the sleeve of Dex's shirt. "Do you really believe that?"

"I do. Some people come to the Lord quickly. Others come slowly over a period of time. Jesus has been courting Katie for a long time. She just hasn't agreed to go out with Him yet." Dex grinned. "All those times Katie mentioned God, the Spirit was calling to her. The fact that Janie and I are in her life is the work of a sovereign God who refuses to give up on your little girl."

"What do you mean?"

Dex briefly related the story of how Janie had been compelled to pray for Katie back in high school. "So I'm sure it's no accident that Katie now works for me. My mom, Janie, and my grandmother all feel a burden to pray for her and reach out to her. And, of course, I feel that desire as well. I just have to be more careful about it."

"I can't believe this!" She twirled her black hair around her index finger. "I do recall Katie talking about someone in high school that had a different outlook than everybody else. Of course, I blew it off as nonsense." Her eyes glazed.

"Daria, are you still with me?" asked Dex politely.

"Oh, yeah, I was just thinking about something." She faced her daughter's employer and smiled. "I do feel better now that you've told me all this. It takes a little getting used to, to think that He's been calling to my little girl all these years."

"Well, now that you know, you can join Him in His work. That's what God wants from His children."

"What does He want?"

Dex again tried to think of an explanation Daria could relate to. "Like any parent, God is most pleased when His kids agree to help out around the house, so to speak. I know that makes my parents happy. It's part of being a family. When kids go off and do their own thing, they get into trouble. Instead, they should be a vital part of the family unit. When everybody pitches in, things get done smoothly."

"I think I get what you're saying. God has chores for His kids to do. Like when I used to make Katie clean up her room. I was so pleased when she did it without moaning and groaning."

"Exactly!"

"So how do we know what jobs we're supposed to be doing?"

Dex twisted his mouth in thought. "That's where it gets a little tricky. Some things are obvious. He definitely wants us to pray. So now you can join us in praying for Katie's salvation."

"Okay, that's easy enough. What else?"

"We have to be a light to Katie which means we have to be living examples of the Word, of Jesus. Unfortunately, that's not always as easy to do as it sounds."

"Then how can we do it?"

Dex liked Daria's enthusiasm. It was refreshing to be around a new convert. "We try to live out the life of Christ in front of Katie. That means being kind, loving, compassionate, faithful, patient. There's a list in the book of Galatians. Do you have a Bible?"

Daria stood up and raced into another room. She came back beaming and holding a brand new leather-bound Bible. "Your mom took me to a bookstore yesterday after we left the café and bought this for me. Nobody's ever done anything like that for me before." She sat back down next to Dex. "Can you show me that list?"

Dex didn't hide his pleasure at her eagerness.

With both of their heads buried in the book of Galatians, Dexter Matheson and Daria Montgomery discussed ways they could be living testaments for Jesus Christ.

34

❄

KEVIN HOLLAND PUT THE PHONE back on its cradle. "Man," he murmured, "Why did it happen so close to Christmas?" Then a noise in the lobby told him Katie had arrived. She was humming a Christmas carol. He had been a bit apprehensive when Dex hired someone with no office experience. He was glad now that he had trusted his friend's instincts. Katie was definitely an asset to the company. As to what she was doing to his partner's heart, Kevin could only speculate. He rose to say good morning to his secretary.

"You sure sound in a festive mood today, Katie."

"Yeah, they're playing Christmas songs on the radio. It's hard not to get pulled into a happy mood with 'Jingle Bells' serenading you all the way to work." She hung her coat on the rack and put her lunch in the refrigerator. "I've been eating out a good bit—and enjoying it, too—but I've decided to be a little more frugal. Haven't even begun my Christmas shopping." She smiled. "So, Kevin, is Dex here yet? I've got some ideas for Dennis Grayson's project."

Kevin stared down at the floor. "No, in fact, I just got off the phone with him. He's not coming in today."

"He's not sick, is he?"

"No." Kevin scratched his head. "Miss Ellie died last night."

"What—" Tears formed in her eyes.

"I'm sorry, Katie. I know you had grown to love her. We all did."

Katie backed up until she bumped into her desk. "But, I just saw her on Thanksgiving and she was fine. How could she . . . I mean she can't be . . ." Katie picked at the edge of her sweater.

Kevin had a good working relationship with Katie, but this was so personal that he felt a little off-balance. "She died peacefully, at home. I think that was what she wanted."

Katie was having difficulty disguising the sobs rising in her chest. "But, I just met her. I haven't had . . . enough time to . . . get to know her." She threw her hands over her face and ran to the restroom.

Kevin stood helpless in the lobby. When she came out, she rushed to the coat rack, pulled on her coat and gloves, grabbed her purse, and headed for the door. "You can fire me if you want, Kevin, but I've got to go."

Kevin watched as the door closed behind her. "Don't worry, Katie," he murmured, "your job here is secure." He then glanced at his secretary's desk and saw several appointments listed on the calendar for that day. Grinning, he added, "I certainly won't fire you, Katie Montgomery, but I have a feeling I'm going to miss you an awful lot today."

❄ ❄ ❄

Katie pulled into the Matheson's driveway and almost backed up when she saw several cars crowded in. Only when she saw Dex's and Janie's cars did she decide to stay. Johanna McKinnon answered the door. Katie's face turned red. What was she supposed to say to this pregnant woman? Johanna just reached out and pulled her into the foyer.

"Katie, I'm so glad you came! Miss Ellie would be pleased to know you're here!"

"I heard . . . Kevin told me Dex had called . . ." Katie stumbled over her words. "I wanted to come. Miss Ellie was so nice and—"

"Miss Ellie cared for you so much, Katie," Johanna sniffled, then added graciously, "Here, let me take your coat."

"Thanks, I didn't want to intrude; I just wanted to—"

"Oh, you're not intruding at all! Come on back to the kitchen."

She took Katie's hand. "Mom, look who came by."

At the kitchen table Lydia Matheson sat looking elegant and beautiful in spite of her reddened eyes. Katie silently wondered where that kind of grace came from.

"Katie, how sweet of you to come." Lydia indicated the chair to her left and Katie sat down.

"I was so shocked when Kevin told me what happened. I wanted to come by and—"

"I'm so glad you did."

Katie was startled by a crying sound.

Johanna stood. "That's Emily waking. I'll go see to her."

Lydia watched Johanna leave. "They came last night when we knew Miss Ellie wouldn't make it 'til morning."

Katie gulped. "How'd she . . . die?"

"The same way she did everything—smiling and praising God." She shook her head. "I'm going to miss her."

"Me, too, "whispered Katie.

Kendall stuck her head into the kitchen. "Mom, do you know if the Gardners have moved? Oh, hi, Katie." Kendall addressed her mother again. "The number we have for the Gardners is coming up disconnected. Any suggestions?"

Lydia thought a moment. "Try looking in your father's book, in his office downstairs."

"Okay." Kendall whizzed past the two ladies seated in the kitchen. Lydia grinned.

"Kendall is such a blessing to me. She's so efficient." Lydia rose and picked up the coffee pot. "Would you care for some coffee or tea?"

"No, thanks." Katie felt uneasy. "Maybe I should go."

"No, please. I'll be sitting here all by myself."

Shyly, Katie said, "I saw several cars outside; I assumed lots of people were here."

"Oh, there will be very soon. Everett, Brady, and Dex went to the funeral home to make all the arrangements; Sasha is upstairs with Janie and Jake; Johanna's in with Emily; and Kendall . . . well you saw her. Bruce had to check in at work. Right now it's kind of quiet." Lydia's face momentarily lit up and she motioned Katie to follow her. "I just remembered something, Katie. Come on."

They walked to Miss Ellie's room, but Katie hesitated.

"I . . . I'm having trouble believing she's gone."

Lydia gave the slender girl a motherly embrace. "I know, sweetie. It's hard, but it's gonna be all right." She pulled back and looked into Katie's face. "Miss Ellie's not really gone. She's just not here where we can see her."

Katie sniffed. "I guess you're talking about heaven?"

"Yes, I am," said Lydia matter-of-factly.

"Miss Ellie said Leland was there living in his mansion."

Lydia laughed. "That's right!" Her eyes began to sparkle. "And now Miss Ellie is in *her* mansion. I can just see them now—reunited after all this time."

"So you really believe they're together now?"

"I do, Katie. I believe it with all my heart."

"I hope you're right. I hate to think of Miss Ellie any other way than happy."

"Oh, she's happy all right. She loved God more than anybody I know. She spent her entire life serving Him and now she gets to see Him face-to-face. It's what she's been longing for, what we're all longing for. Some of us have to stick around to finish the work."

"I don't understand."

Lydia laughed softly. "Well, we all have work to do to spread God's love and forgiveness and mercy—all those things Miss Ellie radiated." She snapped her fingers in the air. "And there's one thing I can do right now." Then she took the antique frame off the nightstand, and gazed at the photograph of herself and Everett on their wedding day.

Katie felt she was intruding on a private moment. "It's a beautiful picture. It brought tears to my eyes when I first saw it. Miss Ellie told me how you two started your life together."

"That explains why Miss Ellie wanted you to have it."

"What?"

"Miss Ellie asked me to give this to you. I couldn't imagine why she'd want you to have a picture of Everett and me; but she said you'd understand. Here, it's yours."

Katie unashamedly wiped the tears from her eyes. "I can't . . . it's too personal . . . it should stay in the family."

Once again Lydia wrapped her arms around the young girl. She stroked her hair and whispered, "It was one of her last requests, Katie. You know how stubborn she can be. If you don't take it, she might come back and make you take it!"

Katie laughed. "Maybe I won't take it, so she'll have to come back."

Lydia placed her hands on Katie's tear-streaked cheeks. "Miss Ellie's not here now, Katie, but I am. Will I do?"

Katie fell into her arms, held on tightly, and released the torrent of tears she had bottled up inside.

❊ ❊ ❊

The second floor of the Matheson's home was every bit as exquisite as the first floor, but Katie didn't care about such trivialities on this day. She supposed that, once again, Miss Ellie had been right. People were more important than buildings. Dex had echoed the same sentiment. All people, rich or poor, would some day end up like Miss Ellie—dead.

Katie stood at the half-opened door of Janie's bedroom. Janie sat on the bed, reading something.

"Janie, may I come in?" Janie looked up and smiled.

"Katie! I didn't know you were here. Come on in."

"Sasha said you wouldn't mind if I came up."

"Not at all. I don't like to be alone much when I'm sad."

"I came over when Kevin told me what happened." Katie gently sat down on the bed and swiftly perused the room. She was surprised at the sophistication of the black and cream décor with splashes of pink here and there. Katie had expected Janie's room to be more lively and bright. Instead, she found mature elegance enveloping her. But then again, Janie Matheson was full of surprises. Katie picked up a needlepoint pillow and studied the intricate detail.

"This is pretty. Did somebody make it for you?"

"No, I did it myself. Don't look at it too closely; you'll see all the mistakes." She laughed, but her heart wasn't in it.

"Where did you learn how to do needlepoint?" Katie examined the pretty pink rose on the black background.

"Miss Ellie taught me when I was just a kid. We'd sit together for hours working on projects and just talking and talking. Oh, Katie, I don't know what I'm going to do without her! I can't imagine coming home and not finding her here asking me about my day or what I was studying in the Bible or what I thought about certain subjects. She always talked to me about stuff that matters, and she always challenged me to think about issues and why I believed what I believed."

Katie bit her lip and stared out the window. It was still snowing. "Yeah. I only knew her for a short time; but she told me once that she didn't have time to beat around the bush, so she just came right out and said what was on her mind. I'm glad she did that because instead of talking about trivial things like you usually do when you first meet somebody, I feel like I got to know her in one afternoon. And loved her, too."

Janie cocked her head. "That was Miss Ellie all right: straight to the point. It makes me wonder why we're not all more like that."

"What do you mean?"

"Well, I wonder why we spend so much time talking about unimportant stuff when people all around us are probably hurting and want to talk about major stuff. But we hide our true feelings."

"Little things are easier to talk about."

"Well, maybe so," replied Janie as she tossed the pillow aside, "but who knows, this could be our last day on earth. We could die in a car accident or get hit by a bus or something. Just because we're young doesn't mean we should be shallow. I know Miss Ellie wouldn't want that for me—or for you." Janie looked straight into Katie's eyes. "She loved you, too."

Katie was barely able to choke out her response. "I know. She told me I should consider myself a part of the family."

"Oh, Katie," cried Janie as she reached over to hug her friend, "you *are* part of the family."

Katie was sobbing now, not knowing how to respond.

"I'm sorry, Katie. I didn't mean to make you cry. Here, let me get you a tissue." Janie reached over to the night table and grabbed a box. "I need one as badly as you do! And to think I actually thought I was finished crying!"

Janie looked thoughtful. "You know, you wouldn't think I'd be so emotional about this since I kind of knew it was going to happen."

"You mean because Miss Ellie was so old?"

Janie cocked her head. "Well, partly; but also because two weeks ago I dreamed Miss Ellie was going to die. I think God was trying to prepare me for it."

Katie was stunned. "You . . . you believe . . . in dreams?"

Janie twisted her mouth. "If you mean, do I believe in all of that psychological interpretation of dreams, the answer is no. But if you mean that sometimes our dreams are God's way of teaching us something or reminding us of something, the answer is yes."

"Really?" Katie thought of her nocturnal companion Kaleo. Could there be a higher purpose for his recurring existence in her dreams? Or was he merely the result of an overactive imagination and a guilty conscience?

"You sound surprised."

Katie looked away, thinking. Did Kaleo come from God or

some malevolent force? She shuddered.

"Do you dream much, Katie?"

"Not that much; at least I don't usually remember, if I do."
She hoped she sounded convincing. Janie seemed satisfied with her
answers, but pursued the conversation.

"Dad always says God has to talk to me while I'm asleep
because that's the only time I'm ever quiet enough to listen!"

Katie laughed along with her friend, but she didn't find the
statement all that funny. *Could it be that God sent Kaleo because I
wouldn't listen to Him any other way? Could He really care that much
about communicating with me?* It was easier to believe that God was
tracking her down to punish her for her unforgivable sins. She had
concluded that if God couldn't catch her, He couldn't punish her.

Janie sobered again. "That's another area of my life I'd like to
change and be a really good listener like Miss Ellie. She knew when to
talk and when to sit back and listen—especially to God."

"I've heard people say that, but I don't get it. How can you hear
something that's not audible?"

Janie stiffened with excitement. "Well, God is spirit, not flesh
and blood, so you have to listen with your spirit."

Katie crossed her arms. "But isn't that simply your mind filling
up with its own thoughts?"

Janie situated herself cross-legged on the bed and turned to face
Katie. "I suppose apart from faith in God, it is just your own human
wisdom. But," she continued slowly, "if you have the faith to believe
God exists, He'll speak to you and give you His wisdom. The Bible
says if you seek God with all your heart you will find Him. You have to
believe He's there and He's real and that He loves you."

Katie licked her lips. "So you just believe He's there and you
can hear Him?" This was too easy. Spiritual things were supposed to
be complex and dramatic. Janie was talking about having a simple
conversation with a supreme being. It didn't compute.

"Why would God want to have a conversation with a mere

human anyway? And if He did, wouldn't He only want to talk with the really religious people?"

Janie's eyes shone. "No, Katie, that's the beauty of the gospel. Jesus was God's Son, but He took the form of a simple carpenter. He completely humbled Himself. If it weren't for Jesus, God would be out of our reach." Her eyes filled with tears. "Oh, Katie, He was God's Son, His perfect Son. He knew no sin, but He took our sin upon His shoulders and died so we could stand before a perfect God and know Him and be known by Him."

Confusion crossed Katie's face, but there was no animosity or rejection reflected there. Janie continued.

"See, Katie, God made the ultimate sacrifice—one that would last for all time."

Curiosity had taken over Katie. "So what was it?"

"Well, you know the story of the virgin Mary, the shepherds, the Magi and all that, don't you?"

Katie nodded her head. She'd been hearing all the familiar Christmas carols on the radio for several weeks.

"Jesus came to earth and lived as a man, but He was totally perfect. He never sinned, not even once. Still, He was put to death on the cross. Jesus was tortured and beaten, then His hands and feet were nailed to the cross." Janie shuddered, then continued. "See, Katie, once Jesus was sacrificed on the cross, no other sacrifices had to be made. It was finished. The payment for man's sin had been made. All that was left for a person to do was to look up at the cross and believe this was God's true Son and be saved. It's that simple."

Katie fidgeted with a pillow. "So that's it? You just believe that stuff about the cross and you can hear God?"

"Katie, what is it exactly that you want to know? Remember, Miss Ellie would want you to be honest."

Katie sighed. How could she put her emotions into words? How could she describe the longings of her heart? "I don't know, Janie. I don't know what I want. I just know life should have more meaning than it does right now." She stood up and walked to the window. "You talked about it at Kevin's wedding—how your life had meaning and purpose because of God, but I suppose I don't even know what that is."

She turned and looked at her friend. She saw Miss Ellie staring back at her through the eyes of her granddaughter. "Wow, Janie, you sure do look like your grandmother."

Janie got up, walked over to Katie and hugged her. "That's the nicest thing you could say to me right now!" She pulled back and reached for Katie's hands and held them in her own. "Katie, Jesus wants your life to have meaning and purpose, and He longs to give you both of those. And it really is simple—all you have to do is believe that everything I've told you is true." Janie sighed and looked down, finally letting go of Katie's hands. "I may not have said it very eloquently, but everything I've said is true; it's in the Bible. Don't believe it because I've said it, Katie; believe it because God said it."

Katie stared back out the window and watched the snow accumulate on the Matheson's front lawn. It was a pretty, serene picture. "If it's all so simple, how come it doesn't feel simple?"

Janie slowly released her breath. "I think maybe because you're fighting it. Look, Katie, nobody can make you have peace with God. All we can do is let you know it's there waiting for you. The reason you're feeling confused inside is because God is calling out to you. His Spirit is trying to get your attention."

Janie groaned and ran her hands through her hair. "Oh! I sound like I'm preaching to you, and I didn't want to do that! But there is one more thing I want to say and then I promise I won't keep pressing the issue. Katie, please, be honest with God. Tell Him everything; don't hold anything back. Whatever you hold back is only going to keep you from having a relationship with Him. You can't keep secrets from your best friend and still expect the friendship to be strong. It's the same way with God." She looked at Katie as if trying to read her face. Katie's expression was guarded.

"There, that's all I'm going to say. But I'll be praying."

Katie cleared her throat. "What exactly are you gonna pray about?"

Janie smiled, put her arm around her friend's shoulders and began leading her toward the door. "I'm not sure—whatever God tells me to pray about, I guess."

Now Katie smiled. Saucily, she asked, "Are you gonna have to go to sleep to find out what God wants you to pray?"

Laughing, Janie replied. "Just until I grow up and become more like Miss Ellie! But I will pray, Katie. I promise you that. Now, let's go get something to eat. I'm starving!"

Katie sighed. "Me too."

35
٭

KATIE SHED HER COAT, cast her gloves and purse onto the nearest chair, and made a beeline for the bedroom. She could hardly wait to get out of her dressy clothes. Was it because she hated the panty hose and high heels or because she had to wear them to watch Miss Ellie's body lowered into the cold, hard ground?

Nothing prepared Katie for the surge of emotions that overtook her when she saw the coffin sitting at the front of South Madison Community Church. Then, she didn't think she would be able to contain herself as she listened to the message of Pastor Andy Powell. He spoke of the glories of heaven waiting for those who believe in the saving power of Jesus Christ. If it hadn't been for the comforting arm of Dex or the warm smiles and soothing embraces of the rest of the family, Katie would surely have fled the scene.

But for all that anxiety, nothing compared to the moment when she exited the front doors of the church and ran smack into Carolyn Grady. Apparently, Carolyn and the Mathesons went to church together and were all chummy with each other! Katie shuddered. She vaguely recalled Dex making a quick introduction and telling Katie that Carolyn ran a local crisis pregnancy center. *Like he needed to tell me that.*

"Why, God, can't I get away from this guilt? It's like it's stalking me!" She ripped her dress off, tossed it on the floor, and pulled on faded jeans and an old flannel shirt.

In the kitchen Katie snatched a soda from the refrigerator and retrieved a bag of candy-coated chocolates from the cupboard. Popping a handful of the colorful pebbles into her mouth, Katie recalled how gracious Carolyn Grady had been. She never let on that she knew Katie, though Katie saw a flicker of recognition in her eyes. She had gracefully extended her hand to Katie with the expected "It's nice to meet you." Katie had wanted to die—especially noting the pride in Dex's voice as he related Carolyn's occupation.

She picked up the CD Dex had lent her. The cover showed that Watson guy from the concert, staring out a window as if contemplating some great truth. Or maybe he was just watching the world go by. Katie had done her share of that. She tossed the CD back onto the stereo cabinet and sank into a pale-green and pink plaid chair. She didn't need to hear the song to feel its sting. The lyrics never left her heart.

> Why are the days so lonely
> Where can a heart go free?
> And who will dry the tears that no one's seen?

Who would dry Katie's tears? She thought she had always been so good at disguising them, but somehow Miss Ellie and all the others had seen right through her façade.

Katie sang the words, daring herself to believe them.

> Whisper the words of a prayer
> and you'll find Him there
> Arms open wide, love in His eyes.
> Jesus—He meets you where you are.
> Jesus—He heals your secret scars.
> All the love you're longing for is Jesus
> The friend of a wounded heart.

Janie said to be honest with God. But revealing her secret heart would surely make those "arms open wide" close tightly—shutting her out forever. Some truths were too risky, better left unsaid. The Matheson's God surely wouldn't accept someone as stained as Katie Montgomery.

And what about Dex? She couldn't escape her growing feelings for the eldest Matheson son. If God wouldn't accept her, would Dex? Could he love her if he found out what she had done? A huge stone wall separated her—not only from an angry, righteous God—but also from the man with whom she now found herself feeling desperately and hopelessly in love.

They both expect too much from me! I'll never measure up! Katie tossed her empty soda can onto the coffee table and wadded up the now-empty candy bag. She deliberated about opening another bag of her favorite chocolate indulgence and probably would have had the doorbell not rung at that very moment. Katie trudged to the door, not in the mood for company or for deflecting a pushy salesman.

"Mama! What are you doing here?"

Daria stood there, smiling. She never visited, especially unannounced. And she was holding two suitcases.

"Mama, what's going on?"

"I've left Lou. Can I stay with you, please?"

"Uh . . . sure. Come . . . come on in."

"Katie, I want you to be sure this is okay. I know you've gotten used to this being your place; and if you don't wanna share it with me, I totally understand."

Katie couldn't put her finger on it, but something was different with Daria. Her walls had crumbled. Her eyes held an innocence Katie had never seen. It was disconcerting.

"Mama, don't be silly. Of course you can stay. Where else would you go?" Katie braced herself for a fiery retort. Daria just laughed and set her bags down in the living room.

"Well, now that's a good question. If you hadn't wanted me to stay, I'm not sure where I'd've gone. But I would've found someplace."

"Mama, what happened? Did Lou hit you or anything?"

"Oh, no! Lou's not like that."

"If he's so nice, why did you walk out on him?" Daria had never deserted a man in her life. The guy had always left.

Daria shifted from one foot to the other. "We had a disagreement that couldn't be resolved under the same roof. And since it's Lou's roof, I was the one who needed to leave. Do you mind if I get something to drink?"

"Uh, no, of course not. . . . So, did you two split for good, or are you just taking a break?"

Daria poured herself a root beer. "I think it's a permanent split. Wow, this place looks even better than last time."

"Uh, thanks. Mama, is there something you're not telling me?"

Daria eyed the crumpled candy bag and cola can on the coffee table, the coat crumpled on a chair. "There's something *you're* not telling *me*. You never leave messes like this."

"You're changing the subject, Mama. Are you gonna tell me the truth?"

Daria smirked. "Are you?"

Nervously Katie giggled. "What's gotten into you?"

"Well, I think we both know I've been way overdue in the personality adjustment category."

Katie flopped down on the sofa and scratched her head. "I don't know what to say. This is totally strange."

Daria picked up Katie's coat and purse, hung them on the coat rack, and then sat down.

"Why not tell me what's bothering you?" Daria asked.

"How do you know something's bothering me?"

"I've known you your whole life, and you never leave anything layin' around like that. Where you got that quality from, I'm not sure, but this . . ."

"Well, then you'd better not go into the bedroom."

"What?" Daria up and hurried to the bedroom. There, in a confused mass by the bed lay a wrinkled green dress, a pair of pantyhose, and two black high-heeled shoes. Daria feigned horror. "Oh, my! This is serious. Maybe I should take you to the hospital. You must be ill to mess up two rooms."

"Am I really that much of a neat freak?"

"'Fraid so, sweetie. You're borderline neurotic, I think."

"Well, I have a good excuse."

Daria waited, but her daughter hesitated. "What is it, Katie? You can tell me, whatever it is."

"It's just that . . . I know you think I shouldn't get mixed up with the Mathesons, but . . . Miss Ellie, the grandmother . . . she died and today was the funeral." Her mother wouldn't understand the other burdens weighing on her.

Daria reached out for Katie's hand. "Oh, Katie, I'm sorry. I know I've said a lot of things about Dex and his family, but I know you care for them."

Katie was surprised to see genuine compassion in her mother's eyes. Her own filled with tears. "I didn't want to cry anymore, but I can't seem to stop. I feel silly carrying on like this since I didn't even know her that well, but—"

"Katie, it's okay to feel sad. You've always been a sensitive person." Daria put a protective arm around her daughter.

Katie sniffed. "I always thought you wanted me to be strong and confident."

Daria shook her head. "I s'pose I thought that was the best way to be—don't let anybody hurt you; hurt them first. I always seemed to be on the receiving end of the hurt, and I wanted life to be different for you." She sighed. "I tried to make you something you're not. I hope you'll forgive me."

"Forgive you?" Katie was having difficulty comprehending. This was unlike anything she'd ever heard from her mother. "Um, sure I'll forgive you. . . . But it's not necessary, Mama. You haven't done anything wrong. You just wanted my life to be better than yours, that's all."

Daria stood up and paced back and forth across the small living room. "But the way I went about it was all wrong. I thought I knew so much! I thought I had it all figured out. Lydia said forgivin' yourself is sometimes the hardest part—"

"Lydia? Who's that, Mama?" Katie demanded, stunned.

Daria stopped her pacing and answered hesitantly. "I've been tryin' to figure out how to tell you. I didn't mean to blurt it out."

"Tell me what, Mama?" Katie's voice was shaky.

"Katie," began Daria tremulously, "I know I've said a lot of really stupid things about God and religion in the past; but I want you to know I was wrong. God is real, and Lydia Matheson introduced me to Him about two weeks ago."

Silence filled the room.

"Katie, say something, please."

"What . . . how do you know Lydia Matheson?"

Daria sat down opposite her daughter. "I don't think you're gonna be too happy about what I have to tell you."

"Try me."

"Okay, here goes." Daria took a deep breath. "After our lunch date a couple weeks ago I couldn't stop worryin' about how I just knew you were gonna fall hard for Dex. When I saw the two of you together at the office, I could tell somethin' was going on. The way he looked at you . . . well, it reminded me so much of your father." She pressed her hands to her face. "Oh, Katie, I got so scared for you. I knew he was gonna break your heart like T.J. did mine. I didn't want you to end up like me, so I . . . I—"

"What exactly did you do?"

Daria tried to laugh. "I actually called up Lydia Matheson and asked to meet with her if you can believe that! We met at the same café where you and I had lunch that day."

"Mama, why would you do such a thing? And she agreed to meet with you? But why didn't she say anything to me? I've talked with her several times since then." Was this some kind of conspiracy?

"Don't be angry with her, sweetie. I asked her not to say anything. I wanted to tell you myself."

"You said this all happened over two weeks ago!"

Again, Daria rose and paced the living room. "I know, I know. I just didn't want to make anymore mistakes. God knows I've made enough of those for two lifetimes. Then I tried to talk to Lou about it, and that didn't go very well, obviously." She indicated the suitcases. "I was afraid you might react the same way he did."

Curiosity gripped Katie. "What did you tell him?"

"I told him I had come to realize that God is real and that He wants to know me and make me His child." She looked at her daughter's confused face. "Oh, Katie, there was such freedom when I came to understand that I didn't have to figure everything out on my own. God has figured it all out for us! I feel like a weight was lifted off my shoulders!"

Katie knew what that weight felt like. But all she could think of now was that her mother was nothing but a contradiction in terms. All those times she thwarted Katie's spiritual interests, just to go behind her back and claim it for herself!

As sarcastically as she could, Katie said, "So, you just believed God is real, and now all your problems have disappeared? I'm supposed to believe that! You sound like Janie."

"Please don't be angry. I was afraid you would be."

"Why shouldn't I be angry?" shouted Katie. "I told you nothing was going on between Dex and me. I can't imagine what Lydia must think of me now! How am I supposed to face her or any of the others for that matter?" Suddenly her face fell. "What about Dex? He must know about this which means he knows how I feel about him! Mama, how could you do this? How can I face him?"

In her tantrum, Katie failed to realize she'd been around the entire Matheson family during the past two weeks and they hadn't treated her any different.

Gently, Daria continued. "To be honest with you, Katie, Lydia and I hardly even talked about you. I don't think she knows how you feel about Dex. I . . . um . . . didn't exactly get around to that. You see, I literally started blubbering . . . going on about T.J. and all the pain in my life. I'm embarrassed myself, just thinking about it. But Lydia was such a good listener, she never condemned me or made me feel like I wasn't on the same level with her, which I was sure she would. But you were right. I misjudged them, and I was wrong. Lydia Matheson is the nicest person I ever met."

"So you didn't talk about me at all?"

"It's all kind of fuzzy in my mind, but I don't think so. At least not about your feelings for Dex. I mostly rambled on about my life and what a terrible mother I'd been, and then Lydia started telling me about Jesus and how He wanted to take all my pain away. I couldn't believe it; it sounded too good to be true. But Lydia even had a little pocket Bible in her purse, and she showed me the verses herself. Well, I couldn't turn away after seeing that. I was more than happy to get rid of all the grief I've been carrying around."

"So how did you do it?" asked the ever-practical Katie.

"I bowed my head and talked to God right there in the restaurant. I told Him I didn't have a clue how to make my life better, but that if He did, I'd listen and do what He said." She shrugged her shoulders. "I know it sounds silly."

"That's it? Then what happened?" For Daria to be so changed, Katie was sure lightning must have struck.

Daria leaned back and sighed. "It's hard to explain. For the first time I can ever remember, I felt hope. I suddenly knew I was loved and that I would never be alone. Lydia said a man named Paul had scales fall from his eyes so He could see the Truth; that's kind of how it was with me, I guess—oh, I don't mean actual scales or anything, but there might as well have been. I saw my life so clear, and I didn't like what I saw." Daria shuddered at the memory, then she reached over and grabbed her daughter's hand. "Katie, right at that moment I would have trusted anybody who could take away the sickness I felt when I saw my life for what it was. I thank God that He was the One who was there."

"But, Mama, your life wasn't all that bad, was it?" pleaded

Katie. "I mean, sure, you've made mistakes, but who hasn't? You just haven't found the right guy yet, and maybe a better job. You never enjoyed checking groceries. But you always had me; that should count for something, shouldn't it?"

Daria smiled sadly at her daughter's logic. "Look, sweetie, I'm not talkin' about my circumstances; I'm talkin' about the way I felt inside. If I'd found the perfect guy I still couldn't be happy. And I had the perfect daughter, but that didn't change me." She reached over and caressed Katie's face. "Or I coulda got the perfect job; or better yet, I could inherit ten million dollars and never have to work another day in my life; but it still wouldn't change anything, at least not anything that matters."

Daria ran her fingers through her long dark hair. "When I say I saw my life for what it was, I mean I saw me for what I was. Oh, Katie, I saw the most bitter, angry, ugly person. It literally scared me. I sat there in that booth shakin' like a kitten in a storm! But then Lydia told me Jesus could give me peace and hope." She closed her eyes. "Somethin' deep inside me actually believed what she said."

"But Mama, how did you know it was real?"

Daria exhaled. "This is gonna sound strange, but I saw this scene in my head. It didn't last long; I guess you could say it was kinda like a dream—only I was awake."

"A dream? What kind of a dream?" This was the second time Katie had heard someone connect dreams with God.

"Well." Daria noted her daughter's sudden interest. "I saw myself standing in the middle of a desert-like land. And there was a big hole—like a valley—and a bunch of people lined up around the edge of it. Then I looked down and saw this man nailed to a cross at the bottom of the hole." Tears filled her eyes. "Katie, He looked up at me—I can't even describe how it made me feel when His eyes caught mine. Even though all these other people were standin' around, He sought out me. And those eyes were incredible." She chuckled. "I always thought T.J. Nichols had the most beautiful eyes in the world, but not anymore! They were nothin' compared to these! When I looked back at Him I could literally feel the love pouring out of Him and into me. He didn't even seem concerned about the pain He was in. All He cared about was me, that I was okay and that I wasn't hurting anymore. It was indescribable! I never knew anyone so loving or so unselfish." Daria wiped her eyes. "I knew I could trust Him."

Katie sat speechless. Something had happened to her mother and it was real. Finally she found her voice. "Did you tell Lydia what you saw in your mind?"

"Yeah. She said it was God's way of confirming my belief. She said the way the crucifixion happened was on a hill, not in a valley; but perhaps the vision was given to show me how Jesus had to humble himself to pay for my sins."

"So you believe God spoke to you through that vision?"

"That's what worked with me. I think God does whatever He can to make a person listen, to get their attention. I needed to see a man who would give up His life for me, one that would lower himself for me—even though I don't deserve it." She shook her head in amazement.

Katie's mind whirled with all she was hearing. Denying that Kaleo could have been sent to her from God Himself was getting harder and harder to do. But why a wolf? And what did he want from her? Everything Kaleo asked her to do was painful and unnerving, like walking through the door to the unknown or having to confront that mangled baby. God seemed bent on taking Katie through hell before letting her into heaven. Still, it was worth considering. But right now, she had to deal with her mother.

"Mama, is that why you left Lou? Because you want to do what God wants? Did He tell you to leave him?"

Daria pursed her lips. "Yeah, in a manner of speaking. I didn't hear a voice or see a vision, but I've been reading in the Bible. There was this woman who was caught sleeping with a man who wasn't her husband. A bunch of men who didn't like Jesus asked him what they should do to a woman like that. I think they wanted to stone her."

Katie was shocked. "What did He say to do?"

"He said they should only kill her if they were totally sinless themselves. Of course, none of them were; so they all left. I really like that part."

"So that just left Jesus and the woman?"

"Yeah. Jesus told her to go and sin no more. Well, those words jumped off the page right into my face. I knew that's what I had to do. I had to go—you know, leave the place I was in—and then I had to sin no more. I can't live the way I used to, Katie. It would break Jesus' heart."

Katie had no clue what to say. She'd been telling her mother for years that she didn't need a man to be happy, but she never listened.

"Katie," spoke Daria quietly, "about the way I always lived my life—I need to ask you to forgive me for that."

"What are you talking about?"

"It hurts me to think of the kind of . . ." Daria twisted her hands in her lap. "I've been a terrible example for you, Katie. I've had men in and out of our home all your life. I sure haven't been much of a mother for you. I'm so ashamed." She hung her head and whispered, "Please forgive me, Katie."

Katie threw her arms around her mom and wept with her. "It's okay, Mama, I love you. I always have."

Katie longed for the peace her mother had. To have her secret scars healed, her heart set free, to experience all the love she had ever longed for. Daria Montgomery's wounded heart was finally whole. But could Katie's be healed as easily? She wanted to believe it could. But the path was clouded and the way was constricted by that grotesque, misshapen little baby.

Only two choices remained for Katie Montgomery—she could turn away, or she could face the aborted child. Katie shivered despite her mother's warm embrace.

36

DEXTER MATHESON COULDN'T TELL whether Katie was happy, sad, or ambivalent about the news she had just shared with him. He was admittedly surprised that Daria had walked out on Lou. Oh, he knew it would happen eventually. But sometimes people needed a little more time to adjust their life to line up with the Word of God. She was certainly an interesting woman.

And so was her daughter. Unfortunately, Katie was still confused about spiritual things. So Dex treaded lightly.

"So, is it working out all right for you—having your mom living with you again? I know you were enjoying your independence."

Katie shifted in her seat. "Yeah, that's what's so weird. Mom's being great about everything. She's still working at the Pic-n-Save on the other side of town, but she doesn't complain about the drive or the traffic or the long hours—which, for my mom, is a miracle."

Dex enjoyed hearing the report. "Well, that's good. Do you think she's gonna stay at your place for long?"

"I don't know." Katie licked her lips. "Part of me wants her to stay, but another part is afraid things will end up like they were before with me having to take care of her all the time. I didn't mind it so much back then; but now that I've gotten used to not having to do it, I don't want to go back."

"That's only natural, I suppose." Dex toyed with a pencil and nervously spoke what was on his mind. "Have the two of you talked about what happened to your mom?"

Katie looked away, reminded of her mom's initial reason for

calling Lydia. "Yeah, some. She talks about it all the time, and she's always reading that Bible your mom bought for her."

Again, Dex was having trouble reading Katie's thoughts. He decided he'd better go another route. "Have you decided how you're going to spend Christmas yet?"

"I think Mom wants to stay at home and have a quiet Christmas, just the two of us, to make up for all the other botched Christmases. Why? Are you gonna force me to come to your house like you did on Thanksgiving?" Her eyes sparkled, and Dex was relieved to see her smile. He held his hands up in mock surrender.

"No way, not this time!" He tried to hide his disappointment; he had secretly hoped Katie and Daria would accept Lydia's invitation for Christmas dinner. He managed a sincere smile. "Although you have to admit I did get a good-looking office out of the deal, didn't I?"

Katie gave a satisfied glance around the room. It did look good. The light taupe color of the walls beautifully set off the newly-painted white shelves behind Dex's desk. The addition of some green houseplants livened up the space as well. Katie even found a spacious throw rug with a busy green, purple, and red design to lend just the right splash of color without making it too feminine. All in all, it had been a success. She even enjoyed the lingering scent of the new paint. It was a reminder of the time they had spent together.

"Yeah, I think we did a pretty good job in here. Now, if we can get Kevin to agree, we can tackle his office next."

Dex laughed. "Not much chance of that. He hates decorating more than I do! I think we might have to sneak in and do it one night after he leaves and surprise him."

"Well, I'm all for it, but not until after the holidays."

"I agree. It's getting harder to concentrate on work. The closer it gets to Christmas, the more I start acting like a kid!" He made a funny face, and Katie laughed. "Come January our spare time's gonna be taken up with Dennis's mission project."

"Wow, it's hard to believe it's almost a new year. So much has happened this year."

Dex looked at his secretary quizzically. "Would you say it's been a good year for you, Katie?"

"Yes! I enjoy working here so much more than the Pic-n-Save."

Dex gave his employee a concerned look. "I hope you're not gonna spend all your days off working for Mr. Brinker."

"Don't worry. After finals at school, I'll need a break."

"Good. Sometimes I think you work too hard." He wanted to see Katie spend more time enjoying life instead of burying herself in it. And, he wanted to see her enjoying it with him. That's really all he wanted for Christmas.

Katie chewed her lip. "Speaking of work, look at this." She reached into her purse and pulled out a brochure. She placed it on her boss's desk. "I thought you might be interested. Consider this an early Christmas present."

Dex picked up the pamphlet. He read the words, "'University of Wisconsin School of Interior Design.'" He looked up. "Katie, does this mean what I think it means?"

"Yep, I talked with an advisor. I've already signed up for my first class; it's just an introductory course, but it should help me decide if interior decorating is right for me."

Dex had come around to the other side of his desk. "Oh, Katie, this is great, and I know you're gonna love it."

"I hope you're right, 'cause this course isn't gonna help me at all if I decide to stay in the business department."

"Don't worry about that." Dex pulled Katie into a standing position. "I'll tell you what: my Christmas present to you will be the cost of this class. That way you don't have to worry about losing the credit."

"Dex, I can't let you do that! It's too much." She felt dizzy over the generosity of his offer. "It's . . . I could never—"

"I want to do it, Katie." Dex pulled Katie into his arms. "I've got a gut feeling this is what you should be doing."

Katie's voice was muffled against Dex's shoulder. "Nobody has ever done anything like this for me."

"Oh, Katie." He pulled away just far enough to see her face. "I wish I could do more."

She shook her head. "No, I don't deserve this much." Tears were slowly slipping down her cheeks.

Dex cupped her face in both of his hands, and with his thumbs, he gently wiped her tears. "You deserve so much more, Katie."

He lowered his head and very softly kissed her lips. Katie felt his lips touch hers; then she felt his arms slide around her shoulders until they were pulling her body toward his. She melted against him, clutching the front of his shirt in her hands. Katie Montgomery had not been kissed in a long time, but never had she been kissed like this, so considerately and so tenderly. It was all so natural that she wasn't even aware of when she began kissing him back. Long before Katie was ready for it to end Dex pulled away, but his hands continued to stroke her hair. His eyes were fixed on his hands as if he were mesmerized by the way the strands of light brown hair slipped through his fingers.

Dexter Matheson silently conceded it was time for this stolen moment to slip away as well. He had to fight every natural desire coursing through his body to end it, but he did. He took a step backward but remained close enough to enclose her shaking hands within his.

"Katie, I'm so sorry. I didn't mean for that to happen."

Katie stared at their joined hands.

Dex lifted her chin forcing her to look at him. "Katie, I admit I find you attractive." He gave her that crooked grin she loved. "But I had no right to kiss you."

Katie blushed. "No, I'm sorry. I shouldn't have—"

"Katie, I'm the jerk here, okay? Don't you take the blame for something that isn't your fault."

"But . . . but I should have stopped you or something."

Dex leaned back against his desk and crossed his arms. "Look, I think we both know there's been an attraction between us for a while now. Would you agree; or am I wrong?"

Katie shook her head. "No, you're not wrong."

Dex could barely hear her. He had made her uncomfortable. Somehow he had to let her off the hook so she'd stop blaming herself. But just how was he supposed to do that? He settled on the easy way out, even though it wasn't the complete truth.

"Katie, you're wonderful and beautiful and talented. That's why I got so excited about your design class. I think you'd be great at decorating. I just got a little carried away."

"It's okay, Dex. You don't have to explain." She inched toward the door. She didn't particularly want to hear what was coming next, so she said it for him. "I know there can never be anything between us. Really, it's okay."

"No, it's not!" Dex stepped behind her and closed the door, thwarting her escape. "I'm not gonna have you leave here thinking we could never date because you're not good enough for me. But that's what you're thinking, isn't it?"

She nodded her head.

He took her hand and led her back to the chair she had been sitting in. He knelt in front of her, never once letting go of her hand. "Katie, it has nothing to do with you. It's all me. You know what happened with Ally. I don't think I could go through that again—especially if it were you that got hurt. I couldn't bear that."

Katie wanted to bolt the room but was conscious of Dex's hand firmly pressing on hers. She sat still and silent.

Dex studied the back of Katie's hand while he caressed it with his thumb. "I hope this hasn't messed things up between us. We can't forget that you work here. I don't want you feeling awkward around me."

"I won't," whispered Katie.

Dex cocked his head and grinned. "Are you sure, Katie?"

How Katie loved that grin! It was impossible for her to resist, so she grinned as well. "No, I'm not sure."

"Well, then, we're gonna have to figure out some way to make sure we don't feel strange around each other."

"We could pretend it never happened," offered Katie.

He let go of her hand, and stood up. He walked around the desk to his chair. "I guess we could do that, but I for one don't want to forget that kiss."

Katie blushed. Even in embarrassing moments Dex had a way of making her feel special. And she knew she'd never forget that kiss.

"I'll tell you what, Katie. Since we agree the attraction is mutual, why don't we just take it real slow? We can keep doing things together like we have been—you know in a group as friends. Maybe someday soon I'll feel like I'm ready to date again, and we can talk about it. But I don't want to get ahead of myself."

Katie nodded her head. It was disappointing, but better than a total rejection. "Sure, I understand."

"And, Katie, if you want to go out with someone else, that's okay, too." It hurt Dex to say it, but he had to be fair. "You shouldn't have to put your life on hold until I get my emotions sorted out."

Katie swallowed the lump in her throat. "Okay."

She was obviously upset. Maybe her feelings for him were stronger than he had imagined, Dex thought. This pleased his fleshly desires, but pained his spirit. He didn't want Katie pining for him if there was no future for them.

He tried to give Katie a reassuring smile. "I'm really glad you're gonna be taking that design class. And my offer to pick up the tab is still good."

"You don't have to." They were talking about something else, finally. Katie could breathe a little easier.

"I know, but I want to. After all, I'm the one who suggested it in the first place. This way if it doesn't work out, you won't have lost anything but a little time."

"Yeah, but still . . . it's so generous, and well, I didn't get you anything nearly that . . . that . . . grand."

Dex leaned forward. "I thought signing up for the class was my Christmas present. You mean there's more?" When Katie smiled suspiciously and nodded, Dex added, "I love presents, Katie, and now my curiosity is up. You're gonna have to tell me what it is."

Grateful to have their familiar camaraderie back, Katie pursed her lips and shook her head. "No way, Matheson. You're gonna have to wait like all the other good little boys."

"Whoever said I was a good little boy?"

Katie laughed. "Nobody." She stood up, faced him and spoke in a serious tone. "Nobody had to tell me that, Dex. I knew it the first time I walked into this office." With that she exited the room and closed the door behind her.

Dex closed his eyes and clasped his hands on his desktop. And he prayed. He prayed hard.

❄ ❄ ❄

"Thanks for meeting me on such short notice, Andy."

"No, problem, Dex." The pastor blew on his coffee to cool it. "As long as you're buying lunch I'll meet anytime."

Dex laughed and got right to the point. They were both busy men. When he finished relating what had happened that morning, he commented, "I know kissing her wasn't the right thing to do, but it happened before I was even aware of it."

"Well, you're right; it wasn't the wisest choice you could have made. But at least you stopped at one kiss."

"No easy thing to do." Dex looked chagrined. "Andy, I know I keep saying it, but I don't know how much more I can take."

Andy was sympathetic. "I know, buddy, I know. Just because I'm married with three kids doesn't mean I don't remember what it's like to be young and single. Just keep reminding yourself that God doesn't give us more than we can handle."

"I know, I know." Dex ran his fingers through his hair and took a sip of coffee. "I keep thinking about how I've tried so hard not to hurt Katie, and then I go and kiss her. She's probably more confused than ever about me. And she was pretty shook up when I told her I wasn't ready to date yet."

"Which isn't exactly the truth, I might point out."

"Yeah. But what was I supposed to do? Tell her 'I can't date you until you accept Jesus as your Savior'?"

"Why not? It is the truth."

Dex let out a loud sigh. "But I don't want her to think I'm using God to manipulate her into doing something she's not ready for. No, I think she's been considering spiritual things, especially since her mom's conversion; but something's holding her back."

"We'll just have to keep the faith and believe God is going to get through to her yet," said Andy.

"I guess I'm getting impatient. Especially after that kiss!"

Andy laughed. "Boy, we can't have you running around kissing girls you're not even dating!"

Dex laughed, too, as he bit into his club sandwich. He had been right. Having lunch with his pastor was exactly what he needed.

✻ ✻ ✻

Katie forgot her lunch that morning, so she drove home to get it, still trying to save money by not eating out. She decided she'd prop her feet up and watch TV while she ate. She spotted her mom's Bible on the coffee table. Hesitantly, she picked it up. She couldn't remember if she'd ever held a Bible before. Carolyn Grady had given her a copy of the New Testament that day at the pregnancy center, but not seeing how it could be any help to her, she had thrown it away.

Katie flipped through the pages, not knowing where to begin. Apparently this book contained life-altering words, but she didn't know how to access them. Her mother had talked about the gospels so she flipped to the Table of Contents to try and find them. Nothing was listed under that name, so she scanned the page and her eyes fell on First and Second Peter. That was where the "cast your anxiety" verse was. She eagerly found the page.

She read the first couple of paragraphs. Apparently, this was a letter written by a man named Peter to a bunch of people who believed in Jesus. Peter was telling them not to be discouraged though life was hard. He said their faith would be strengthened because of their trials. Katie vaguely recalled Dex saying something similar on Thanksgiving, so she kept reading. One verse caught her attention: "Though you have not seen him, you love him; and even though you do not see him now, you believe in him and are filled with an inexpressible and glorious joy."

"That describes Mama perfectly!" spoke Katie out loud. "So you don't have to see Jesus with your eyes to know Him!"

Katie was excited that she was understanding some of what she was reading. She had always assumed the Bible was off-limits to most people; only religious fanatics could read and understand it.

She continued reading until she looked at her watch some 45 minutes later. "Oh, no! I'm gonna be late!" She carefully put Daria's Bible right where she had found it. She didn't want her mom to know she'd been reading it.

All the way back to work she thought about the last verse she had read. It made her uncomfortable, but she couldn't push it from her mind. She thought about talking it over with Dex, but after what had happened that morning, she didn't have the nerve. By the time she reached DesignLink, she had determined to forget all about it.

Finally, though, her discomfiture got the best of her. She knocked on Kevin's half-open door.

"Yeah? Whatcha need, Katie?"

"I was wondering if I could ask you a question."

"Sure, come on in." He quickly cleared the extra chair of a pile of files, books, and printout sheets.

Katie scratched her head in her nervousness. "I had a question about the Bible. I thought maybe you could help."

Kevin almost dropped the folder he held but caught it just in time. "I'll do my best. I'm no scholar. What is it?"

"I was wondering . . . exactly what does God consider evil? I mean I know it's wrong to murder and steal and all, but there must be more to it than that."

Kevin sat back in his chair and puffed his cheeks before answering. "I suppose anything contrary to God's Word would be considered evil in His sight. That's why we have the Bible, so we'll know what's right and wrong. Face it, Katie, without some kind of guidebook, we'd be all messed up."

"But how can God help if He only cares for people who do what is right?"

"I don't follow you."

"I read this verse—maybe I misunderstood it—but it said God only hears the prayers of the righteous and He turns away from those who do evil. So, if someone has been doing evil—or has done evil in the past—what hope do they have?"

Kevin squinted his eyes, as if trying to ascertain where Katie was coming from.

"No matter what people do, Katie, God will forgive them if they believe He exists and sincerely tell Him they're sorry. The only thing that keeps a person from receiving God's forgiveness is unbelief."

Katie tried to grasp the full import of Kevin's statement. "So, the evil people the verse was talking about are the ones who do bad things and don't feel remorse?"

"Yeah. The Spirit of God will convict you of your sin—meaning you'll no longer be able to do evil without thinking twice about it. When that conviction happens, you have two choices. You can turn to God and ask Him to forgive you and change your life or you can reject the Spirit. He never forces Himself on anybody. He lets us choose. Some people wait until they're on their death bed before seeing their need for repentance. But the forgiveness is still the same, whether it comes now or later."

Katie wondered aloud, "Why not just live your life however you want and repent at the end? Then you wouldn't have to feel bad every time you did something wrong." This made sense to Katie.

Kevin, however, didn't agree. "Because then you'd miss all the blessings God has for you. There's a joy that can only come when we have fellowship with God—that means having a relationship with Him here on earth. People who reject God may appear happy on the outside, but deep down in their soul is an empty place that can only be filled with God."

Katie nodded. She understood. She had lived that way for a long time—feeling empty and meaningless. "My mom said she hated her life but didn't even know it for a long time. Then, when she really looked at it, she was willing to do anything to change it."

"I heard she decided to follow Jesus. That's great. She no longer has to be a slave to her past life. She can be free."

"Slave? She was never anybody's slave."

"Well, not literally. I just meant that before we accept Christ as our Savior, we're trapped in a world of sin. We can't get out by ourselves. Even if we try, the Bible says our efforts are like dirty rags in God's eyes."

This offended Katie. She liked to think of herself as a good person. Other than a couple of dark stains she had tried to live an upright life. Now Kevin was saying her life was nothing more than a discarded old dish towel.

"That sounds pretty harsh, doesn't it?" Kevin added.

Katie nodded.

"I know how you feel. I've been saved for over fifteen years, and I still find myself falling into the trap of thinking I can make God happy as long as I'm a good little boy." He shook his head. "But God only looks at you as righteous when you look at His Son and say, 'I believe Jesus Christ is the only way to find favor with You, Lord.

Forgive me for ever thinking anything else.'"

Stunned, Katie stiffened in her seat. Apparently this God didn't cut any slack to his followers at all. It was either totally Him or nothing. "Whoa! That's a lot to think about."

"But considering the eternal consequences, it's worth it."

Katie involuntarily shivered. God was ruthless. He could at least acknowledge some of the good she had accomplished. She had worked so hard and overcome so much!

"Well, thanks for your time, Kevin. I'd better get back to work." She stood up to leave.

"Katie, you know I'll talk with you about this anytime. So will Dex."

She nodded silently.

Just as she returned to her desk, Dex came in. He was smiling, but this time it irritated Katie.

"Hey, Katie," he said as he stopped to browse through the mail stacked on her desk.

"Hi." Her voice was flat.

"Did you have a good lunch?"

"Yeah, it was fine."

Dex stared at her for a moment before noticing Kevin out of the corner of his eye subtly signaling for Dex to leave their secretary alone. Something had gone on while he was out, and Dexter Matheson was extremely anxious to find out what it was.

37

❋

DARIA MONTGMERY WATCHED HER DAUGHTER munch a bowl of Corn Flakes. As always, she was astounded by Katie's natural beauty and grace—even the way she lifted the spoon to her mouth was poetry in motion. *Lord, thank You for giving me such a wonderful daughter. Help me be a good mom, and help her to see her need for You.*

Praying for Katie, Daria walked into the kitchen and grabbed her own cereal bowl and filled it. "Morning, sweetie."

Katie glanced up. "Good morning. You look pretty today." Katie's gaze swept over her mother's black knee-length skirt, white turtleneck, and red, gray, and black plaid vest. Quite a departure from Daria's usual tight jeans and even tighter sweater.

Daria grinned self-consciously. "Thanks. I went shopping the other day. It's about time I started dressing my age."

Katie swallowed a mouthful of milk. "It suits you." She was still trying to get used to the "new and improved" Daria. She had even cut her hair. She had always worn it about midway down her back, but now it was barely above the shoulders and curled under on the ends. Wispy bangs swept over her forehead, softening her face and making her appear younger. Katie smiled. "So, are you going out or something?"

"I'm just goin' to church, then out to lunch." She nonchalantly glanced at her daughter. "You could come, too."

Katie got up and put her bowl in the sink. "No, I think I'll pass. I was planning on refinishing that antique table for Dex. I'm running out of time. Christmas is right around the corner." When Katie and

Dex had painted his office, they agreed that he needed a small table for his fax machine since it took up so much space on his desk. However, they had run out of money after buying the paint, paint supplies, new shelving, and area rug. So, when Katie stumbled upon a rickety tray table at a second-hand store, she knew it was the perfect gift for her boss. She had already stripped, reinforced, and primed it; now it was ready to finish with a mahogany stain. She was then going to stencil it with some geometric figures in the same colors as those in the rug they had purchased. She couldn't wait to see the finished product and Dex's reaction when she gave it to him.

Chewing cereal, Daria tried not to let her disappointment show. "Yeah, it's creeping up on us, isn't it? You know, I heard they're having a Christmas Eve program at the church—mostly singing. Maybe you'd like to go to that with me. It sounds like fun, and then we could come back here and turn the tree lights on and stay up all night watching old Christmas movies. What's that one you like to watch every year?"

"*It's a Wonderful Life*," replied Katie in a bored tone.

"Yeah, that's it! What do you say?"

Katie hadn't missed the eagerness in her mother's voice. Part of her wanted to agree just to please Daria, but another part reminded her that it was safer to stay away from South Madison Community Church—far, far away. "I don't know, Mama. I told Mr. Brinker I'd consider working for him. You know how everyone always wants Christmas Eve and Christmas Day off; he said he could probably use me—and give me holiday pay. I hate to pass that up."

"But it's Christmas!"

"And when has that ever meant anything to you?"

Daria bit her lip. "Never, I guess," she whispered. "Until now." She got up slowly and walked over to Katie and touched her on the shoulder. "I'm sorry you've had to endure a lot of lousy Christmases, sweetie. I can't change the past, but maybe I can do something to make the future better. I'm not gonna force you to do anything. You're a grown woman and can make your own decisions. If you want to work, that's fine. But I want you to know I'd like to spend this Christmas with you, just the two of us. I won't make any other plans until you let me know what you decide, okay?"

Katie simply nodded her head. Her mother's kindness made it difficult to think straight.

"And, Katie, no matter what you decide, it'll be okay."

Katie turned her head so her mom wouldn't see the tear about to fall. "Thanks, Mama. I need to get to work on that table." She fled the kitchen and headed to the laundry room where the landlord Mr. Carraway had said she could work. The ventilation was better in there.

Briefly closing her eyes in prayer for her daughter, Daria washed the breakfast dishes and headed out the door to church.

❊　❊　❊

"Daria, wait up!"

Daria turned and saw Dexter Matheson jogging through the church parking lot toward her. She waved.

"Whew! I must be out of shape if a short run like that leaves me winded!" panted Dex as he caught up with Daria.

Daria laughed. Dexter Matheson was anything but out of shape.

"I'm glad I caught you before you went inside. I was wondering if I could speak to you for a minute."

"Sure, no problem." They moved to the entryway of the church, but didn't go inside. "What is it?"

Dex cleared his throat. "I need to apologize to you for something. It's embarrassing." He was clearly uncomfortable.

Daria couldn't imagine what he was talking about but urged him to continue.

"I promised you I would never do anything to hurt Katie. And I certainly didn't mean to, but I'm afraid I didn't keep that promise." He noticed Daria's confused expression. "Did she tell you what happened the other day at work?"

"No, I don't recall anything," said Daria slowly, a little afraid of what Katie's boss might reveal.

Dex lowered his head. "Well, basically, I was a real jerk. Katie was telling me about the design class she signed up for, and I got real excited. I think she'd be a great interior decorator and I've been praying she'd have the confidence to believe she has real talent. Anyway, in my excitement, I gave her a hug and before I knew what I was doing . . . I, um . . . I kissed her." Dex blushed; he dared to meet Daria's eyes. "I'm sorry I did that; I had no right."

Daria grinned. "That's all! You just kissed her? I thought you were gonna say you two had a big fight and you fired her!"

Now Dex laughed, too. "No, nothing like that. But still, I shouldn't have done it. You know I can't pursue a relationship with her right now, no matter how much I want to. I had to tell her that so she wouldn't get the wrong idea."

"You told her it was because she's not a Christian?" Daria was surprised. She was sure Katie would have mentioned that to her—probably to scoff about Christianity.

Dex rubbed the back of his neck. "I didn't exactly tell her the whole truth. I told her I'm attracted to her but that I'm not ready to get involved with anybody because of some past mistakes I've made. She believed me, but I'm pretty sure it hurt her feelings." He scowled and clenched his fists. "Oh, I am so mad at myself! I never should have done that!"

Daria was sympathetic to the young man in front of her. "Dex, you do know Katie cares for you, don't you?" She thought of the hours her daughter had spent—and was spending at that moment—on Dex's Christmas present.

Dex eyed the older woman sheepishly. "I was hoping so, but I wasn't sure. Then after the stunt I pulled the other day, I wouldn't blame her for never wanting to see me again."

Daria shook her head. "I can tell you that's not the case. Look, my daughter—she has no confidence at all." Daria's countenance fell. "I suppose I'm to blame for the way she feels. She won't even let herself believe somebody like you would ever fall for somebody like her."

"I know. I mentioned that very thing to her and told her it wasn't true. But I don't think I convinced her. I feel torn, Daria; I mean, I don't want her thinking she's not good enough for me; but I can't pretend everything's fine, either."

Daria reached out and touched his arm. "Dex, please don't give up on Katie. She is so close to believing. But she's got some things she's afraid to deal with and they're keeping her from turning to Jesus. I know she wants to. But she's too angry and confused to listen to me." Daria's eyes brightened. "I'll bet she'd listen to you. Don't be afraid to push her a little. Katie is so cautious she may never get there on her own."

Dex nodded. "I just don't want to drive her away."

"Oh, I think it'd take a Mack truck to drive Katie away from you." When Dex's jaw dropped, she laughed. "Don't look so surprised! When we Montgomery women fall, we fall hard! Now, if you'll excuse me, I'm going to church. I think they already started; I can hear the praise team singing."

She walked over and opened the door of the church. Normally, Dex would have jumped to open it for her but he was pre-occupied. Daria didn't even have to wonder where his thoughts were. She smiled as she entered the sanctuary.

Daria gathered her purse, Bible, and church bulletin. She was still thinking about a verse that Pastor Powell mentioned during the sermon. He had quoted something from 2 Timothy saying that Christians weren't supposed to be afraid; instead they were supposed to have power and love in their lives.

With those thoughts echoing in her brain, Daria Montgomery

swallowed her fear and made a beeline for the person sitting a few rows over. She had overheard someone say the tall woman with the brown hair ran a crisis pregnancy center.

Daria had only been home for a few minutes when she heard Katie come in the front door. She stiffened and prayed God would give her wisdom. She tried desperately to recall everything Carolyn Grady had shared with her at lunch. She had been astounded to learn Katie had actually talked with the woman before having her abortion. Daria was again reminded—and comforted—that God truly had been seeking out her daughter for a long time.

"Hi, how's the table coming?"

"Pretty good," answered Katie glancing at her paint-stained T-shirt. "I've still got a ways to go. I got thirsty." She indicated the cola in her hand. "It was time for a break." She noticed that her mom had changed into a pair of gray sweatpants and an old sweatshirt. "Have you been home long?"

"No, not too long." She watched as Katie sauntered into the living room and clicked on the TV. Daria swallowed hard and forced herself to calmly sit down. "I had a real nice lunch with a lady from church."

"Yeah? Good, I'm glad," replied Katie never taking her eyes from the television. "You'd think there'd be something good to watch on a Sunday afternoon, maybe an old movie."

"You always were picky about what you watched," offered Daria, searching for courage to say what was on her mind. "Uh, I think you know the lady I had lunch with."

"Oh? What's her name?" Katie showed mild interest.

"Carolyn Grady."

Katie almost dropped the remote control. "Carolyn Grady." She spoke slowly. "I . . . I don't think I know her."

"Well, she remembers you."

Katie got up, not bothering to shut off the TV. A fuzzy pink bunny banging on a drum flitted across the screen demonstrating the endurance of some kind of battery.

"I'm gonna go back down and work on that table."

"I wish you'd stay here and talk."

Katie's hand was on the doorknob. She stood still. "What exactly did you want to talk about, Mama?"

Daria took a deep breath. "I thought maybe you'd like to tell me some of your feelings about the abortion."

Katie whirled around to face her mother. "My feelings! You want to talk about my feelings! You sure didn't want to that day at lunch, did you? Let's see, I believe your exact words were 'What's done is done; nothing can change that.'"

Daria knew this wouldn't be easy, but the sting of her daughter's words was sharper than she had anticipated. "I shouldn't have said that. We can't change what happened, but we can at least talk about it so it won't destroy our future."

Katie had never felt rage like she did right then. An uncontrollable force rose inside her starting at her feet and not stopping until it completely consumed her. She wanted to strike out at something. If she had been standing closer to her mother, she might have hit her. Finding no outlet for her anger, she fisted her hands in tight balls and lashed verbally.

"So, now you're attacking my life and saying it's no good, huh? Well, I'll have you know I'm working as hard as I can to avoid ending up like you. You're not exactly the person who should be giving advice, you know."

"I know, Katie," Daria sobbed. "But please let's just—"

"Please, let's just do what, Mama? You know, it occurs to me that you want everything on your terms. If you don't want to talk about something, we don't talk about it. If you do want to talk about it, then we do. If you don't want to talk about God, then we don't. But if you change your mind and do want to talk about God, then that's all we talk about! And, let's not forget this one: if you want me to have an abortion, then that's it! No need to discuss other options! No, it's always been your way or no way. Who do you think you are, Mama? Why do you think you have all the answers? And why do you think you can control my life and judge whether or not I'm happy?" Katie gestured wildly. "This is my home now, Mama. You walked out. Why do you think you can just waltz back in and start telling me what all is wrong with my life? You've got some nerve!" Katie was now frantically pacing; her body felt like it was electrically charged. She stopped long enough to cross her arms tightly over her chest and face her distraught mother. "Why, Mama, why are you doing this to me?"

Daria choked out the words. "Because I love you."

Katie bellowed and resumed the frenetic pacing. "Ha! That's a good one, Mama. You've got a really funny way of showing love. Most mothers show love by supporting their children. But not you! No way! You have challenged me on every decision I've ever made. You laugh at me because I want to study interior decorating. You send me on a guilt trip because I want to spend Thanksgiving with friends instead of with you. You call me foolish because I dare to consider the possibility that God exists or that somebody like Dexter Matheson might actually fall in love with somebody like me." She put her hands on her hips and laughed sarcastically. "You know, you tell me all the time how wonderful I am, but you sure don't act like you believe it."

Daria was struggling to keep herself from falling apart. Her heart felt like it was in a million little pieces. "Katie . . . I am so sorry . . . I . . . I think . . . that . . . that you are so—"

"Oh, save it, Mama. I don't even want to hear another apology. That's all you've been doing lately. If you're so sorry, then tell me why you've never been there for me? What did I ever do to make you so opposed to me?" Katie was sobbing almost as hard as her mother.

"Oh, baby," said Daria as she moved toward her daughter who was now leaning against the front door. "I'm not opposed to you. You have always been right—about everything. I was wrong—so, so wrong." She reached to hug Katie.

"Don't touch me!" shouted Katie. She slid down, her anger melting and giving way to sorrow the closer she got to the floor. "Leave me alone, Mama. You want too much from me." Through her tears, she looked up. "I can't be what you want me to be. I tried, I really did." She sounded like a little girl. "I tried to be brave and strong. I told myself I was doing the right thing, that it would only hurt for a little while." Her eyes grew round. "But those people at the clinic, they were wrong. They said it would be painless, but it still hurts so bad. I just want the pain to go away. But it never does."

Daria knelt beside her daughter. She didn't try to hug her, just put her arm on Katie's shoulder. "I know, baby."

"Even when I sleep, the pain is there. No matter where I go, it's there. And when I hear a baby crying, it's like a knife tearing through my flesh. It hurts so much worse than I thought it would. Carolyn tried to tell me; Memphis tried to tell me as well. But I didn't listen. I kept thinking if I was strong enough or smart enough or busy enough then the pain couldn't get hold of me." She locked gazes with her mother. "But it hunts me down, Mama, it hunts me down. I can't get away from it. I try, but it's always there. I just want it to go away." She clutched at Daria's arm. "Make it go away, Mama, please. If you love me, then do this one thing for me. Please!"

Daria's mind raced. She knew the only One who could take away Katie's pain was Jesus Christ. She longed to tell her all about Him, but something held her back. Then she remembered the pamphlets in her purse that Carolyn had given to her describing post-abortion stress. She could pull those out and show them to Katie. Everything her daughter was feeling was described in the one called *When the Pain Won't Go Away*. But again, a small, quiet voice admonished Daria to be patient and wait. There'd be time for that later.

For now, Daria Montgomery put her arms around her weeping child and held her, gently rocking her to the sound of the ticking clock hanging above their heads.

38

❄

KATIE LOOKED OVER HER BOSS'S SHOULDER at the blueprints on his desk. His musky cologne made her head swim; but she tried to force herself to focus on what Dex was saying.

"I know I said I wasn't gonna work on Dennis' project until after the holidays, but I couldn't sleep last night, so I did this." He indicated the computer drawing spread out in front of him. "If we knock this wall out, and put in a dividing wall here, we'll have better use of the space. What do you think?"

Katie nodded her head. "Yeah, and you could make this wall a bookcase. That would eliminate a lot of clutter and keep Dennis from having to purchase a separate piece of furniture for storage. The kids could keep their supplies and toys there."

Still looking at the blueprint, he nodded approval and muttered, "That's good, Katie, that's real good. What about the kitchen area? It needs to be opened up quite a bit or the kids will have to sit on top of one another just to eat!"

"We certainly can't have that, can we?" Dex and Katie looked up to see who was speaking. Lydia and Janie stood in the doorwary.

"Mom, Janie! We didn't hear you come in."

Lydia laughed. "Obviously not! Kevin told us to come on back here. What are you two so engrossed in anyway?"

Dex leaned back and put his hands behind his head. "This is Dennis Grayson's downtown mission project. Katie's been giving me pointers on space management."

Katie blushed, thinking Dex was merely being kind.

"Well," Janie piped up, "I'm afraid you're going to have to get along without her for the rest of the day." She walked over and slipped her arm through Katie's.

Dex grinned. "So today's the day, huh?"

"And there's nothing you can do about it," said Janie.

Katie looked from one Matheson face to another, not comprehending what was going on. "Would someone like to explain all this to me?" she asked.

Dex laughed. "This is a tradition with the females in my family. Mom kidnaps her daughters sometime during the week before Christmas and takes them shopping for their presents." He looked at Katie. "You might as well go along for the ride. Don't fight it."

"But . . . I have work to do. I have to schedule some appointments for the week after Christmas. I have to—"

"I'm not totally helpless. I do still remember how to use a telephone." Dex stood up, grabbed Katie's arm and pushed her toward the door while Janie pulled from the other side.

"But . . . I can't leave—"

"Oh, yes you can," said Lydia firmly while she winked at her son. "I'm still your boss's mother, you know. He has to obey me or he may get switches in his stocking!"

"Ouch, that's cruel, Mom!" laughed Dex.

"Well, a mother has to do what a mother has to do."

❋ ❋ ❋

Katie stared at her plate of half-eaten chicken fettuccine. The salad had been huge; the bread sticks kept appearing out of nowhere; and Janie was already talking about dessert. (She kept mentioning something about ordering the most delicious chocolate roulage to be found in all of Wisconsin.)

Lydia eyed her newly-acquired "daughter". "Don't you like your food, Katie? You've barely touched it."

"Oh, yes, it's delicious. I just don't know how I can finish it all. I keep eating, but it's like the food is multiplying."

Janie laughed. "I know, but it doesn't stop me." She made a face. "At this rate, I'll be big as a blimp before New Years!"

Katie giggled. Apparently all the Mathesons had high metabolisms; they were always eating but never seemed to gain weight.

"I was thinking we could head over to Hilldale Mall and do our shopping there. How does that sound?" asked Lydia.

Janie's eyes rounded. "That would be great! I haven't been there in ages. I say we do it—but only after dessert!"

"Great," replied Lydia. "What about you, Katie?"

Katie swallowed a drink of tea. "Um . . . I don't really know what to say." Everything was high-priced at Hilldale.

Lydia reached over and patted her hand. "Katie, it's the holidays. I want to treat my girls to a special time. That's why I do this every year." She smiled as if recalling a fond memory. "I can remember my mother taking me out Christmas shopping when I was little. It was such a wonderful time—I always looked forward to it. Back then people dressed up when they went to town. Not like now where people go to the mall almost every other day. No, this was an event you prepared for and spent the entire day doing."

Intrigued, Katie asked, "What would you do?" She felt an attraction to days past and enjoyed learning about the different lifestyles of different time periods.

"We'd get up early and Mama would dress me in my best wool skirt and matching crew-neck sweater with a little lace collar. We didn't have a lot of money, but every woman and little girl back then had to have a dressy coat with gloves and hat to match." She paused before resuming her narrative. "After we were bundled up, we'd ride the bus all the way to downtown Chicago and begin our day of shopping. We'd shop for my father and brothers in the morning, and then we'd go to the café at the Marshall Field's store and have the most wonderful lunch! My favorite was the turkey with pecan stuffing and then, of course, I'd always ask if I could have a huge piece of black forest cake for dessert." She grinned slyly. "I usually got it, unless I had misbehaved or something."

"I can't imagine you ever misbehaving," said Katie.

Janie howled and then looked embarrassed as she realized how loud she had been. "Sorry, but I couldn't help it. Katie, you just don't know Mom all that well yet."

"Don't pay any attention to her, Katie." Lydia smiled.

Janie leaned over and whispered to her friend, loudly enough for her mother to hear. "Later I'll tell you some stunts Mom pulled when she was a kid. Grandma told me lots of stories, but I'll wait until after we get our presents."

"A wise decision on your part," retorted Lydia. "Now, where was I? Oh yes, after lunch would be the best part of the trip because then I would get to go up to the toy department on the third floor of Marshall Fields and pick out my Christmas gift. Most of my presents were practical—school supplies, clothes, or shoes. But my mother always left enough money to buy me one special gift, something totally frivolous I'd get to pick out all by myself."

"What would you usually ask for?" Katie wondered.

Lydia's eyes misted over. "Oh, just getting to go was a treat in itself. The stores back then always put in big toy departments just for the season, and it was like a fairyland for a kid. We didn't have massive toy stores like today, so kids had to wait all year to go and peruse the aisles filled with the latest and greatest new toys. And there were always extravagant window displays with animated Christmas scenes. I could stand for hours and look at everything!"

Janie wiped a tear from her eye. "Grandma really loved Christmas." She looked over at Katie. "Grandma Dexter died when I was twelve, but I can still remember her playing the piano and singing Christmas hymns on Christmas Eve."

Lydia sighed. "Now we don't have Miss Ellie either."

Katie was experiencing a strange comfortableness in this conversation. For the first time in her life she had somebody to mourn and miss; and as sad as that was, it gave her the anchor and heritage she had longed for in her drifting life. Without embarrassment she brushed her own tears away. "I still forget sometimes that Miss Ellie is gone. The other day I put her name on my list of people to buy presents for. It hurt all over again when I had to cross her off."

"I know," sniffed Lydia. "I do the same kinds of things—like setting a place for her at dinner or going to her room to ask her a question. Christmas won't be the same without her." Lydia took a deep breath and straightened her back. "Which is another reason why I want to make this an extra special trip for the two of you. When you lose someone close to you, it's more important than ever to hold on to the precious memories and traditions we have. That way, we can still feel like they're right here with us. That's why I enjoy these annual shopping trips so much. I like knowing I'm passing down a little piece of history and heritage from my mother to my girls."

"Mom, you never told Katie what gift you would pick."

"Oh, I guess I did forget that part, huh?" laughed Lydia. "Well, no matter what kind of new-fangled toy was put on the market, I'd always go straight for the dolls. My favorite and most cherished one was a Madame Alexander bride doll I got for Christmas when I was ten. She was the most beautiful thing I had ever laid eyes on. The minute I saw her, I knew she was meant to be mine."

Lydia glanced at her two young companions to make sure she wasn't boring them. She was struck by the fascination registered on Katie's face. "Do you collect dolls, Katie?"

"What . . . um, no . . . it's not that," said Katie knowing she was rambling. "I just think it's nice that you have all these traditions and memories." She lowered her head.

Lydia and Janie exchanged glances. Lydia reached across the table and held Katie's hand. "Honey, it's never too late to start traditions or build memories."

Katie looked into Lydia's eyes. "Is that your way of telling me to stay home and spend Christmas with my mom?"

Lydia grinned. "Katie, your mother is trying her best to reach out to you."

Katie slowly let out her breath and tried to make sense of her conflicting emotions. "I've been pretty rough on her, I guess. But it's hard to go from one way of living to another just like . . ." she said as she snapped her fingers, "that."

"True; but did you ever stop to think that it's hard for your mom, too? She's changed on the inside because of trusting Christ, but the outside doesn't change without a lot of effort. She's working hard to make life different, and she needs your support."

"I know you're right, Lydia."

"So, what do you think you'll decide to do?" asked Janie.

"Part of me wants to stay home and try to feel like a real family, but part of me wants to go to your house and spend Christmas there. It's kind of ironic, isn't it?"

Janie looked confused. "How come?"

"Dex had to practically drag me to your place for Thanksgiving, and now that's the only place I want to be."

"Your mom was invited, too; you could both come."

"Yeah, I guess so, but I think I'm gonna decline." Resolve crept into Katie's voice. "Staying home feels right." She shuddered. She was getting closer and closer to painful territory. But she didn't want to fight it anymore. Too much was at stake. She forced herself to smile. "I'll have to make sure I can rent a copy of *It's a Wonderful Life*. Mama said she'd like to watch it with me this year."

"See," enthused Lydia, "you already have your first Montgomery family tradition: watching *It's a Wonderful Life!*"

Katie chuckled. "So it would seem."

Lydia's face broke into a conspiratorial grin. "And I know just where our first stop is going to be after dessert."

"Where?" chimed Janie and Katie simultaneously.

"We're going to the video store and buying Katie her very own copy of that movie. No more renting it every year."

"Then let's hurry and order dessert!" Katie's appetite had returned.

Katie lay awake re-living the afternoon of shopping and pampering. Lydia hadn't been kidding when she said she wanted the day to be special. The three ladies had manicures—Katie's first ever—and then tried on clothes in every store in the mall (or so it had seemed). Lydia insisted Katie stop looking at price tags and pick out what she wanted. No easy task; everything was gorgeous. She finally settled on a lissome, gray crepe skirt sporting lavender-and-ecru berries and topped it with a dusty-lavender blouse of the softest silk Katie ever had the pleasure of feeling. To accessorize the ensemble, Lydia suggested a tan leather western-style belt which added just the hint of casualness. She stood in front of the dressing room mirror and imagined her hair swept up with a tortoise shell clip. Then Katie had flung her arms around Lydia and uttered at least a dozen thank-yous.

Janie had opted for a bright red two-piece skirt set boasting a flattering hip-length jacket with a Peter Pan collar and dainty flower-shaped buttons up the front. Katie had been astounded at how elegant and mature her friend could look. The girls agreed they would wear their new outfits to the Christmas Eve service at South Madison Community Church.

Katie rolled over. Daria insisted on sleeping on the sofa. The old Daria would have sauntered in and plopped down on the bed without asking. The woman in Katie's living room was not the same woman who had moved into this apartment with Rick McBride more than eight years earlier. Katie knew the change was all because of the man named Jesus. Fatigue fast overtaking her, Katie closed her eyes and muttered a semi-audible prayer. *Lord, please don't let my mama down. She's changed everything for You.*

Katie went directly to sleep and slept dreamlessly for the first time in months.

39

❅

STANDING IN THE HALLWAY of the office, Katie debated as to how to go about giving Dex his Christmas present. She had hoped to arrive at work before him, put the table in his office, thereby surprising him with it when he walked in. However, he had ruined that plan by getting to the office first. She had seen his Jeep as soon as she pulled into the parking lot. Now, she wasn't sure what to do. Tomorrow was Christmas Eve so they wouldn't be working. She would see him at the Christmas Eve church service but didn't want to drag the table there and present it to him in front of all those people. So she simply stood in the hallway wringing her hands.

Finally, she turned to head back to her desk and bumped right into Kevin, who was coming out of his own office. "Whoa! Sorry about that, Katie."

"No, I'm sorry. I shouldn't have been standing there."

Kevin sensed something was on his secretary's mind. He winked slightly. "Why don't you let me buy you a cup of coffee? It's the least I can do after running over you the way I did." He gestured for her to lead the way to the snack area.

"I'll tell you what," replied Katie over her shoulder, "if you make it a cup of tea, you've got a deal."

"That's right," Kevin asserted, "I keep forgetting you don't like coffee." He pulled a chair out for her and Katie sat down. "Let's see, cream and sugar?"

"No, just sugar is fine," answered Katie.

Kevin saw her distraction and smiled. "There, that should be how you like it."

"Thanks," she replied as she blindly reached for the cup of steaming liquid. As she was about to take her first sip, she realized she wasn't holding the usual plain white mug she kept at the office. Her eyes grew large as she beheld a beautiful bone china cup with deep red and yellow flowers etched on the side. The saucer in front of her was trimmed with the same floral motif. She looked at Kevin. "Where did this come from?"

Kevin Holland laughed in his deep baritone. "Let's just say I didn't really forget you don't like coffee. Rachel suggested you might enjoy something fancier to drink out of."

"This is so pretty. I've never had anything like this." She turned the saucer over and saw that it was an English pattern called Old Country Roses. "Thank you, Kevin, and tell Rachel thank you as well. It was nice of her to think of me."

Kevin reached into the cabinet where they kept the office's meager culinary supplies. "Here, we also got this for you." He handed her a boxed assortment of flavored teas.

Katie accepted the proffered gift. "Wow, look at all the different flavors. The boxes are so pretty that I'm not gonna want to open them! Again, thank you, Kevin."

"No problem. I think Rachel feels a little sorry for you having to work with two guys every day. She was hoping to add some elegance to your workday."

"Well, this will definitely do it. I love it. The pattern is so pretty. It's exactly what I would have picked out for myself." She shook her head in amazement. "I must have the two best bosses in the world." She was quick to add, "And the best boss's wife, too. Rachel didn't have to get me anything. This is about the nicest Christmas I've ever had what with Dex paying for my decorating class and now this. Not to mention the Christmas bonus in my last paycheck. Boy, has that come in handy! In fact . . ." She got up and went to her desk and pulled out a small package from one of the drawers. "That bonus helped me buy this for you and Rachel." Suddenly she felt a wave of embarrassment. She knew her gift for the Hollands wasn't nearly as expensive as what they had given her. "It's . . . it's not much, but I thought you might like it."

Kevin opened the package and pulled out a gold, heart-shaped ornament. It had "Our First Christmas Together" inscribed on the front and "Kevin and Rachel" engraved on the back.

"Katie, this is great!"

"You probably have lots of First Christmas ornaments."

"No. Maybe two others, but they're nothing like this."

"It opens up like a locket so you can put in a wedding picture."

"Hey, this is great! Rachel's gonna love it."

"What's Rachel gonna love?" inquired Dex as he made his way toward the coffee pot. "After that phone conversation I just had, I'm in desperate need of a strong jolt of caffeine. Some clients, it seems, are a little short on Christmas cheer."

"Look at this, Dex. Katie got this for Rachel and me."

"Hey, pretty nice. And Katie, what'd you think about the tea stuff? That was pretty nice, too, huh?"

"I love it!" gushed Katie. "I think the tea even tastes better when it's served in such a pretty cup!"

"Well, in that case, you'd better let me borrow it 'cause I still can't make a decent pot of coffee!"

"Sorry, buddy, but Rachel gave me strict instructions that this was to be Katie's cup and only Katie's cup."

Dex feigned antagonism. "What's this? You've been married less than two months and she's already running our business! Come on, partner, that's pitiful!"

Kevin slapped his friend on the back. "Yeah, Dex, and I'm gonna count myself blessed because of it."

Dex winked at Katie. "Ooo! Good answer. Spoken just like an old married man!"

"That's *happily* old married man, my friend! Now, if the two of you will excuse me, I'm gonna go get some work done." He turned to leave. "Thanks again, Katie."

"You're welcome, and thanks for my gift as well."

Katie stared into her cup of tea. She still tended to feel awkward in Dex's presence if they weren't discussing work.

He sat down in the chair opposite his secretary. "So, you looking forward to having a few days off?" Christmas was on Friday, so, by taking Christmas Eve off, they would have a four-day weekend.

Katie nodded her head. "Sure."

"Are you gonna work at the grocery store?"

"Not until Saturday, and then I'll only pull half a shift. But Mama has to work that day, too, so it all evens out."

"Well, I guess I should get back to work—tie up a few loose ends before the long weekend." Dex stood up and stretched.

"Um . . . if you have a few minutes, there's . . . um . . . something I wanted to show you." Katie was embarrassed.

"Sure, what is it?"

Katie stood up and began speaking rapidly, sounding more like Janie than herself. "I was gonna bring it in this morning so it would be here when you got here, but then you were already here and there was no way I could do it without you noticing me, so it's still out in the car." She looked at her boss with uncertainty.

Dex held his hands up. "Slow down! I have no idea what you're talking about." He laughed.

Katie laughed as well, finally relaxing. "Just put your coat on, Boss, and follow me."

Dex did as he was instructed and found himself standing outside in the snow next to Katie's little blue Toyota.

She fumbled with her keys until she was able to unlock the hatchback. She lifted the door, and Dex could see some sort of wooden object with a bright red bow stuck to it. He looked at her questioningly.

"I had a hard time making it fit in there, so good luck trying to get it out."

Dex looked from Katie to the car and back to Katie again. "I don't understand."

"It's your Christmas present."

"My Christmas present?"

Katie giggled. "Here, help me get it out of the car." After they had succeeded, without causing damage to the car or the table, Dex set the newly-refinished table down on the snow-covered sidewalk and stood back to get a good look at it.

"Did you make this?"

Katie rolled her eyes. "I didn't construct the table, if that's what you're asking. I'm a secretary, remember, not a carpenter." Her eyes were twinkling; she was enjoying the surprised look on his face. "I found it at a second-hand store; it was in pretty bad shape so I got a great deal on it. I took it home, reinforced it, stripped the original paint, and then stained and stenciled it. That's all."

"That's all?" asked Dex incredulously. He slid his hand up and down the sides of the table studying the intricacies of the carving as well as Katie's handiwork.

"Well? Do you like it? It's for your fax machine."

"How can you ask that? It's beautiful." Katie's face glowed with pleasure and an equal amount of embarrassment.

"You should be proud of this. The stenciling even matches the pattern of my rug perfectly. That had to take a tremendous amount of time and effort. Not to mention the prep work. It's as smooth as glass. I can't imagine how many hours it must have taken you to sand and stain such a detailed piece of furniture."

"Then you're pleased?"

Katie wondered why he hesitated to answer. He wasn't smiling. And when he spoke, his words caught her off guard.

"So this is why you've been turning Janie down when she invites you to go out." He rubbed his chin as he stared blankly at his Christmas present, the big red bow gleaming against the white snow.

"Katie, I love the table, but you shouldn't have gone to all that trouble."

"Oh, I like doing this kind of work."

Dex frowned. "No, you're missing the point. You're always doing this kind of thing—for me or for the office or for your own apartment. I wish you'd learn to relax a little bit. You're gonna work yourself into an early grave."

Katie instantly stiffened. "That's not true." She was barely able to squeak out the words. "It's not as bad as you make it sound." She mentally recalled all the times she had turned down invitations from Janie—even her mom—to stay home and . . . and . . . do what? *Hide*, said a little voice in the back of her mind. *You hide so nobody will know the real you.* She pushed the unbidden voice aside.

"You said yourself I'm good at this sort of thing."

"Well, it doesn't mean you have to do it all the time. There is such a thing as fun, you know, Katie." He grinned.

Katie didn't know how to argue with his calm logic and even calmer demeanor. "But I think projects like this are fun." She tried to match his even tone of voice.

"I know I'm not communicating my point very well. I just hate to think that you went to all this trouble for me. It's not necessary. I don't need fancy gifts like this from you. An ornament like you gave Kevin would have been fine."

Katie flashed him a fiery gaze, struggling to keep her voice level. "Seeing as how you're not married, I didn't think it would have been appropriate!" She shifted her stance, arms akimbo. She looked like she might pounce any moment.

"You're angry."

"And you're a genius!" She spat the words at him.

Dex ran his fingers through his hair. He took a deep breath. "I'm sorry I've upset you. Truly, I didn't mean to, but . . . Well, I get the feeling that sometimes you avoid people, that you think it's easier to lock yourself away and never come out. I don't like to think of you living that way."

She angrily tapped her foot in the snow. "Then stop thinking about it! Besides, you don't know anything about the way I live my life. I do what I have to do to survive! Not everybody can have the perfect little life you have, Dexter Matheson!" Closing her eyes in an attempt to compose her raging emotions, Katie spoke softly and mechanically, pronouncing each word distinctly. "I like my life just the way it is." She wanted to tell him to mind his own business but couldn't bring herself to say the words. Knowing he cared enough to even consider how she spent her time brought a much-needed measure of comfort to her lonely, struggling soul. She repeated, "I like my life. Everything is fine."

"Really? Katie, you work a full time job, you go to school part time, you work at the grocery store part time, you put in extra hours here, which you don't want me to pay you for. Then, in your spare time—which isn't much—you study or work on some project. What are you trying to prove?"

Taking a deep breath to keep her own temper from boiling over, Katie straightened her back and pursed her lips before speaking. "I'm not trying to prove anything! I was trying to be nice! I'm sorry if that offends you." She pulled her coat tighter across her chest. "It's a table for crying out loud, a stupid table! That's all! If you don't want it, I'll take it home with me. I'm sure I can find some place to put it."

Again Dex ran his hands through his hair. His voice was filled with exasperation. "Katie, I didn't mean that to sound the way it did." He saw that she was reaching for the table, her intention obviously to load it back into her car. He grabbed her arm. "Katie, please don't—"

"Let go of me," she snapped as she jerked her arm free.

"No! I won't." This time he grabbed both of her arms and forced her to face him. "I'm not gonna let you go, Katie. I figured you'd know that by now."

"I don't know anything where you're concerned!"

He loosened his grip, but not enough to let her escape. "Look, once again I've been a first-class jerk. It's just that I get the feeling you're trying so hard to prove yourself to me when you don't have to. Have I done something to make you think that way?"

She shook her head, not willing to meet his eyes.

"Has Kevin?"

Again she shook her head.

"Then why not relax a little? Your job is safe. You don't have to keep working the way you have been. I can't even tell you how valuable you are to us. And as for me . . . well . . . you certainly don't have to try and earn favor where I'm concerned." Dex looked at Katie's glistening eyes and cringed.

Katie shivered in the cold.

"Come here." He pulled her into his arms and held her tightly. "Katie, please forgive me for making you cry. I love the table; really, I do. I'll treasure it."

"Then why did you say those things?" Her voice was muffled, but the hurt came through loud and clear.

He groaned and winced. "I know your life has been tough, and I hate to add to that. In fact, I'd love to see you sit back and take the time to notice the good things around you instead of always burying yourself in some kind of work."

Katie was thinking the best thing she knew in life was embracing her at that very moment. She pulled slightly away and toyed with the pocket on the front of Dex's jacket. "My life is better now than it's been in a long time. You just don't see it because you haven't known me that long. There was a time when . . . when—"

"When what?" coaxed Dex.

Katie looked down. "Nothing."

Dex lifted her chin. "What were you gonna say?"

Mentally calculating her options, Katie carefully considered how to respond. "It's nothing. I was just going to say that there was a time when I didn't even have a hobby. I did nothing at all in my spare time." She thought back to those four years after high school. Her life

had existed solely of work at the Pic-n-Save and occasional classes at
the university. The time in between was a blur. What had she done?
Watch TV? Read books? Sleep? Study? She couldn't remember what
had filled the hours. But she had very little to show for it. She was
certain Dex would be repulsed by such an existence. She chose not to
look at him and strained to sound lighthearted. "At least I'm doing
something constructive now."

"I guess you're right; I haven't known you long. But long
enough to know that I want more for you than you probably want
for yourself." He rubbed her upper arms. "Now come on, let's get this
table inside. It's cold out here!"

She nodded and followed Dex into the DesignLink office.

"Where do you think we should put it?"

Katie warmed at his use of the pronoun *we*. She glanced around
the room. "Maybe to the right of your desk. That way you can reach
it without having to get up."

Dex grinned his crooked grin. "My thoughts exactly!" He
quickly cleared the spot and placed it in its new home. He situated the
fax machine on top and stepped back to evaluate the new addition.
"Looks good. What do you think?" He turned to his secretary.

"So you're not mad at me anymore?"

He motioned for her to sit down while he leaned against his
desk. "Katie, I wasn't mad. How can I explain this to you?" He
searched the ceiling for answers before looking back at a very vulnerable Katie. "You did a beautiful job on the table. I'm honored that
you went to all that trouble for me. I'm obviously not worth it. The
things I said to you out there came from my own frustration, not
anything you did."

"I wanted to do something nice for you because you've been
so good to me."

He smiled, his heart quietly breaking with love for the girl
sitting in front of him. "You could have given me a paper clip and
I'd have loved it, Katie."

She smiled in spite of her confusion. "That certainly would have been a lot cheaper and a lot quicker."

"And it wouldn't have made me like you any more or less."

"But you do like the table, don't you? I mean 'cause if you don't I can take it back and get you that paper clip you wanted." Her eyes sparkled.

"Oh, no!" He held his hands up to stop her. "You're not touching that table. A very special person gave it to me, and I wouldn't part with it for all the paper clips in the world!"

Katie giggled, then grew serious. "Dex, what do you mean, you want more for me than I want for myself?"

Dex's face grew somber. "Katie, there's a way you can be free from all that you're struggling with. That's the life I want for you—one where you're not always running and hiding. See, God wants us to have peace. And we can have it, but . . . it comes at a high price."

"What . . . What's the price?"

Dex knelt in front of her chair, and took her hands in his. "The price is your life as you know it now." This wasn't what she expected to hear. "You've got to let it go—all of it."

Silence lingered. Katie was the first to break it. "Janie said the same thing. She said not to hold anything back."

"Whatever you hold back is only gonna haunt you."

"I know," whispered Katie.

Dex rubbed the back of her hands with his thumbs. "Sure, there are struggles in life; God knows I've got my fair share. But life itself isn't meant to be fought against—not like you're fighting it. You're trying to prove you can beat it, that you can overcome it. Satan and the world preach that lie, and it's just plain wrong. They tell you it's all about power and being in control. But power and control belong to God alone. He gives us what we need when we need it. We just have to ask and wait." He stood up. "Trust me, Katie. I've tried both ways of living—my way and God's way. And it's no contest. God's way is the only way. I'm not gonna lie to you. It's all or nothing where God is concerned."

Katie Montgomery stared into the hopeful, blue eyes of her boss. He was like Kaleo—persistently waiting for her. She knew Dex was attracted to her—he had admitted that much to her himself—but why did all this other stuff matter to him? Most guys would have been happy just to go out with her and get what they could. Then they'd leave. Like Eric had done. Like her father had done.

No, Dexter Matheson had never been like that. He would never ask her for anything. He would never take anything from her. He didn't even want her spending her time doing things for him. No, he didn't want anything from her. But his God did. His God wanted everything she had—including things Katie would prefer to forget about, if she could. But she knew she would never forget. That thought made her grimace. Fervently, she chewed her bottom lip.

Dex broke into her musings. "Have I scared you?"

She looked away and spoke softly. "Maybe a little."

"God is kind of scary until you get to know Him. It's part of His power. If He didn't have power, we wouldn't be in awe of Him." He reached out and gently turned her face toward him. "It's good to be afraid, Katie. The Bible says that fear of the Lord is the beginning of wisdom. So don't fight the feelings stirring inside you. Ask God about them. He'll be there for you. And I'll be here, too, if you need me."

"I'm glad," she half-whispered.

He leaned over and kissed her on the cheek. "Merry Christmas, Katie." As he stood up, he pulled something from his shirt pocket. "This is for you." He handed her a white envelope with her name scrawled on the front of it.

"I don't understand."

He laughed. "Now you sound like me! It's your Christmas present. I was gonna give it to you tomorrow night at church; but since you've already given me my gift, I figured why not." He motioned toward the envelope. "Open it."

"But . . . you said the price of my class was my gift."

He smiled slyly. "I know, and it is. This was something I just couldn't pass up. Now come on, open it."

She did, and pulled out two tickets. "What are these?"

"Well, what do they say?"

"Stars on Ice," she read. "You mean—?"

"That's right. I heard on the radio the other day that the show's coming to the Dane County Coliseum in February. They had advance tickets on sell, so I picked up a couple for you. Look." He pointed to the small print on the top ticket. "These seats are practically on the ice. I've heard it's a totally different feel when you're that close."

Katie was speechless. Not fifteen minutes ago she was sure he was upset with her and wouldn't want anything else to do with her, and now he was giving her tickets to an ice skating show!

"I . . . I don't know what to say."

"Just say Merry Christmas!"

Katie jumped out of her chair and embraced him. "Merry Christmas, Dex. And thank you." She pulled back so she could see his face. "Thank you for everything."

He looked like he wanted to kiss her. But he didn't. "You're welcome, Katie. You're very welcome."

Katie turned to leave his office, then stopped. "Dex?"

"Yeah?"

"I noticed there are two tickets to the show. I know it's still early and all, but would you go with me?"

"Only if you really want me to. I mean, you could take Janie or your mom. . . . Or another guy."

Katie didn't even hear his last comment. "No, I think it has to be you. You're the only one who knows how I feel about ice skating. I've never shared that with anybody else."

"Katie, I would be hono
red. In fact, I'll count the days."

"Good," she sighed, "so will I."

40

✴

STANDING IN THE KITCHEN doorway, Katie suppressed a smile over her mom's contant "bird vigil."

"How's it look, Mama?"

For the fifth time in the last half hour Daria opened the oven door to check the turkey breast roasting inside. Lydia Matheson had promised this was a guaranteed recipe.

Daria grinned. "Well, so far so good . . . I think."

"When should it be ready? I'm starting to get hungry."

Daria glanced at the clock. "Should be ready by 5:30. We can eat, clean up, and get to the church by 7:00."

"Sounds good." Katie walked through the kitchen, grabbing a roll on her way. She'd been a bit skeptical when Daria first approached her with the idea of cooking a big traditional meal on Christmas Eve so they'd have plenty of leftovers for Christmas day. They planned to do nothing but lie around and watch TV on December 25.

But, her mom had worked in the kitchen for hours and seemed to be enjoying it; she wouldn't even let Katie do a chore as simple as chopping an onion. Daria had been a woman on a mission. Katie hoped for her mother's sake everything tasted as good as it smelled.

Just as Katie reached for a magazine to leaf through, the doorbell rang. "I'll get it," she called to her mother.

Katie was greeted by an enthusiastic "Merry Christmas" before she got the door completely opened. "Janie! What are you doing here? Come on in."

"I came to spread some Christmas cheer!" Without waiting for an invitation, Janie Matheson set down one of the two bags she was holding, marched into the kitchen, and gave Daria a hug. "What's cooking that smells so great!"

Daria laughed. "It should. It's your mother's recipe."

"Oh, speaking of my mom; here, she sent this." She held out a package wrapped in bright red cellophane with a plaid ribbon. "During the holidays Mom always bakes loaves of cranberry bread for family and friends."

Daria took the loaf. "Oh, this'll be perfect for breakfast tomorrow. Katie and I made a pact that we aren't doing any kind of work at all tomorrow. We're vegging out all day!"

"Ooo! Can I come over and hang out with you guys?"

"Sure," replied Daria.

"Yeah, Janie. You know you're welcome," added Katie.

Janie smiled but shook her head. "I can't. I think everybody in the northern United States with the last name Matheson is planning to be at our house. I'm kind of obligated."

Katie laughed. "Then you'll be in your element, won't you? There's nothing you like better than a big party."

Janie cocked her head. "You're right about that. Besides, a lot of people I haven't seen in years will be coming. That should be fun." Her eyes sparkled. "And tons of kids! That's always the best part of Christmas. You get to play with all those toys and nobody looks at you funny! And, of course," she added, "I like it when kids are around because then I'm not the shortest person in the room!"

Katie and Daria both laughed. "Janie, do you want some hot chocolate or tea or anything?" inquired Katie.

Janie gave a quick glance at her watch. "I'd like to, but I've still got a few stops to make. I'll have to hurry if I'm gonna make it to church on time." She walked back to the living room. "But there is one more thing I need to do while I'm here." She picked up the large gold and white gift bag she had deposited earlier. A picture of a Victorian angel adorned the front and sparkly gold tissue paper stuck out the top. "Here, Katie. This is for you. Merry Christmas."

Katie reached for the package thinking it was too beautiful to open. "Janie, you didn't have to get me anything."

Janie rolled her eyes. "Well, of course I did! I love giving presents!" She turned toward Daria who had joined them in the living room. "You should see the bracelet Katie got for me when we were out shopping with my mom the other day. It's gorgeous. She bought it to go with the red suit Mom got me." Suddenly her eyes lit up. "Oh, you'll be able to see it tonight at church. I'll have it on."

Daria smiled. "I can hardly wait. Katie tried to describe it to me, but I'm the kind of person who needs to see something up close." She sat down on the sofa next to her daughter, anxious for her to open her present. Lydia had told her about it on the phone. "Come on, sweetie, open your gift."

Katie slowly pulled the tissue paper back and peered inside. She saw some white fabric, but she couldn't make out what it was.

Janie implored her meticulous friend to get on with it.

"Okay," laughed Katie and pulled the object out. She stared at it blankly for a moment; then understanding dawned.

"Janie . . . I can't take this . . . you'd give this to me?"

"Yes, silly, I want you to have it. Mom and I agreed it should go to you." She smiled. "The two of you can share it and consider yourselves honorary Mathesons."

Daria reached out and touched the silky white cloth only slightly colored with age. "It sure is a beautiful doll, Katie. Look at that veil. It even has little pearls edging it."

"It's . . . it's beautiful. I've never seen a more beautiful doll." She touched the delicate little wedding dress with something akin to reverence. "But . . . but Janie, I can't take this. It's too much." She turned pleading eyes to her friend.

Janie sighed. "Mom said you'd react like this. She said you wouldn't want to take it."

"It's not that I don't want the doll; but I don't feel . . . worthy. It should belong to you or your sisters."

Janie turned to Daria. "Is she always like this?"

Daria shrugged. "Yeah, that's just the way Katie is."

"Well," stated Janie matter-of-factly, "the doll is yours now, Katie; there's nothing you can do about it."

"But don't you want it?"

"Let's see if I can explain this." Janie cocked her head, considering how to begin. "My sisters and I grew up hearing Mom's stories about how Grandma would take her Christmas shopping each year. Even though we love those stories, I think we cherish the time spent with Mom every year even more. We like the idea that we're carrying on the tradition and that someday, Lord willing, we'll pass it on to our own children." She paused for a breath. "Well, I got the doll when I turned ten. That's how old Mom was when she got it. So, for the last ten years it's been displayed in my room. I'm surprised you didn't see it that day when you were there, Katie."

"I was a little distracted," said Katie remembering the awful day she had learned of Miss Ellie's death.

"What made you decide you wanted Katie to have the doll?" asked Daria.

"I suppose," said Janie thoughtfully, "it was the look on Katie's face the other day at lunch when Mom was retelling the story. I decided right then to give it to her, but I wanted to check with Mom before I did. So that night I talked to her about it, and she said the same thought had occurred to her, but she didn't know how to bring the subject up with me. We both laughed, assuming the idea must have come from God." Janie looked triumphantly at Katie. "So you see, Katie, you have to take it. God wants you to have it; and if I were you, I wouldn't argue with God!" She and Daria laughed.

Katie didn't see anything funny. She was too busy struggling with feelings of unworthiness. Why were these people trusting her with their precious heirlooms? First, Miss Ellie had insisted Katie have the photo of Everett and Lydia, and now, the doll. Not to mention

Dex's generosity in paying for her design class.

"The last thing I want to do is to make you feel uncomfortable. But I've had an entire lifetime with my family and only gotten to know you recently. I guess you could say the doll is to make up for all those years. I wish I could have known you and spent time with you these past ten years, but since I can't change the way it is, the least I can do is give you the doll. Oh! I just remembered! Mom put a note in here for you." She shuffled through the tissue paper. "Here it is." She handed Katie a small envelope with the same angel motif.

Carefully, Katie opened the card and read: "For the daughter of my heart. Merry Christmas. I love you. Lydia."

"I don't deserve this.

"Don't you see, Katie," said Janie, "that's what Christmas is about. The world didn't deserve a Savior, but it got the best gift of all. So maybe when you look at the doll it can remind you of that."

Daria's eyes filled with tears. "I know it'll make me think of that, Janie." She stood up and gave the small girl a hug. "You and your family have been so kind to us."

Janie, always ready for a good cry, didn't even try to stop the tears from flowing. She hugged Daria back. "Merry Christmas," was all she could manage to say.

"You, too, sweetie," said Daria, having difficulty keeping her emotions under control. She tugged on Katie's hand until she, too, joined them for a group hug.

At that moment the oven timer buzzed. They laughed.

"The turkey's ready!" cried Daria as she hurried to the kitchen to check on the fruits of her culinary labors.

"Well, I've got to run," said Janie. "Enjoy your dinner. I'll see you in a little while."

Closing the door after Janie, Katie again stood staring at her mom. The past week had seemed unreal—a shopping spree, a best friend, a wonderful boss, and now her mom in the kitchen fixing Christmas Eve dinner! Could it be possible that the God of the universe had a soft spot for Katie Montgomery?

✳ ✳ ✳

Later that evening, Katie was humming the tune to "Angels We Have Heard on High" as she carefully hung her new print skirt and lavender blouse in the closet. Her fingers lingered on the soft, silky fabric. Never having been preoccupied with her appearance, Katie had to admit she had felt beautiful tonight. Perhaps it was the new clothes. Perhaps it was the spirit of the Christmas season. Or perhaps because for the first time since she could remember, she felt loved.

She flopped on the bed, grabbing a pillow and hugging it tightly. Her mind wandered to the church service that evening. It hadn't been long—people were anxious to get home to their own families and own traditions—but it had been beautiful. The lights were dimmed and the glow of several candles illuminated the sanctuary with what Katie could only describe as a holy serenity. Of course, it helped that she had been surrounded by people she could now unashamedly consider to be family. The Mathesons occupied two entire rows in the church, and Daria and Katie were included.

At church that night she could reach out and touch Lydia's sleeve knowing she would have her attention; she could hear Everett, Dex, and Brady behind her singing the Christmas hymns in their deep, rich voices; she could turn and see her mother—her mother!—praying silently as the pastor prayed aloud; and she could see Janie, the sister of her heart, smiling at her from the end of the pew.

And she could see the cross at the front of the church. Katie wondered if maybe that was the key to it all.

"Katie, can I come in?"

Katie sat up and saw her mother in the doorway. "Sure."

"Whatcha doin'?"

Katie still hugged the pillow. "Oh, just thinking."

Holding something behind her back, Daria sat on the edge of the bed. "Yeah, a lot's been going on lately, huh?"

"Yeah. You really outdid yourself with the meal."

Daria beamed. "Thanks, sweetie. I hope I can do a lot more cooking from now on." She made a face. "But I'm gonna have to get some more recipes from Lydia, or we'll be eating turkey and dressing every day of the new year!"

"Well, it would beat my usual frozen dinners!"

Daria motioned toward the kitchen. "I've got some hot chocolate going. I thought we could have some with our dessert and watch the movie now if you want."

"Sure," replied Katie. "I just need to get changed." She was wearing only her slip. She stood up to get her pajamas.

"Um," stammered Daria, "I got this for you." She held out a package. "Just a little something; it's probably stupid."

"What is it?" asked Katie.

Daria looked embarrassed. "I picked it up the other day on a whim. I don't know what made me do it. Here, open it. If you don't like it, you can just tell me."

"I thought we weren't exchanging gifts 'til tomorrow."

"I know," said Daria, "but it'd be better if you opened this one tonight. I've got some more for tomorrow."

Katie untied the little red ribbon and unfastened the paper. She pulled out a pair of red and green plaid flannel lounge pants and a white thermal top with a matching plaid teddy bear pattern stitched onto the front. "These are so cute! And I needed some more, too. My old ones were practically obscene!" she laughed. "Thank you, Mama. I love them. . . . What is it? Why the strange look on your face?"

"I did something, and I hope you won't think it's too silly. I . . . bought me a pair just like yours." She looked away, obviously blushing. "I thought we could both put 'em on tonight while we watched the movie. You know, have mother and daughter matching pajamas. Stupid idea, huh?"

"I think it's a great idea, Mama. Let's do it!"

Daria breathed a sigh of relief.

41

※

DRIVING TO WORK Katie had difficulty sorting through her emotions. Was she angry or scared? Embarrassed or frustrated? The dream she had the night before wasn't helping.

She had dreamed that the doorway to her bedroom was engulfed in flames. In the dream she jumped on her bed screaming for help. Through the raging flames she saw everybody she loved—Janie, Dex, Lydia, Everett, Daria—but they couldn't reach her. Only Kaleo was on her side of the fire.

Just like in the dream she had right after her abortion, Kaleo grabbed Katie's hand and pulled her—not away from, but toward the fire. The flames seared her skin. She screamed. It was too painful. She pulled back, but not before she saw the pleading looks on the faces of her loved ones. They wanted her to come to them.

And then she saw her. For a split second, Katie forgot all about the scorching heat and took a couple of steps toward the door, where Daria was holding a tiny, mangled infant. Daria held the baby out to her. Katie reached out, unable to control the growing desire to embrace her little, broken daughter. Even in her deformed condition, the infant seemed to know Katie was her mother and seemed to long to be cuddled close to the breast of the woman who had first nourished her, the only home in this world she had ever known.

As Katie was about to step into the fire, a white-hot flame flashed in her face. She jumped back. Kaleo moved closer toward her, entreating her not to be afraid.

"But I am afraid! I am!" Katie had screamed.

Fear not, Katie, for I have redeemed you; I have summoned you by name; you are mine. When you pass through the waters, I will be with you; and when you pass through the rivers, they will not sweep over you. When you walk through the fire, you will not be burned; the flames will not set you ablaze.

Katie stared at the gray wolf. His mouth had not moved, yet he had spoken. Kaleo nudged her toward the door and the fire; but, despite the intense heat and the warm, gentle voice, Katie's feet froze to the floor. Disgusted by her self-inflicted fear, Katie threw herself onto the bed and covered her head with her pillow, waiting for the fire to consume her. She dared to peek out at her wolf-friend. Kaleo stepped into the midst of the fire as it fast encroached upon the bed.

Then she saw Daria turn and hand her baby to Dex who rocked it and whispered sweet words of comfort into the little one's ear. Daria called with outstretched arms, "Katie, please come home. We're all waiting for you. Don't be afraid."

"No, Mama, I can't!" Smoke filled the room.

Kaleo limped out of the other side of the fire. He was badly burned, his body scarred and one leg burned completely off. But he was free. Katie was all alone. Then all went black.

That was all she could remember of the dream.

Absent-mindedly, Katie navigated the turn into DesignLink's parking lot, not anxious to get to work. She parked but didn't exit the vehicle. Instead, she reached over to the passenger seat and picked up the pamphlet her mother had given her that morning.

Why had Daria chosen this particular day to bring up the subject of her abortion? Daria Montgomery, for all of her faults, had surprised Katie with her silence the last couple of weeks. Since that day before Christmas when Katie had broken down and cried, she had been waiting for her mother to preach to her or at least insist she go and talk with Carolyn Grady. But she hadn't said a word. Until today. And even then, she said very little. She simply sat down at the table, laid the pamphlet in front of her daughter, and very softly told Katie she ought to look over the information and to call her at work if she needed to talk. Katie had grabbed the pamphlet, lied about being late for work, and had run out the door.

Now she sat staring at the little booklet: *When the Pain Won't Go Away—Dealing with the Aftereffects of Abortion.* Memphis Blue had said that she was going to have to heal and that it probably wouldn't be easy. Was that what Kaleo had been trying to get her to do all along? To heal? She turned to the first page. She began reading the story of a girl named Laurie who had chosen to have an abortion. Katie realized she could have been reading her own story. Oh, the circumstances were different, but the emotions were the same. She read how Laurie had suppressed her emotions so she wouldn't cause anyone else any pain while she was silently dying on the inside. She read how Laurie had felt unlovable because of what she had done. Katie was well-acquainted with that feeling. Maybe she *was* always trying to prove she was good enough, just like Dex said. She continued to read.

She came to a description of "post-abortion trauma," something Katie had never heard of before. But she recognized the symptoms listed: feelings of betrayal, bitterness, depression, distrust, guilt, shame; recurring nightmares, low self-esteem, avoidance of babies and pregnant women.

Katie continued reading far enough to discover that if a woman had five or more of the symptoms, she most likely was having difficulty recovering from her choice to abort.

So it was true. Her abortion had never been a settled matter in her mind. Oh, she had tried hard to convince herself it was—but guilt had been hounding her since that decisive day years earlier. If she opened the door to that guilt now, would she be able to overcome it? Or would it overcome her?

Taking the practical approach, Katie decided she would have to wait until later to think about it. She had responsibilities. Dex and Kevin were waiting for her and would expect her to be professional and efficient. *Put the abortion stuff on hold for a while,* she told herself as she concealed the booklet in her purse and opened the door of DesignLink. She took off her coat and gloves and went to make herself a cup of tea. Seeing Kevin through his half-open door, she smiled and waved at him, calling out a cheery, "Good morning!" She noticed Dex's office door was closed. *He must be on the phone or working at the computer.* She reached for her china cup, pondered the tea flavors, and opted for blackberry. A fruity flavor might liven up the dreary, gray day. The sky was threatening snow again.

Waiting for the water to boil, she sauntered over to her desk to check the day's appointments. She turned her desk calendar to the correct day; usually she did that the night before, but she must have forgotten yesterday. It wasn't a particularly busy day as far as appointments were concerned so she mentally noted it would be a good day to do the housekeeping chores: dusting, vacuuming, watering the plants, clean out the refrigerator; and, of course, filing.

The water reached a boil and she poured it into her cup, added a spoonful of sugar, and bounced the teabag up and down in the scalding water. She'd have to let it cool. She didn't like things too hot.

It wasn't until she set her cup on her desk that she saw what day was written on her calendar: January 15. She shivered, oblivious to the steam rising from her teacup; she turned deathly pale. She didn't even hear Dex come up beside her.

"I thought I heard you out here. I was on the phone."

No response.

"Katie? Are you okay?"

Dex stood right next to his secretary and reached for her arm. "Maybe you should sit down. You look kind of pale." Gently he guided her to her seat. "Katie? What is it?"

Katie didn't notice the worried look on Dex's face. She said, "I . . . I . . . uh . . . it's the 15th."

"Yeah, it's the 15th. . . . What's going on?"

She didn't respond for a moment, then said, "I think I'd better

401

go." She stood, reaching for her coat.

"Can't you tell me what's wrong?"

"I have to get out of here." Before he could stop her, Katie fled the office and drove off in her little blue Toyota.

❉ ❉ ❉

Daria Montgomery eyed the clock, realizing a delay would make her late for work; but she picked up the phone anyway and dialed Lydia Matheson's number. It rang twice.

"Hello?"

"Lydia, it's me, Daria. I'm sorry to call so early, but I need you to pray. You see, today's the day, and I'm worried; I'm not sure how she's gonna react. I may have pushed her too soon this morning at breakfast. I just wanted to help, but—"

"Whoa! Daria, slow down. First, it's never too early to call with a prayer need; and second, who am I praying for?"

Daria breathed a sigh of relief. "Katie."

"Okay. Can you tell me what the problem is?"

"Well, I can't tell you all the details. I'm sorry."

"No, that's fine. I understand. What can you tell me?"

"Oh, Lydia, Katie's been running from God for several years now. She's afraid of His wrath, I think. She needs to understand His forgiveness—I mean really understand it. And for reasons I can't go into right now, I think today is gonna be especially hard on her." Daria didn't mention the significance of the date and what had occurred exactly five years earlier. Nor did she bring up the terrible cries she heard coming from her daughter's room in the night.

Daria had been asking God to show her the right time to approach Katie about the guilt suffocating her. She didn't know if it truly had been God prompting her or her own frustrated heart yearning to do something to help her daughter.

"So, Lydia," Daria said, "please just pray that Katie will stop running and finally meet God face to face. If she'd only stand still long enough, I know she'd see the same love and forgiveness I saw that day when you first told me about Christ. I want this so much for her; I can hardly stand it."

"Of course I'll pray for her, Daria. And I'll call Everett and have him pray as well. But right now why don't you and I pray? Maybe that would ease your mind a little."

And it did, for the moment. But Daria Montgomery had a difficult time at work that day. No matter how hard she tried to keep her mind on the price of the various grocery items she was scanning, it always wandered instead to the spiritual battle being waged inside her daughter's soul.

❋ ❋ ❋

Wandering aimlessly through West Towne Mall, Katie tried to keep her mind distracted. However, she had no spending money left after the holidays, and shopping was frustrating when you couldn't afford to buy anything.

Katie sighed as she strolled the aisles of The Lang Store gift shop, her eyes perusing the various knick-knacks and decorative items filling the shelves. She found the rustic wooden floors and soothing scents of the shop comforting. She picked up a pink pillar candle and breathed deeply of its mellow, flowery scent. The thought came to her that the color would have worked beautifully in a little girl's room—her little girl's room. She set it down with a thud on the shelf.

"I've got to stop thinking about this," she muttered.

"Can I help you, dear? All our candles are half-priced."

Katie jerked her head up and looked at the salesperson, an older woman with gray hair and pudgy cheeks. "Uh, no, ma'am. I'm just looking today, killing time mostly."

"Well, let me know if I can help you with anything."

She started toward the exit. "I need to be going." Katie didn't want anyone to get too close to her today, not even a sweet saleslady. Maybe shopping wasn't such a good idea.

Out in the mall area, she felt the first pangs of hunger. Since she had no cash, she decided to head home and eat there. Maybe loafing in front of the TV would be what she needed.

* * *

"Mom, it's Dex."

"Hi, Son. What's up?"

"Well, I'm a little worried about Katie. You haven't heard from her, have you?"

"No, not today. Why?"

"She came to work as usual, but then she left without any explanation." He frowned. "Is Janie around?"

"She's got classes all day and won't be home 'til four."

"Hmm. I thought maybe Katie had confided in her."

"Dex, Daria phoned me this morning. She was afraid today was going to be hard on Katie for some reason. She wouldn't tell me why; she just asked me to pray that Katie would finally stop running and come face to face with God."

"Really? She didn't indicate what the problem was?"

"No, but she sounded frantic."

"What do you think I should do, Mom?"

"There's not much you can do except pray. If Katie wants to talk to you, she'll seek you out."

"Thanks, Mom. If you hear anything, let me know."

Dex hung up the phone feeling more concerned than ever. He'd have to take his mother's advice and pray and wait, but he figured it was going to be a long day.

* * *

Changed into jeans and a sweater, Katie added the finishing touches to her salad. As she put the ranch dressing back in the refrigerator, she noticed the light blinking on her phone. Curiosity got the better of her and she punched the button.

"Katie, it's Dex. I was hoping to talk to you. You had me a little worried with the way you left the office this morning. Are you okay? If you're there, please pick up the phone." A pause. "C'mon, Katie, where are you? Please let me hear from you soon. I'll be waiting."

Katie closed her eyes. She longed to run into his arms and have him tell her everything was going to be okay. But was it? What would he do when he found out the truth about her? She stifled the cry she felt forming in her chest.

She grabbed her salad, walked to the living room, and clicked on the TV, hoping it would serve as a better distraction than the mall had. Crunching on a mouthful of iceberg lettuce, remote control in hand, Katie vetoed several news programs, a lewd music video, an old western movie, and a cooking show.

She surfed the channels until her attention was caught by an attractive middle-aged woman dressed in a tailored indigo suit with large gold buttons down the front of the jacket. She was talking with an older man who seemed captivated by what she was saying. Katie turned the volume up.

"I worked as a nurse in an abortion clinic for nine years before my eyes were opened to the truth. And when they finally opened, I was horrified at what I saw, at what I had been a part of. I knew that by working in the abortion industry I might as well have been slapping God in the face."

"Explain what you mean by 'slapping God in the face.'"

"Well, in the book of Acts, chapter 17, Paul teaches that God made the entire world and that He is the one who gives life and breath to all people. He goes on to say that God determines the time and place each person should live and that only through Him can a person truly live and move and even have their being. We are, in essence, God's offspring. But, by choosing to abort, a woman and those who counsel her to make that decision, are saying they disagree with God's plan, that He's wrong and they know a better way. When we accept this viewpoint, we begin to do shocking, unthinkable things—like deciding who has the right to live or not."

"Did things at the clinic shock you?"

Katie held her breath as the woman on the screen answered. "I think what shocked me then—and still shocks me today—is the total denial that these are *babies* being aborted. As an abortion nurse, I was coached to always refer to them as fetuses or unwanted pregnancy tissue." Emotion was etched on her face. "Then one day I saw very clearly that it was much more than tissue. It was a tiny little person."

The host leaned closer and gently asked, "What happened to make you realize this?"

"Well, one of my jobs was inspecting aborted tissue. Infection could occur if any body parts were left inside the mother's uterus. We had to be careful. I inspected thousands of body parts over the course of my time there, but one particular day—I'll never forget this for as long as I live—I looked down at the little arms, legs, torso, and head lying there. And they were all arranged perfectly in the shape of a baby." She closed her eyes. "But they were lifeless—disconnected from each other and from the mother who was supposed to be nourishing them into a healthy little person. I stepped back in horror unable to take my eyes off of that mangled little body. Finally, I turned and ran out of there, and never went back."

The woman shook her head for emphasis. "From that moment on, I knew that what I had done was help women kill their babies. I had gone to seminars where I learned techniques for persuading women to do this, much like you would learn how to close a business deal." She pursed her lips in self-disgust. "It was all so clinical and sterile. The reality of what we were doing was cloaked in medical terminology and humanistic jargon. God's Truth was deliberately omitted. I could no longer deny, though, that those were babies."

Katie's thoughts turned to Margaret Kilgore. Katie had longed to believe she really cared about her, that she wanted to help her. Had she just been "closing the deal" with Katie's baby as the collateral? The very notion wrenched her stomach.

"That is an incredible story." The host commented. "God reaching you in such an environment is miraculous."

"I found out later that several faithful believers had been praying for me. I hate to think where I'd be today if somebody hadn't cared enough about me or those babies to pray."

Katie clicked off the TV and stared at the blackened screen. Her eyes filled with tears as she allowed herself to consider the possible truth of what she had just heard. *Did I really kill my baby? Am I a . . . a murderer? Is there a God who is the giver of life? What does He think of me now?*

Having God angry with you was enough to make anybody squirm. It was time to get up and move. Katie rose from the couch, dumped her dirty dishes into the sink and headed out, never hearing how the abortion nurse found peace in Jesus. But it's hard to hear anything when you're running.

❅ ❅ ❅

Katie drove around mindlessly, but she began to feel guilty about running out on her bosses. *I should go back to the office and finish at least some work. But they're sure to ask questions.* She parked across the street out of sight and waited. She hoped neither of her bosses would work late.

Shortly after six o'clock, both Dex and Kevin came out the front door, locked it, bid one another good-bye, and went their separate ways. As the two men's cars pulled out of the parking lot, Katie breathed a sigh of relief.

"All right, girl, time to get to work and at least do a little something productive today. Tomorrow we'll pretend none of this happened." Katie pulled into the parking lot.

She cringed, recalling her rash behavior. Seeing the date on the calendar had unexpectedly jolted her into some kind of emotional breakdown. Hopefully, she was past it now—at least until this same time next year; but today seemed to have enough trouble of its own.

42

IN A WHIRLWIND OF ACTIVITY Katie watered the plants, cleaned the refrigerator, dusted the furniture, and filed the paperwork. All she had left to do was vacuum and clean the bathroom. Not looking forward to the next task, Katie grabbed the walk-man from her desk drawer. She hummed along with the upbeat tape as she pushed and pulled the vacuum cleaner across the beige carpeting. So intent was she that she didn't hear the front door open or her boss steal up beside her.

※　※　※

Dex—grateful to finally know where Katie was—didn't think about the possibility of frightening her with his presence. He tapped her on the shoulder and called her name.

Katie jumped and Dex would have laughed but for her stricken look. He clicked the machine off.

"Katie, thank God you're okay."

Katie pulled off the headphones and placed her hand over her wildly beating heart and took a few deep breaths. "Whether or not I'm okay is debatable. I think I may have just had a massive coronary." She looked up at her boss. "What are you doing here?"

Now Dex smiled. Seeing Katie acting like her old self again was a balm for his heart. "Sorry, didn't mean to scare you so bad. I just came by to pick up some plans I left, so I can look them over before my meeting tomorrow morning."

"Do you ever do anything besides work?"

"Well, I could ask you the same thing." Dex eyed her sheepishly. "Of course, you didn't do much work today."

Katie's defenses went up.

"No. I'm sorry about that. I had no right to run out on you that way, but I'm making up for it now. I've almost finished everything I would have done this afternoon." She began winding up the vacuum cleaner cord. "All that's left is the bathroom." She cast a sidelong glance at her boss. "I could clean your office if you want me to."

"You're doing it again, Katie, did you know that?"

"Doing what?"

"You're hiding behind your work, that's what."

Katie thrust the vacuum to the side. "I am not." Dex could be so arrogant. "I'm simply doing my job!"

"Well, some things are more important than your job."

"Look, if you want to fire me for leaving, just do it."

Dex wanted to shake her; she could be so insufferable. "I don't want to fire you and you know it!"

Katie's eyes blazed. "Maybe to me nothing is more important than my job. Some of us have to struggle for a living. We're not all like you. I've been trying to tell you how different we are for a long time, but you just won't listen."

Dex rubbed the back of his neck. His voice was tight. "This has nothing to do with how different we are, Katie. It has to do with the way you keep running from everything and everybody that matters. You don't have to—"

"Since when did having to endure a critical commentary on my life become part of my job description?"

"Why won't you talk to me?" Dex yelled. He was past the point of exasperation. Why couldn't he make her see she could trust him? "I know something's going on. Why are you pushing me away? All day I've worried and prayed for you."

"I never asked you to do that."

Dex stared into her flashing eyes. How did it come to this? This was not the way he had played out the scene in his head. He thought

Katie would confide in him and he would finally have the opportunity to break through her walls.

Had Dex taken the time to examine his feelings, he would have discovered that his pride had been hurt. But in the heat of an argument, there's not much time for self-examination. Retaliation comes much more naturally and easily.

"No, you never asked me to. And right now I can't figure out why I bothered! If you want to live your life closed up in a shell, that's fine with me. Go ahead and shut the rest of us out. Forget about how Miss Ellie loved you and how my mom and dad practically consider you one of their own kids. And, of course, forget about Janie. Who needs her friendship anyway? In fact, you don't need any of us, do you, Katie?" He ran his hand through his hair. "Well, that's fine. It would make my life a whole lot easier!" He stomped into his office and grabbed the plans. As he passed back through the lobby, he turned and faced his secretary. "You can stay here and work all night if you want to, Katie. It makes no difference to me!"

❄ ❄ ❄

Katie watched him slam the door behind him. He disappeared into the black night.

Dexter Matheson had said his life would be better off without her. She knew she had been saying that very thing to him for a long time, but it hurt a lot more coming from him. She pushed the vacuum into the utility closet with a shove and reached for the bucket, mop, sponge, and ammonia. She made her way into the small lavatory and began to scrub the sink, brushing away the tear trickling down her cheek.

"It's better this way," she told herself. "Now I won't have to worry about fitting in to his world anymore." She wiped another tear, thinking about Dex's harsh words. Katie's breathing became labored. She filled the bucket with water and added ammonia. After thrusting the mop into the sudsy water, she mopped the small tiled floor, each stroke becoming more vigorous than the one before.

"It doesn't matter; it doesn't matter," chanted Katie, hoping the mantra would calm her struggling soul and mend her tattered emotions. "It doesn't matter; it doesn't matter."

Finally, she threw the mop down and sank to her knees. "Then why does it hurt so much!" she cried. "I'm so tired; I want the fears and the doubts to go away. I can't take this pain anymore!" She rocked methodically back and forth, her hands spread on the floor in front of her. She kept seeing Dex walking away from her and slamming the door to all of her dreams. "No! I don't want to be alone! Oh, God, help me . . ."

Slowly, through her veil of tears, Katie began to see that Dex was right. She was running—and had been for years. But how could she stop? Running was all she knew.

Then there danced through Katie's mind an image of a smiling white-haired lady telling her to search until she had her answers and placing into Katie's palm a small card that said "Cast all your anxiety on him because he cares for you."

"Oh, how I want to believe that," she whispered through broken sobs. She thought how the lady was like Miss Ellie. They both saw straight into her soul. "Oh, Miss Ellie, I wish you were here."

Katie sat up as a question posed itself in her mind. What would she do if Miss Ellie were still alive? She longed to sit and listen to the stories of faith and family.

As if operating on automatic, Katie walked to the lobby, grabbed her keys and left the DesignLink office. It never occurred to her that she had left her cleaning supplies in the bathroom or that she had forgotten her jacket. Mentally, Katie was no longer at DesignLink. She was at long last taking that sweet old lady's advice and searching, desperately searching, for a refuge from her torment. And she was determined to find it as quickly as her little blue Toyota could get her there.

Dex entered his apartment and threw the architectural plans across the room. "Why? Why did I have to be so stupid and lose my temper like that?" Self loathing filled him.

He fell to his knees in the middle of his living room and cried out to his heavenly Father. He couldn't find words to articulate his feelings; his prayer sounded like a garbled message coming over a static-filled line. He was confident, however, that his groanings were perfectly clear to his Savior who would plead to the Father on his behalf for forgiveness and for protection for the girl named Katie.

Oblivious to the falling snow and half-blinded by tears, Katie navigated her car down the winding road and into the dimly-lit driveway. Shifting the gear into park, she got out of the car and stumbled to the door. As she hesitated, the accumulating snow dampened her hair and clothing. She peered into the window and could see lights on in the back of the house. She gathered her courage and knocked.

Everett, who had been watching the news with Lydia, motioned for his wife to keep her seat while he answered the door. Who would be arriving unannounced at such a late hour?

He opened the door and Katie flew past him and threw herself into Lydia's arms. Curiosity had gotten the better of his wife and she had followed him to greet their unexpected visitor. What a relief to see Katie.

"There, there," soothed Lydia as she stroked Katie's hair. "Come into the family room. We have a fire going."

Katie allowed herself to be led, never letting go of Lydia's hand. "I'm sorry to come so late."

"Shhh, don't you worry about that." She directed Katie to the hearth where the shivering girl immediately fell to her knees and began warming her hands. Lydia grabbed an afghan off the rocking chair and put it around Katie's shoulders, then whispered to her husband, "Go call Daria."

Everett left to make the call, but he hurried back, just as anxious as Lydia to know Katie was okay. Returning, he found his wife pressing a hot cup of tea into Katie's hands.

"Drink this, it'll warm you up quicker than anything."

"Th-thank you. I didn't realize how cold I was."

"Well," interjected Everett, "the temperature's been dropping all day. They're predicting a heavy snowstorm. We were just watching the weather when you came."

Katie turned pitiful eyes toward her boss's father. "I'm sorry, I shouldn't have disturbed you." She gingerly set her steaming cup down and began to rise. "I should go."

"No you will not!" spoke Everett emphatically. "I will not let you leave this house while it's snowing this hard. I'm just thankful you made it here okay."

Katie turned to Lydia who nodded in agreement. "Everett's right. You're right where you need to be. In fact, I believe God led you here."

Katie shook her head violently. "No, you're wrong. God wouldn't lead me anywhere! He hates me; I just know it. I wish I could take it all back, but I can't! No matter what I do or where I go, it's there to haunt me. I . . . I . . . I can't change it no matter how much I want to. But I'm sorry! I really am sorry. Oh, God, why did I do it?"

Katie was nearing hysteria. Lydia sank to her knees and wrapped her arms around the crying girl.

Katie shrugged free. "No, you don't know what I've done! You . . . you couldn't possibly understand!"

Lydia and Everett shared a concerned glance. "Whatever it is," stated Lydia with much more calm than she felt, "we can surely talk about it. You know we love you, Katie."

"That's right." Everett hunkered down beside his wife.

Shaking her head, trying to hold back the torrent of tears, Katie kept repeating, "No, no, no. You wouldn't if you knew the truth. It's just like Dex said. You'd all be better off without me. I'm not worth it."

"I can't believe Dex would say that," Lydia exclaimed

"Oh, he said it all right," choked out Katie.

"No, he didn't," responded Everett, feeling his anger rising toward his eldest son.

"There must be some explanation. He would never deliberately be that cruel." Lydia turned toward her husband, unsure of what to do or say next.

"He did say it!" Katie practically screamed. "And he was right! You've all been so nice to me and I don't deserve it!"

In tears herself, Lydia tried once again to put her arms around Katie, this time with success. "I'm sorry Dex hurt you, Katie. I'm so sorry. I can't imagine what he was thinking."

"Dex would never want to hurt Katie!"

Everett, Lydia, and Katie all three turned to the doorway of the room. There stood Janie. Her tears spilled over. She sniffed loudly and repeated, "Dex wouldn't hurt you, Katie. He loves you. He's been in love with you for months."

Silence hung over the room. Lydia looked questioningly at her husband. He simply nodded his head.

After an eternity Katie spoke. She rocked back and forth in Lydia's arms. "He can't love me, he can't love me."

"Why can't he, Katie? Why can't Dex love you?" asked Lydia as she gently guided Katie's chin toward her.

"Because I killed my baby. Oh, God, I killed my baby!" She covered her face with her hands in shame. "I knew what I was doing, but I did it anyway."

It was quiet. Janie walked toward Katie with outstretched arms. "Oh, Katie." Janie looked into Katie's bewildered eyes. "Katie; I love you. I'm just sorry I haven't been a better friend to you."

"Wh-what do you mean? Y-you've been the best friend I've ever had," choked out Katie.

Everett and Lydia looked questioningly at their daughter. Wiping a solitary tear from her cheek, Janie took a deep breath and answered her friend. "I've always struggled with my mouth. I never seem to know when to shut up. But, in your case, Katie, I think I haven't said enough."

"Didn't you hear me, Janie? I had an abortion."

On the verge of crying again, Janie nodded her head. "I know. I also know that you had it back in high school, the second semester of your senior year. Right?"

"H-how did you know that? I've never told a soul except my mother."

"That day you sat with me in the lunchroom at school I knew something was weighing on you. But I was too afraid to push." Sorrow crossed her face. "Maybe if I had pushed a little, you wouldn't be hurting so much right now."

"No, Janie, no! Don't blame yourself for my mistakes. I knew it was wrong, but I didn't see any other way out." She pushed the hair back from her face. "And now I'm gonna have to live with it for the rest of my life."

Lydia said, "It seems to me you've suffered enough."

"No," cried Katie, "never enough. Nothing could make up for what I've done." She buried her face in her hands again.

"That's where you're wrong, Katie," interjected Janie. She glanced over at her father who was on his knees praying.

Everett Matheson shared a smile with his Savior and continued to pray.

✳ ✳ ✳

"Katie," spoke Janie softly, placing her hand on her friend's shoulder. "Nothing can change the past; you're right about that. But as far as God not forgiving you, you're wrong. If you believe in Jesus and what

He did on the cross, the Bible says you can be reconciled to God."

"Reconciled? Wh-what?" Katie's voice faltered, but she was willing to reach for any lifeline at this point.

"It means," said Lydia, "you can be a friend of God's if you believe His Son died for your sins—not just because you had an abortion but for every time you've done anything contrary to His word or His ways."

Katie looked hopeful. "Why would God want to be my friend if He knows the despicable things I've done?" She shook her head again. "I don't deserve His friendship or anyone else's." She looked at Lydia and Janie, wondering that they hadn't kicked her out of the house yet.

"But, Katie, that's the beauty of God's grace and His forgiveness. If we deserved it, it wouldn't be so special." Janie's eyes pleaded with Katie to understand.

"Like what you said on Christmas Eve? That the world didn't deserve a savior, but God sent one anyway?"

"Yes! Exactly!" enthused Janie.

Lydia reached over and grasped Katie's hand. "Oh, Katie, no one can fathom the love of God—how high, how wide, how long, or how deep it is. He only wants to love you; but He can't as long as sin stands between you and Him."

"But . . . it's already been done; I can't go back and change it! It'll always be there!" Katie's voice was frantic.

"Christ can erase it, Katie." Lydia spoke firmly. "That's why He came. He can't change the fact that you have sinned, but He has already taken your punishment." She stared into Katie's eyes. "Everything you fear God is going to do to you has already been done. All the fury you deserve, all the humiliation, all the anger—it was unleashed on Christ on the cross. Katie, don't you see? Christ walked through the fire for you."

The fire! Katie's thoughts rewound to the dream she'd had the night before. She had been so afraid of that fire; but it was the only way to the other side, where all the people she loved were waiting. Now Lydia was telling her Someone else was willing to go in her place. And that Someone was Jesus.

"Jesus," Katie whispered inaudibly.

Lydia sat back on her heels. She didn't know what else to say. From this point on it was strictly up to Katie to believe or reject. Salvation was a gift, freely given and freely received.

Janie leaned back as well to give her friend some breathing room. "Never forget that you're loved, Katie. By us and by God. Nothing will ever change that."

Katie rubbed her face with her hands. She was exhausted, but also restless, and very tired of being restless.

"So, what do I do now? I'm tired of running and pretending. But it's all I know how to do."

All three Mathesons breathed a sigh of relief. Katie was tired of running!

"Just talk to God, Katie, and tell Him everything. Don't hold anything back."

Katie managed a small smile. "Like you told me on the day Miss Ellie died. You've been telling me what to do all along; I just haven't listened." She pursed her lips.

"People around you may have been planting seeds," said Lydia, "but God is the One who makes them grow when He knows they're ready to grow. His timing is perfect, and I know that whatever you've gone through these past years, no matter how painful it's been, can be redeemed and used for good in God's kingdom. But right now all that matters is that you're ready to make a change. You've got to move out from under all this guilt."

Katie looked questioningly at Lydia and Janie and then glanced over at Everett as well. "Do I do it now? Right here?" She still wasn't sure what was expected of her.

"Sure, we'll go through it with you if you want. Or you can do it privately."

"Please don't leave." She grabbed Janie's hand and squeezed Lydia's. "I'm finished trying to do things by myself."

They formed a circle, holding hands. Lydia prayed aloud that Katie would finally open her heart to her heavenly Father.

And then she did.

"God, my name is Katie, and I want to tell You I'm sorry for what I've done. I . . . I killed my baby when I knew it was wrong. I've tried to do things my way for such a long time, and I'm sorry. But Lydia and Janie and my mom have been telling me that You still love me. I . . . um . . . I confess that I find that a little hard to believe, but I do want to believe it. I've never wanted anything more in my whole life. I know Jesus never did anything wrong." Katie paused to wipe the tears that had begun accumulating again. "I know He was perfect, and I surely don't understand why You would want me if You already had a perfect child. But I hope You do because, well, see, if You don't help me, I don't think anyone can. And if that's true, then I don't want to live anymore. So please, even though I don't deserve it, would you accept me? Would You forgive me and show me how to do things Your way? Please!"

Katie sniffed and Everett handed her a tissue. Embarrassed, she blew her nose. "Welcome home, Katie," he said.

"Wh-what do you mean?" Katie dabbed at her eyes.

Everett smiled. "What I mean is that you are now part of God's family. He's your Father and you're His child."

Katie's eyes grew round. "Really? Just like that?"

"Just like that. You've been adopted by the Creator of the universe. The Bible says that 'to those who believed in his name, he gave the right to become children of God.' By acknowledging that Jesus is Lord, you've secured your inheritance in the kingdom of God." Everett smiled.

"Oh, Katie, that was so beautiful, so honest and real!" Janie threw her arms around a confused Katie.

"But, isn't there something else I need to do or say?"

"Nope," answered Everett. "Salvation is a gift, pure and simple. If you truly desire it and ask for it, it's yours."

"And I heard you do all of that tonight, Katie." Lydia was wiping her own eyes as well. "Now you begin your journey of faith along with the rest of us."

"But how will I know what to do?"

Everett laughed. "Well, you certainly don't have to do anything tonight. It's practically midnight!"

"Oh my, it is, isn't it?" echoed Lydia. "I think the first thing would be to get a good night's sleep. We can talk tomorrow about how different your life is going to be."

Everett helped his wife to a standing position. "Lydia's right, Katie, and I'm going to insist you stay here tonight." He glanced out the window and saw the snow was still falling. "It's too late for you to be out on those icy roads."

"But I don't have any of my things."

Lydia put her arm around Katie's shoulders. "Don't worry. We've still got a lot of Kendall's things upstairs. We can find something for you to sleep in and wear tomorrow."

Katie's eyes grew very round. "Oh no! I just realized my mom doesn't know where I am! She'll be worried sick!"

"Actually, Katie, I called her earlier, right after you arrived. I told her you were safe and sound and that we weren't about to let you leave."

Surprising herself, Katie flung her arms around Everett, who was just as surprised. He knew he was being hugged for more than making a simple phone call. He kissed the top of Katie's head. "Good night, Katie. Sleep well."

She pulled her head back and looked at this older man she adored. He wasn't her father, but then she'd never even known her real dad. She figured this one would do just fine. She closed her eyes, thankful that God had put such wonderful people into her life.

"You know, Everett," she told him, "I think maybe I will sleep well tonight. For the first time in my life."

✳ ✳ ✳

Everett watched as his wife launched into her nightly routine. For all of her spontaneity, Lydia Matheson was quite the creature of habit when it came to her bedtime ritual. He smiled and mentally announced each of his wife's tasks. *First, we brush the hair, then we wash the face and apply our night cream, then we brush the teeth. Next we stare at our teeth in the mirror and decide if we have the time and energy to floss. Usually we don't. Tonight is no exception. We then turn out the bathroom light and come to bed.* Right on cue, Lydia entered the bedroom.

"What does that smug look on your face mean?"

"Oh, nothing. I was just admiring my wife, that's all."

"You're making fun of my little nightly routine, huh?"

"Well," grinned Everett, "maybe." He sobered for a moment. "Actually, I was wondering why you're not chattering on about Katie. After Daria accepted Christ you couldn't talk about anything else."

Lydia stared at her husband and bit her lip. She plopped down on the bed and pulled the covers up around her. Tears began to form in the corners of her eyes.

"I suppose I'm a little ashamed of myself." She sighed.

"Ashamed? Whatever for?"

"Oh, Everett," she sobbed as her husband's arms encircled her petite frame. "I'm ashamed of the thoughts I had when Katie told us she had an abortion! For a brief moment I was . . . I was repulsed. I wanted to slap her or tell her to leave or something! I know it's wrong, but it's how I felt."

Everett slowly stroked his wife's hair. "I know, baby. I guess I felt a little of that, too."

Lydia looked up. "You did?"

"You and I love babies so much. It's hard to imagine someone deliberately killing one for their own selfish reasons."

Lydia sniffed. "I know, but I thought I was past those judgmen-

420

tal attitudes by now." She waved her hand in the air. "I mean, we've supported Carolyn and the Pregnancy Center for years! I assumed I knew everything there was to know about abortion. Can you get any more arrogant than that?"

Everett rubbed his tired eyes. "Don't be too hard on yourself, honey. You're forgetting that all of our experience with abortion has been purely philosophical, never personal."

"Until tonight, you mean."

"Yes. And remember what Carolyn said. Statistics show that close to one out of six women in the church have had abortions, but they're too ashamed to let anybody know."

"They're too ashamed because they're afraid people will respond exactly like I did tonight!"

"Well, whatever you might have been thinking and feeling on the inside, you certainly didn't show it on the outside. Katie obviously felt secure enough with us to make the biggest decision of her life right downstairs in our family room."

Lydia wiped her eyes and blew her nose. "That's true. And I really am thrilled about it."

Everett pulled her chin toward him and stared into his wife's face. "Are you thrilled enough to perhaps have Katie Montgomery as a daughter-in-law someday?"

"What?" Lydia stared back at her husband.

"What Janie said downstairs is true. Dex has been in love with Katie for months. He just couldn't do anything about it because she wasn't a believer. But now she is."

"But does Dex know about the abortion?"

"No, I'm pretty sure he doesn't. He's known something was eating away at her, but he's had no idea what it was."

"Do you think it'll change his feelings toward her?"

Everett studied his wife's features. "Do you want it to make a difference?"

"Why would you ask that?"

"Let's be honest, Lydia. If you're struggling with this, it would be a lot easier if Katie weren't in the picture."

Lydia thought hard. Finally, with resolve in her voice, she spoke. "No, Everett, I don't want it to make a difference. A couple of months ago, I believed God wanted me to reach out to Katie, and I still believe it today. She's already like a part of our family, with or without a relationship with Dex."

"So, you can love her and not hang this over her head?"

"Yes, I can, and I will. And I'm gonna thank God for showing me this sin in my life."

Everett nodded. "I guess that's why we have to continually pray Psalm 139: 'Search me, O God, and know my heart; test me and know my anxious thoughts. See if there be any offensive way in me, and lead me in the way everlasting.'"

"Yes." Lydia snuggled next to her husband. No matter what came up in their lives, there was always a word from the Scriptures to comfort them and see them through.

Both husband and wife slept well that night.

✻ ✻ ✻

Katie was pulling back the covers to Janie's bed when the younger girl returned from the bathroom.

"Are you sure you don't mind sharing your bed with me, Janie? I can sleep down the hall in Kendall's old room."

"Are you kidding? She still has all those boxes stacked up in there. Besides, I'd rather have you here with me. I've always considered you a sister anyway, so this just makes it official." She grinned hugely. "In more ways than one."

"What do you mean?"

"Well, you've always been a sister of my heart, but now you're a sister of my spirit as well. We're both the adopted children of God, so that makes it official. We're family!"

Katie smiled. Janie was always so full of life and she still had the most beautiful smile Katie had ever seen.

"Janie, can I ask you a question?"

"Sure," she chirped as she set her alarm clock. She had an 8:00 class in the morning, and it was already past midnight.

Katie cleared her throat and spoke shyly. "I was just wondering about what you said downstairs. . . . you know, about Dex. I know I probably shouldn't be thinking about him right now . . . I mean with everything else that's happened . . . maybe I shouldn't even ask."

"Are you kidding? I've been waiting for you to ask! I've had to keep my brother's secret for over six months. Not an easy task!"

Katie laughed. "Well, you certainly never hinted or anything. I had no idea he felt that way about me. I mean, I hoped, and I knew he was attracted to me, but . . ." She shook her head.

Janie cocked her head. "You do understand why he couldn't tell you, don't you?"

"Kind of, I guess."

"He never wanted to hurt you, Katie. Dex isn't like that. But the Bible's pretty clear about a believer not marrying an unbeliever. So Dex had to tread lightly."

Katie was astonished that Janie had brought up marriage. She and Dex had never even been on a date! "It's not like he's gonna propose to me or anything!"

Janie cocked her head. "Well, no, but Mom and Dad always taught us that the reason for dating somebody is to see if they might be the mate God wants you to have. So it doesn't make any sense to get involved with someone who doesn't share your faith because that's the most important part of a relationship."

Katie dropped her head. "It may not matter anyway."

"Why would you say that?" demanded Janie.

"Janie, let's be realistic. When Dex finds out what I've done he may not want anything to do with me." She shuddered. "I've seen him around his niece and nephew and talking to Johanna's unborn baby. I'd be a fool to think my abortion wouldn't matter to him."

Janie bit her lip and avoided Katie's eyes.

"Janie, what's wrong?"

Slumping her shoulders and exhaling loudly, Janie confessed. "I'm sorry if I've overstepped my bounds in this, Katie; it's just that I love you so much and I love Dex so much. I've waited so long for the two of you to be able to be together."

"What are you talking about?"

"It's my mouth again. But I only had good intentions! Please don't be mad at me!"

"Mad at you? For what? Just tell me."

"Well, when I got home from school today, Mom told me Dex had called and said he was worried about you because you had left work unexpectedly but wouldn't say why. So, I tried calling your apartment, but there was no answer. Then I kind of got worried, too."

She took a deep breath. "Then tonight I found out why you were so upset. But Dex didn't know. He was still at his place worrying about you. I knew he'd be thrilled about your decision to trust Christ. I guess I got a little excited because, well . . ." She gulped. "When you were in the bathroom, I ran downstairs and called Dex."

Stunned, Katie sat down hard on the bed. "Um . . . how much . . . exactly how much did you tell him?"

It was Janie's turn to stammer. "I . . . um . . . told him . . . pretty much everything."

Katie's expression sank.

"I'm sorry, Katie. I know I shouldn't have. But I've watched my brother struggle for so long with dating and relationships that I couldn't help myself. I jumped in without thinking. Forgive me, please."

Katie was speechless. Dex knew her secret. What did this mean? She was almost afraid to find out. She turned toward her friend. Seeing Janie's pleading eyes, she couldn't help but smile.

"You're incredible, Janie, did you know that?"

Janie's eyes lit up. "No, and I'm not sure I believe it. I just want to make sure you're not mad at me. Am I forgiven?"

Katie sighed. "I don't know much about this Christian life, but I'm pretty sure I'm supposed to forgive people, so I guess you're off the hook."

"Oh, thank you! Now I'll be able to sleep better." She climbed into the bed and fluffed her pillow. "Good night."

"Not so fast, sister. You're not getting any sleep until you tell me what your brother said."

Janie laughed out loud. "So, you *are* interested?"

Katie collapsed onto the bed. "If you don't tell me what he said, I might have to strangle you!"

"Okay, okay! There's no need for violence!" She scooted higher in the bed. "First, he was just glad to know you were here. He'd been praying constantly. When I told him about the abortion, he was shocked; but then I told him how you'd asked God to forgive you in the name of Jesus."

"What did he say?"

"Naturally, he was relieved, to put it mildly. He did say, however, that he knew he'd have to do a lot of thinking about it all, but he couldn't wait to see you and talk everything over with you—you know, get it all out in the open."

Katie's countenance reflected the worry she was feeling. "Janie, how do I face him now? How do I walk into the office tomorrow morning knowing that he knows everything?"

Janie smiled her famous smile. "You don't have to worry. He said for you not to come in to work tomorrow but to stay here. And after he finishes his morning appointment, he's coming over to see you. He said this is more important than work. I think he plans on spending the day with you; that is, if you want him to." She glanced at her friend.

Katie felt her eyes filling with tears. "Yes, Janie, I do."

"Good!"

The two girls hugged quickly before shutting out the light. Katie was amazed that the darkness was nothing more to her than the absence of light. No more trying desperately to hide and escape. No more fear of nightmares and the unknown. Just tranquility.

Even if she and Dex couldn't work out their relationship, she was slowly becoming more and more aware of another important relationship in her life—one even more important than Dexter Matheson. For the second time that night, in a voice no other person could hear, Katie whispered, "Jesus." With that name on her lips, she drifted into much-needed sleep.

43

❋

OUTSIDE THE MATHESON'S BREAKFAST ROOM window the sun glistened off newly-fallen snow, providing a perfect backdrop for Katie's thoughts as she sat meditating. Lydia had invited Katie to join her for her daily devotional time after Everett and Janie had left for the office and for school. Katie had gladly accepted, eager to begin her walk of faith.

Now she glanced at the Bible on the table, open to the verses Lydia had shared with her. Alone in the house (Lydia made a quick run to the grocery store), Katie read the first part of Psalm 30 aloud.

I will exalt you, O Lord, for you lifted me out of the
depths and did not let my enemies gloat over me.
O Lord my God, I called to you for help and you healed
me.
O Lord, you brought me up from the grave; you spared
me from going down into the pit.
Sing to the Lord, you saints of his; praise his holy name.
For his anger lasts only a moment; but his favor lasts a
lifetime; weeping may remain for a night, but rejoicing
comes in the morning.

She had lived so long in gravelike fear, doubt, and insecurity. But God had answered her cry for help. Her grave had been opened and she had come forth. Now all she wanted to do was praise her God. Her time of weeping was gone, just like last night's snowstorm. For the first time in her life, the sun shone down on Katie Montgomery. She cried tears of joy.

❄ ❄ ❄

Dex found her there. She obviously hadn't heard him come in. He
hesitated to disturb her. But his sleep hadn't been as peaceful as hers.
His was filled with anticipation of finally talking as a fellow believer
with the girl he loved.

"Katie?" he called softly.

"Oh!" She looked flustered. "I didn't hear you come in."

"I know I shouldn't have sneaked in, but I've been pretty
anxious to see you." He slid into a chair across from her, smiling. "I
can't even tell you what my client and I discussed this morning."

Katie looked at him over the rim of her teacup. "And just what
were you thinking about instead?"

"You have to ask?"

"Maybe I just want to hear you say it."

Dex stood up and held his hand out to her. "How 'bout if we
go for a little snow walk and talk all about it?"

Cautiously, Katie put her hand into his. "I'd like that."

Snuggled into coats, hats, and gloves, Katie and Dex traipsed
down to the shore of the lake behind the house.

"I remember the last time we came out here together," said Dex
as they reached the water's edge.

"Mmm . . . so do I. Thanksgiving."

"I told you a lot of really personal stuff that day."

"Yeah, you did. I can't remember if I ever thanked you for
trusting me with your deepest thoughts and secrets."

"I guess I should ask you if you think you can trust me with
yours," responded Dex, trepidation filling his voice.

Katie faced him squarely. "You've been trying to get me to open
up to you ever since we met. I'm sorry it's taken me so long; but if you
still want to know me, I'm ready."

Dexter Matheson's arms encircled Katie's slim frame. "Yes, I still
want to know you, everything about you—starting with the verse you
were reading when I interrupted you."

Katie pulled away to look at his shining eyes.

"Oh, Dex, I don't have to be afraid of God anymore! His anger is gone, but His favor lasts a lifetime!"

Dex hugged her again, this time lifting her feet off of the snowy ground. "Yes. And it's just beginning for us, Katie."

Katie slipped into her apartment, glad to find her mother home. Daria sat on the sofa pretending to be interested in a documentary about ancient Rome. She immediately clicked off the TV when she saw her daughter's face.

"So, you're okay; you're really okay?" asked Daria, getting up and walking toward Katie.

"I'm more than okay, Mama. I'm better than I've ever been. You were right. It's like a huge weight has been lifted off my shoulders. I feel like I could even fly if I needed to!"

"So then it's really true? You've trusted Christ?"

Katie barely had time to nod before Daria wrapped her arms around her and sobbed, "My baby, my precious baby. Thank you, God. Thank you, Jesus."

Finally, after Daria's emotions calmed somewhat, mother and daughter sat across from each other and talked, really talked for the first time in their lives.

"So, you've discussed all this with Dex?" asked Daria.

"As much as we could squeeze into one afternoon. I'm still amazed that his feelings are so strong for me."

"Well, I'm not," chimed Daria. "God had His hand in this from the beginning."

"Don't get too far ahead of yourself, Mama. Dex and I still have a long way to go. He explained that we need to get to know each other and . . ." She hung her head. "And deal with the abortion."

"What did he say you should do?"

Katie sighed. "He suggested we go and talk to Carolyn Grady."

Katie met her mother's eyes. "It's gonna be so hard for me to do that, Mama. I should have listened to her five years ago, but I didn't. It still hurts to think about it."

Daria reached for her daughter's hand. "I know, sweetie, I know. It hurts me, too. But I'm glad Dex wants the two of you to talk about it. I think it'll help."

"I guess just because I've admitted it and asked for forgiveness doesn't mean the healing is finished. I probably have a lot of unresolved feelings. And Dex, too. He said Carolyn leads a group for people who are in relationships with women who have had abortions. He said he thought it might be a good idea if he went—just to make sure he was really dealing with it instead of pretending everything was fine. It would be pretty easy to do that without realizing it."

Katie looked up and saw her mother crying.

"Mama, what's the matter? What did I say wrong?"

Daria waved her hand in the air. "Nothing at all. I'm just so glad Dex is willing to do that for you. And, well . . . I've already talked to Carolyn about that class myself."

Katie's eyes grew large. "You have?"

Daria nodded. "Yeah. I think I have unresolved issues about it, too. I'm the one who told you to do it. I didn't even want to discuss any other options." She broke down at that point and buried her face in her hands. "That was my granddaughter! But I won't get to see her until heaven!"

Katie went to her mother. She cupped Daria's face in her hands and forced her to look at her. In a broken but firm voice, she said, "Mama, God will not leave us in this pain. He will heal us. We have no choice but to trust Him. We've tried everything else, and nothing worked." She wiped her eyes. "We're just gonna have to trust Him, Mama," she repeated, "because that's what faith is. And faith is all we really have."

Daria nodded her assent. "And it's enough, Katie."

❄ ❄ ❄

Five weeks later Katie and Dex exited the Dane County Coliseum hand in hand. The night was cold, but the stars were out and Katie couldn't have asked for a better evening—or for better company.

"That was incredible, Dex, sitting so close to the rink."

"Yeah, it was pretty spectacular."

"I could hear the blades scratching against the ice! It gave me a new appreciation for the athleticism of the sport. I've always focused on the artistry of it; but after tonight, I realize just how much strength and endurance it takes."

Dex grinned. "So, I take it you enjoyed the show."

Katie laughed coyly. "Oh, it was all right. And since I didn't have anything better to do—"

Dex scooped her up in his arms and ran toward a snowbank at the edge of the parking lot.

"Dex, no!" Her cry fell on deaf ears, and Katie found herself immersed in a pile of fluffy white snow. She looked up at Dex as she tried to graciously expel the snow from her mouth. Dex just laughed.

"That's what you get for toying with my affections!"

Katie brushed snow off herself and made a face at Dex.

After a few moments he took pity and held out his hand to assist her to a standing position. Then, when she clasped his hand, he found himself face-first in the same snowbank.

He didn't mind. In fact, he would have been disappointed if she hadn't done it. Propping himself on one elbow in the snow, Dex said for the first time, "I love you, Katie Montgomery." She smiled back at him.

"Dex, do you remember on Thanksgiving when I told you how I had always dreamed about being an ice skater—how I wanted to be graceful and glide across the rink bringing the audience to its feet? I wanted to jump high into the air and accomplish great feats."

"Yeah, I remember. I learned more about you from that one conversation than anything else, I think."

431

"Well, I don't feel that way anymore."

He tucked a flyaway strand of hair behind her ear. "You don't? Why not?" he asked gently.

"Because," she answered very carefully, "I think I'd much rather stay here on solid ground with you."

For the second time in his life, Dex leaned over and kissed Katie. But this time he didn't apologize.

EPILOGUE

✴

FOR THE FIFTH TIME KATIE CHECKED her appearance in the mirror
backstage. Carolyn would be introducing her in a few minutes. While
she waited, Katie would just take time for a quick peek through the
curtains at the packed banquet room of people waiting to hear her
tell her story.

There in the audience sat Memphis Blue, ethereal as ever in
a sapphire silk dress. Katie eyed her own tailored suit. She'd never
have Memphis's style. But she was more than happy to settle for
her friendship. She gave a quick thank-you to God as she mentally
recalled how Memphis had helped her through those early days of
healing—always asking just the right questions and always ready with
a listening ear.

Katie scanned the room and found other familiar faces, each
one loved and treasured—for their sense of humor, their creative
genius, their inexhaustible work ethic, or their generosity in supporting the Pregnancy Information Center. Many people gave up countless
precious hours volunteering to help frightened, young women make
decisions that wouldn't haunt them for the rest of their lives.

Katie didn't need to start crying now, not when her turn to
speak was so near. She never had liked speaking in front of an audience. But Carolyn insisted she was ready. And Carolyn had never led
her astray.

Then Katie spotted a large round table near the front of the
banquet room. She was amazed that it now took an entire table to
seat her family. Once it had only been she and Daria. But Dex had

been right. It was better to have people to share your life, the bad
as well as the good. Now she could look out and see her mother
and father-in-law, her two older sisters-in-law with their husbands, her
brother-in-law Brady and Sasha, and of course, Janie, who was not
only her sister but her closest friend.

Katie's eyes then rested on her mother nestled between Everett
and Bruce McKinnon. Daria Montgomery was beautiful. Katie bit
her lip. Nobody had been more of an inspiration to her the last few
years. Daria had changed every aspect of her life to please her Savior.
And God blessed her for it. He had even opened up the unlikely
door for Daria to become a manager at the new Pic-n-Save in the
neighborhood of McFarland.

The past five years Katie and Daria had learned to walk the
road of faith side by side. Together they navigated the winding paths,
sometimes stumbling but always picking one another up. Mostly,
however, they simply kept a steady and even pace. But, occasionally,
when they felt the Spirit leading them to do so, they would break into
a run—no longer running away, but running instead toward the prize
that awaited them. Tonight was just such a night for Katie. She never
ceased to be amazed at the surprises God had for her.

Daria did her fair share of surprising as well. Katie marveled at
her mother's refusal of several nice men in the church who showed an
interest in her. Katie found it exciting to think of her mother finally
married to a nice, God-fearing man, but Daria had other ideas. She
told Katie that she had spent so many years with so many different
men that now she wanted to remain completely faithful to Jesus. He
was all she needed.

And Katie had been supportive of Daria's decision. But still,
there was that nice Carl Wilkinson, the widower with three grown
children. *Who knows, just maybe God will work that one out.* Either
way, Katie could ask for no more than her mother's happiness. And
she already had that.

Katie feared her heart might not be able to contain itself,

looking at that wonderful man sitting on the far side of Lydia. He had loved her, married her, supported her, and been a magnificent father to their beautiful little son. He had even insisted Katie set up one corner of DesignLink as "baby central" so she could continue working part time as a decorator without having to give up time with little Leland. (They called him Lee for short.) When Katie mentioned that it might interfere with work, Dex only grinned and replied with his standard comeback that some things are more important than work. And how could she argue with that? She now knew that to be so true.

That was one of the truths she hoped to share with her audience tonight. And she was about to have her opportunity. Carolyn Grady was introducing her.

Katie walked as gracefully as she could to the microphone, praying God would calm her rapidly beating heart. It came to her right as she hugged Carolyn that this was the reason she had suffered through all the guilt and fear. Lydia had said that perhaps God would show her how to redeem the years her sin had stolen. Once again, He had proven faithful and poured out His favor. He was taking her sin and pain and using it for good. Maybe her story would help one girl—one cold, lonely, scared young girl—turn her life around and give it to the One who had desired it all along.

Katie's only regret was that her precious baby girl had been sacrificed. It still brought agony to Katie's heart to think she wouldn't see Carina (her "dear little one") until God called her home, but she was comforted with the knowledge that her daughter had never been separated from Jesus. She never had to endure the struggles of this life.

Katie remembered the first time she had viewed her abortion as a sacrifice. She had told Dex how a wolf named Kaleo had repeatedly shown up in her dreams trying to get her to follow him. Dex offhandedly commented that the Greek word for "call" or "invite" is *kaleo*. Katie immediately knew the faithful wolf had been sent to her by God to invite her to follow him. If only she hadn't waited so long!

After her own conversion Daria had assured Katie that God would reach people any way He could. Daria had needed to see a man who was willing to humble Himself to show His love. Katie had needed to see someone who was willing to give His life in order to forgive the unforgivable.

In Katie's last dream of him, Kaleo, like all wolves, had been more than willing to sacrifice a leg in order to escape a trap. Life was what mattered to him—even if it were lived maimed. Katie understood that now. Kaleo had relentlessly invited her to live, really live. His life on the other side of the fire had been worth the heat of the flames.

Kaleo had been a precious gift to Katie—a messenger sent to call her home. Although the gray wolf ceased appearing in her dreams after her conversion, Katie knew he had been replaced with One far greater who would never leave her.

One glorious day in the future she would touch the precious scars sustained on her behalf. Every time she walked beside her Savior, she would be reminded of the spear that pierced his side—all for her. And every time she put her hand into His, she would feel the wound made by the cruel hammer and piercing nail. And when she knelt at His feet to tell Him how much she loved Him she would see the scars of the nails that held her Savior to that old wooden cross. Any fire she had to walk through was nothing compared to what He had endured for her.

She would keep her eyes on that cross and finish the race given her to run. She would be faithful to the end and claim the prize purchased for her on that hill called Calvary. And she would start on this night by opening her heart and revealing her own scars. She vowed to tell her story as God allowed her to do so and help people as God put them into her path.

She stepped up to the microphone and smiled at the audience before her.

"Hello, my name is Katie, and ten years ago I had an abortion."

ABOUT THE AUTHOR

Tracey Langford, a graduate of the University of Alabama at Birmingham (B.S., Secondary Education), has taught high school English. She and her singer/songwriter husband, Jon Langford, reside in Alabama. They frequently collaborate on song writing, with Tracey writing lyrics to the music Jon composes. Tracey and Jon are the parents of seven-year-old quadruplets, two boys and two girls, whom Tracey homeschools.

This is Tracey's first novel.

You may visit the Langford's website at <www.jonlangford.com>.

ACKNOWLEDGMENTS

I would like to thank the following people for the part they have played in either making this book what it needs to be or making me what I need to be; and in some cases, both. Thank you to:

Jan Monski —for taking so much of your valuable time to help me. God bless you and your entire staff at Sav-A-Life.

Allen Bean —for your willingness to read that original manuscript and still offer encouragement!

Catherine Lawton —for taking a chance on both Katie and me.

Stu and Fran Swindle (my parents) —for all the Wednesdays you tirelessly babysit my kids so I can get out of the house. Much of this book was written on those days; suffice it to say, without the two of you, it probably still wouldn't be finished!

Randy Hofheins —for so faithfully praying and for always asking, "How's the book going?"

Lisa McCarrell —for knowing me for so long and still being my friend!

Alison Bailey —for being the friend I needed so desperately. God is good! The fact that you love to read as much if not more than I do is icing on the cake (chocolate, of course).

Patty McKinnon —for so often being the voice of encouragement. Thanks also for the tour of Madison and all the laughs that went with it. But most of all, thank you for being that special friend that comes along once in a lifetime. I look forward to an eternity of heavenly tea parties with you!

Martin, Stephen, Hannah, and Abigail Langford (my kids) —for being such wonderful children that I was actually able to finish this book! Thanks for teaching me what it means to love. (I'm still learning!) Also, thanks for all the prayers that "Mommy would find a publisher." You may not have understood what you were praying for, but God understood every bit of it.

Jon Langford (my husband) —for believing long before I did that I could write this book and for wanting me to do it. ("I must stay tuned in to you.") But mostly for making life so much fun. I'm glad we get to go through it together.

My Savior —for holding it all together, me included.

— Tracey Langford
June, 2003

This book may be ordered direct from the publisher :

970.371.9530
FAX 970.351.8240

MAIL ORDERS:

CLADACH PUBLISHING
PO BOX 336144
GREELEY, CO 80633

WEB ORDERS:

WWW.CLADACH.com

Ask about quantity discounts for nonprofits.